ANTHONY TR

THE COMPLETE SHO

VOLUME

2

THE CHRISTMAS STORIES

EDITED, WITH AN INTRODUCTION, BY
BETTY BREYER
FOREWORD BY
JOANNA TROLLOPE

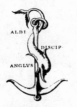

LONDON
WILLIAM PICKERING
1990

First published by Texas Christian University Press
This edition with revisions published by
Pickering & Chatto (Publishers) Limited,
17 Pall Mall, London, SW1Y 5NB

British Library Cataloguing in Publication Data
Trollope, Anthony, *1815–1882*
   Anthony Trollope: the complete short stories
   Vol. 2, the christmas stories.
   I. Title   II. Breyer, Betty
   823'.8 [F]

ISBN 1–85196–701–X

Printed and bound in Great Britain by
Redwood Press Limited
Melksham

Foreword

Between them, Prince Albert and Charles Dickens have most emphatically dictated our perception of the high Victorian Christmas. Anthony Trollope, however, took quite another view. Not for him 'that pretty German toy – the Christmas tree'; not for him the soppy little children and the sentimental old grandfathers; not for him the tinsel and candles and general Pecksniffian high jinks. No indeed.

'Nothing', he wrote weightily in his Autobiography, 'can be more distasteful to me than to have to give a relish of Christmas to what I write. I feel the humbug implied by the nature of the order. A Christmas story, in the proper sense, should be the ebullition of some mind anxious to instil others with a desire for Christmas religious thought or Christmas festivities – or, better still, Christmas charity.'

Trollope's view of Christmas, and the attendant special stories that became such a Victorian rage, was – if a touch pompous – both vigorous and honest. His Christmas stories were intended – as all his stories were – to be examinations of those 'little lacerations of the spirit' that he understood so well. The function of Christmas in these tales is to throw into fleeting high relief the dilemmas of his characters being tested against their own moral and social codes. Christmas, Trollope is saying, reminds us of our better selves and obliges us to obey them – but, oh, the struggle!

There are eight of these Christmas stories, four written towards the end of Trollope's life. In only two of them, 'The Mistletoe Bough' and 'Christmas Day at Kirkby Cottage', do we get what we expect to find – a family story with a mild moral, a happy ending and a moderate description of hanging holly in the church and mistletoe in the hall. Both these are love stories, their narratives sustained by the heroines' agonies over tiny problems – a state of female mind Trollope always and inexplicably found endearing.

The other stories put romantic love in second place, or even, as in 'Christmas at Thompson Hall', almost dismiss it entirely. Rather than providing narrative, its function is to form one of the horns of the Christmas-accentuated dilemma on which Trollope has speared his characters. Should Nora Field, in 'The Widow's Mite', obey the desires of her lover, or the commands of her conscience? Should the two heroines of Plumplington regard themselves primarily as dutiful daughters or loyal promised wives?

I say that these dilemmas are Christmas accentuated; but some of them are hardly even that. In two of the stories – the intriguing 'The Two Generals' and the dark 'Catherine Carmichael' – Christmas plays no more significant a part than that of a tolling bell, a measure of time to mark each new and significant step in the narrative. Only in 'The Widow's Mite', an exploration of the true nature of charity, do we feel that the situation has indeed been brought about by Christmas, and that the warm, well-fed inhabitants of Plumstock Rectory can hardly swallow their mince pies for thinking of the consequences of the cotton famine on the poor of nearby Liverpool.

There are even, in this collection of stories which one would expect to be so orthodox, some jokers in the pack, and entirely unrelated jokers at that. 'Christmas at Thompson Hall', the account of a woman's difficulties in getting a peevish husband back to England for family celebrations, starts with a long and extraordinary sequence in a Paris hotel, a mixture of farce and pathos, which serves in the end as no more than a clumsy and overbearing lump of plot. 'The Two Generals', set in Kentucky during the American Civil War, is a slightly Boys' Own Paper tale of brotherly blood finally proving itself thicker than water, with Christmas not much more than the convenient provider of dramatic weather for the Confederate brother to struggle home in. As for 'Catherine Carmichael', a brutal story set in the New Zealand outback, we are taken into an alarming and inarticulate world where Christmas is virtually ignored as being a mockery of the raw reality of life.

In only one of the tales do we see Trollope's full and familiar benevolence – a benevolence we might be forgiven for expecting in double measure in Christmas stories. This is 'The Two Heroines of Plumplington', published after his death, and full of those quietly ironic portraits of human absurdity of which he was such a master. As a story, it could have been set at any time of the year, but the two triumphant girls in it are finally rewarded by a Christmas dinner at which their fathers and lovers are, at least for the sake of the season, reconciled.

Yet, even as they sit around the festive table, replete with harmony and plum pudding, there is a suggestion – just the merest suggestion – that in the background Trollope is whispering, 'Humbug'.

JOANNA TROLLOPE

Contents

Introduction

IT IS BEST TO BE CANDID about this volume. Trollope seems to have been somewhat contradictory in his attitude toward Christmas stories. In his autobiography he expressed a certain dislike for them, yet near the end of his career many of the short stories he wrote were Christmas stories. So whether Trollope himself would approve such a collection is open to question. But it is a question that can be answered perhaps only in the context of his whole artistic career.

Anthony Trollope (1815-1882) is perhaps best known for his novels of clerical life set in Barsetshire, that county which he added forever to the map of England. His novels with their stable and solid world have become a benchmark of the Victorian age. Even at the time of his death in 1882 his work was hailed by one of his most perceptive critics, R. H. Hutton, as "helping us to revive the past." In part his gift for faithfully recreating his world comes from what Henry James in *Partial Portraits* called his "complete understanding of the usual." In part it comes from the fact that Trollope was himself a thoroughly Victorian man. Bustling, energetic, inquisitive, and incredibly industrious, he was bluff in his public manner, hearty and generous-spirited in his private life, and indefatigable in his duty to his career as a novelist and his career as a postal official. For James Russell Lowell, whom he met in Boston, he was "a big, red-faced, rather underbred Englishman of the bald-with-spectacles type." But Julian Hawthorne, more observant than his fellow American, paints a slightly different picture in his *Confessions and Criticisms*: "He was a quick-tempered man, and the ardour and hurry of his temperament made him seem more so than he really was: but he was never more angry than he was forgiving and generous. He was hurt by little things, and little things pleased him; he was suspicious and perverse, but in a manner that rather endeared him to you than otherwise."

If Trollope had a private credo, it must have been these words he wrote in *Rachel Ray*: ". . . ease of spirit come from action only, and the world's dignity is given to those who do the world's work. Let no man put his neck from out of the collar till in truth he can no longer draw the weight attached to it." His own capacity for work seemed almost limitless. His career as a postal official lasted twenty-five years and sent him trudging along muddy Wiltshire lanes, walking through Irish hamlets, riding across Central America on a donkey, and sailing off to Egypt, Jamaica, and the United States. In addition to working and travelling for the GPO, he travelled the length and breadth of Europe on holidays, to South Africa to write a travel book, to Ceylon, to Australia, and twice across the United States. Such a career is enough to make any man's life a full and active one, but for almost forty years Trollope was also working at another career. From 1843 to 1882 he wrote forty-seven novels, five travel books, numerous magazine articles, and forty-two short stories. He once wrote with broad humor to his friend Alfred Austin, later poet laureate: "I cannot believe the Old Testament because labour is spoken of as the *evil* consequence of the Fall of Man. My only doubt as to finding a heaven for myself at last arises from the fear that the disembodied and beatified spirits will not want novels."

Trollope had already written eight novels including *The Warden, Barchester Towers, Dr. Thorne,* and *The Three Clerks* when he began writing short stories in 1859, and in 1860, when the first of his stories was published, his novel *Framley Parsonage* was making him one of the most popular novelists in England. Though he continued to publish short stories during the rest of his life, most of them were written between 1860 and 1870. Many of the stories written during these ten years were based on his own experiences and observations while "banging about the world" (as one observer called it) and while editing *St. Paul's Magazine*. These stories reflect his insatiable curiosity about life and his shrewd, but amused, observations of himself and others. As Michael Sadleir has pointed out in his *Anthony Trollope: A Commentary*, Trollope relished the "small calamities of life and often recorded them in his stories with the understanding of a man who has witnessed and experienced such dilemmas."

After 1870, although Trollope still travelled extensively and continued to write at least one novel every year as well as travel books and magazine articles, he wrote only eight short stories. Four of the eight are Christmas stories included in this volume. Gradually he began to curtail his working schedule, and by 1880, two years before his death, he answered a request for a magazine article by saying: "I am accustomed to write Christmas stories for magazines, but not to do other literary work." At sixty-five he at last had resigned himself to the fact that he could no longer work as he had before. But still he wrote his novels with that workmanlike precision and pace that he had ever used, dictating them to his niece as his health began to fail. On November 3, 1882, he suffered a stroke at the home of his brother-in-law and died on the evening of December 6. His last short stories, "Not If I Know It" and "The Two Heroines of Plumplington," were published posthumously. About these stories Trollope has left no comment, but it is interesting to note that one of them is set in Barsetshire and that both of them are Christmas stories.

The formal Christmas story was a Victorian invention. The Victorians added many of their own trappings to the celebration of Christmas. The older, more sedate trimmings of Christmas— the feast, the pudding, the holly — were augmented by tinsel, tapers, "that pretty German toy — a Christmas tree" as Dickens called it, and the Christmas story. Gaily illustrated annuals were published for the Christmas season, authors liked nothing better than to have their books come out for the Christmas market, and journals and magazines printed supplements and special Christmas editions with pictures, holiday poems, and Christmas stories. The nineteenth century middle class, the magazine-reading public, learned to demand year after year fare with a Christmas flavor. Christmas, after all, was that time of year in which the rigors of progressive pragmatism could be laid aside briefly for the softness of sentimentalism and the high celebration of the Family, that most hallowed of all Victorian traditions. And Dickens, who popularized the Christmas story with *A Christmas Carol* written in 1843 (the year Trollope began writing his first novel, *The Macdermots of Ballycloran*), was successful because his story was not only a sentimental celebration of Christian virtues but a sentimental celebration of the Family as well.

Dickens's Christmas stories, as might be expected, are very different from those of Trollope. Some of his shorter pieces are little more than impressionistic sketches which evoke mood, scene, and emotional response. His more formal Christmas stories are only slightly disguised parables held together with fantasy, symbolism, and sentimentality. There is little effort to develop character beyond the delineation of a single quality which can become part of the symbolism. There is little effort to develop the action beyond the demands of the moral exegesis. For Dickens the purpose of the Christmas story was to teach a moral lesson and instruct his readers (often young readers) in the values of those virtues of generousity, compassion, and love which the season taught. While he succeeded in telling a captivating and appealing tale in A *Christmas Carol*, he failed in, for example, *The Battle of Life* because that story lacks the straightforward appeal to sentiment and precise categorization of virtues and sins which is substituted for characterization and plot in A *Christmas Carol* and because it lacks the moral focus which unifies his more successful story *The Chimes*. Dickens appears to have regarded the stories in something of the same light as the morality play, and where he achieves that unity of intent that is characteristic of a morality play he has been successful.

In *An Autobiography* (written in 1875-6 and published after his death), Trollope comments on Dickens's and his own Christmas stories: "Nothing can be more distasteful to me than to have to give a relish of Christmas to what I write. I feel the humbug implied by the nature of the order. A Christmas story, in the proper sense, should be the ebullition of some mind anxious to instil others with a desire for Christmas religious thought, or Christmas festivities, — or, better still with Christmas charity. Such was the case with Dickens when he wrote his two first Christmas stories. But since that the things written annually — all of which have been fixed to Christmas like children's toys to a Christmas tree — have had no real savour of Christmas about them. I had done two or three before. Alas! at this very moment I have one to write, which I have promised to supply within three weeks of this time, — the picture-makers always require a long interval, — as to which I have in vain been cudgelling my brain for the last month. I can't send away the order to another shop, but I do not know how I shall ever get the coffin made."

Although there is a great deal of satirical self-deprecating humor in this passage, it does tell us something about Trollope's evaluation of Dickens's Christmas stories and about his attitude toward his own. About Dickens's stories Trollope recognized that they were not all successful because all of them were not written with that necessary honesty of purpose and unity of intent of which he speaks in his autobiography. The "real savour of Christmas" requires something more than a Christmas setting, kind hearts, and sentiments. The writer, as he said often, must write because he "has a story to tell, not because he has to tell a story." The Christmas story, if its writer is not honestly concerned with the values of the Christmas message, becomes just another piece of humbug — a decoration attached to Christmas by the slenderest thread.

It is clear that he disliked Christmas stories that were meant to decorate magazines and journals like Christmas ornaments. On the other hand, he was sometimes asked to write stories with "the relish of Christmas." He was quite certain that he could not write the kind of story that Dickens produced — those stories full of spirits, ghosts, and small children of incongruous virtues. The reluctance to write Christmas stories that he expresses in the passage above, though it is exaggerated for effect, is nonetheless genuine. Trollope's concern was how to avoid the humbug and have an honest story to tell. In order to do so he turned to the world he knew best. He relied on a familiar, tangible reality — that beef and ale world Hawthorne talked about in his novels — where men and women must live with the knowledge that good and evil are not abstractions for speculation, but necessary elements of their daily life. He recorded with both comedy and pathos those conflicts of men and women which arise from the human condition. And in his Christmas stories that spirit of Christmas charity of which he spoke was translated into the attempt of ordinary people to live as best they could in an imperfect world by a perfect law. Although these stories are set at Christmas time, their claim on Christmas comes not from the setting but from the characters themselves and their awareness

that the season imposes a special demand upon them to be charitable beyond the usual and at peace with those around them,
not only in the great conflicts, but in the small dilemmas as well.

For Trollope it was the seemingly small, daily dilemmas that
often went as far as anything else in defining man's life. He tells
us in his essay "A Walk in a Wood": "It is not the sorrows but
the annoyances of life which impede. Were I told that the bank
had broken in which my little all was kept for me I could sit
down and write my love story with almost a sublimated vision of
love; but to discover that I had given half a sovereign instead of
sixpence to a cabman would render a great effort necessary before
I could find the fitting words for a lover. These little lacerations
of the spirit, not the deep wounds, make the difficulty." Like the
other side of Wordsworth's "little unremembered acts of kindness," Trollope's "little lacerations of the spirit" can be the better or worse part of a good man's life. From the little "annoyances
of life" come the situations he creates to test the moral and social
codes of his generation. He saw in the small and trivial matters of
life the measure by which man is most often taken. Small and
trivial matters are, indeed, important because in the final analy-
sis they determine how a man lives his life. Moreover, Trollope's
concern was to show how men and women cope with being
human and fallible in a world whose rules presuppose perfection
and infallibility. His talent for the interpretation of the commonplace rests on a balance between a perfect world of abstract
rules and a real world in which as he said "things are always very
far from being perfect." Man, after all, must live in this balance.
It is there, between fallibility and infallibility, that he must seek
to reconcile himself, and it is this balance that Trollope captures
in his stories.

"The Mistletoe Bough," "The Widow's Mite," and "The Two
Generals" come from the first period of his short stories and were
included in the two volumes of *Tales of All Countries*. The stories
are set in Westmoreland, Cheshire, and Frankfort, Kentucky,
respectively. Trollope made it a point of pride that he was acquainted with the settings of these stories. Westmoreland and
Cheshire he knew from his work as a postal surveyor and Frankfort, Kentucky, he had visited in 1861 when he toured the
United States for his travel book *North America*. Both "The

Mistletoe Bough" and "The Two Generals," in very different ways, show his perceptive handling of the complexities of human relationships, but among all his stories there is no finer study of the nature of true Christian charity than "The Widow's Mite." Here he wrote with delicacy and humor of the difficulties and rewards of practicing that perfect rule of giving taught by the parable of the widow's mite.

Among the Christmas stories of his later period, there is much variety of setting, tone, and theme. But each in its way portrays ordinary men and women caught between the demands of conscience and human imperfections. It is part of Trollope's charm and talent that he could make the commonplace exceptional and interesting, that he could be accurate in his details without making those details tedious, and that he could handle themes that would not have been tolerated from another pen. "Catherine Carmichael," published here for the first time since its original publication in 1878, is such a story as only Trollope could have written. Taut with emotional and sexual tensions, it tells the story of a young woman trapped between her hatred of her husband and her love for another man. It is one of the few stories whose grim and demanding world is not relieved by that touch of satire of which he was so fond. Its mood and tone might give credence to the theory of his increasingly dark vision of the world if it were not for the last of his short stories, "The Two Heroines of Plumplington." Published posthumously in *Good Cheer*, the Christmas issue of *Good Words* in 1882, it is both unique and representative of his work. It is unique because it is the only one of his short stories set in Barsetshire; it is representative because it expounds his favorite theme, the politics of love and society. The story comes after a lifetime spent observing and recording with keenly accurate details the habits of men and women in the ways of the world. He was, as Sadleir has said, socially speaking the wisest of English novelists, and it is that social wisdom which makes "The Two Heroines of Plumplington" the culmination of the comic war waged in the name of social politics.

Trollope's style is for the most part plain and unadorned, seldom relying on the figurative, but sensitive to the cadence of his characters — compact or expansive as the action or mood demands. His characters are always recognizable. He never allowed himself the luxury of forgetting human nature, nor did he allow his characters to falsify the humanity he gave them. He made their vanities accessible to all men and their virtues within reach. His tone was ever that of the human apologist, of one who knew that man is neither very good nor very bad, but a compendium of common desires, practical emotions, obvious failings, and winsome virtues. And he preached his sermon, even to the last, that he should make "virtue alluring and vice ugly, while he charmed his readers instead of wearying them."

The Mistletoe Bough

L ET THE BOYS HAVE IT if they like it," said Mrs. Garrow, pleading to her only daughter on behalf of her two sons.

"Pray don't, mamma," said Elizabeth Garrow. "It only means romping. To me all that is detestable; and I am sure it is not the sort of thing that Miss Holmes would like."

"We always had it at Christmas when we were young."

"But, mamma, the world is so changed!"

The point in dispute was one very delicate in its nature, hardly to be discussed in all its bearings even in fiction, and the very mention of which between a mother and daughter showed a great amount of close confidence between them. It was no less than this, — should that branch of mistletoe which Frank Garrow had brought home with him out of the Lowther woods be hung up on Christmas Eve in the dining-room at Thwaite Hall, according to his wishes, or should permission for such hanging be positively refused? It was clearly a thing not to be done after such a discussion, and therefore the decision given by Mrs. Garrow was against it.

I am inclined to think that Miss Garrow was right in saying that the world is changed as touching mistletoe boughs. Kissing, I fear, is less innocent now than it used to be when our grandmothers were alive, and we have become more fastidious in our amusements. Nevertheless, I think that she laid herself fairly open to the raillery with which her brothers attacked her.

"'Honi soit qui mal y pense,'" said Frank, who was eighteen. "Nobody will want to kiss you, my Lady Fineairs," said Harry, who was just a year younger.

"Because you choose to be a Puritan there are to be no more cakes and ale in the house," said Frank.

"'Still waters run deep,' we all know that," said Harry.

The boys had not been present when the matter was discussed and decided between Mrs. Garrow and her daughter, nor had the mother been present when those little amenities had passed between the brother and sister.

"Only that mamma has said it, and I wouldn't seem to go against her," said Frank, "I'd ask my father. He wouldn't give way to such nonsense, I know."

Elizabeth turned away without answering, and left the room. Her eyes were full of tears, but she would not let her brothers see that they had vexed her. They were only two days home from school, and for the last week before their coming all her thoughts had been to prepare for their Christmas pleasures. She had arranged their rooms, making everything warm and pretty. Out of her own pocket she had bought a shotbelt for one and skates for the other. She had told the old groom that her pony was to belong exclusively to Master Harry for the holidays, and now Harry told her that "still waters run deep." She had been driven to the use of all her eloquence in inducing her father to purchase that gun for Frank, and now Frank called her a Puritan. And why? She did not choose that a mistletoe bough should be hung in her father's hall when Godfrey Holmes was coming there to visit him. She could not explain this to Frank, but Frank might have had the wit to understand it. But Frank was thinking only of Patty Coverdale, a blue-eyed little romp of sixteen, who, with her sister Kate, was coming from Penrith to spend the Christmas at Thwaite Hall. Elizabeth left the room with her slow, graceful step, hiding her tears — hiding all emotion, as, latterly, she had taught herself that it was feminine to do. "There goes my 'Lady Fineairs'!" said Harry, sending his shrill voice after her.

Thwaite Hall was not a place of much pretension. It was a moderate-sized house, surrounded by pretty gardens and shrubberies, close down upon the River Eamont, on the Westmorland side of the river, looking over to a lovely wooded bank in Cum-

2

berland. All the world knows that the Eamont runs out of Ulleswater, dividing the two counties, passing under Penrith Bridge and by the old ruins of Brougham Castle, below which it joins the Eden. Thwaite Hall nestled down close upon the clear rocky stream, about halfway between Ulleswater and Penrith, and had been built just at a bend of the river. The windows of the dining-parlour and of the drawing-room stood at right angles to each other, and yet each commanded a reach of the stream. Immediately from a side door of the house steps were cut down through the red rock to the water's edge, and here a small boat was always moored to a chain. The chain was stretched across the river, fixed on to staples driven into the rock on either side, and thus the boat was pulled backwards and forwards over the stream without aid from oars or paddles. From the opposite side a path led through the wood and across the fields to Penrith, and this was the route commonly used between Thwaite Hall and the town.

Major Garrow was a retired officer of Engineers who had seen service in all parts of the world, and was now spending the evening of his days on a small property which had come to him from his father. He held in his own hands about forty acres of land, and he was the owner of one small farm close by, which was let to a tenant. That, together with his halfpay and the interest of his wife's thousand pounds, sufficed to educate his children, and keep the wolf at a comfortable distance from his door. He himself was a spare thin man, with quiet, lazy, literary habits. He had done the work of life, but had so done it as to permit of his enjoying that which was left to him. His sole remaining care was the establishment of his children, and, as far as he could see, he had no ground for anticipating disappointment. They were clever, good-looking, well-disposed young people, and, upon the whole, it may be said that the sun shone brightly on Thwaite Hall. Of Mrs. Garrow it may certainly be said that she deserved such sunshine.

In years past it had been the practice of the family to have some sort of gathering at Thwaite Hall during Christmas. Godfrey Holmes had been left under the care of Major Garrow, and, as he had always spent his Christmas holidays with his guardian, this, perhaps, had given rise to the practice. Then the Coverdales were cousins of the Garrows, and they had usually been there as children. At the Christmas last past the custom had been broken, for young Holmes had been abroad. Previous to that they had all been children, except him. But, now that they were to meet again, they were no longer children. Elizabeth, at any rate, was not so, for she had already counted nineteen summers. And Isabella Holmes was coming. Isabella was two years older than Elizabeth, and had been educated in Brussels. Moreover, she was comparatively a stranger at Thwaite Hall, never having been at those early Christmas meetings.

And now I must take permission to begin my story by telling a lady's secret. Elizabeth Garrow had already been in love with Godfrey Holmes; — or perhaps it might be more becoming to say that Godfrey Holmes had already been in love with her. They had already been engaged. And, alas! they had already agreed that that engagement should be broken off. Young Holmes was now twenty-seven years of age, and was employed in a bank at Liverpool, — not as a clerk, but as assistant manager, with a large salary. He was a man well to do in the world, who had money also of his own, and who might afford to marry. Some two years since, on the eve of his leaving Thwaite Hall, he had, with low doubting whisper, told Elizabeth that he loved her, and she had flown trembling to her mother. "Godfrey, my boy," the Major had said to him, as he parted with him the next morning, "Bessy is only a child, and too young to think of this yet." At the next Christmas Godfrey was in Italy, and the thing was gone by; so at least the father and mother said to each other. But the young people had met in the summer, and one joyful letter had come from the girl home to her mother — "I have accepted him, dearest, dearest, mamma! I do love him! But don't tell papa yet, for I have not quite accepted him. I think I am sure, but I am not quite sure. I am not quite sure about him." And then, two days after that, there had come a letter that was not at all joyful — "Dearest mamma, — It is not to be. It is not written in the book. We have both agreed that it will not do. I am so glad that you have not told dear papa, for I could never make him understand. You will understand, for I shall tell you everything, down to his very words. But we have agreed that there shall be no quarrel. It shall be exactly as it was; and he will come at Christmas all the same. It would never do that he and papa should be separated; nor could we now put off Isabella. It is better so in every way, for there is, and need be, no quarrel. We still like each other. I am sure I like him; but I know that I should not make him happy as his wife. He says it is my fault. I, at any rate, have never told him that I thought it his." From all which it will be seen that the confidence between the mother and daughter was very close.

Elizabeth Garrow was a very good girl, but it might almost be a question whether she was not too good. She had learned, or thought that she had learned, that most girls are vapid, silly, and useless — given chiefly to pleasure-seeking and a hankering after lovers, — and she had resolved that she would not be such a one. Industry, self-denial, and a religious purpose in life, were the tasks which she set herself; and she went about the performance of them with much courage. But such tasks, though they are excellently well adapted to fit a young lady for the work of living, may also, if carried too far, have the effect of unfitting her for that work. When Elizabeth Garrow made up her mind that the finding of a husband was not the *summum bonum* of life, she did very well. It is very well that a young lady should feel herself capable of going through the world happily without one. But in teaching herself thus she also taught herself to think that there was a certain merit in refusing herself the natural delight of a lover, even though the possession of the lover were compatible with all her duties to herself, her father and mother, and the world at large. It was not that she had determined to have no lover. She made no such resolve, and when the proper lover came he was admitted to her heart. But she declared to herself, unconsciously, that she must put a guard upon herself lest she should be betrayed into weakness by her own happiness. She had resolved that in loving her lord she would not worship him, and that in giving her heart she would only so give it as it should be given to a human creature like herself. She had acted on these high resolves, and hence it had come to pass, not unnaturally, that Mr. Godfrey Holmes had told her that it was "her fault." She had resolved not to worship her lover, and he, perhaps, had resolved that he would be worshipped.

She was a pretty, fair girl, with soft dark brown hair, and soft long dark eyelashes. Her grey eyes were tender and lustrous, her face was oval, and the lines of her cheek and chin perfect in their symmetry. She was generally quiet in her demeanour; but when stirred she could rouse herself to great energy, and speak with feeling and almost with fire. Her fault was too great a reverence for martyrdom in general, and a feeling, of which she was unconscious, that it became a young woman to be unhappy in secret — that it became a young woman, I might rather say, to have a source of unhappiness hidden from the world in general and endured without any flaw to her outward cheerfulness. We know the story of the Spartan boy who held the fox under his tunic. The fox was biting him into the very entrails, but the young hero spoke never a word. Now, Bessy Garrow was inclined to think that it was a good thing to have a fox always biting, so that the torment caused no ruffle to her outward smiles. Now, at this moment the fox within her bosom was biting her sore enough, but she bore it without flinching.

"If you would rather that he should not come I will have it arranged," her mother said to her.

"Not for worlds!" she had answered; "I should never think well of myself again."

Her mother had changed her own mind more than once as to the conduct in this matter which it might be best for her to follow, thinking solely of her daughter's welfare. "If he comes they will be reconciled, and she will be happy," had been her first idea. But then there was a stern fixedness of purpose in Bessy's words when she spoke of Mr. Holmes which had expelled this hope, and Mrs. Garrow had for a while thought it better that the young man should not come. But Bessy would not permit this. It would vex her father, put out of course the arrangements of other people, and display weakness on her own part. He should come, and she would endure without flinching while the fox gnawed at her heart.

That battle of the mistletoe had been fought on the morning before Christmas Day, and the Holmeses came on Christmas Eve. Isabella was comparatively a stranger, and therefore received at first the greater share of attention. She and Elizabeth had once seen each other, and for the last year or two had corresponded, but personally they had never been intimate. Unfortunately for Elizabeth that story of Godfrey's offer and acceptance had been communicated to Isabella, as had of course the immediately subsequent story of their separation. But now it would be impossible to avoid the subject in conversation. "Dearest Isabella, let it be as though it never had been," she had said in one of her letters. But sometimes it is very difficult to let things be as though they never had been.

The first evening passed over very well. The two Coverdale girls were there, and there was much talking and merry laughter, rather juvenile in its nature, but, on the whole, none the worse for that. Isabella Holmes was a fine, tall, handsome girl, good-humoured and well disposed to be pleased, rather Frenchified in her manners, and quite able to take care of herself. But she was not above round games, and did not turn up her nose at the boys. Godfrey behaved himself excellently, talking much to the Major, but by no means avoiding Miss Garrow. Mrs. Garrow, though she had known him since he was a boy, had taken an aversion to him since he had quarrelled with her daughter; but there was no room on this first night for showing such aversion, and everything went off well.

"Godfrey is very much improved," the Major said to his wife that night.

"Do you think so?"

"Indeed, I do. He has filled out and become a fine man."

"In personal appearance you mean. Yes, he is well-looking enough."

"And in his manner, too. He is doing uncommonly well at Liverpool, I can tell you; and if he should think of Bessy" —

"There is nothing of that sort," said Mrs. Garrow.

"He did speak to me, you know — two years ago. Bessy was too young then, and so, indeed, was he. But if she likes him" —

"I don't think she does."

"Then there's an end of it." And so they went to bed.

"Frank," said the sister to her elder brother, knocking at his door when they had all gone up-stairs, "may I come in, if you're not in bed yet?"

"In bed!" said he, looking up with some little pride from his Greek book. "I've one hundred and fifty lines to do before I can get to bed. It'll be two, I suppose. I've got to read uncommon hard these holidays. I've only one more half, you know, and then" —

"Don't overdo it, Frank."

"No. I won't overdo it. I mean to take one day a week as a holiday, and work eight hours a day on the other five. That will be forty hours a week, and will give me just two hundred hours for the holiday. I've got it all down here on a table. That will be a hundred and five for Greek play, forty for algebra" — And so he explained to her the exact destiny of all his long hours of proposed labour. He had as yet been home a day and a half, and had succeeded in drawing out with red lines and blue figures the table which he showed her. "If I can do that it will be pretty well; won't it?"

"But, Frank, you have come for your holidays, to enjoy yourself?"

"But a fellow must work nowadays."

"Don't overdo it, dear; that's all. But, Frank, I could not sleep if I went to bed without speaking to you. You made me unhappy to-day."

"Did I, Bessy?"

"You called me a Puritan, and then you quoted that ill-natured French proverb at me. Do you really believe that your sister thinks evil, Frank?" And as she spoke she put her arm caressingly round his neck.

"Of course I don't."

"Then why say so? Harry is so much younger and so thoughtless that I can bear what he says without so much suffering. But if you and I are not friends I shall be very wretched. If you knew how I have looked forward to your coming home!"

"I did not mean to vex you, and I won't say such things again."

"There's my own Frank! What I said to mamma I said because I thought it right; but you must not say that I am a Puritan. I would do anything in my power to make your holidays bright and pleasant. I know that boys require so much more to amuse them than girls do. Good night, dearest. Pray don't overdo yourself with work, and do take care of your eyes." So saying, she kissed him, and went her way. In twenty minutes after that he had gone to sleep over his book, and, when he woke up to find the candle guttering down, he resolved that he would not begin his measured hours till Christmas Day was fairly over.

The morning of Christmas Day passed very quietly. They all went to church, and then sat round the fire chatting till the four o'clock dinner was ready. The Coverdale girls thought it was rather more dull than former Thwaite Hall festivities, and Frank was seen to yawn. But then everybody knows that the real fun of Christmas never begins till the day itself be passed. The beef and pudding are ponderous, and unless there be absolute children in the party there is a difficulty in grafting any special afternoon amusements on the Sunday pursuits of the morning. In the evening they were to have a dance; — that had been distinctly promised to Patty Coverdale; but the dance would not commence till eight. The beef and pudding were ponderous, but with due efforts they were overcome and disappeared. The glass of port was sipped, the almonds and raisins were nibbled, and then the ladies left the room. Ten minutes after that Elizabeth found herself seated with Isabella Holmes over the fire in her father's little bookroom. It was not by her that this meeting was arranged, for she dreaded such a constrained confidence; but it could not be avoided, and, perhaps, it might be as well now as hereafter.

"Bessy," said the elder girl, "I am dying to be alone with you for a moment."

"Well; you shall not die — that is, if being alone with me will save you."

"I have so much to say to you, and, if you have any true friendship in you, you also will have so much to say to me."

Miss Garrow, perhaps, had no true friendship in her at the moment, for she would gladly have avoided saying anything had that been possible. But in order to prove that she was not deficient in friendship, she gave her friend her hand.

"And now tell me everything about Godfrey," said Isabella.

"Dear Bella, I have nothing to tell, literally nothing."

"That is nonsense. Stop a moment, dear, and understand that I do not mean to offend you. It cannot be that you have nothing to tell if you choose to tell it. You are not the girl to have accepted Godfrey without loving him, nor is he the man to have asked you without loving you. When you wrote me word that you had changed your mind, as you might about a dress, of course

9

I knew you had not told me all. Now I insist upon knowing it —
that is, if we are to be friends. I would not speak a word to
Godfrey till I had seen you, in order that I might hear your story
first."

"Indeed, Bella, there is no story to tell."

"Then I must ask him."

"If you wish to play the part of a true friend to me you will let
the matter pass by and say nothing. You must understand that,
circumstanced as we are, your brother's visit here —. What I
mean is, that it is very difficult for me to act and speak exactly as
I should do, and a few unfortunate words spoken may make my
position unendurable."

"Will you answer me one question?"

"I cannot tell. I think I will."

"Do you love him?" For a moment or two Bessy remained
silent, striving to arrange her words so that they should contain
no falsehood, and yet betray no truth. "Ah! I see you do,"
continued Miss Holmes. "But of course you do. Why else did you
accept him?"

"I fancied that I did, as young ladies do sometimes fancy."

"And will you say that you do not, now?" Again Bessy was
silent, and then her friend rose from her seat. "I see it all," she
said. "What a pity it was that you both had not some friend like
me by you at the time! But perhaps it may not be too late."

I need not repeat at length all the protestations which were
poured forth with hot energy by poor Bessy. She endeavoured to
explain how great had been the difficulty of her position. This
Christmas visit had been arranged before that unhappy affair at
Liverpool had occurred. Isabella's visit had been partly one of
business, it being necessary that certain money affairs should be
arranged between her, her brother, and the Major. "I determined," said Bessy, "not to let my own feelings stand in the way,
and hoped that things might settle down to their former friendly
footing. I already fear that I have been wrong, but it will be
ungenerous in you to punish me." Then she went on to say that
if anybody attempted to interfere with her she should at once go
away to her mother's sister, who lived at Hexham, in Northum-
berland.

Then came the dance, and the hearts of Kate and Patty

Coverdale were at last made happy. But here again poor Bessy was made to understand how terribly difficult was this experiment of entertaining on a footing of friendship a lover with whom she had quarrelled only a month or two before. That she must as a necessity become the partner of Godfrey Holmes she had already calculated, and so much she was prepared to endure. Her brothers would, of course, dance with the Coverdale girls; and her father would, of course, stand up with Isabella. There was no other possible arrangement, — at any rate as a beginning. She had schooled herself, too, as to the way in which she would speak to him on the occasion, and how she would remain mistress of herself and of her thoughts. But when the time came the difficulty was almost too much for her.

"You do not care much for dancing, if I remember?" said he.

"Oh yes, I do. Not as Patty Coverdale does; it's a passion with her. But then I'm older than Patty Coverdale." After that he was silent for a minute or two.

"It seems so odd for me to be here again," he said. It was odd. She felt that it was odd. But he ought not to have said so.

"Two years make a great difference; the boys have grown so much."

"Yes; and there are other things."

"Bella was never here before, — at least not with you."

"No; but I did not exactly mean that. All that would not make the place so strange. But your mother seems altered to me —. She used to be almost like my own mother."

"I suppose she finds that you are a more formidable person as you grow older. It was all very well scolding you when you were a clerk in the bank, but it does not do to scold the manager. Those are the penalties men pay for becoming great."

"It is not my greatness that stands in my way, but" —

"Then I'm sure I cannot say what it is. But Patty will scold you if you do not mind the figure, though you were the whole board of directors packed into one."

When Bessy went to bed that night she began to feel that she had attempted too much. "Mamma," she said, "could I not make some excuse, and go away to aunt Mary?"

"What, now!"

"Yes, mamma. Now — to-morrow. I need not say that it will

make me unhappy to be away at such a time; but I begin to think
that it will be better."

"What will papa say?"

"You must tell him all."

"And aunt Mary must be told, also. You would not like that.
Has he said anything?"

"No, nothing; — very little, that is. But Bella has spoken to
me. Oh! mamma, I think we have been wrong in this: that is, I
have been wrong. I feel as though I should disgrace myself, and
turn the whole party here into a misfortune."

It would be dreadful, that telling of the story, even though her
mother should undertake the task. "I will remain if it be possible," she said; "but, mamma, if I wish to go, you will not stop
me?" Her mother promised that she would not stop her, but
strongly advised her to stand her ground.

On the following morning, when she came downstairs before
breakfast, she found Frank standing in the hall with his gun, of
which he was trying the lock. "It is not loaded, is it, Frank?" said
she.

"Oh dear no! No one thinks of loading nowadays till one has
got out of the house. Directly after breakfast I am going across
with Godfrey to the back of Greystock to see after some moor
fowl. He asked me to go, and I couldn't well refuse."

"Of course not. Why should you?"

"It will be deuced hard work to make up the time. I was to
have been up at four this morning, but that alarum went off and
never woke me. However, I shall be able to do something to-
night."

"Don't make a slavery of your holidays, Frank. What's the
good of having a new gun if you're not to enjoy it?"

"It's not the new gun. I'm not such a child as that comes to.
But you see Godfrey is here, and one ought to be civil to him. I'll
tell you what I want you girls to do, Bessy. You must come and
meet us on our way home. Come over in the boat, and along the
path to the Patterdale road. We'll be there under the hill at
about five."

"And, if you are not there, are we to wait in the snow?"

"Don't make difficulties, Bessy. I tell you we will be there. We
are to go in the cart, and so shall have plenty of time."

"And how do you know the other girls will go?"

"Why, to tell you the truth, Patty Coverdale has promised. As for Miss Holmes, if she won't, why, you must leave her at home with mamma. But Kate and Patty can't come without you."

"Your discretion has found that out, has it?"

"Well, Patty says so. But you will come, won't you, Bessy? As for waiting, it's all nonsense. Of course you can walk on. But we'll be at the stile by five. I've got my watch, you know." And then Bessy promised him. What would she not have done for him that was in her power to do?

"Go! of course I'll go!" said Miss Holmes; "I'm up to anything. I'd have gone with them in the morning, and have taken a gun, if they had asked me. But, by-the-by, I'd better not."

"Why not?" said Patty, who was hardly yet without fear lest something should mar the expedition.

"What will three gentlemen do with four ladies?"

"Oh, I forgot," said Patty, innocently.

"I'm sure I don't care," said Kate. "You may have Harry if you like."

"Thank you for nothing," said Miss Holmes. "I want one for myself. It's all very well for you to make the offer; but what should I do if Harry wouldn't have me? There are two sides, you know, to every bargain."

"I'm sure he isn't anything to me," said Kate. "Why, he is not quite seventeen yet."

"Poor boy! What a shame to dispose of him so soon! We'll let him off for a year or two; won't we, Miss Coverdale? But as there seems, by acknowledgment, to be one beau with unappropriated services" —

"I'm sure I have appropriated nobody," said Patty, "and don't intend."

"Godfrey, then, is the only knight whose services are claimed," said Miss Holmes, looking at Bessy. Bessy made no immediate answer with either her eyes or tongue, but when the Coverdales were gone she took her new friend to task.

"How can you fill those young girls' heads with such nonsense?"

"Nature has done that, my dear."

"But Nature should be trained, should it not? You will make

them think that those foolish boys are in love with them."

"They'll be sure to think that without any teaching from me. The foolish boys, as you call them, will look after that themselves. It seems to me that the foolish boys know what they are about better than some of their elders." And then, after a moment's pause, she added, "As for my brother, I have no patience with him."

"Pray do not discuss your brother," said Bessy. "And, Bella, unless you wish to drive me away, pray do not speak of him and me together as you did just now."

"Are you so bad as that, that the slightest commonplace joke upsets you? Would not his services be due to you as a matter of course? If you are so sore about it you will betray your secret."

"I have no secret — none, at least, from you, or from mamma; and, indeed, none from him. We were both very foolish, thinking that we knew each other and our own hearts, when we knew neither."

"I hate to hear people talk of knowing their hearts. My idea is that, if you like a young man, and he asks you to marry him, you ought to have him — that is, if there's enough to live on. I don't know what more is wanted. But girls are getting to talk and think as though they were to send their hearts through some fiery furnace of trial before they give them up to a husband's keeping. I'm not at all sure that the French fashion is not the best, and that these things shouldn't be managed by the fathers and mothers, or perhaps by the family lawyers. Girls who are so intent upon knowing their own hearts generally end by knowing nobody's hearts but their own, and then they die old maids."

"Better that than give themselves to the keeping of those they don't know or cannot esteem."

"That's a matter of taste. I mean to take the first that comes, so long as he looks like a gentleman and has no less than eight hundred a year. Now, Godfrey does look like a gentleman, and has nearly double that. If I had such a chance I shouldn't think twice of it."

"And if you had not you would not think of it at all."

"That's the way the wind blows, is it?"

"No, no! Oh, Bella, pray, pray leave me alone. Pray do not interfere. There is no wind blowing any way. All that I want is your silence and your sympathy."

"Very well. I will be silent and sympathetic as the grave. Only don't imagine that I am cold as the grave also. I don't exactly appreciate your ideas; but, if I can do no good, I will at any rate endeavour to do no harm."

After lunch, at about three, they started on their walk, and managed to ferry themselves over the river. "Oh, do let me, Bessy," said Kate Coverdale; "I understand all about it. Look here, Miss Holmes. You pull the chain through your hands" —

"And inevitably tear your gloves to pieces," said Miss Holmes. Kate certainly had done so, and did not seem to be particularly well pleased with the accident.

"There's a nasty nail in the chain," she said. "I wonder whv those stupid boys did not tell us."

Of course they reached the trysting-place much too soon, and were very tired of walking up and down to keep their feet warm before the sportsmen came up; but this was their own fault, seeing that they had reached the stile half an hour before the time fixed.

"I never will go anywhere to meet gentlemen again," said Miss Holmes. "It is most preposterous that ladies should be left in the snow for an hour. Well, young men, what sport have you had?"

"I shot the big black cock," said Harry.

"Did you, indeed?" said Kate Coverdale.

"And there are the feathers out of his tail for you. He dropped them in the water, and I had to go in after them up to my middle; but I told you that I would, so I was determined to get them."

"Oh, you silly, silly boy!" said Kate. "But I'll keep them for ever; I will indeed."

This was said a little apart, for Harry had managed to draw the young lady aside before he presented the feathers.

Frank also had his trophies for Patty, and the tale to tell of his own prowess. In that he was a year older than his brother, he was by a year's growth less ready to tender his present to his lady-love openly in the presence of them all; but he found his opportunity; and then he and Patty went on a little in advance. Kate was deep in her consolations to Harry as to his ducking, and thus they four disposed of themselves. Miss Holmes, therefore, and her brother, and Bessy Garrow were left together in the path, and discussed

15

the performances of the day in a manner that exhibited no very ecstatic interest. So they walked for a mile, and by degree the conversation between them dwindled down almost to silence.

"There is nothing I dislike so much as coming out with people younger than myself," said Miss Holmes; "one always feels so old and dull. Listen to those children, there! They make me think myself an old maiden aunt brought out with them to do propriety."

"Patty won't at all approve if she hears you call her a child."

"Nor shall I approve if she treats me like an old woman." And then she stepped on and joined "the children." "I wouldn't spoil even their sport if I could help it," she said to herself. "But with them I shall only be a temporary nuisance. If I remain behind I shall do permanent injury." And thus Bessy and her old lover were left by themselves.

"I hope you will get on well with Bella," said Godfrey, when they had remained silent for a minute or two.

"Oh, yes; she is so good-natured and light-hearted that everybody must like her. But I fear she must find it very dull here."

"She is never dull anywhere; not even at Liverpool, which, for a young lady, I sometimes think is the dullest place on earth. I know it is for a man."

"A man who has work to do can never be dull; can he?"

"Indeed he can; as dull as death. I am so often enough. I have never been very bright there, Bessy, since you left us."

There was nothing in his calling her Bessy, for it had become a habit with him since they were children, and they had formally agreed that everything between them should be as it had been before that foolish whisper of love had been spoken. Indeed, provision had been made by them specially on this point, so that there need be no awkwardness in their mode of addressing each other. Such provision had seemed to be very prudent, but it hardly had the desired effect on the present occasion.

"I don't know what you mean by brightness," she said, after a pause. "Perhaps it is not intended that people's lives should be what you call bright."

"Life ought to be as bright as we can make it."

"It all depends on the meaning of the word. I suppose we are not very bright here at Thwaite Hall; but yet we think ourselves very happy."

"I'm sure you are," said Godfrey. "I very often think of you here."

"We always think of the places where we've been when we were young," said Bessy. Then again they walked on for some way in silence, and Bessy began to increase her pace with the view of catching the children. The present walk to her was anything but bright, and she reflected with dismay that they were still two miles distant from the ferry.

"Bessy," Godfrey said at last; and then he stopped, doubting how he ought to proceed. She, however, did not say a word, but walked on quickly, as though her only hope were in catching the party before her. But they also were walking quickly; for Bella had determined that she would not be caught.

"Bessy, I must speak to you once of what passed between us at Liverpool."

"Must you?" said she.

"Unless you positively forbid it."

"Stop, Godfrey," she said. And they did stop in the path; for now she no longer thought of putting an end to her embarrassment by overtaking her companions. "If any such words are necessary for your comfort it would hardly become me to forbid them. Were I to do so, you might accuse me afterwards of harshness in your own heart. It must be for you to judge whether it is well to reopen a wound that is nearly healed."

"But with me it is not nearly healed. The wound is open always."

"There are some hurts," she said, "which do not admit of an absolute and perfect cure, unless after long years." As she said this she could not but think how much better was his chance of such perfect cure than her own. With her — so she said to herself — such curing was all but impossible; whereas with him it was almost as impossible that the injury should last.

"Bessy," he said — and he again stopped her in the narrow path, standing immediately before on the way — "you remember all the circumstances that made us part?"

"Yes, I think I remember them."

"And you still think that we were right?"

She paused for a moment before she answered him; but it was

17

only for a moment, and then she spoke quite firmly. "Yes, Godfrey, I do. I have thought about it much since then. I have thought, I fear to no good purpose, about aught else. But I have never thought that we had been unwise in that."

"And yet, I think, you loved me?"

"I am bound to confess I did so, as otherwise I must confess myself a liar. I told you at that time that I loved you, and I told you so truly. But it is better — ten times better — that those who love should part, even though they still should love, than that two should be joined together who are incapable of making each other happy. Remember what you told me."

"I do remember."

"You found yourself unhappy in your engagement, and you said that it was my fault."

"Bessy, there is my hand. If you have ceased to love me, there is an end of it; but if you love me still let all that I then said be forgotten."

"Forgotten, Godfrey! How can it be forgotten? You were unhappy, and it was my fault. My fault — as it would be if I tried to solace a sick child with arithmetic, or feed a dog with grass. I had no right to love you, knowing you as I did, and knowing also that my ways would not be your ways. My punishment I understand, and it is not more than I can bear; but I had hoped that your punishment would have been soon over."

"You are too proud, Bessy."

"That is very likely. Frank says that I am a Puritan, and pride was the worst of their sins."

"Too proud and unbending. In marriage should not the man and woman adapt themselves to each other?"

"When they are married, yes; and every girl who thinks of marrying should know that in very much she must adapt herself to her husband. But I do not think that a woman should be the ivy, to take the direction of every branch of the tree to which she clings. If she does so, what can be her own character? But we must go on, or we shall be too late."

"And you will give me no other answer?"

"None other, Godfrey. Have you not just now, at this very moment, told me that I was too proud? Can it be possible that you should wish to tie yourself for life to female pride? And if you tell me that now, at such a moment as this, what would you tell me in the close intimacy of married life, when the trifles of every day would have worn away the courtesies of the guest and lover?"

There was a sharpness of rebuke in this which Godfrey Holmes could not at the moment overcome. Nevertheless, he knew the girl, and understood the workings of her heart and mind. Now, in her present state, she would be unbending, proud, and almost rough. In that she had much to lose in declining the renewed offer which he made her, she would, as it were, continually prompt herself to be harsh and inflexible. Had he been poor, had she not loved him, had not all good things seemed to have attended the promise of such a marriage, she would have been less suspicious of herself in receiving the offer, and more gracious in replying to it. Had he lost all his money before he came back to her she would have taken him at once; or had he been deprived of an eye or become crippled in his legs she would have done so. But, circumstanced as he was, she had no motive to tenderness. There was an organic defect in her character, which, no doubt, was plainly marked by its own bump on her cranium — the bump of philomartyrdom, as it might properly be called. She had shipwrecked her own happiness in rejecting Godfrey Holmes, but it seemed to her to be the proper thing that a well-behaved young lady should shipwreck her own happiness. In the last month or two she had been tossed about by the waters and was nearly drowned. Now there was beautiful land again close to her, and a strong, pleasant hand stretched out to save her; but, though she had suffered terribly among the waves, she still thought it wrong to be saved. It would be so pleasant to take that hand, — so sweet, so joyous, that it surely must be wrong. That was her doctrine; and Godfrey Holmes, though he had hardly analysed the matter, partly understood that it was so; and yet, if once she were landed on that green island, she would be happy. She spoke with scorn of a woman clinging to her husband like ivy to a tree; and yet, were she once married, no woman would cling to her husband with sweeter feminine tenacity than Bessy Garrow. He spoke no further word to her as he walked home, but in handing her down into the ferry-boat he pressed her hand: for a second it seemed as though she had returned his pressure; if so, the action was involuntary, and her hand instantly resumed its stiffness to his touch.

It was late that night when Major Garrow went to his bed-room, but his wife was still up waiting for him. "Well," said she, "what has he said to you? He has been with you above an hour."

"Such stories are never very quickly told," said the father, "and in this case it was necessary to understand him very accurately."

It would be wearisome to repeat all that was said on that night between the Major and Mrs. Garrow as to the offer which had now for a third time been made to their daughter. On that evening, after the ladies had gone, and when the two boys had taken themselves off, Godfrey Holmes had told his tale to his host, and had honestly explained to him what he believed to be the state of his daughter's feelings. "Now you know it all," said he. "I do believe that she loves me; and, if she does, perhaps she may still listen to you." Major Garrow did not then feel sure that he knew it all. But, when he had fully discussed the matter that night with his wife, then he thought that, perhaps, he had arrived at that knowledge.

On the following morning Bessy learned from the maid at an early hour that Godfrey Holmes had left Thwaite Hall and gone back to Liverpool. To the girl she said nothing on the subject; but she felt herself obliged to say a word or two to Bella. "It is his coming that I regret," she said — "that he should have had the trouble and annoyance for nothing. I acknowledge that it was my fault, and I am very sorry."

"It cannot be helped," said Miss Holmes somewhat gravely. "As to his misfortunes, I presume that his journeys between here and Liverpool are not the worst of them."

After breakfast on that day Bessy was summoned into her father's bookroom, and found him there, and her mother also. "Bessy," said he, "sit down, my dear. You know why Godfrey has left us this morning?" Bessy walked round the room so that in sitting she might be close to her mother, and take her mother's hand in her own.

"I suppose I do, papa," she said.

"He was with me late last night, Bessy; and, when he told me what had passed between you, I agreed with him that he had better go."

"It was better that he should go, papa."

"But he has left a message for you."

"A message, papa!"

"Yes, Bessy; and your mother agreed with me that it had better be given to you. It is this, — that, if you will send him word to come again, he will be here by Twelfth Night. He came before on my invitation, but if he returns it must be on yours."

"Oh, papa, I cannot."

"I do not say that you can; but you should think of it calmly before you refuse. You shall give me your answer on New Year's morning."

"Mamma knows that it would be impossible," said Bessy.

"Not impossible, dearest. I do know that it would be a hard thing to do."

"In such a matter you should do what you believe to be right," said her father.

"If I were to ask him here again it would be telling that I would" —

"Exactly, Bessy; it would be telling him that you would be his wife. He would understand it so, and so would your mother and I. It must be understood altogether."

"But, papa, when we were at Liverpool" —

"I have told him everything, dearest," said Mrs. Garrow.

"I think I understand the whole," said the Major; "and in such a matter as this I will give no advice on either side. But you must remember that, in making up your mind, you must think of him as well as of yourself. If you do not love him, — if you feel that as his wife you could not love him, — there is not another word to be said. I need not explain to my daughter that under such circumstances she would be wrong to encourage the visits of a suitor. But your mother says you do love him?"

"Oh, mamma!"

"I will not ask you. But, if you do, — if you have so told him, and allowed him to build up an idea of his life's happiness on such telling, — you will, I think, sin greatly against him by allowing false feminine pride to mar his happiness. When once a girl has confessed to a man that she loves him, the confession and the love together put upon her the burden of a duty towards him which she cannot with impunity throw aside." Then he kissed her, and, bidding her give him a reply on the morning of the New Year, left her with her mother.

She had four days for consideration, and they went past with her by no means easily. Could she have been alone with her mother the struggle would not have been so painful, but there was the necessity that she should talk to Isabella Holmes, and the necessity also that she should not neglect the Coverdales. None could have been kinder than Bella. She did not speak on the subject till the morning of the last day, and then only in a very few words. "Bessy," she said, "as you are great, be merciful!"

"But I am not great, and it would not be mercy," replied Bessy.

"As to that," said Bella, "he has surely a right to his own opinion."

On that evening she was sitting alone in her room when her mother came to her, and her eyes were red with weeping. Pen and paper were before her as though she were resolved to write, but hitherto no word had been written.

"Well, Bessy," said her mother, sitting down close beside her, "is the deed done?"

"What deed, mamma? Who says that I am to do it?"

"The deed is not the writing, but the resolution to write. Five words will be sufficient, if only those five words may be written."

"It is for one's whole life, mamma; for his life as well as my own."

"True, Bessy; that is quite true. But it is equally true whether you bid him come or allow him to remain away. That task of making up one's mind for life must always at last be done in some special moment of that life."

"Mamma, mamma, tell me what I should do."

But this Mrs. Garrow would not do. "I will write the words for you if you like," she said; "but it is you who must resolve that they shall be written. I cannot bid my darling go away and leave me for another home. I can only say that in my heart I do believe that home would be a happy one."

It was morning before the note was written; but when the morning came Bessy had written it and brought it to her mother. "You must take it to papa," she said. Then she went, and hid herself from all eyes till the noon was passed. "Dear Godfrey," —

the letter ran, — "Papa says that you will return on Wednesday if I write to ask you. Do come back to us, — if you wish it. Yours always, Bessy."

"It is as good as though she had filled the sheet," said the Major. But in sending it to Godfrey Holmes he did not omit a few accompanying remarks of his own.

An answer came from Godfrey by return of post, and, on the afternoon of the 6th of January, Frank Garrow drove over to the station at Penrith to meet him. On their way back to Thwaite there grew up a very close confidence between the two future brothers-in-law, and Frank explained with great perspicuity a little plan which he had arranged himself. "As soon as it is dark, so that she won't see, Harry will hang it up in the dining-room" he said; "and mind you go in there before you go anywhere else."

"I am very glad you have come back, Godfrey," said the Major meeting him in the hall. "God bless you, dear Godfrey," said Mrs. Garrow. "You will find Bessy in the dining-room," she whispered; but in so whispering she was quite unconscious of Frank's mistletoe bough.

And so also was Bessy. Nor do I think that she was much more conscious when that interview was over. Godfrey had made all manner of promises to Frank; but when the moment arrived he had found the crisis too important for any special reference to the little bough above his head. Not so, however, Patty Coverdale. "It's a shame," she said, bursting out of the room; "and if I'd known what you had done nothing on earth should have induced me to go in. I will not enter the room again till I know that you have taken it out." Nevertheless, her sister Kate was bold enough to solve the mystery before the evening was over.

"The Mistletoe Bough" appeared for the first time in 1861 in The Christmas Supplement to The Illustrated London News.

Christmas at Thompson Hall

Mrs. Brown's Success

EVERYONE REMEMBERS the severity of the Christmas of 187-. I will not designate the year more closely, lest I should enable those who are too curious to investigate the circumstances of this story, and inquire into details which I do not intend to make known. That winter, however, was especially severe, and the cold of the last ten days of December was more felt, I think, in Paris than in any part of England. It may, indeed, be doubted whether there is any town in any country in which thoroughly bad weather is more afflicting than in the French capital. Snow and hail seem to be colder there, and fires certainly are less warm, than in London. And then there is a feeling among visitors to Paris that Paris ought to be gay; that gaiety, prettiness, and liveliness are its aims, as money, commerce, and general business are the aims of London, — which with its outside sombre darkness does often seem to want an excuse for its ugliness. But on this occasion, at this Christmas of 187-, Paris was neither gay nor pretty nor lively. You could not walk the streets without being ankle deep, not in snow, but in snow that had just become slush; and there were falling throughout the day and night of the 23rd of December a succession of damp half-frozen abominations from the sky which made it almost impossible for men and women to go about their business.

It was at ten o'clock on that evening that an English lady

and gentleman arrived at the Grand Hotel on the Boulevard des Italiens. As I have reasons for concealing the names of this married couple I will call them Mr. and Mrs. Brown. Now I wish it to be understood that in all the general affairs of life this gentleman and this lady lived happily together, with all the amenities which should bind a husband and a wife. Mrs. Brown was one of a wealthy family, and Mr. Brown, when he married her, had been relieved from the necessity of earning his bread. Nevertheless she had at once yielded to him when he expressed a desire to spend the winters of their life in the South of France; and he, though he was by disposition somewhat idle, and but little prone to the energetic occupations of life, would generally allow himself, at other periods of the year, to be carried hither and thither by her, whose more robust nature delighted in the excitement of travelling. But on this occasion there had been a little difference between them.

Early in December an intimation had reached Mrs. Brown at Pau that on the coming Christmas there was to be a great gathering of all the Thompsons in the Thompson family hall at Stratford-le-Bow, and that she who had been a Thompson was desired to join the party with her husband. On this occasion her only sister was desirous of introducing to the family generally a most excellent young man to whom she had recently become engaged. The Thompsons, — the real name, however, is in fact concealed, — were a numerous and a thriving people. There were uncles and cousins and brothers who had all done well in the world, and who were all likely to do better still. One had lately been returned to Parliament for the Essex Flats, and was at the time of which I am writing a conspicuous member of the gallant Conservative majority. It was partly in triumph at this success that the great Christmas gathering of the Thompsons was to be held, and an opinion had been expressed by the legislator himself that should Mrs. Brown, with her husband, fail to join the family on this happy occasion she and he would be regarded as being *fainéant* Thompsons.

Since her marriage, which was an affair now nearly eight years old, Mrs. Brown had never passed a Christmas in England. The desirability of doing so had often been mooted by her. Her very soul craved the festivities of holly and mince-pies. There had ever been meetings of the Thompsons at Thompson Hall, though meetings not so significant, not so important to the family, as this one which was now to be collected. More than once had she expressed a wish to see old Christmas again in the old house among the old faces. But her husband had always pleaded a certain weakness about his throat and chest as a reason for remaining among the delights of Pau. Year after year she had yielded; and now this loud summons had come.

It was not without considerable trouble that she had induced Mr. Brown to come as far as Paris. Most unwillingly had he left Pau; and then, twice on his journey, — both at Bordeaux and Tours, — he had made an attempt to return. From the first moment he had pleaded his throat, and when at last he had consented to make the journey he had stipulated for sleeping at those two towns and at Paris. Mrs. Brown, who, without the slightest feeling of fatigue, could have made the journey from Pau to Stratford without stopping, had assented to everything, — so that they might be at Thompson Hall on Christmas Eve. When Mr. Brown uttered his unavailing complaints at the two first towns at which they stayed, she did not perhaps quite believe all that he said of his own condition. We know how prone the strong are to suspect the weakness of the weak, — as the weak are to be disgusted by the strength of the strong. There were perhaps a few words between them on the journey, but the result had hitherto been in favour of the lady. She had succeeded in bringing Mr. Brown as far as Paris.

Had the occasion been less important, no doubt she would have yielded. The weather had been bad even when they left Pau, but as they had made their way northwards it had become worse and still worse. As they left Tours Mr. Brown, in a hoarse whisper, had declared his conviction that the journey would kill him. Mrs. Brown, however, had unfortunately noticed half an hour before that he had scolded the waiter on the score of an overcharged franc or two with a loud and clear voice. Had she really believed that there was danger, or even

suffering, she would have yielded; — but no woman is satisfied in such a matter to be taken in by false pretences. She
observed that he ate a good dinner on his way to Paris, and
that he took a small glass of cognac with complete relish, —
which a man really suffering from bronchitis surely would not
do. So she persevered, and brought him into Paris, late in the
evening, in the midst of all that slush and snow. Then, as
they sat down to supper, she thought that he did speak
hoarsely, and her loving feminine heart began to misgive her.

But this now was at any rate clear to her, — that he could
not be worse off by going on to London than he would be
should he remain in Paris. If a man is to be ill he had better
be ill in the bosom of his family than at a hotel. What comfort could he have, what relief, in that huge barrack? As for
the cruelty of the weather, London could not be worse than
Paris, and then she thought she had heard that sea air is good
for a sore throat. In that bedroom which had been allotted to
them *au quatrième*, they could not even get a decent fire. It
would in every way be wrong now to forego the great Christmas gathering when nothing could be gained by staying in
Paris.

She had perceived that as her husband became really ill he
became also more tractable and less disputatious. Immediately
after that little glass of cognac he had declared that he would
be_____ if he would go beyond Paris, and she began to
fear that, after all, everything would have been done in vain.
But as they went down to supper between ten and eleven he
was more subdued, and merely remarked that this journey
would, he was sure, be the death of him. It was half-past
eleven when they got back to their bedroom, and then he
seemed to speak with good sense, — and also with much real
apprehension. "If I can't get something to relieve me I know I
shall never make my way on," he said. It was intended that
they should leave the hotel at half-past five the next morning,
so as to arrive at Stratford, travelling by the tidal train, at
half-past seven on Christmas Eve. The early hour, the long
journey, the infamous weather, the prospect of that horrid gulf
between Boulogne and Folkestone, would have been as nothing to Mrs. Brown, had it not been for that settled look of

anguish which had now pervaded her husband's face. "If you don't find something to relieve me I shall never live through it," he said again, sinking back into the questionable comfort of a Parisian hotel arm-chair.

"But, my dear, what can I do?" she asked, almost in tears, standing over him and caressing him. He was a thin, genteel-looking man, with a fine long, soft brown beard, a little bald at the top of the head, but certainly a genteel-looking man. She loved him dearly, and in her softer moods was apt to spoil him with her caresses. "What can I do, my dearie? You know I would do anything if I could. Get into bed, my pet, and be warm, and then to-morrow morning you will be all right." At this moment he was preparing himself for his bed, and she was assisting him. Then she tied a piece of flannel round his throat, and kissed him, and put him in beneath the bed-clothes.

"I'll tell you what you can do," he said very hoarsely. His voice was so bad now that she could hardly hear him. So she crept close to him, and bent over him. She would do anything if he would only say what. Then he told her what was his plan. Down in the salon he had seen a large jar of mustard standing on a sideboard. As he left the room he had observed that this had not been withdrawn with the other appurtenances of the meal. If she could manage to find her way down there, taking with her a handkerchief folded for the purpose, and if she could then appropriate a part of the contents of that jar, and returning with her prize, apply it to his throat, he thought that he could get some relief, so that he might be able to leave his bed the next morning at five. "But I am afraid it will be very disagreeable for you to go down all alone at this time of night," he croaked out in a piteous whisper.

"Of course I'll go," said she. "I don't mind going in the least. Nobody will bite me," and she at once began to fold a clean handkerchief. "I won't be two minutes, my darling, and if there is a grain of mustard in the house I'll have it on your chest almost immediately." She was a woman not easily cowed, and the journey down into the salon was nothing to her. Before she went she tucked the clothes carefully up to his ears, and then she started.

To run along the first corridor till she came to a flight of stairs was easy enough, and easy enough to descend them. Then there was another corridor, and another flight, and a third corridor and a third flight, and she began to think that she was wrong. She found herself in a part of the hotel which she had not hitherto visited, and soon discovered by looking through an open door or two that she had found her way among a set of private sitting-rooms which she had not seen before. Then she tried to make her way back, up the same stairs and through the same passages, so that she might start again. She was beginning to think that she had lost herself altogether, and that she would be able to find neither the salon nor her bedroom, when she happily met the night porter. She was dressed in a loose white dressing gown, with a white net over her loose hair, and with white worsted slippers. I ought perhaps to have described her personal appearance sooner. She was a large woman, with a commanding bust, thought by some to be handsome, after the manner of Juno. But with strangers there was a certain severity of manner about her, — a fortification, as it were, of her virtue against all possible attacks, — a declared determination to maintain at all points, the beautiful character of a British matron, which, much as it had been appreciated at Thompson Hall, had met with some ill-natured criticism among French men and women. At Pau she had been called La Fière Anglaise. The name had reached her own ears and those of her husband. He had been much annoyed, but she had taken it in good part, — and had endeavoured to live up to it. With her husband she could, on occasion, be soft, but she was of opinion that with other men a British matron should be stern. She was now greatly in want of assistance; but, nevertheless, when she met the porter she remembered her character. "I have lost my way wandering through these horrid passages," she said, in her severest tone. This was in answer to some question from him, — some question to which her reply was given very slowly. Then when he asked where Madame wished to go, she paused, again thinking what destination she would announce. No doubt the man could take her back to her bedroom, but if so, the mustard must be renounced, and with the mustard, as she now feared, all hope of reaching Thompson Hall on Christmas Eve. But she, though she was in many respects a brave woman, did not dare to tell the man that she was prowling about the hotel in order that she might

make a midnight raid upon the mustard pot. She paused, therefore, for a moment, that she might collect her thoughts, erecting
her head as she did so in her best Juno fashion, till the porter was
lost in admiration. Thus she gained time to fabricate a tale. She
had, she said, dropped her handkerchief under the supper table;
would he show her the way to the salon, in order that she might
pick it up. But the porter did more than that, and accompanied
her to the room in which she had supped.

Here, of course, there was a prolonged, and, it need hardly be
said, a vain search. The good-natured man insisted on emptying
an enormous receptacle of soiled table-napkins, and on turning
them over one by one, in order that the lady's property might be
found. The lady stood by unhappy, but still patient, and, as the
man was stooping to his work, her eye was on the mustard pot.
There it was, capable of containing enough to blister the throats
of a score of sufferers. She edged off a little towards it while the
man was busy, trying to persuade herself that he would surely
forgive her if she took the mustard, and told him her whole story.
But the descent from her Juno bearing would have been so great!
She must have owned, not only to the quest for mustard, but also
to a fib, — and she could not do it. The porter was at last of
opinion that Madame must have made a mistake, and Madame
acknowledged that she was afraid it was so.

With a longing, lingering eye, with an eye turned back, oh! so
sadly, to the great jar, she left the room, the porter leading the
way. She assured him that she would find it by herself, but he
would not leave her till he had put her on to the proper passage.
The journey seemed to be longer now even than before, but as
she ascended the many stairs she swore to herself that she would
not even yet be baulked of her object. Should her husband want
comfort for his poor throat, and the comfort be there within her
reach, and he not have it? She counted every stair as she went
up, and marked every turn well. She was sure now that she would
know the way, and that she could return to the room without
fault. She would go back to the salon. Even though the man
should encounter her again, she would go boldly forward and
seize the remedy which her poor husband so grievously required.

"Ah, yes," she said, when the porter told her that her room,
No. 333, was in the corridor which they had then reached, "I

31

know it all now. I am so much obliged. Do not come a step
further." He was anxious to accompany her up to the very door,
but she stood in the passage and prevailed. He lingered awhile —
naturally. Unluckily she had brought no money with her, and
could not give him the two-franc piece which he had earned.
Nor could she fetch it from her room, feeling that were she to
return to her husband without the mustard no second attempt
would be possible. The disappointed man turned on his heel at
last, and made his way down the stairs and along the passage. It
seemed to her to be almost an eternity while she listened to his
still audible footsteps. She had gone on, creeping noiselessly up
to the very door of her room, and there she stood, shading the
candle in her hand, till she thought that the man must have
wandered away into some furthest corner of that endless building. Then she turned once more and retraced her steps.

There was no difficulty now as to the way. She knew it, every
stair. At the head of each flight she stood and listened, but not a
sound was to be heard, and then she went on again. Her heart
beat high with anxious desire to achieve her object, and at the
same time with fear. What might have been explained so easily
at first would now be as difficult of explanation. At last she was
in the great public vestibule, which she was now visiting for the
third time, and of which, at her last visit, she had taken the
bearings accurately. The door was there — closed, indeed, but it
opened easily to the hand. In the hall, and on the stairs, and
along the passages, there had been gas, but here there was no
light beyond that given by the little taper which she carried.
When accompanied by the porter she had not feared the darkness, but now there was something in the obscurity which made
her dread to walk the length of the room up to the mustard jar.
She paused, and listened, and trembled. Then she thought of the
glories of Thompson Hall, of the genial warmth of a British
Christmas, of that proud legislator who was her first cousin, and
with a rush she made good the distance, and laid her hand upon
the copious delft. She looked round, but there was no one there;
no sound was heard; not the distant creak of a shoe, not a rattle
from one of those doors. As she paused with her fair hand upon
the top of the jar, while the other held the white cloth on which
the medicinal compound was to be placed, she looked like Lady

Macbeth as she listened at Duncan's chamber door.

There was no doubt as to the sufficiency of the contents. The jar was full nearly up to the lips. The mixture was, no doubt, very different from that good wholesome English mustard which your cook makes fresh for you, with a little water, in two minutes. It was impregnated with a sour odour, and was, to English eyes, unwholesome of colour. But still it was mustard. She seized the horn spoon, and without further delay spread an ample sufficiency on the folded square of the handkerchief. Then she commenced to hurry her return.

But still there was a difficulty, no thought of which had occurred to her before. The candle occupied one hand, so that she had but the other for the sustenance of her treasure. Had she brought a plate or saucer from the salon, it would have been all well. As it was she was obliged to keep her eye intent on her right hand, and to proceed very slowly on her return journey. She was surprised to find what an aptitude the thing had to slip from her grasp. But still she progressed slowly, and was careful not to miss a turning. At last she was safe at her chamber door. There it was, No. 333.

Mrs. Brown's Failure

With her eye still fixed upon her burden, she glanced up at the number of the door — 333. She had been determined all through not to forget that. Then she turned the latch and crept in. The chamber also was dark after the gaslight on the stairs, but that was so much the better. She herself had put out the two candles on the dressing-table before she had left her husband. As she was closing the door behind her she paused, and could hear that he was sleeping. She was well aware that she had been long absent, — quite long enough for a man to fall into slumber who was given that way. She must have been gone, she thought, fully an hour. There had been no end to that turning over of napkins

33

which she had so well known to be altogether vain. She paused at the centre table of the room, still looking at the mustard, which she now delicately dried from off her hand. She had had no idea that it would have been so difficult to carry so light and so small an affair. But there it was, and nothing had been lost. She took some small instrument from the washing-stand, and with the handle collected the flowing fragments into the centre. Then the question occurred to her whether, as her husband was sleeping so sweetly, it would be well to disturb him. She listened again, and felt that the slight murmur of a snore with which her ears were regaled was altogether free from any real malady in the throat. Then it occurred to her, that after all, fatigue perhaps had only made him cross. She bethought herself how, during the whole journey, she had failed to believe in his illness. What meals he had eaten! How thoroughly he had been able to enjoy his full complement of cigars! And then that glass of brandy, against which she had raised her voice slightly in feminine opposition. And now he was sleeping there like an infant, with full, round, perfected, almost sonorous workings of the throat. Who does not know that sound, almost of two rusty bits of iron scratching against each other, which comes from a suffering windpipe? There was no semblance of that here. Why disturb him when he was so thoroughly enjoying that rest which, more certainly than anything else, would fit him for the fatigue of the morrow's journey?

I think that, after all her labour, she would have left the pungent cataplasm on the table, and have crept gently into bed beside him, had not a thought suddenly struck her of the great injury he had been doing her if he were not really ill. To send her down there, in a strange hotel, wandering among the passages, in the middle of the night, subject to the contumely of any one who might meet her, on a commission which, if it were not sanctified by absolute necessity, would be so thoroughly objectionable! At this moment she hardly did believe that he had ever really been ill. Let him have the cataplasm; if not as a remedy, then as a punishment. It could, at any rate, do him no harm. It was with an idea of avenging rather than of justifying the past labours of the night that she proceeded at once to quick action.

Leaving the candle on the table so that she might steady her right hand with the left, she hurried stealthily to the bed-side. Even though he was behaving badly to her, she would not cause him discomfort by waking him roughly. She would do a wife's duty to him as a British matron should. She would not only put the warm mixture on his neck, but would sit carefully by him for twenty minutes, so that she might relieve him from it when the proper period should have come for removing the counter irritation from his throat. There would doubtless be some little difficulty in this, — in collecting the mustard after it had served her purpose. Had she been at home, surrounded by her own comforts, the application would have been made with some delicate linen bag, through which the pungency of the spice would have penetrated with strength sufficient for the purpose. But the circumstance of the occasion had not admitted this. She had, she felt, done wonders in achieving so much success as this which she had obtained. If there should be anything disagreeable in the operation he must submit to it. He had asked for mustard for his throat, and mustard he should have.

As these thoughts passed quickly through her mind, leaning over him in the dark, with her eye fixed on the mixture lest it should slip, she gently raised his flowing beard with her left hand, and with her other inverted rapidly, steadily but very softly fixed the handkerchief on his throat. From the bottom of his chin to the spot at which the collar bones meeting together form the orifice of the chest it covered the whole noble expanse. There was barely time for a glance, but never had she been more conscious of the grand proportions of that manly throat. A sweet feeling of pity came upon her, causing her to determine to relieve his sufferings in the shorter space of fifteen minutes. He had been lying on his back, with his lips apart, and as she held back his beard, that and her hand nearly covered the features of his face. But he made no violent effort to free himself from the encounter. He did not even move an arm or a leg. He simply emitted a snore louder than any that had come before. She was aware that it was not his wont to be so loud — that there was generally something more delicate and perhaps more querulous in his nocturnal voice, but then the present circumstances were exceptional. She dropped the beard very softly — and there on the pillow before her lay the face of a stranger. She had put the mustard plaster on

35

the wrong man.

Not Priam wakened in the dead of night, not Dido when first she learned that AEneas had fled, not Othello when he learned that Desdemona had been chaste, not Medea when she became conscious of her slaughtered children, could have been more struck with horror than was this British matron as she stood for a moment gazing with awe on that stranger's bed. One vain, half-completed, snatching grasp she made at the handkerchief, and then drew back her hand. If she were to touch him would he not wake at once, and find her standing there in his bedroom? And then how could she explain it? By what words could she so quickly make him know the circumstances of that strange occurrence that he should accept it all before he had said a word that might offend her? For a moment she stood all but paralysed after that faint ineffectual movement of her arm. Then he stirred his head uneasily on the pillow, opened wider his lips, and twice in rapid succession snored louder than before. She started back a couple of paces, and with her body placed between him and the candle, with her face averted, but with her hand still resting on the foot of the bed, she endeavoured to think what duty required of her.

She had injured the man. Though she had done it most unwittingly, there could be no doubt but that she had injured him. If for a moment she could be brave, the injury might in truth be little; but how disastrous might be the consequences if she were now in her cowardice to leave him, who could tell? Applied for fifteen or twenty minutes a mustard plaster may be the salvation of a throat ill at ease, but if left there throughout the night upon the neck of a strong man, ailing nothing, only too prone in his strength to slumber soundly, how sad, how painful, for aught she knew how dangerous might be the effects! And surely it was an error which any man with a heart in his bosom would pardon! Judging from what little she had seen of him she thought that he must have a heart in his bosom. Was it not her duty to wake him, and then quietly to extricate him from the embarrassment which she had brought upon him?

But in doing this what words should she use? How should she wake him? How should she make him understand her goodness, her beneficence, her sense of duty, before he should have jumped from the bed and rushed to the bell, and have summoned all above and all below to the rescue? "Sir, do not move, do not stir, do not scream. I have put a mustard plaster on your throat, thinking that you were my husband. As yet no harm has been done. Let me take it off, and then hold your peace for ever." Where is the man of such native constancy and grace of spirit that, at the first moment of waking with a shock, he could hear these words from the mouth of an unknown woman by his bed-side, and at once obey them to the letter? Would he not surely jump from his bed, with that horrid compound falling about him, — from which there could be no complete relief unless he would keep his present attitude without a motion. The picture which presented itself to her mind as to his probable conduct was so terrible that she found herself unable to incur the risk.

Then an idea presented itself to her mind. We all know how in a moment quick thoughts will course through the subtle brain. She would find that porter and send him to explain it all. There should be no concealment now. She would tell the story and would bid him to find the necessary aid. Alas! as she told herself that she would do so, she knew well that she was only running from the danger which it was her duty to encounter. Once again she put out her hand as though to return along the bed. Then thrice he snorted louder than before, and moved up his knee uneasily beneath the clothes as though the sharpness of the mustard were already working upon his skin. She watched him for a moment longer, and then, with the candle in her hand, she fled.

Poor human nature! Had he been an old man, even a middle-aged man, she would not have left him to his unmerited suffer-ings. As it was, though she completely recognised her duty, and knew what justice and goodness demanded of her, she could not do it. But there was still left to her that plan of sending the night-porter to him. It was not till she was out of the room and had gently closed the door behind her, that she began to bethink herself how she had made the mistake. With a glance of her eye she looked up, and then saw the number on the door: 353. Remarking to herself, with a Briton's natural criticism on things French, that those horrid foreigners do not know how to make their figures, she scudded rather than ran along the corridor, and then down some stairs and along another passage, — so that she might not be found in the neighbourhood should the poor man in his agony rush rapidly from his bed.

In the confusion of her first escape she hardly ventured to look for her own passage, — nor did she in the least know how she had lost her way when she came upstairs with the mustard in her hand. But at the present moment her chief object was the night porter. She went on descending till she came again to that vestibule, and looking up at the clock saw that it was now past one. It was not yet midnight when she left her husband, but she was not at all astonished at the lapse of time. It seemed to her as though she had passed a night among these miseries. And, oh, what a night! But there was yet much to be done. She must find that porter, and then return to her own suffering husband. Ah, — what now should she say to him! If he should really be ill, how should she assuage him? And yet how more than ever necessary was it that they should leave that hotel early in the morning, — that they should leave Paris by the very earliest and quickest train that would take them as fugitives from their present dangers! The door of the salon was open, but she had no courage to go in search of a second supply. She would have lacked strength to carry it up the stairs. Where now, oh, where, was that man? From the vestibule she made her way into the hall, but everything seemed to be deserted. Through the glass she could see a light in the court beyond, but she could not bring herself to endeavour even to open the hall doors.

And now she was very cold, — chilled to her very bones. All this had been done at Christmas, and during such severity of weather as had never before been experienced by living Parisians. A feeling of great pity for herself gradually came upon her. What wrong had she done that she should be so grievously punished? Why should she be driven to wander about in this way till her limbs were failing her? And then, so absolutely important as it was that her strength should support her in the morning! The man would not die even though he were left there without aid, to rid himself of the cataplasm as best he might. Was it absolutely necessary that she should disgrace herself?

But she could not even procure the means of disgracing herself, if that telling her story to the night-porter would have been, a disgrace. She did not find him, and at last resolved to make her way back to her own room without further quest. She began to think that she had done all that she could do. No man was ever killed by a mustard plaster on his throat. His discomfort at the worst would not be worse than hers had been — or too probably than that of her poor husband. So she went back up the stairs and along the passages, and made her way on this occasion to the door of her room without any difficulty. The way was so well known to her that she could not but wonder that she had failed before. But now her hands had been empty, and her eyes had been at her full command. She looked up, and there was the number, very manifest on this occasion, — 333. She opened the door most gently, thinking that her husband might be sleeping as soundly as that other man had slept, and she crept into the room.

Mrs. Brown Attempts to Escape ·

But her husband was not sleeping. He was not even in bed, as she had left him. She found him sitting there before the fire-place, on which one half-burned log still retained a spark of what had once pretended to be a fire. Nothing more wretched than his appearance could be imagined. There was a single lighted candle on the table, on which he was leaning with his two elbows, while his head rested between his hands. He had on a dressing-gown over his night-shirt, but otherwise was not clothed. He shivered audibly, or rather shook himself with the cold, and made the table to chatter as she entered the room. Then he groaned, and let his head fall from his hands on to the table. It occurred to her at the moment as she recognised the tone of his querulous voice, and as she saw the form of his neck, that she must have been deaf and blind when she had mistaken that stalwart stranger for her husband. "Oh, my dear," she said, "why are you not in bed?" He answered nothing in words, but only groaned again. "Why did

39

you get up? I left you warm and comfortable."

"Where have you been all night?" he half whispered, half croaked, with an agonising effort.

"I have been looking for the mustard."

"Have been looking all night and haven't found it? Where have you been?"

She refused to speak a word to him till she had got him into bed, and then she told her story. But, alas, that which she told was not the true story! As she was persuading him to go back to his rest, and while she arranged the clothes again around him, she with difficulty made up her mind as to what she would do and what she would say. Living or dying he must be made to start for Thompson Hall at half-past five on the next morning. It was no longer a question of the amenities of Christmas, no longer a mere desire to satisfy the family ambition of her own people, no longer an anxiety to see her new brother-in-law. She was conscious that there was in that house one whom she had deeply injured, and from whose vengeance, even from whose aspect, she must fly. How could she endure to see that face which she was so well sure that she would recognise, or to hear the slightest sound of that voice which would be quite familiar to her ears, though it had never spoken a word in her hearing? She must certainly fly on the wings of the earliest train which would carry her towards the old house; but in order that she might do so she must propitiate her husband.

So she told her story. She had gone forth, as he had bade her, in search of the mustard, and then had suddenly lost her way. Up and down the house she had wandered, perhaps nearly a dozen times. "Had she met no one?" he asked in that raspy, husky whisper. "Surely there must have been some one about the hotel! Nor was it possible that she could have been roaming about all those hours." "Only one hour, my dear," she said. Then there was a question about the duration of time, in which both of them waxed angry, and as she became angry her husband waxed stronger, and as he became violent beneath the clothes the comfortable idea returned to her that he was not perhaps so ill as he would seem to be. She found herself driven to tell him something about the porter, having to account for that lapse of time by explaining how she had driven the poor man to search for the handkerchief which she had never lost.

"Why did you not tell him you wanted the mustard?"

"My dear!"

"Why not? There is nothing to be ashamed of in wanting mustard."

"At one o'clock in the morning! I couldn't do it. To tell you the truth, he wasn't very civil, and I thought that he was, — perhaps a little tipsy. Now, my dear, do go to sleep."

"Why didn't you get the mustard?"

"There was none there, — nowhere at all about the room. I went down again and searched everywhere. That's what took me so long. They always lock up those kind of things at these French hotels. They are too close-fisted to leave anything out. When you first spoke of it I knew that it would be gone when I got there. Now, my dear, do go to sleep, because we positively must start in the morning."

"That is impossible," said he, jumping up in the bed.

"We must go, my dear. I say that we must go. After all that has passed I wouldn't not be with Uncle John and my cousin Robert to-morrow evening for more, — more, — more than I would venture to say."

"Bother!" he exclaimed.

"It's all very well for you to say that, Charles, but you don't know. I say that we must go to-morrow, and we will."

"I do believe you want to kill me, Mary."

"That is very cruel, Charles, and most false, and most unjust. As for making you ill, nothing could be so bad for you as this wretched place, where nobody can get warm either day or night. If anything will cure your throat for you at once it will be the sea air. And only think how much more comfortable they can make you at Thompson Hall than anywhere in this country. I have so set my heart upon it, Charles, that I will do it. If we are not there to-morrow night Uncle John won't consider us as belonging to the family."

"I don't believe a word of it."

"Jane told me so in her letter. I wouldn't let you know before because I thought it so unjust. But that has been the reason why I've been so earnest about it all through."

It was a thousand pities that so good a woman should have

41

been driven by the sad stress of circumstances to tell so many fibs. One after another she was compelled to invent them, that there might be a way open to her of escaping the horrors of a prolonged sojourn in that hotel. At length, after much grumbling, he became silent, and she trusted that he was sleeping. He had not as yet said that he would start at the required hour in the morning, but she was perfectly determined in her own mind that he should be made to do so. As he lay there motionless, and as she wandered about the room pretending to pack her things, she more than once almost resolved that she would tell him everything. Surely then he would be ready to make any effort. But there came upon her an idea that he might perhaps fail to see all the circumstances, and that, so failing, he would insist on remaining that he might tender some apology to the injured gentleman. An apology might have been very well had she not left him there in his misery — but what apology would be possible now? She would have to see him and speak to him, and everyone in the hotel would know every detail of the story. Everyone in France would know that it was she who had gone to the strange man's bedside, and put the mustard plaster on the strange man's throat in the dead of night! She could not tell the story even to her husband, lest even her husband should betray her.

Her own sufferings at the present moment were not light. In her perturbation of mind she had foolishly resolved that she would not herself go to bed. The tragedy of the night had seemed to her too deep for personal comfort. And then how would it be were she to sleep, and have no one to call her? It was imperative that she should have all her powers ready for thoroughly arousing him. It occurred to her that the servant of the hotel would certainly run her too short of time. She had to work for herself and for him too, and therefore she would not sleep. But she was very cold, and she put on first a shawl over her dressing-gown and then a cloak. She could not consume all the remaining hours of the night in packing one bag and one portmanteau, so that at last she sat down on the narrow red cotton velvet sofa, and, looking at her watch, perceived that as yet it was not much past two o'clock. How was she to get through those other three long, tedious, chilly hours?

Then there came a voice from the bed — "Ain't you coming?"

"I hoped you were asleep, my dear."

"I haven't been asleep at all. You'd better come, if you don't mean to make yourself as ill as I am."

"You are not so very bad, are you, darling?"

"I don't know what you call bad. I never felt my throat so choked in my life before!" Still as she listened she thought that she remembered his throat to have been more choked. If the husband of her bosom could play with her feelings and deceive her on such an occasion as this, — then, then, — then she thought that she would rather not have any husband of her bosom at all. But she did creep into bed, and lay down beside him without saying another word.

Of course she slept, but her sleep was not the sleep of the blest. At every striking of the clock in the quadrangle she would start up in alarm, fearing that she had let the time go by. Though the night was so short it was very long to her. But he slept like an infant. She could hear from his breathing that he was not quite so well as she could wish him to be, but still he was resting in beautiful tranquility. Not once did he move when she started up, as she did so frequently. Orders had been given and repeated over and over again that they should be called at five. The man in the office had almost been angry as he assured Mrs. Brown for the fourth time that Monsieur and Madame would most assuredly be wakened at the appointed time. But still she would trust no one, and was up and about the room before the clock had struck half-past four.

In her heart of hearts she was very tender towards her husband. Now, in order that he might feel a gleam of warmth while he was dressing himself, she collected together the fragments of half-burned wood, and endeavoured to make a little fire. Then she took out from her bag a small pot, and a patent lamp, and some chocolate, and prepared for him a warm drink, so that he might have it instantly as he was awakened. She would do anything for him in the way of ministering to his comfort — only he must go! Yes, he certainly must go!

And then she wondered how that strange man was bearing himself at the present moment. She would fain have ministered to him too had it been possible; but ah! — it was so impossible! Probably before this he would have been aroused from his troubled slumbers. But then — how aroused? At what time in the night would the burning heat upon his chest have awakened him to a sense of torture which must have been so altogether incomprehensible to him? Her strong imagination showed to her a clear picture of the scene, — clear, though it must have been done in the dark. How he must have tossed and hurled himself under the clothes; how those strong knees must have worked themselves up and down before the potent god of sleep would allow him to return to perfect consciousness; how his fingers, restrained by no reason, would have trampled over his feverish throat, scattering everywhere that unhappy poultice! Then when he should have sat up wide awake, but still in the dark — with her mind's eye she saw it all — feeling that some fire as from the infernal regions had fallen upon him but whence he would know not, how fiercely wild would be the working of his spirit! Ah, now she knew, now she felt, now she acknowledged how bound she had been to awaken him at the moment, whatever might have been the personal inconvenience to herself! In such a position what would he do — or rather what had he done? She could follow much of it in her own thoughts; — how he would scramble madly from his bed, and with one hand still on his throat, would snatch hurriedly at the matches with the other. How the light would come, and how then he would rush to the mirror. Ah, what a sight he would behold! She could see it all to the last widespread daub.

But she could not see, she could not tell herself, what in such a position a man would do; — at any rate, not what that man would do. Her husband, she thought, would tell his wife, and then the two of them, between them, would — put up with it. There are misfortunes which, if they be published, are simply aggravated by ridicule. But she remembered the features of the stranger as she had seen them at that instant in which she had dropped his beard, and she thought that there was a ferocity in them, a certain tenacity of self-importance, which would not permit their owner to endure such treatment in silence. Would he not storm and rage, and ring the bell, and call all Paris to witness his revenge?

But the storming and the raging had not reached her yet, and now it wanted but a quarter to five. In three-quarters of an hour they would be in that demi-omnibus which they had ordered for themselves, and in half-an-hour after that they would be flying towards Thompson Hall. Then she allowed herself to think of those coming comforts, — of those comforts so sweet, if only they would come! That very day now present to her was the 24th December, and on that very evening she would be sitting in Christmas joy among all her uncles and cousins, holding her new brother-in-law affectionately by the hand. Oh, what a change from Pandemonium to Paradise; — from that wretched room, from that miserable house in which there was such ample cause for fear, to all the domestic Christmas bliss of the home of the Thompsons! She resolved that she would not, at any rate, be deterred by any light opposition on the part of her husband. "It wants just a quarter to five," she said, putting her hand steadily upon his shoulder, "and I'll get a cup of chocolate for you, so that you may get up comfortably."

"I've been thinking about it," he said, rubbing his eyes with the back of his hands. "It will be so much better to go over by the mail train to-night. We should be in time for Christmas just the same."

"That will not do at all," she answered, energetically. "Come, Charles, after all the trouble do not disappoint me."

"It is such a horrid grind."

"Think what I have gone through, — what I have done for you! In twelve hours we shall be there, among them all. You won't be so little like a man as not to go on now." He threw himself back upon the bed, and tried to readjust the clothes round his neck. "No, Charles, no," she continued; "not if I know it. Take your chocolate and get up. There is not a moment to be lost." With that she laid her hand upon his shoulder, and made him clearly understand that he would not be allowed to take further rest in that bed.

Grumbling, sulky, coughing continually, and declaring that life under such circumstances was not worth having, he did at last get up and dress himself. When once she saw that he was obeying her she became again tender to him, and certainly took much more than her own share of the trouble of the proceedings. Long before the time was up she was ready, and the porter had been summoned to take the luggage down stairs. When the man

45

came she was rejoiced to see that it was not he whom she had met among the passages during her nocturnal rambles. He shouldered the box, and told them that they would find coffee and bread and butter in the small *salle-à-manger* below.

"I told you that it would be so, when you would boil that stuff," said the ungrateful man, who had nevertheless swallowed the hot chocolate when it was given to him.

They followed their luggage down into the hall; but as she went, at every step, the lady looked around her. She dreaded the sight of that porter of the night; she feared lest some potential authority of the hotel should come to her and ask her some horrid question; but of all her fears her greatest fear was that there should arise before her an apparition of that face which she had seen recumbent on its pillow.

As they passed the door of the great salon, Mr. Brown looked in. "Why, there it is still!" said he.

"What?" said she, trembling in every limb.

"The mustard-pot!"

"They have put it in there since," she exclaimed energetically, in her despair. "But never mind. The omnibus is here. Come away." And she absolutely took him by the arm.

But at that moment a door behind them opened, and Mrs. Brown heard herself called by her name. And there was the night-porter, — with a handkerchief in his hand. But the further doings of that morning must be told in a further chapter.

Mrs. Brown Does Escape

It had been visible to Mrs. Brown from the first moment of her arrival on the ground floor that "something was the matter," if we may be allowed to use such a phrase; and she felt all but convinced that this something had reference to her. She fancied that the people of the hotel were looking at her as she swallowed, or tried to swallow, her coffee. When her husband was paying the bill there was something disagreeable in the eye of the man who was taking the money. Her sufferings were very great, and no one sympathised with her. Her husband was quite at his ease, except that he was complaining of the cold. When she was anxious to get him out into the carriage, he still stood there leisurely, arranging shawl after shawl around his throat. "You can do that quite as well in the omnibus," she had just said to him very crossly, when there appeared upon the scene through a side door that very porter whom she dreaded, with a soiled pocket-handkerchief in his hand.

Even before the sound of her own name met her ears Mrs. Brown knew it all. She understood the full horror of her position from that man's hostile face, and from the little article which he held in his hand. If during the watches of the night she had had money in her pocket, if she had made a friend of this greedy fellow by well-timed liberality, all might have been so different! But she reflected that she had allowed him to go unfee'd after all his trouble, and she knew that he was her enemy. It was the handkerchief that she feared. She thought that she might have brazened out anything but that. No one had seen her enter or leave that strange man's room. No one had seen her dip her hands in that jar. She had, no doubt, been found wandering about the house while the slumberer had been made to suffer so strangely, and there might have been suspicion, and perhaps accusation. But she would have been ready with frequent protestations to deny all charges made against her, and, though no one might have believed her, no one could have convicted her. Here, however, was evidence against which she would be unable to stand for a moment. At the first glance she acknowledged the potency of that damning morsel of linen.

During all the horrors of the night she had never given a thought to the handkerchief, and yet she ought to have known that the evidence it would bring against her was palpable and certain. Her name, "M. Brown," was plainly written on the corner. What a fool she had been not to have thought of this! Had she but remembered the plain marking which she, as a careful, well-conducted, British matron, had put upon all her clothes, she would at any hazard have recovered the article. Oh that she had waked the man, or bribed the porter, or even told

47

her husband! But now she was, as it were, friendless, without support, without a word that she could say in her own defence, convicted of having committed this assault upon a strange man as he slept in his own bedroom, and then of having left him! The thing must be explained by the truth; but how to explain such truth, how to tell such story in a way to satisfy injured folk, and she with barely time sufficient to catch the train! Then it occurred to her that they could have no legal right to stop her because the pocket-handkerchief had been found in a strange gentleman's bedroom. "Yes, it is mine," she said, turning to her husband, as the porter, with a loud voice, asked if she were not Madame Brown. "Take it, Charles, and come on." Mr. Brown naturally stood still in astonishment. He did put out his hand, but the porter would not allow the evidence to pass so readily out of his custody.

"What does it all mean?" asked Mr. Brown.

"A gentleman has been — eh — eh —. Something has been done to a gentleman in his bedroom," said the clerk.

"Something done to a gentleman!" repeated Mr. Brown.

"Something very bad indeed," said the porter. "Look here," and he showed the condition of the handkerchief.

"Charles, we shall lose the train," said the affrighted wife.

"What the mischief does it all mean?" demanded the husband.

"Did Madame go into the gentleman's room?" asked the clerk. Then there was an awful silence, and all eyes were fixed upon the lady.

"What does it all mean?" demanded the husband. "Did you go into anybody's room?"

"I did," said Mrs. Brown with much dignity, looking round upon her enemies as a stag at bay will look upon the hounds which are attacking him. "Give me the handkerchief." But the night porter quickly put it behind his back. "Charles, we cannot allow ourselves to be delayed. You shall write a letter to the keeper of the hotel, explaining it all." Then she essayed to swim out, through the front door, into the courtyard in which the vehicle was waiting for them. But three or four men and women interposed themselves, and even her husband did not seem quite ready to continue his journey. "To-night is Christmas Eve," said Mrs. Brown, "and we shall not be at Thompson Hall! Think of my sister!"

"Why did you go into the man's bedroom, my dear?" whispered Mr. Brown in English.

But the porter heard the whisper, and understood the language; — the porter who had not been "tipped." "Ye'es; — vy?" asked the porter.

"It was a mistake, Charles; there is not a moment to lose. I can explain it all to you in the carriage." Then the clerk suggested that Madame had better postpone her journey a little. The gentleman upstairs had certainly been very badly treated, and had demanded to know why so great an outrage had been perpetrated. The clerk said that he did not wish to send for the police — here Mrs. Brown gasped terribly and threw herself on her husband's shoulder, — but he did not think he could allow the party to go till the gentleman upstairs had received some satisfaction. It had now become clearly impossible that the journey could be made by the early train. Even Mrs. Brown gave it up herself, and demanded of her husband that she should be taken back to her bedroom.

"But what is to be said to the gentleman?" asked the porter.

Of course it was impossible that Mrs. Brown should be made to tell her story there in the presence of them all. The clerk, when he found he had succeeded in preventing her from leaving the house, was satisfied with a promise from Mr. Brown that he would inquire from his wife what were these mysterious circumstances, and would then come down to the office and give some explanation. If it were necessary, he would see the strange gentleman, — whom he now ascertained to be a certain Mr. Jones returning from the east of Europe. He learned also that this Mr. Jones had been most anxious to travel by that very morning train which he and his wife had intended to use, — that Mr. Jones had been most particular in giving his orders accordingly, but that at the last moment he had declared himself to be unable even to dress himself, because of the injury which had been done him during the night. When Mr. Brown heard this from the clerk just before he was allowed to take his wife upstairs, while she was sitting on a sofa in a corner with her face hidden, a look of awful gloom came over his own countenance. What could it be that his wife had done to the gentleman of so terrible a nature? "You had better come up with me," he said to her with marital severity, and the poor cowed woman went with him tamely as might have done some patient Grizel. Not a word was spoken till they were in the room and the door was locked. "Now," said he, "what does it all mean?"

It was not till nearly two hours had passed that Mr. Brown came down the stairs very slowly, — turning it all over in his mind. He had now gradually heard the absolute and exact truth, and had very gradually learned to believe it. It was first necessary that he should understand that his wife had told him many fibs during the night; but, as she constantly alleged to him when he complained of her conduct in this respect, they had all been told on his behalf. Had she not struggled to get the mustard for his comfort, and when she had secured the prize had she not hurried to put it on, — as she had fondly thought, — his throat? And though she had fibbed to him afterwards, had she not done so in order that he might not be troubled? "You are not angry with me because I was in that man's room?" she asked, looking full into his eyes, but not quite without a sob. He paused a moment, and then declared, with something of a true husband's confidence in his tone, that he was not in the least angry with her on that account. Then she kissed him, and bade him remember that after all no one could really injure them. "What harm has been done, Charles? The gentleman won't die because he has had a mustard plaster on his throat. The worst is about Uncle John and dear Jane. They do think so much of Christmas Eve at Thompson Hall!"

Mr. Brown, when he again found himself in the clerk's office, requested that his card might be taken up to Mr. Jones. Mr. Jones had sent down his own card, which was handed to Mr. Brown: "Mr. Barnaby Jones." "And how was it all, sir?" asked the clerk, in a whisper — a whisper which had at the same time something of authoritative demand and something also of submissive respect. The clerk of course was anxious to know the mystery. It is hardly too much to say that every one in that vast hotel was by this time anxious to have the mystery unravelled. But Mr. Brown would tell nothing to any one. "It is merely a matter to be explained between me and Mr. Jones," he said. The card was taken upstairs, and after a while he was ushered into

Mr. Jones' room. It was, of course, that very 353 with which the reader is already acquainted. There was a fire burning, and the remains of Mr. Jones' breakfast were on the table. He was sitting in his dressing-gown and slippers, with his shirt open in the front, and a silk handkerchief very loosely covering his throat. Mr. Brown, as he entered the room, of course looked with considerable anxiety at the gentleman of whose condition he had heard so sad an account; but he could only observe some considerable stiffness of movement and demeanour as Mr. Jones turned his head round to greet him.

"This has been a very disagreeable accident, Mr. Jones," said the husband of the lady.

"Accident! I don't know how it could have been an accident. It has been a most — most — most — a most monstrous, — er, — er, — I must say, interference with a gentleman's privacy, and personal comfort."

"Quite so, Mr. Jones, but, — on the part of the lady, who is my wife——"

"So I understand. I myself am about to become a married man, and I can understand what your feelings must be. I wish to say as little as possible to harrow them." Here Mr. Brown bowed. "But, — there's the fact. She did do it."

"She thought it was — me!"

"What!"

"I give you my word as a gentleman, Mr. Jones. When she was putting that mess upon you she thought it was me! She did, indeed."

Mr. Jones looked at his new acquaintance and shook his head. He did not think it possible that any woman would make such a mistake as that.

"I had a very bad sore throat," continued Mr. Brown, "and indeed you may perceive it still," — in saying this, he perhaps aggravated a little sign of his distemper, "and I asked Mrs. Brown to go down and get one, — just what she put on you."

"I wish you'd had it," said Mr. Jones, putting his hand up to his neck.

"I wish I had, — for your sake as well as mine, — and for hers, poor woman. I don't know when she will get over the shock."

"I don't know when I shall. And it has stopped me on my

journey. I was to have been to-night, this very night, this Christmas Eve, with the young lady I am engaged to marry. Of course I couldn't travel. The extent of the injury done nobody can imagine at present."

"It has been just as bad to me, sir. We were to have been with our family this Christmas Eve. There were particular reasons, — most particular. We were only hindered from going by hearing of your condition."

"Why did she come into my room at all? I can't understand that. A lady always knows her own room at an hotel."

"353 — that's yours; 333 — that's ours. Don't you see how easy it was? She had lost her way, and she was a little afraid lest the thing should fall down."

"I wish it had, with all my heart."

"That's how it was. Now I'm sure, Mr. Jones, you'll take a lady's apology. It was a most unfortunate mistake, — most unfortunate; but what more can be said?"

Mr. Jones gave himself up to reflection for a few moments before he replied to this. He supposed that he was bound to believe the story as far as it went. At any rate, he did not know how he could say that he did not believe it. It seemed to him to be almost incredible, — especially incredible in regard to that personal mistake, for, except that they both had long beards and brown beards, Mr. Jones thought that there was no point of resemblance between himself and Mr. Brown. But still, even that, he felt, must be accepted. But then why had he been left, deserted, to undergo all those torments? "She found out her mistake at last, I suppose?" he said.

"Oh, yes."

"Why didn't she wake a fellow and take it off again?"

"Ah!"

"She can't have cared very much for a man's comfort when she went away and left him like that."

"Ah! there was the difficulty, Mr. Jones."

"Difficulty! Who was it that had done it? To come to me, in my bedroom, in the middle of the night and put that thing on me, and then leave it there and say nothing about it! It seems to me deuced like a practical joke."

"No, Mr. Jones!"

"That's the way I look at it," said Mr. Jones, plucking up his courage.

"There isn't a woman in all England, or in all France, less likely to do such a thing than my wife. She's as steady as a rock, Mr. Jones, and would no more go into another gentleman's bedroom in joke than —— Oh dear no! You're going to be a married man yourself."

"Unless all this makes a difference," said Mr. Jones, almost in tears. "I had sworn that I would be with her this Christmas Eve."

"Oh, Mr. Jones, I cannot believe that will interfere with your happiness. How could you think that your wife, as is to be, would do such a thing as that in joke?"

"She wouldn't do it at all; — joke or anyway."

"How can you tell what accident might happen to any one?"

"She'd have wakened the man then afterwards. I'm sure she would. She would never have left him to suffer in that way. Her heart is too soft. Why didn't she send you to wake me, and explain it all. That's what my Jane would have done; and I should have gone and wakened him. But the whole thing is impossible," he said, shaking his head as he remembered that he and his Jane were not in a condition as yet to undergo any such mutual trouble. At last Mr. Jones was brought to acknowledge that nothing more could be done. The lady sent her apology, and told her story, and he must bear the trouble and inconvenience to which she had subjected him. He still, however, had his own opinion about her conduct generally, and could not be brought to give any sign of amity. He simply bowed when Mr. Brown was hoping to induce him to shake hands, and sent no word of pardon to the great offender.

The matter, however, was so far concluded that there was no further question of police interference, nor any doubt but that the lady with her husband was to be allowed to leave Paris by the night train. The nature of the accident probably became known to all. Mr. Brown was interrogated by many, and though he professed to declare that he would answer no question, nevertheless he found it better to tell the clerk something of the truth than to allow the matter to be shrouded in mystery. It is to be feared that Mr. Jones, who did not once show himself through the day, but who employed the hours in endeavouring to assuage the injury done him, still lived in the conviction that the lady had played a practical joke on him. But the subject of such a joke never talks about it, and Mr. Jones could not be induced to speak even by friendly adherence of the night porter.

Mrs. Brown also clung to the seclusion of her own bedroom, never once stirring from it till the time came in which she was to be taken down to the omnibus. Upstairs she ate her meals, and upstairs she passed her time in packing and unpacking, and in requesting that telegrams might be sent repeatedly to Thompson Hall. In the course of the day two such telegrams were sent, in the latter of which the Thompson family were assured that the Browns would arrive, probably in time for breakfast on Christmas Day, certainly in time for church. She asked more than once tenderly after Mr. Jones's welfare, but could obtain no information. "He was very cross, and that's all I know about it," said Mr. Brown. Then she made a remark as to the gentleman's Christian name, which appeared on the card as "Barnaby." "My sister's husband's name will be Burnaby," she said. "And this man's Christian name is Barnaby; that's all the difference," said her husband, with ill-timed jocularity.

We all know how people under a cloud are apt to fail in asserting their personal dignity. On the former day a separate vehicle had been ordered by Mr. Brown to take himself and his wife to the station, but now, after his misfortunes, he contented himself with such provision as the people at the hotel might make for him. At the appointed hour he brought his wife down, thickly veiled. There were many strangers as she passed through the hall, ready to look at the lady who had done that wonderful thing in the dead of night, but none could see a feature of her face as she stepped across the hall, and was hurried into the omnibus. And there were many eyes also on Mr. Jones, who followed her very quickly, for he also, in spite of his sufferings, was leaving Paris on the evening in order that he might be with his English friends on Christmas Day. He, as he went through the crowd, assumed an air of great dignity, to which, perhaps, something was added by his endeavours, as he walked, to save his poor throat from irritation. He, too, got into the same omnibus, stumbling over the feet of his enemy in the dark. At the station they got their tickets, one close after the other, and then were brought into each other's presence in the waiting-room. I think it must be acknowledged that here Mr. Jones was conscious not only of her presence, but of her consciousness of his presence, and that he assumed an attitude, as though he should have said, "Now do you think it possible for me to believe that you mistook me for your husband?" She was perfectly quiet, but sat through that quarter of an hour with her face continually veiled. Mr. Brown made some little overture of conversation to Mr. Jones, but Mr. Jones, though he did mutter some reply, showed plainly enough that he had no desire for further intercourse. Then came the accustomed stampede, the awful rush, the internecine struggle in which seats had to be found. Seats, I fancy, are regularly found, even by the most tardy, but it always appears that every British father and every British husband is actuated at these stormy moments by a conviction that unless he prove himself a very Hercules he and his daughters and his wife will be left desolate in Paris. Mr. Brown was quite Herculean, carrying two bags and a hat-box in his own hands, besides the cloaks, the coats, the rugs, the sticks, and the umbrellas. But when he had got himself and his wife well seated, with their faces to the engine, with a corner seat for her, — there was Mr. Jones immediately opposite to her. Mr. Jones, as soon as he perceived the inconvenience of his position, made a scramble for another place, but he was too late. In that contiguity the journey as far as Dover had to be made. She, poor woman, never once took up her veil. There he sat, without closing an eye, stiff as a ramrod, sometimes showing by little uneasy gestures that the trouble at his neck was still there, but never speaking a word, and hardly moving a limb.

Crossing from Calais to Dover the lady was, of course, separated from her victim. The passage was very bad, and she more than once reminded her husband how well it would have been with them now had they pursued their journey as she had intended, — as though they had been detained in Paris by his fault! Mr. Jones, as he laid himself down on his back, gave himself up to wondering whether any man before him had ever been made subject to such absolute injustice. Now and again he put his hand up to his own beard, and began to doubt whether it could have been moved, as it must have been moved, without waking him. What if chloroform had been used? Many such suspicions crossed his mind during the misery of that passage.

They were again together in the same railway carriage from Dover to London. They had now got used to the close neighbourhood, and knew how to endure each the presence of the other. But as yet Mr. Jones had never seen the lady's face. He longed to know what were the features of the woman who had been so blind — if indeed that story were true. Or if it were not true, of what like was the woman who would dare in the middle of the night to play such a trick as that. But still she kept her veil close over her face.

From Cannon Street the Browns took their departure in a cab for the Liverpool Street Station, whence they would be conveyed by the Eastern Counties Railway to Stratford. Now at any rate their troubles were over. They would be in ample time, not only for Christmas Day church, but for Christmas Day breakfast. "It will be just the same as getting in there last night," said Mr. Brown, as he walked across the platform to place his wife in the carriage for Stratford. She entered it first, and as she did so there she saw Mr. Jones seated in the corner! Hitherto she had borne his presence well, but now she could not restrain herself from a little start and a little scream. He bowed his head very slightly, as though acknowledging the compliment, and then down she dropped her veil. When they arrived at Stratford, the journey being over in a quarter of an hour, Jones was out of the carriage even before the Browns.

"There is Uncle John's carriage," said Mrs. Brown, thinking that now, at any rate, she would be able to free herself from the presence of this terrible stranger. No doubt he was a handsome man to look at, but on no face so sternly hostile had she ever before fixed her eyes. She did not, perhaps, reflect that the owner of no other face had ever been so deeply injured by herself.

Mrs. Brown at Thompson Hall

"Please, sir, we were to ask for Mr. Jones," said the servant, putting his head into the carriage after both Mr. and Mrs. Brown had seated themselves.

"Mr. Jones!" exclaimed the husband.

"Why ask for Mr. Jones?" demanded the wife. The servant was about to tender some explanation when Mr. Jones stepped up and said that he was Mr. Jones. "We are going to Thompson Hall," said the lady with great vigour.

"So am I," said Mr. Jones, with much dignity. It was, however, arranged that he should sit with the coachman, as there was a rumble behind for the other servant. The luggage was put into a cart, and away all went for Thompson Hall.

"What do you think about it, Mary," whispered Mr. Brown, after a pause. He was evidently awe-struck by the horror of the occasion.

"I cannot make it out at all. What do you think?"

"I don't know what to think. Jones going to Thompson Hall!"

"He's a very good-looking young man," said Mrs. Brown.

"Well; — that's as people think. A stiff, stuck-up fellow, I should say. Up to this moment he has never forgiven you for what you did to him."

"Would you have forgiven his wife, Charles, if she'd done it to you?"

"He hasn't got a wife, — yet."

"How do you know?"

"He is coming home now to be married," said Mr. Brown. "He expects to meet the young lady this very Christmas Day. He told me so. That was one of the reasons why he was so angry at being stopped by what you did last night."

"I suppose he knows Uncle John, or he wouldn't be going to the Hall," said Mrs. Brown.

"I can't make it out," said Mr. Brown, shaking his head.

"He looks quite like a gentleman," said Mrs. Brown, "though he has been so stiff. Jones! Barnaby Jones! You're sure it was Barnaby?"

"That was the name on the card."

"Not Burnaby?" asked Mrs. Brown.

"It was Barnaby Jones on the card, — just the same as 'Barnaby Rudge,' and as for looking like a gentleman, I'm by no means quite so sure. A gentleman takes an apology when it's offered."

"Perhaps, my dear, that depends on the condition of his throat. If you had had a mustard plaster on all night, you might not have liked it. But here we are at Thompson Hall at last."

Thompson Hall was an old brick mansion, standing within a huge iron gate, with a gravel sweep before it. It had stood there before Stratford was a town, or even a suburb, and had then been known by the name Bow Place. But it had been in the hands of the present family for the last thirty years, and was now known far and wide as Thompson Hall, — a comfortable, roomy, old-fashioned place, perhaps a little dark and dull to look at, but much more substantially built than most of our modern villas. Mrs. Brown jumped with alacrity from the carriage, and with a quick step entered the home of her forefathers. Her husband followed her more leisurely, but he, too, felt that he was at home at Thompson Hall. Then Mr. Jones walked in also; — but he looked as though he were not at all at home. It was still very early, and no one of the family was as yet down. In these circumstances it was almost necessary that something should be said to Mr. Jones.

"Do you know Mr. Thompson?" asked Mr. Brown.

"I never had the pleasure of seeing him, — as yet," answered Mr. Jones, very stiffly.

"Oh, — I didn't know; — because you said you were coming here."

"And I have come here. Are you friends of Mr. Thompson?"

"Oh, dear, yes," said Mrs. Brown. "I was a Thompson myself before I married."

"Oh, — indeed!" said Mr. Jones. "How very odd; — very odd indeed."

During this time the luggage was being brought into the house, and two old family servants were offering them assistance. Would the new comers like to go up to their bedrooms? Then the housekeeper, Mrs. Green, intimated with a wink that Miss Jane would, she was sure, be down quite immediately. The present moment, however, was still very unpleasant. The lady probably had made her guess as to the mystery; but the two gentlemen were still altogether in the dark. Mrs. Brown had no doubt declared her parentage, but Mr. Jones, with such a multitude of strange facts crowding on his mind, had been slow to understand her. Being somewhat suspicious by nature he was beginning to think whether possibly the mustard had been put by this lady on his throat with some reference to his connexion with Thompson Hall. Could it be that she, for some reason of her own, had wished to prevent his coming, and had contrived this untoward stratagem out of her brain? or had she wished to make him ridiculous to the Thompson family, — to whom, as a family, he was at present unknown? It was becoming more and more improbable to him that the whole thing should have been an accident. When, after the first horrid torments of that morning in which he had in his agony invoked the assistance of the night-porter, he had begun to reflect on his situation, he had determined that it would be better that nothing further should be said about it. What would life be worth to him if he were to be known wherever he went as the man who had been mustard-plastered in the middle of the night by a strange lady? The worst of a practical joke is that the remembrance of the absurd condition sticks so long to the sufferer! At the hotel that night-porter, who had possessed himself of the handkerchief and had read the name and had connected that name with the occupant of 333 whom he had found wandering about the house with some strange purpose, had not permitted the thing to sleep. The porter had pressed the matter home against the Browns, and had produced the interview which has been recorded. But during the whole of that day Mr. Jones had been resolving that he would never again either think of the Browns or speak of them. A great injury had been done to him, — a most outrageous injustice; — but it was a thing which had to be endured. A horrid woman had come across him like a nightmare. All he could do was to endeavour to forget the terrible visitation. Such had been his resolve, — in making which he had passed that long day in Paris. And now the Browns had stuck to him from the moment of his leaving his room! He had been forced to travel with them, but had travelled with them as a stranger. He had tried to comfort himself with the reflection that at every fresh stage he would shake them off. In one railway after another the vicinity had been bad, — but still they were strangers. Now he found himself in the same house with them, — where of course the story would be told. Had not the thing been done on purpose that the story might be told there at Thompson Hall?

Mrs. Brown had acceded to the proposition of the housekeeper, and was about to be taken to her room when there was heard a sound of footsteps along the passage above and on the stairs, and a young lady came bounding on to the scene. "You have all of you come a quarter of an hour earlier than we thought possible," said the young lady. "I did so mean to be up to receive you!" With that she passed her sister on the stairs, — for the young lady was Miss Jane Thompson, sister to our Mrs. Brown, — and hurried down into the hall. Here Mr. Brown, who had ever been on affectionate terms with his sister-in-law, put himself forward to receive her embraces; but she, apparently not noticing him in her ardour, rushed on and threw herself on to the breast of the other gentleman. "This is my Charles," she said. "Oh, Charles, I thought you never would be here."

Mr. Charles Burnaby Jones, for such was his name since he had inherited the Jones property in Pembrokeshire, received into his arms the ardent girl of his heart with all that love, and devotion to which she was entitled, but could not do so without some external shrinking from her embrace. "Oh, Charles, what is it?" she said.

"Nothing, dearest — only — only —." Then he looked piteously up into Mrs. Brown's face, as though imploring her not to tell the story.

"Perhaps, Jane, you had better introduce us," said Mrs. Brown.

"Introduce you! I thought you had been travelling together, and staying at the same hotel — and all that."

"So we have; but people may be in the same hotel without knowing each other. And we have travelled all the way home with Mr. Jones without in the least knowing who he was."

"How very odd! Do you mean you have never spoken?"

"Not a word," said Mrs. Brown.

"I do so hope you'll love each other," said Jane.

"It shan't be my fault if we don't," said Mrs. Brown.

"I'm sure it shan't be mine," said Mr. Brown, tendering his hand to the other gentleman. The various feelings of the moment were too much for Mr. Jones, and he could not respond quite as he should have done. But as he was taken upstairs to his room he determined that he would make the best of it.

The owner of the house was old Uncle John. He was a bachelor, and with him lived various members of the family. There was the great Thompson of them all, Cousin Robert, who was now member of Parliament for the Essex Flats, and young John, as a certain enterprising Thompson of the age of forty was usually called, and then there was old Aunt Bess, and among other young branches there was Miss Jane Thompson who was now engaged to marry Mr. Charles Burnaby Jones. As it happened, no other member of the family had as yet seen Mr. Burnaby Jones, and he, being by nature of a retiring disposition, felt himself to be ill at ease when he came into the breakfast parlour among all the Thompsons. He was known to be a gentleman of good family and ample means, and all the Thompsons had approved of the match, but during that first Christmas breakfast he did not seem to accept his condition jovially. His own Jane sat beside him, but then on the other side sat Mrs. Brown. She assumed an immediate intimacy, — as women know how to do on such occasions, — being determined from the very first to regard her sister's husband as a brother; but he still feared her. She was still to him the woman who had come to him in the dead of night with that horrid mixture, — and had then left him.

"It was so odd that both of you should have been detained on the very same day," said Jane.

"Yes, it was odd," said Mrs. Brown, with a smile, looking round upon her neighbour.

"It was abominably bad weather, you know," said Brown.

"But you were both so determined to come," said the old gentleman. "When we got the two telegrams at the same moment, we were sure that there had been some agreement between you."

"Not exactly an agreement," said Mrs. Brown; whereupon Mr. Jones looked as grim as death.

"I'm sure there is something more than we understand yet," said the member of Parliament.

Then they all went to church, as a united family ought to do on Christmas Day, and came home to a fine old English early dinner at three o'clock, — a sirloin of beef a foot-and-a-half broad, a turkey as big as an ostrich, a plum pudding bigger than the turkey, and two or three dozen mince-pies. "That's a very large bit of beef," said Mr. Jones, who had not lived much in England latterly. "It won't look so large," said the old gentleman, "when all our friends downstairs have had their say to it." "A plum-pudding on Christmas Day can't be too big," he said again, "if the cook will but take time enough over it. I never knew a bit go to waste yet."

By this time there had been some explanation as to past events between the two sisters. Mrs. Brown had indeed told Jane all about it, how ill her husband had been, how she had been forced to go down and look for the mustard, and then what she had done with the mustard. "I don't think they are a bit alike you know, Mary, if you mean that," said Jane.

"Well, no; perhaps not quite alike. I only saw his beard, you know. No doubt it was stupid, but I did it."

"Why didn't you take it off again?" asked the sister.

"Oh, Jane, if you'd only think of it? Could you!" Then of course all that occurred was explained, how they had been stopped on their journey, how Brown had made the best apology in his power, and how Jones had travelled with them and had never spoken a word. The gentleman had only taken his new name a week since but of course had had his new card printed immediately. "I'm sure I should have thought of it if they hadn't made a mistake with the first name. Charles said it was like Barnaby Rudge."

"Not at all like Barnaby Rudge," said Jane; "Charles Burnaby Jones is a very good name."

"Very good indeed, — and I'm sure that after a little bit he won't be at all the worse for the accident."

Before dinner the secret had been told no further, but still there had crept about among the Thompsons, and, indeed, downstairs also, among the retainers, a feeling that there was a secret. The old housekeeper was sure that Miss Mary, as she still called Mrs. Brown, had something to tell if she could only be induced to tell it, and that this something had reference to Mr. Jones' personal comfort. The head of the family, who was a sharp old gentleman, felt this also, and the member of Parliament, who had an idea that he specially should never be kept in the dark, was almost angry. Mr. Jones, suffering from some kindred feeling throughout the dinner, remained silent and unhappy. When two or three toasts had been drunk, — the Queen's health, the old gentleman's health, the young couple's health, Brown's health, and the general health of all the Thompsons, then tongues were loosened and a question was asked, "I know that there has been something doing in Paris between these young people that we haven't heard as yet," said the uncle. Then Mrs. Brown laughed, and Jane, laughing too, gave Mr. Jones to understand that she at any rate knew all about it.

"If there is a mystery I hope it will be told at once," said the member of Parliament, angrily.

"Come, Brown, what is it?" asked another male cousin.

"Well, there was an accident. I'd rather Jones should tell," said he.

Jones's brow became blacker than thunder, but he did not say a word. "You mustn't be angry with Mary," Jane whispered into her lover's ear.

"Come, Mary, you never were slow at talking," said the uncle.

"I do hate this kind of thing," said the member of Parliament.

"I will tell it all," said Mrs. Brown, very nearly in tears, or else pretending to be very nearly in tears. "I know I was very wrong, and I do beg his pardon, and if he won't say that he forgives me I never shall be happy again." Then she clasped her hands, and, turning round, looked him piteously in the face.

"Oh yes; I do forgive you," said Mr. Jones.

"My brother," said she, throwing her arms round him and kissing him. He recoiled from the embrace, but I think that he attempted to return the kiss. "And now I will tell the whole story," said Mrs. Brown. And she told it, acknowledging her fault with true contrition, and swearing that she would atone for it by life-long sisterly devotion.

"And you mustard-plastered the wrong man!" said the old gentleman, almost rolling off his chair with delight.

"I did," said Mrs. Brown, sobbing, "and I think that no woman ever suffered as I suffered."

"And Jones wouldn't let you leave the hotel?"

"It was the handkerchief stopped us," said Brown.

"If it had turned out to be anybody else," said the member of Parliament, "the results might have been most serious, — not to say discreditable."

"That's nonsense, Robert," said Mrs. Brown, who was disposed to resent the use of so severe a word, even from the legislator cousin.

"In a strange gentleman's bedroom!" he continued. "It only shows that what I have always said is quite true. You should never go to bed in a strange house without locking your door."

Nevertheless it was a very jovial meeting, and before the evening was over Mr. Jones was happy, and had been brought to acknowledge that the mustard-plaster would probably not do him any permanent injury.

"Christmas at Thompson Hall" appeared for the first time in 1876 in the Christmas number of The Graphic.

Christmas Day at Kirkby Cottage

What Maurice Archer Said about Christmas

A FTER ALL, CHRISTMAS is a bore!"

"Even though you should think so, Mr. Archer, pray do not say so here."

"But it is."

"I am very sorry that you should feel like that; but pray do not say anything so very horrible."

"Why not? and why is it horrible? You know very well what I mean."

"I do not want to know what you mean; and it would make papa very unhappy if he were to hear you."

"A great deal of beef is roasted, and a great deal of pudding is boiled, and then people try to be jolly by eating more than usual. The consequence is, they get very sleepy, and want to go to bed an hour before the proper time. That's Christmas."

He who made this speech was a young man about twenty-three years old, and the other personage in the dialogue was a young lady, who might be, perhaps, three years his junior. The "papa" to whom the lady had alluded was the Rev. John Lownd, parson of Kirkby Cliffe, in Craven, and the scene was the parsonage library, as pleasant a little room as you would wish to see, in which the young man who thought Christmas to be a bore was at present sitting over the fire, in the parson's arm chair, with a novel in his hand, which he had been reading till he was interrupted by the parson's daughter. It was nearly time for him to dress for dinner, and the young lady was already dressed. She had entered the room on the pretext of looking for some book or paper, but perhaps her main object may have been to ask for some assistance from Maurice Archer in the work of decorating the parish church. The necessary ivy and holly branches had been collected, and the work was to be performed on the morrow. The day following would be Christmas Day. It must be acknowledged, that Mr. Archer had not accepted the proposition made to him very graciously.

Maurice Archer was a young man as to whose future career in life many of his elder friends shook their heads and expressed much fear. It was not that his conduct was dangerously bad, or that he spent his money too fast, but that he was abominably conceited, so said these elder friends; and then there was the unfortunate fact of his being altogether beyond control. He had neither father, nor mother, nor uncle, nor guardian. He was the owner of a small property not far from Kirkby Cliffe, which gave him an income of some six or seven hundred a year, and he had altogether declined any of the professions which had been suggested to him. He had, in the course of the year now coming to a close, taken his degree at Oxford, with some academical honours, which were not high enough to confer distinction, and had already positively refused to be ordained, although, would he do so, a small living would be at his disposal on the death of a septuagenarian cousin. He intended, he said, to farm a portion of his own land, and had already begun to make amicable arrangements for buying up the interest of one of his two tenants. The rector of Kirkby Cliffe, the Rev. John Lownd, had been among his father's dearest friends, and he was now the parson's guest for the Christmas.

There had been many doubts in the parsonage before the young man had been invited. Mrs. Lownd had considered that the visit would be dangerous. Their family consisted of two daughters, the youngest of whom was still a child; but Isabel was turned twenty, and if a young man were brought into the house, would it not follow, as a matter of course, that she should fall in love with him? That was the mother's first argument. "Young people don't always fall in love," said the father. "But people will say that he is brought here on purpose," said the mother, using her second argument. The parson, who in family matters generally had his own way, expressed an opinion that if they were to be governed by what other people might choose to say, their course of action would be very limited indeed. As for his girl, he did not think she would ever give her heart to any man before it had been asked; and as for the young man, — whose father had been for over thirty years his dearest friend, — if he chose to fall in love, he must run his chance, like other young men. Mr. Lownd declared he knew nothing against him, except that he was, perhaps, a little self-willed; and so Maurice Archer came to Kirkby Cliffe, intending to spend two months in the same house with Isabel Lownd.

Hitherto, as far as the parents or the neighbours saw, — and in their endeavours to see, the neighbours were very diligent, — there had been no love-making. Between Mabel, the young daughter, and Maurice, there had grown up a violent friendship, — so much so, that Mabel, who was fourteen, declared that Maurice Archer was "the jolliest person" in the world. She called him Maurice, as did Mr. and Mrs. Lownd; and to Maurice, of course, she was Mabel. But between Isabel and Maurice it was always Miss Lownd and Mr. Archer, as was proper. It was so, at least, with this difference, that each of them had got into a way of dropping, when possible, the other's name.

It was acknowledged throughout Craven, — which my readers of course know to be a district in the northern portion of the West Riding of Yorkshire, of which Skipton is the capital, — that Isabel Lownd was a very pretty girl. There were those who thought that Mary Manniwick, of Barden, excelled her; and others, again, expressed a preference for Fanny Grange, the pink-cheeked daughter of the surgeon at Giggleswick. No attempt shall here be made to award the palm of superior merit; but it shall be asserted boldly, that no man need desire a prettier girl with whom to fall in love than was

67

Isabel Lownd. She was tall, active, fair, the very picture of feminine health, with bright gray eyes, a perfectly beautiful nose, — as is common to almost all girls belonging to Craven, — a mouth by no means delicately small, but eager, eloquent, and full of spirit, a well-formed short chin, with a dimple, and light brown hair, which was worn plainly smoothed over her brows, and fell in short curls behind her head. Of Maurice Archer it cannot be said that he was handsome. He had a snub nose; and a man so visaged can hardly be good-looking, though a girl with a snub nose may be very pretty. But he was a well-made young fellow, having a look of power about him, with dark-brown hair, cut very short, close shorn, with clear but rather small blue eyes, and an expression of countenance which allowed no one for a moment to think that he was weak in character, or a fool. His own place, called Hundlewick Hall, was about five miles from the parsonage. He had been there four or five times a week since his arrival at Kirkby Cliffe, and had already made arrangements for his own entrance upon the land in the following September. If a marriage were to come of it, the arrangement would be one very comfortable for the father and mother at Kirkby Cliffe. Mrs. Lownd had already admitted as much as that to herself, though she still trembled for her girl. Girls are so prone to lose their hearts, whereas the young men of these days are so very cautious and hard! That, at least, was Mrs. Lownd's idea of girls and young men; and even at this present moment she was hardly happy about her child. Maurice, she was sure, had spoken never a word that might not have been proclaimed from the church tower; but her girl, she thought, was not quite the same as she had been before the young man had come among them. She was somewhat less easy in her manner, more preoccupied, and seemed to labour under a conviction that the presence in the house of Maurice Archer must alter the nature of her life. Of course it had altered the nature of her life, and of course she thought a great deal of Maurice Archer.

It had been chiefly at Mabel's instigation that Isabel had invited the co-operation of her father's visitor in the adornment of the church for Christmas Day. Isabel had expressed her opinion that Mr. Archer didn't care a bit about such things, but Mabel declared that she had already extracted a promise from him. "He'll do anything I ask him," said Mabel, proudly. Isabel, however, had not cared to undertake the work in such company, simply under her sister's management, and had proffered the request herself. Maurice had not declined the task, — had indeed promised his assistance in some indifferent fashion, — but had accompanied his promise by a suggestion that Christmas was a bore! Isabel had rebuked him, and then he had explained. But his explanation, in Isabel's view of the case, only made the matter worse. Christmas to her was a very great affair indeed, — a festival to which the roast beef and the plum pudding were, no doubt, very necessary; but not by any means the essence, as he had chosen to consider them. Christmas a bore! No; a man who thought Christmas to be a bore should never be more to her than a mere acquaintance. She listened to his explanation, and then left the room, almost indignantly. Maurice, when she was gone, looked after her, and then read a page of his novel; but he was thinking of Isabel, and not of the book. It was quite true that he had never said a word to her that might not have been declared from the church tower; but, nevertheless, he had thought about her a good deal. Those were days on which he was sure that he was in love with her, and would make her his wife. Then there came days on which he ridiculed himself for the idea. And now and then there was a day on which he asked himself whether he was sure that she would take him were he to ask her. There was sometimes an air with her, some little trick of the body, a manner of carrying her head when in his presence, which he was not physiognomist enough to investigate, but which in some way suggested doubts to him. It was on such occasions as this that he was most in love with her; and now she had left the room with that particular motion of her head which seemed almost to betoken contempt.

"If you mean to do anything before dinner you'd better do it at once," said the parson, opening the door. Maurice jumped up, and in ten minutes was dressed and down in the dining-room. Isabel was there, but did not greet him. "You'll come and help us to-morrow," said Mabel, taking him by the arm and whispering to him.

"Of course I will," said Maurice.

"And you won't go to Hundlewick again till after Christmas?"

"It won't take up the whole day to put up the holly."

"Yes it will, — to do it nicely, — and nobody ever does any work the day before Christmas."

"Except the cook," suggested Maurice. Isabel, who heard the words, assumed that look of which he was already afraid, but said not a word. Then dinner was announced, and he gave his arm to the parson's wife.

Not a word was said about Christmas that evening. Isabel had threatened the young man with her father's displeasure on account of his expressed opinion as to the festival being a bore, but Mr. Lownd was not himself one who talked a great deal about any Church festival. Indeed, it may be doubted whether his more enthusiastic daughter did not in her heart think him almost too indifferent on the subject. In the decorations of the church he, being an elderly man, and one with other duties to perform, would of course take no part. When the day came he would preach, no doubt, an appropriate sermon, would then eat his own roast beef and pudding with his ordinary appetite, would afterwards, if allowed to do so, sink into his arm-chair behind his book, — and then, for him, Christmas would be over. In all this there was no disrespect for the day, but it was hardly an enthusiastic observance. Isabel desired to greet the morning of her Saviour's birth with some special demonstration of joy. Perhaps from year to year she was somewhat disappointed, — but never before had it been hinted to her that Christmas was a bore.

On the following morning the work was to be commenced immediately after breakfast. The same thing had been done so often at Kirkby Cliffe, that the rector was quite used to it. David Drum, the clerk, who was also schoolmaster, and Barty Crossgrain, the parsonage gardener, would devote their services to the work in hand throughout the whole day, under the direction of Isabel. Mabel would of course be there assisting, as would also two daughters of a neighbouring farmer. Mrs. Lownd would go down to the church about eleven, and stay till one, when the whole party would come up to the parsonage for refreshment. Mrs. Lownd would not return to the work, but the others would remain there till it was finished, which finishing was never accomplished till candles had been burned in the church for a couple of hours. Then there would be more refreshments; but on this special day the parsonage dinner was never comfortable and orderly. The rector bore it all with good humour, but no one could say that he was enthusiastic in the matter. Mabel, who delighted in going up ladders, and leaning over the pulpit, and finding herself in all those odd parts of the church to which her imagination would stray during her father's sermons, but which were ordinarily inaccessible to her, took great delight in the work. And perhaps Isabel's delight had commenced with similar feelings. Immediately after breakfast, which was much hurried on the occasion, she put on her hat and hurried down to the church, without a word to Maurice on the subject. There was another whisper from Mabel, which was answered also with a whisper, and then Mabel also went. Maurice took up his novel, and seated himself comfortably by the parlour fire.

But again he did not read a word. Why had Isabel made herself so disagreeable, and why had she perked up her head as she left the room in that self-sufficient way, as though she was determined to show him that she did not want his assistance? Of course, she had understood well enough that he had not intended to say that the ceremonial observance of the day was a bore. He had spoken of the beef and the pudding, and she had chosen to pretend to misunderstand him. He would not go near the church. And as for his love, and his half-formed resolution to make her his wife, he would get over it altogether. If there were one thing more fixed with him than another, it was that on no consideration would he marry a girl who should give herself airs. Among them they might decorate the church as they pleased, and when he should see their handywork, — as he would do, of course, during the services of Christmas Day, — he would pass it by without a remark. So resolving, he again turned over a page or two of his novel, and then remembered that he was bound, at any rate, to keep his promise to his friend Mabel. Assuring himself that it was on that plea that he went, and on no other, he sauntered down to the church.

Kirkby Cliffe Church

Kirkby Cliffe Church stands close upon the River Wharfe, about a quarter of a mile from the parsonage, which is on a steep hill-side running down from the moors to the stream. A prettier little church or graveyard you shall hardly find in England. Here, no large influx of population has necessitated the removal of the last home of the parishioners from beneath the shelter of the parish church. Every inhabitant of Kirkby Cliffe has, when dead, the privilege of rest among those green hillocks. Within the building is still room for tablets commemorative of the rectors and their wives and families, for there are none others in the parish to whom such honour is accorded. Without the walls, here and there, stand the tombstones of the farmers; while the undistinguished graves of the peasants lie about in clusters which, solemn though they be, are still picturesque. The church itself is old, and may probably be doomed before long to that kind of destruction which is called restoration; but hitherto it has been allowed to stand beneath all its weight of ivy, and has known but little change during the last two hundred years. Its old oak pews, and ancient exalted reading-desk and pulpit are offensive to many who come to see the spot; but Isabel Lownd is of opinion that neither the one nor the other could be touched, in the way of change, without profanation.

In the very porch Maurice Archer met Mabel, with her arms full of ivy branches, attended by David Drum. "So you have come at last, Master Maurice?" she said.

"Come at last! Is that all the thanks I get? Now let me see what it is you're going to do. Is your sister here?"

"Of course she is. Barty is up in the pulpit, sticking holly branches round the sounding-board, and she is with him."

"T' boorde's that rotten an' maaky, it'll be doon on Miss Is'bel's heede, an' Barty Crossgrain ain't more than or'nary saft-handed," said the clerk.

They entered the church, and there it was, just as Mabel had said. The old gardener was standing on the rail of the pulpit, and Isabel was beneath, handing up to him nails and boughs, and giving him directions as to their disposal. "Naa, miss, naa; it wonot do that a-way," said Barty. "Thou'll ha' me o'er on to t'stances — thou wilt, that a-gait. Lard-a-mussy, miss, thou munnot clim' up, or thou'lt be doon, and brek thee banes, thee ull!" So saying, Barty Crossgrain, who had contented himself with remonstrating when called upon by his young mistress to imperil his own neck, jumped on to the floor of the pulpit and took hold of the young lady by both her ankles. As he did so, he looked up at her with anxious eyes, and steadied himself on his own feet, as though it might become necessary for him to per-form some great feat of activity. All this Maurice Archer saw, and Isabel saw that he saw it. She was not well pleased at know-ing that he should see her in that position, held by the legs by the old gardener, and from which she could only extricate herself by putting her hand on the old man's neck as she jumped down from her perch. But she did jump down, and then began to scold Crossgrain, as though the awkwardness had come from fault of his.

"I've come to help, in spite of the hard words you said to me yesterday, Miss Lownd," said Maurice, standing on the lower steps of the pulpit. "Couldn't I get up and do the things at the top?" But Isabel thought that Mr. Archer could not get up and "do the things at the top." The wood was so far decayed that they must abandon the idea of ornamenting the sounding-board, and so both Crossgrain and Isabel descended into the body of the church.

Things did not go comfortably with them for the next hour. Isabel had certainly invited his co-operation, and therefore could not tell him to go away; and yet, such was her present feeling towards him, she could not employ him profitably, and with ease to herself. She was somewhat angry with him, and more angry with herself. It was not only that she had spoken hard words to him, as he had accused her of doing, but that, after the speaking of the hard words, she had been distant and cold in her manner to him. And yet he was so much to her! she liked him so well! — and though she had never dreamed of admitting to herself that she was in love with him, yet — yet it would be so pleasant to have the opportunity of asking herself whether she could not love him, should he ever give her a fair and open opportunity of searching her own heart on the matter. There had now sprung up some half-quarrel between them, and it was impossible that it could be set aside by any action on her part. She could not be otherwise than cold and haughty in her demeanour to him. Any attempt at reconciliation must come from him, and the longer that she continued to be cold and haughty, the less chance there was that it would come. And yet she knew that she had been right to rebuke him for what he had said. "Christmas a bore!" She would rather lose his friendship for ever than hear such words from his mouth, without letting him know what she thought of them. Now he was there with her, and his coming could not but be taken as a sign of repentance. Yet she could not soften her manners to him, and become intimate with him, and playful, as had been her wont. He was allowed to pull about the masses of ivy, and to stick up branches of holly here and there at discretion; but what he did was done under Mabel's direction, and not under hers, — with the aid of one of the farmer's daughters, and not with her aid. In silence she continued to work round the chancel and communion-table, with Crossgrain, while Archer, Mabel, and David Drum used their taste and diligence in the nave and aisles of the little church. Then Mrs. Lownd came among them, and things went more easily; but hardly a word had been spoken between Isabel and Maurice when, after sundry hints from David Drum as to the lateness of the hour, they left the church and went up to the parsonage for their luncheon.

Isabel stoutly walked on first, as though determined to show that she had no other idea in her head but that of reaching the parsonage as quickly as possible. Perhaps Maurice Archer had the same idea, for he followed her. Then he soon found that he was so far in advance of Mrs. Lownd and the old gardener as to be sure of three minutes' uninterrupted conversation; for Mabel remained with her mother, making earnest supplication as to the expenditure of certain yards of green silk tape, which she declared to be necessary for the due performance of the work which they had in hand. "Miss Lownd," said Maurice, "I think you are a little hard upon me."

"In what way, Mr. Archer?"

"You asked me to come down to the church, and you haven't

spoken to me all the time I was there."

"I asked you to come and work, not to talk," she said.

"You asked me to come and work with you."

"I don't think that I said any such thing; and you came at Mabel's request, and not at mine. When I asked you, you told me it was all — a bore. Indeed you said much worse than that. I certainly did not mean to ask you again. Mabel asked you, and you came to oblige her. She talked to you, for I heard her; and I was half disposed to tell her not to laugh so much, and to remember that she was in church."

"I did not laugh, Miss Lownd."

"I was not listening especially to you."

"Confess, now," he said after a pause; "don't you know that you misinterpreted me yesterday, and that you took what I said in a different spirit from my own."

"No; I do not know it."

"But you did. I was speaking of the holiday part of Christmas, which consists of pudding and beef, and is surely subject to ridicule, if one chooses to ridicule pudding and beef. You answered me as though I had spoken slightingly of the religious feeling which belongs to the day."

"You said that the whole thing was —; I won't repeat the word. Why should pudding and beef be a bore to you, when it is prepared as a sign that there shall be plenty on that day for people who perhaps don't have plenty on any other day of the year? The meaning of it is, that you don't like it all, because that which gives unusual enjoyment to poor people, who very seldom have any pleasure, is tedious to you. I don't like you for feeling it to be tedious. There! that's the truth. I don't mean to be uncivil, but ——"

"You are very uncivil."

"What am I to say, when you come and ask me?"

"I do not well know how you could be more uncivil, Miss Lownd. Of course it is the commonest thing in the world, that one person should dislike another. It occurs every day, and people know it of each other. I can perceive very well that you dislike me, and I have no reason to be angry with you for disliking me. You have a right to dislike me, if your mind runs that way. But it is very unusual for one person to tell another so to his

75

face, — and more unusual to say so to a guest." Maurice Archer, as he said this, spoke with a degree of solemnity to which she was not at all accustomed, so that she became frightened at what she had said. And not only was she frightened, but very unhappy also. She did not quite know whether she had or had not told him plainly that she disliked him, but she was quite sure that she had not intended to do so. She had been determined to scold him, — to let him see that, however much of real friendship there might be between them, she would speak her mind plainly, if he offended her; but she certainly had not desired to give him cause for lasting wrath against her. "However," continued Maurice, "perhaps the truth is best after all, though it is so very unusual to hear such truths spoken."

"I didn't mean to be uncivil," stammered Isabel.

"But you meant to be true?"

"I meant to say what I felt about Christmas Day." Then she paused a moment. "If I have offended you, I beg your pardon."

He looked at her and saw that her eyes were full of tears, and his heart was at once softened towards her. Should he say a word to her, to let her know that there was, — or, at any rate, that henceforth there should be no offence? But it occurred to him that if he did so, that word would mean so much, and would lead perhaps to the saying of other words, which ought not to be shown without forethought. And now, too, they were within the parsonage gate, and there was no time for speaking. "You will go down again after lunch?" he asked.

"I don't know; — not if I can help it. Here's Papa." She had begged his pardon, — had humbled herself before him. And he had not said a word in acknowledgment of the grace she had done him. She almost thought that she did dislike him, — really dislike him. Of course he had known what she meant, and he had chosen to misunderstand her and to take her, as it were, at an advantage. In her difficulty she had abjectly apologized to him, and he had not even deigned to express himself as satisfied with what she had done. She had known him to be conceited and masterful; but that, she had thought, she could forgive, believing it to be the common way with men, — imagining, perhaps, that a man was only the more worthy of love on account of such fault; but now she found that he was ungenerous

76

also, and deficient in that chivalry without which a man can hardly appear at advantage in a woman's eyes. She went on into the house, merely touching her father's arm, as she passed him, and hurried up to her own room. "Is there anything wrong with Isabel?" asked Mr. Lownd.

"She has worked too hard, I think, and is tired," said Maurice.

Within ten minutes they were all assembled in the dining-room, and Mabel was loud in her narrative of the doings of the morning. Barty Crossgrain and David Drum had both declared the sounding-board to be so old that it mustn't even be touched, and she was greatly afraid that it would tumble down some day and "squash papa" in the pulpit. The rector ridiculed the idea of any such disaster; and then there came a full description of the morning's scene, and of Barty's fears lest Isabel should "brek her banes." "His own wig was almost off," said Mabel, "and he gave Isabel such a lug by the leg that she very nearly had to jump into his arms."

"I didn't do anything of the kind," said Isabel.

"You had better leave the sounding-board alone," said the parson.

"We have left it alone, papa," said Isabel, with great dignity. "There are some other things that can't be done this year." For Isabel was becoming tired of her task, and would not have re-turned to the church at all could she have avoided it.

"What other things?" demanded Mabel, who was as enthusiastic as ever. "We can finish all the rest. Why shouldn't we finish it? We are ever so much more forward than we were last year, when David and Barty went to dinner. We've finished the Granby-Moore pew, and we never used to get to that till after luncheon." But Mabel on this occasion had all the enthusiasm to herself. The two farmer's daughters, who had been brought up to the parsonage as usual, never on such occasions uttered a word. Mrs. Lownd had completed her part of the work; Maurice could not trust himself to speak on the subject; and Isabel was dumb. Luncheon, however, was soon over, and something must be done. The four girls of course returned to their labours, but Maurice did not go with them, nor did he make any excuse for not doing so.

"I shall walk over to Hundlewick before dinner," he said, as

77

soon as they were all moving. The rector suggested that he would hardly be back in time. "Oh, yes; ten miles — two hours and a half; and I shall have two hours there besides. I must see what they are doing with our own church, and how they mean to keep Christmas there. I'm not quite sure that I shan't go over there again tomorrow." Even Mabel felt that there was something wrong, and said not a word in opposition to this wicked desertion.

He did walk to Hundlewick and back again, and when at Hundlewick he visited the church, though the church was a mile beyond his own farm. And he added something to the store provided for the beef and pudding of those who lived upon his own land; but of this he said nothing on his return to Kirkby Cliffe. He walked his dozen miles, and saw what was being done about the place, and visited the cottages of some who knew him, and yet was back at the parsonage in time for dinner. And during his walk he turned many things over in his thoughts, and endeavoured to make up his mind on one or two points. Isabel had never looked so pretty as when she jumped down into the pulpit, unless it was when she was begging his pardon for her want of courtesy to him. And though she had been, as he described it to himself, "rather down upon him," in regard to what he had said of Christmas, did he not like her the better for having an opinion of her own? And then, as he had stood for a few minutes leaning on his own gate, and looking at his own house at Hundlewick, it had occurred to him that he could hardly live there without a companion. After that he had walked back again, and was dressed for dinner, and in the drawing-room before any one of the family.

With poor Isabel the afternoon had gone much less satisfactorily. She found that she almost hated her work, that she really had a headache, and that she could put no heart into what she was doing. She was cross to Mabel, and almost surly to David Drum and Barty Crossgrain. The two farmer's daughters were allowed to do almost what they pleased with the holly branches, — a state of things which was most unusual, — and then Isabel, on her return to the parsonage, declared her intention of going to bed! Mrs. Lownd, who had never before known her to do such a thing, was perfectly shocked. Go to bed, and not come down the whole of Christmas Eve! But Isabel was resolute. With a bad headache she would be better in bed than up. Were she to attempt to shake it off, she would be ill the next day. She did not want anything to eat, and would not take anything. No; she would not have any tea, but would go to bed at once. And to bed she went.

She was thoroughly discontented with herself, and felt that Maurice had, as it were, made up his mind against her forever. She hardly knew whether to be angry with herself or with him; but she did know very well that she had not intended really to quarrel with him. Of course she had been in earnest in what she had said; but he had taken her words as signifying so much more than she had intended! If he chose to quarrel with her, of course he must; but a friend could not, she was sure, care for her a great deal who would really be angry with her for such a trifle. Of course this friend did not care for her at all, — not the least, or he would not treat her so savagely. He had been quite savage to her, and she hated him for it. And yet she hated herself almost more. What right could she have had first to scold him, and then to tell him to his face that she disliked him? Of course he had gone away to Hundlewick. She would not have been a bit surprised if he had stayed there and never come back again. But he did come back, and she hated herself as she heard their voices as they all went in to dinner without her. It seemed to her that his voice was more cheery than ever. Last night and all the morning he had been silent and almost sullen, but now, the moment that she was away, he could talk and be full of spirits. She heard Mabel's ringing laughter downstairs, and she almost hated Mabel. It seemed to her that everybody was gay and happy because she was upstairs in her bed, and ill. Then there came a peal of laughter. She was glad that she was upstairs in bed, and ill. Nobody would have laughed, nobody would have been gay, had she been there. Maurice Archer liked them all, except her, — she was sure of that. And what could be more natural after her conduct to him? She had taken upon herself to lecture him, and of course he had not chosen to endure it. But of one thing she was quite sure, as she lay there, wretched in her solitude, — that now she would never alter her demeanour to him. He had chosen to be cold to her, and she would be like frozen ice to him.

Again and again she heard their voices, and then, sobbing on her pillow, she fell asleep.

Showing How Isabel Lownd Told a Lie

On the following morning, — Christmas morning, — when she woke, her headache was gone, and she was able, as she dressed, to make some stern resolutions. The ecstasy of her sorrow was over, and she could see how foolish she had been to grieve as she had grieved. After all, what had she lost, or what harm had she done? She had never fancied that the young man was her lover, and she had never wished, — so she now told herself, — that he should become her lover. If one thing was plainer to her than another, it was this — that they two were not fitted for each other. She had sometimes whispered to herself, that if she were to marry at all, she would fain marry a clergyman. Now, no man could be more unlike a clergyman than Maurice Archer. He was, she thought, irreverent, and at no pains to keep his want of reverence out of sight, even in that house. He had said that Christmas was a bore, which, to her thinking, was abominable. Was she so poor a creature as to go to bed and cry for a man who had given her no sign that he even liked her, and of whose ways she disapproved so greatly, that even were he to offer her his hand she would certainly refuse it? She consoled herself for the folly of the preceding evening by assuring herself that she had really worked in the church till she was ill, and that she would have gone to bed, and must have gone to bed, had Maurice Archer never been seen or heard of at the parsonage. Other people went to bed when they had headaches, and why should not she? Then she resolved, as she dressed, that there should be no signs of illness, nor bit of ill-humour on her, on this sacred day. She would appear among them all full of mirth and happiness, and would laugh at the attack brought upon her by Barty Crossgrain's sudden fear in the pulpit; and she would greet Maurice Archer with all possible cordiality, wishing him a merry Christmas as she gave him her hand, and would make him understand in a moment that she had altogether forgotten their mutual bickerings. He should understand that, or should, at least, understand that she willed that it should all be regarded as forgotten. What was he to her, that any thought of him should be allowed to perplex her mind on such a day as this?

She went downstairs, knowing that she was the first up in the house, — the first, excepting the servants. She went into Mabel's room, and kissing her sister, who was only half awake, wished her many, many, many happy Christmases.

"Oh, Bell," said Mabel, "I do so hope you are better!"

"Of course I am better. Of course I am well. There is nothing for a headache like having twelve hours round of sleep. I don't know what made me so tired and so bad."

"I thought it was something Maurice said," suggested Mabel.

"Oh, dear, no. I think Barty had more to do with it than Mr. Archer. The old fellow frightened me so when he made me think I was falling down. But get up, dear. Papa is in his room, and he'll be ready for prayers before you."

Then she descended to the kitchen, and offered her good wishes to all the servants. To Barty, who always breakfasted there on Christmas mornings, she was especially kind, and said something civil about his work in the church.

"She'll 'bout brek her little heart for t' young mon there, an' he's naa true t' her," said Barty, as soon as Miss Lownd had closed the kitchen door; showing, perhaps, that he knew more of the matter concerning herself than she did.

She then went into the parlour to prepare the breakfast, and to put a little present, which she had made for her father, on his plate; — when, whom should she see but Maurice Archer!

It was a fact known to all the household, and a fact that had not recommended him at all to Isabel, that Maurice never did come downstairs in time for morning prayers. He was always the last; and, though in most respects a very active man, seemed to be almost a sluggard in regard to lying in bed late. As far as she could remember at the moment, he had never been present at prayers a single morning since the first after his arrival at the

81

parsonage, when shame, and a natural feeling of strangeness in the house, had brought him out of his bed. Now he was there half an hour before the appointed time, and during that half-hour she was doomed to be alone with him. But her courage did not for a moment desert her.

"This is a wonder!" she said, as she took his hand. "You will have a long Christmas Day, but I sincerely hope that it may be a happy one."

"That depends on you," said he.

"I'll do everything I can," she answered. "You shall only have a very little bit of roast beef, and the unfortunate pudding shan't be brought near you." Then she looked in his face, and saw that his manner was very serious, — almost solemn, — and quite unlike his usual ways. "Is anything wrong?" she asked.

"I don't know; I hope not. There are things which one has to say which seem to be so very difficult when the time comes. Miss Lownd, I want you to love me."

"What!" She started back as she made the exclamation, as though some terrible proposition had wounded her ears. If she had ever dreamed of his asking for her love, she had dreamed of it as a thing that future days might possibly produce; — when he should be altogether settled at Hundlewick, and when they should have got to know each other intimately by the association of years.

"Yes, I want you to love me, and to be my wife. I don't know how to tell you; but I love you better than anything and every-thing in the world, — better than all the world put together. I have done so from the first moment that I saw you; I have. I knew how it would be the very first instant I saw your dear face, and every word you have spoken, and every look out of your eyes, has made me love you more and more. If I offended you yesterday, I will beg your pardon."

"Oh, no," she said.

"I wish I had bitten my tongue out before I had said what I did about Christmas Day. I do, indeed. I only meant, in a half-joking way, to — to — to ——. But I ought to have known you wouldn't like it, and I beg your pardon. Tell me, Isabel, do you think that you can love me?"

Not half an hour since she had made up her mind that, even

were he to propose to her, — which she then knew to be absolutely impossible, — she would certainly refuse him. He was not the sort of man for whom she would be a fitting wife; and she had made up her mind also, at the same time, that she did not at all care for him, and that he certainly did not in the least care for her. And now the offer had absolutely been made to her! Then came across her mind an idea that he ought in the first place to have gone to her father; but as to that she was not quite sure. Be that as it might, there he was, and she must give him some answer. As for thinking about it, that was altogether beyond her. The shock to her was too great to allow of her thinking. After some fashion, which afterwards was quite unintelligible to herself, it seemed to her, at that moment, that duty, and maidenly reserve, and filial obedience, all required her to reject him instantly. Indeed, to have accepted him would have been quite beyond her power. "Dear Isabel," said he, "may I hope that some day you will love me?"

"Oh, Mr. Archer, don't," she said. "Do not ask me."

"Why should I not ask you?"

"It can never be." This she said quite plainly, and in a voice that seemed to him to settle his fate forever; and yet at the moment her heart was full of love towards him. Though she could not think, she could feel. Of course she loved him. At the very moment in which she was telling him that it could never be, she was elated by an almost ecstatic triumph, as she remembered all her fears, and now knew that the man was at her feet.

When a girl first receives the homage of a man's love, and receives it from one whom, whether she loves him or not, she thoroughly respects, her earliest feeling is one of victory, — such a feeling as warmed the heart of a conqueror in the Olympian games. He is the spoil of her spear, the fruit of her prowess, the quarry brought down by her own bow and arrow. She, too, by some power of her own which she is hitherto quite unable to analyze, has stricken a man to the very heart, so as to compel him for the moment to follow wherever she may lead him. So it was with Isabel Lownd as she stood there, conscious of the eager gaze which was fixed upon her face, and fully alive to the anxious tones of her lover's voice. And yet she could only deny him. Afterwards, when she thought of it, she could not imagine why it had been so with her; but, in spite of her great love, she continued to tell herself that there was some obstacle which could never be overcome, — or was it that a certain maidenly reserve sat so strong within her bosom that she could not bring herself to own to him that he was dear to her?

"Never!" exclaimed Maurice, despondently.

"Oh, no!"

"But why not? I will be very frank with you, dear. I did think you liked me a little before that affair in the study." Like him a little! Oh, how she had loved him! She knew it now, and yet not for worlds could she tell him so. "You are not still angry with me, Isabel?"

"No; not angry."

"Why should you say never? Dear Isabel, cannot you try to love me?" Then he attempted to take her hand, but she recoiled at once from his touch, and did feel something of anger against him in that he should thus refuse to take her word. She knew not what it was that she desired of him, but certainly he should not attempt to take her hand, when she told him plainly that she could not love him. A red spot rose to each of her cheeks as again he pressed her. "Do you really mean that you can never, never love me?" She muttered some answer, she knew not what, and then he turned from her, and stood looking out upon the snow which had fallen during the night. She kept her ground for a few seconds, and then escaped through the door, and up to her own bedroom. When once there, she burst out into tears. Could it be possible that she had thrown away forever her own happiness, because she had been too silly to give a true answer to an honest question? And was this the enjoyment and content which she had promised herself for Christmas Day? But surely, surely he would come to her again. If he really loved her as he had declared, if it was true that ever since his arrival at Kirkby Cliffe he had thought of her as his wife, he would not abandon her because in the first tumult of her surprise she had lacked courage to own to him the truth; and then in the midst of her tears there came upon her that delicious recognition of a triumph which, whatever be the victory won, causes such elation to the heart! Nothing, at any rate, could rob her of this — that he had loved her. Then, as a thought suddenly struck her, she ran quickly across the passage, and in a moment was upstairs, telling her tale with her mother's arm close folded round her waist.

In the meantime Mr. Lownd had gone down to the parlour, and had found Maurice still looking out upon the snow. He, too, with some gentle sarcasm, had congratulated the young man on his early rising, as he expressed the ordinary wish of the day. "Yes," said Maurice, "I had something special to do. Many happy Christmases, sir! I don't know much about its being happy to me."

"Why, what ails you?"

"It's a nasty sort of day, isn't it?"said Maurice.

"Does that trouble you? I rather like a little snow on Christmas Day. It has a pleasant, old-fashioned look. And there isn't enough to keep even an old woman at home."

"I dare say not," said Maurice, who was still beating about the bush, having something to tell, but not knowing how to tell it. "Mr. Lownd, I should have come to you first, if it hadn't been for an accident."

"Come to me first! What accident?"

"Yes; only I found Miss Lownd down here this morning, and I asked her to be my wife. You needn't be unhappy about it, sir. She refused me point blank."

"You must have startled her, Maurice. You have startled me, at any rate."

"There was nothing of that sort, Mr. Lownd. She took it all very easily. I think she does take things easily." Poor Isabel! "She just told me plainly that it never could be so, and then she walked out of the room."

"I don't think she expected it, Maurice."

"Oh, dear no! I'm quite sure she didn't. She hadn't thought about me any more than if I were an old dog. I suppose men do make fools of themselves sometimes. I shall get over it, sir."

"Oh, I hope so."

"I shall give up the idea of living here. I couldn't do that. I shall probably sell the property, and go to Africa."

"Go to Africa!"

"Well, yes. It's as good a place as any other, I suppose. It's wild, and a long way off, and all that kind of thing. As this is Christmas, I had better stay here to-day, I suppose."

"Of course you will."

"If you don't mind, I'll be off early to-morrow, sir. It's a kind of thing, you know, that does flurry a man. And then my being here may be disagreeable to her; — not that I suppose she thinks about me any more than if I were an old cow."

It need hardly be remarked that the rector was a much older man than Maurice Archer, and that he therefore knew the world much better. Nor was he in love. And he had, moreover, the advantage of a much closer knowledge of the young lady's character than could be possessed by the lover. And, as it happened, during the last week, he had been fretted by fears expressed by his wife, — fears which were altogether opposed to Archer's present despondency and African resolutions. Mrs. Lownd had been uneasy, — almost more than uneasy, — lest poor dear Isabel should be stricken at her heart; whereas, in regard to that young man, she didn't believe that he cared a bit for her girl. He ought not to have been brought into the house. But he was there, and what could they do? The rector was of the opinion that things would come straight, — that they would be straightened not by any lover's propensities on the part of his guest, as to which he protested himself to be altogether indifferent, but by his girl's good sense. His Isabel would never allow herself to be seriously affected by a regard for a young man who had made no overtures to her. That was the rector's argument; and perhaps, within his own mind, it was backed by a feeling that, were she so weak, she must stand the consequence. To him it seemed to be an absurd degree of caution that two young people should not be brought together in the same house lest one should fall in love with the other. And he had seen no symptoms of such love. Nevertheless his wife had fretted him, and he had been uneasy. Now the shoe was altogether on the other foot. The young man was the despondent lover, and was asserting that he must go instantly to Africa, because the young lady treated him like an old dog, and thought no more about him than of an old cow.

A father in such a position can hardly venture to hold out hopes to a lover, even though he may approve of the man as a suitor for his daughter's hand. He cannot answer for his girl, nor can he very well urge upon a lover the expediency of renewing his suit. In this case Mr. Lownd did think, that in spite of the cruel, determined obduracy which his daughter was said to have displayed, she might probably be softened by constancy and perseverance. But he knew nothing of the circumstances, and could only suggest that Maurice should not take his place for the first stage on his way to Africa quite at once. "I do not think you need hurry away because of Isabel," he said, with a gentle smile.

"I couldn't stand it, — I couldn't indeed," said Maurice, impetuously. "I hope I didn't do wrong in speaking to her when I found her here this morning. If you had come first I should have told you."

"I could only have referred you to her, my dear boy. Come — here they are; and now we will have prayers." As he spoke, Mrs. Lownd entered the room, followed closely by Mabel, and then at a little distance by Isabel. The three maid-servants were standing behind in a line, ready to come in for prayers. Maurice could not but feel that Mrs. Lownd's manner to him was especially affectionate; for, in truth, hitherto she had kept somewhat aloof from him, as though he had been a ravening wolf. Now she held him by the hand, and had a spark of motherly affection in her eyes, as she, too, repeated her Christmas greeting. It might well be so, thought Maurice. Of course she would be more kind to him than ordinary, if she knew that he was a poor blighted individual. It was a thing of course that Isabel should have told her mother, equally a thing of course that he should be pitied and treated tenderly. But on the next day he would be off. Such tenderness as that would kill him.

As they sat at breakfast, they all tried to be very gracious to each other. Mabel was sharp enough to know that something special had happened, but could not quite be sure what it was. Isabel struggled very hard to make little speeches about the day, but cannot be said to have succeeded well. Her mother, who had known at once how it was with her child, and had required no positive answers to direct questions to enable her to assume that Isabel was now devoted to her lover, had told her girl that if the man's love were worth having, he would surely ask her again. "I don't think he will, mamma," Isabel had whispered, with her face half-hidden on her mother's arm. "He must be very unlike other men if he does not," Mrs. Lownd had said, resolving that the opportunity should not be wanting. Now she was very gracious to Maurice, speaking before him as though he were quite one of the family. Her trembling maternal heart had feared him, while she thought that he might be a ravening wolf, who would steal away her daughter's heart, leaving nothing in return; but now that he had proved himself willing to enter the fold as a useful domestic sheep, nothing could be too good for him. The parson himself, seeing all this, understanding every turn in his wife's mind, and painfully anxious that no word might be spoken which should seem to entrap his guest, strove diligently to talk as though nothing was amiss. He spoke of his sermon, and of David Drum, and of the allowance of pudding that was to be given to the inmates of the neighbouring poor-house. There had been a subscription, so as to relieve the rates from the burden of the plum-pudding, and Mr. Lownd thought that the farmers had not been sufficiently liberal. "There's Furness, at Loversloup, gave us half-a-crown. I told him he ought to be ashamed of himself. He declared to me to my face that if he could find puddings for his own bairns, that was enough for him."

"The richest farmer in these parts, Maurice," said Mrs. Lownd.

"He holds above three hundred acres of land, and could stock double as many, if he had them," said the would-be indignant rector, who was thinking a great deal more of his daughter than of the poor-house festival. Maurice answered him with a word or two, but found it very hard to assume any interest in the question of the pudding. Isabel was more hard-hearted, he thought, than even Farmer Furness, of Loversloup. And why should he trouble himself about these people, — he, who intended to sell his acres, and go away to Africa? But he smiled and made some reply, and buttered his toast, and struggled hard to seem as though nothing ailed him.

The parson went down to church before his wife, and Mabel went with him. "Is anything wrong with Maurice Archer?" she asked her father.

"Nothing, I hope," said he.

"Because he doesn't seem to be able to talk this morning."

"Everybody isn't a chatter-box like you, Mab."

"I don't think I chatter more than mamma, or Bell. Do you know, papa, I think Bell has quarrelled with Maurice Archer."

"I hope not. I should be very sorry that there should be any quarrelling at all — particularly on this day. Well, I think you've done it very nicely; and it is none the worse because you've left the sounding-board alone." Then Mabel went over to David Drum's cottage, and asked after the condition of Mrs. Drum's plum-pudding.

No one had ventured to ask Maurice Archer whether he would stay in church for the sacrament, but he did. Let us hope that no undue motive of pleasing Isabel Lownd had any effect upon him at such a time. But it did please her. Let us hope also that, as she knelt beside her lover at the low railing, her young heart was not too full of her love. That she had been thinking of him throughout her father's sermon, — thinking of him, then resolving that she would think of him no more, and then thinking of him more than ever, — must be admitted. When her mother had told her that he would come again to her, she had not attempted to assert that, were he to do so, she would again reject him. Her mother knew all her secret, and, should he not come again, her mother would know that she was heart-broken. She had told him positively that she would never love him. She had so told him, knowing well that at the very moment he was dearer to her than all the world beside. Why had she been so wicked as to lie to him? And if now she were punished for her lie by his silence, would she not be served properly? Her mind ran much more on the subject of this great sin which she had committed on that very morning, — that sin against one who loved her so well, and who desired to do good to her, — than on those general arguments in favour of Christian kindness and forbearance which the preacher drew from the texts applicable to Christmas Day. All her father's eloquence was nothing to her. On ordinary occasions he had no more devoted listener; but, on this morning, she could only exercise her spirit by repenting her own unchristian conduct. And then he came and knelt beside her at that sacred moment! It was impossible that he should forgive her, because he could not know that she had sinned against him.

There were certain visits to her poorer friends in the immediate village which, according to custom, she would make after church. When Maurice and Mrs. Lownd went up to the parsonage, she and Mabel made their usual round. They all welcomed her, but they felt that she was not quite herself with them, and even Mabel asked her what ailed her.

"Why should anything ail me? — only I don't like walking in the snow."

Then Mabel took courage. "If there is a secret, Bell, pray tell me. I would tell you any secret."

"I don't know what you mean," said Isabel, almost crossly.

"Is there a secret, Bell? I'm sure there is a secret about Maurice."

"Don't, — don't," said Isabel.

"I do like Maurice so much. Don't you like him?"

"Pray do not talk about him, Mabel."

"I believe he is in love with you, Bell; and, if he is, I think you ought to be in love with him. I don't know how you could have anybody nicer. And he is going to live at Hundlewick, which would be such great fun. Would not papa like it?"

"I don't know. Oh, dear! — oh, dear!" Then she burst out into tears, and walking out of the village, told Mabel the whole truth. Mabel heard it with consternation, and expressed her opinion that, in these circumstances, Maurice would never ask again to make her his wife.

"Then I shall die," said Isabel, frankly.

Showing How Isabel Lownd Repented Her Fault

In spite of her piteous condition and near prospect of death, Isabel Lownd completed her round of visits among her old friends. That Christmas should be kept in some way by every inhabitant of Kirkby Cliffe, was a thing of course. The district is not poor, and plenty on that day was rarely wanting. But Parson Lownd was not what we call a rich man; and there was no resident squire in the parish. The farmers, comprehending well their own privileges, and aware that the obligation of gentle living did not lie on them, were inclined to be close-fisted; and thus there was sometimes a difficulty in providing for the old and the infirm. There was a certain ancient widow in the village, of the name of Mucklewort, who was troubled with three orphan grandchildren and a lame daughter; and Isabel had, some days since, expressed a fear up at the parsonage that the good things of this world might be scarce in the old widow's cottage. Something had, of course, been done for the old woman, but not enough, as Isabel had thought. "My dear," her mother had said, "it is no use trying to make very poor people think that they are not poor."

"It is only one day in the year," Isabel had pleaded.

"What you give in excess to one, you take from another," replied Mrs. Lownd, with the stern wisdom which experience teaches. Poor Isabel could say nothing further, but had feared greatly that the rations in Mrs. Mucklewort's abode would be deficient. She now entered the cottage, and found the whole family at that moment preparing themselves for the consumption of a great Christmas banquet. Mrs. Mucklewort, whose temper was not always the best in the world, was radiant. The children were silent, open-eyed, expectant, and solemn. The lame aunt was in the act of transferring a large lump of beef, which seemed to be commingled in a most inartistic way with potatoes and cabbage, out of a pot on to the family dish. At any rate there was plenty; for no five appetites — had the five all been masculine, adult, and yet youthful — could, by any feats of strength, have emptied that dish at a sitting. And Isabel knew well that there had been pudding. She herself had sent the pudding; but that, as she was well aware, had not been allowed to abide its fate till this late hour of the day. "I'm glad you're all so well employed," said Isabel. "I thought you had done dinner long ago. I won't stop a minute now."

The old woman got up from her chair, and nodded her head, and held out her withered old hand to be shaken. The children opened their mouths wider than ever, and hoped there might be no great delay. The lame aunt curtseyed and explained the circumstances. "Beef, Miss Isabel, do take a mortal time t' boil; and it ain't no wise good for t' bairns to have it any ways raw." To this opinion Isabel gave her full assent, and expressed her gratification that the amount of beef should be sufficient to require so

91

much cooking. Then the truth came out. "Muster Archer just sent us over from Rowdy's a meal's meat with a vengence; God bless him!" "God bless him!" crooned out the old woman, and the children muttered some unintelligible sound, as though aware that duty required them to express some Amen to the prayer of their elders. Now Rowdy was the butcher living at Grassington, some six miles away, — for at Kirkby Cliffe there was no butcher. Isabel smiled all round upon them sweetly, with her eyes full of tears, and then left the cottage without a word.

He had done this because she had expressed a wish that these people should be kindly treated, — had done it without a syllable spoken to her or to any one, — had taken trouble, sending all the way to Grassington for Mrs. Mucklewort's beef! No doubt he had given other people beef, and had whispered no word of his kindness to any one at the rectory. And yet she had taken upon herself to rebuke him, because he had not cared for Christmas Day! As she walked along, silent, holding Mabel's hand, it seemed to her that of all men he was the most perfect. She had rebuked him, and had then told him — with incredible falseness — that she did not like him; and after that, when he had proposed to her in the kindest, noblest manner, she had rejected him, — almost as though he had not been good enough for her! She felt now as though she would like to bite the tongue out of her head for such misbehavior.

"Was not that nice of him?" said Mabel. But Isabel could not answer the question. "I always thought he was like that," continued the younger sister. "If he were my lover, I'd do anything he asked me, because he is so good-natured."

"Don't talk to me," said Isabel. And Mabel, who comprehended something of the condition of her sister's mind, did not say another word on their way back to the parsonage.

It was the rule of the house that on Christmas Day they should dine at four o'clock; — a rule which almost justified the very strong expression with which Maurice first offended the young lady whom he loved. To dine at one or two o'clock is a practice which has its recommendations. It suits the appetite, is healthy, and divides the day into two equal halves, so that no man so dining fancies that his dinner should bring to him an end of his usual occupations. And to dine at six, seven, or eight is well adapted to serve several purposes of life. It is convenient, as inducing that gentle lethargy which will sometimes follow the pleasant act of eating at a time when the work of the day is done; and it is both fashionable and comfortable. But to dine at four is almost worse than not to dine at all. The rule, however, existed at Kirkby Cliffe parsonage in regard to this one special day in the year, and was always obeyed.

On this occasion Isabel did not see her lover from the moment in which he left her at the church door till they met at table. She had been with her mother, but her mother had said not a word to her about Maurice. Isabel knew very well that they two had walked home together from the church, and she had thought that her best chance lay in the possibility that he would have spoken of what had occurred during the walk. Had this been so, surely her mother would have told her; but not a word had been said; and even with her mother Isabel had been too shamefaced to ask a question. In truth, Isabel's name had not been mentioned between them, nor had any allusion been made to what had taken place during the morning. Mrs. Lownd had been too wise and too wary, — too well aware of what was really due to her daughter, — to bring up the subject herself; and he had been silent, subdued, and almost sullen. If he could not get an acknowledgment of affection from the girl herself, he certainly would not endeavour to extract a cold compliance by the mother's aid. Africa, and a disruption of all the plans of his life, would be better to him than that. But Mrs. Lownd knew very well how it was with him; knew how it was with them both; and was aware that in such a condition things should be allowed to arrange themselves. At dinner, both she and the rector were full of mirth and good humour, and Mabel, with great glee, told the story of Mrs. Muckelwort's dinner. "I don't want to destroy your pleasure," she said, bobbing her head at Maurice; "but it did look so nasty! Beef should always be roast beef on Christmas Day."

"I told the butcher it was to be roast beef," said Maurice, sadly.

"I dare say the little Muckelworts would just as soon have it boiled," said Mrs. Lownd. "Beef is beef to them, and a pot for boiling is an easy apparatus."

"If you had beef, Miss Mab, only once or twice a year," said her father, "you would not care whether it were roast or boiled." But Isabel spoke not a word. She was most anxious to join the conversation about Mrs. Mucklewort, and would have liked much to give testimony to the generosity displayed in regard to quantity; but she found that she could not do it. She was absolutely dumb. Maurice Archer did speak, making, every now and then, a terrible effort to be jocose; but Isabel from first to last was silent. Only by silence could she refrain from a renewed deluge of tears.

In the evening two or three girls came in with their younger brothers, the children of farmers of the better class in the neighbourhood, and the usual attempts were made at jollity. Games were set on foot, in which even the rector joined, instead of going to sleep behind his book, and Mabel, still conscious of her sister's wounds, did her very best to promote the sports. There was blindman's-buff, and hide and seek, and snapdragon, and forfeits, and a certain game with music and chairs, — very prejudicial to the chairs, — in which it was everybody's object to sit down as quickly as possible when the music stopped. In the game Isabel insisted on playing, because she could do that alone. But even to do this was too much for her. The sudden pause could hardly be made without a certain hilarity of spirit, and her spirits were unequal to any exertion. Maurice went through his work like a man, was blinded, did his forfeits, and jostled for the chairs with the greatest diligence; but in the midst of it all he, too, was as solemn as a judge, and never once spoke a single word to Isabel. Mrs. Lownd, who usually was not herself much given to the playing of games, did on this occasion make an effort, and absolutely consented to cry the forfeits; but Mabel was wonderfully quiet, so that the farmer's daughters hardly perceived that there was anything amiss.

It came to pass, after a while, that Isabel had retreated to her room, — not for the night, as it was as yet hardly eight o'clock, — and she certainly would not disappear till the visitors had taken their departure, — a ceremony which was sure to take place with the greatest punctuality at ten, after an early supper. But she had escaped for a while, and in the meantime some frolic was going on which demanded the absence of one of the party from the room, in order that mysteries might be arranged of which the absent one should remain in ignorance. Maurice was thus banished, and desired to remain in desolation for the space of five minutes; but, just as he had taken up his position, Isabel descended with slow, solemn steps, and found him standing at her father's study door. She was passing on, and had almost entered the drawing-room, when he called her. "Miss Lownd," he said. Isabel stopped, but did not speak; she was absolutely' beyond speaking. The excitement of the day had been so great, that she was all but overcome by it, and doubted, herself, whether she would be able to keep up appearances till the supper should be over, and she should be relieved for the night. "Would you let me say one word to you?" said Maurice. She bowed her head and went with him into the study.

Five minutes had been allowed for the arrangement of the mysteries, and at the end of the five minutes Maurice was authorized, by the rules of the game, to return to the room. But he did not come, and upon Mabel's suggesting that possibly he might not be able to see his watch in the dark, she was sent to fetch him. She burst into the study, and there she found the truant and her sister, very close, standing together on the hearthrug. "I didn't know you were here, Bell," she exclaimed. Whereupon Maurice, as she declared afterwards, jumped round the table after her, and took her in his arms and kissed her. "But you must come," said Mabel, who accepted the embrace with perfect goodwill.

"Of course you must. Do go, pray, and I'll follow, — almost immediately." Mabel perceived at once that her sister had altogether recovered her voice.

"I'll tell 'em you're coming," said Mabel, vanishing.

"You must go now," said Isabel. "They'll all be away soon, and then you can talk about it." As she spoke, he was standing with his arm round her waist, and Isabel Lownd was the happiest girl in all Craven.

Mrs. Lownd knew all about it from the moment in which Maurice Archer's prolonged absence had become cause of complaint among the players. Her mind had been intent upon the matter, and she had become well aware that it was only necessary that the two young people should be alone together for a few moments. Mabel had entertained great hopes, thinking, however, that perhaps three or four years must be passed in melancholy gloomy doubts before the path of true love could be made to run smooth; but the light had shone upon her as soon as she saw them standing together. The parson knew nothing about it till the supper was over. Then, when the front door was open, and the farmer's daughters had been cautioned not to get themselves more wet than they could help in the falling snow, Maurice said a word to his future father-in-law. "She has consented at last, sir. I hope you have nothing to say against it."

"Not a word," said the parson, grasping the young man's hand, and remembering as he did so, the extension of the time over which that phrase "at last" was supposed to spread itself.

Maurice had been promised some further opportunity of "talking about it," and of course claimed a fulfillment of the promise. There was a difficulty about it, as Isabel, having now been assured of her happiness, was anxious to talk about it all to her mother rather than to him; but he was imperative, and there came at last for him a quarter of an hour of delicious triumph in that very spot on which he had been so scolded for saying that Christmas was a bore. "You were so very sudden," said Isabel, excusing herself for her conduct in the morning.

"But you did love me?"

"If I do now, that ought to be enough for you. But I did, and I've been so unhappy since; and I thought that, perhaps, you would never speak to me again. But it was all your fault; you were so sudden. And then you ought to have asked papa first, — you know you ought. But, Maurice, you will promise me one thing. You won't ever again say that Christmas Day is a bore!"

"Christmas Day at Kirkby Cottage" appeared for the first time in 1870 in Routledge's Christmas Annual.

The Two Heroines
of Plumplington

I

The Two Girls

N THE LITTLE TOWN of Plumplington last year, just
about this time of the year, — it was in November, — the
ladies and gentlemen forming the Plumplington Society were
much exercised as to the affairs of two young ladies. They
were both the only daughters of two elderly gentlemen, well
known and greatly respected in Plumplington. All the world
may not know that Plumplington is the second town in
Barsetshire, and though it sends no member to Parliament, as
does Silverbridge, it has a population of over 20,000 souls,
and three separate banks. Of one of these Mr. Greenmantle is
the manager, and is reputed to have shares in the bank. At
any rate he is known to be a warm man. His daughter Emily
is supposed to be the heiress of all he possesses, and has been
regarded as a fitting match by many of the sons of the country
gentlemen around. It was rumoured a short time since that
young Harry Gresham was likely to ask her hand in marriage,
and Mr. Greenmantle was supposed at the time to have been
very willing to entertain the idea. Whether Mr. Gresham has
ever asked or not, Emily Greenmantle did not incline her ear
that way, and it came out while the affair was being discussed
in Plumplington circles that the young lady much preferred
one Mr. Philip Hughes. Now Philip Hughes was a very prom-

ising young man, but was at the time no more than a cashier
in her father's bank. It become known at once that Mr.
Greenmantle was very angry. Mr. Greenmantle was a man
who carried himself with a dignified and handsome demeanour, but he was one of whom those who knew him used
to declare that it would be found very difficult to turn him
from his purpose. It might not be possible that he should succeed with Harry Gresham, but it was considered out of the
question that he should give his girl and his money to such a
man as Philip Hughes.

The other of these elderly gentlemen is Mr. Hickory Peppercorn. It cannot be said that Mr. Hickory Peppercorn had
ever been put on a par with Mr. Greenmantle. No one could
suppose that Mr. Peppercorn had ever sat down to dinner in
company with Mr. and Miss Greenmantle. Neither did Mr. or
Miss Peppercorn expect to be asked on the festive occasion of
one of Mr. Greenmantle's dinners. But Miss Peppercorn was
not unfrequently made welcome to Miss Greenmantle's five
o'clock tea-table; and in many of the affairs of the town the
two young ladies were seen associated together. They were
both very active in the schools, and stood nearly equal in the
good graces of old Dr. Freeborn. There was, perhaps, a little
jealousy on this account in the bosom of Mr. Greenmantle,
who was pervaded perhaps by an idea that Dr. Freeborn
thought too much of himself. There never was a quarrel, as
Mr. Greenmantle was a good churchman; but there was a
jealousy. Mr. Greenmantle's family sank into insignificance if
you looked beyond his grandfather; but Dr. Freeborn could
talk glibly of his ancestors in the time of Charles I. And it
certainly was the fact that Dr. Freeborn would speak of the
two young ladies in one and the same breath.

Now Mr. Hickory Peppercorn was in truth nearly as warm a
man as his neighbour, and he was one who was specially
proud of being warm. He was a foreman, — or rather more
than foreman, — a kind of top sawyer in the brewery establishment of Messrs. Du Boung and Co., a firm which has an
establishment also in the town of Silverbridge. His position in
the world may be described by declaring that he always wears
a dark-coloured tweed coat and trousers, and a chimney-pot

hat. It is almost impossible to say too much that is good of Mr. Peppercorn. His one great fault has been already designated. He was and still is very fond of his money. He does not talk much about it; but it is to be feared that it dwells too constantly on his mind. As a servant to the firm he is honesty and constancy itself. He is a man of such a nature that by means of his very presence all the partners can be allowed to go to bed if they wish it. And there is not a man in the establishment who does not know him to be good and true. He understands all the systems of brewing, and his very existence in the brewery is a proof that Messrs. Du Boung and Co. are prosperous.

He has one daughter, Polly, to whom he is so thoroughly devoted that all the other girls in Plumplington envy her. If anything is to be done Polly is asked to go to her father, and if Polly does go to her father the thing is done. As far as money is concerned it is not known that Mr. Peppercorn ever refused Polly anything. It is the pride of his heart that Polly shall be, at any rate, as well dressed as Emily Greenmantle. In truth nearly double as much is spent on her clothes, all of which Polly accepts without a word to show her pride. Her father does not say much, but now and again a sigh does escape him. Then it came out, as a blow to Plumplington, that Polly too had a lover. And the last person in Plumplington who heard the news was Mr. Peppercorn. It seemed from his demeanour, when he first heard the tidings, that he had not expected that any such accident would ever happen. And yet Polly Peppercorn was a very pretty, bright girl of one-and-twenty of whom the wonder was, — if it was true, — that she had never already had a lover. She looked to be the very girl for lovers, and she looked also to be one quite able to keep a lover in his place.

Emily Greenmantle's lover was a two-months'-old story when Polly's lover became known to the public. There was a young man in Barchester who came over on Thursdays dealing with Mr. Peppercorn for malt. He was a fine stalwart young fellow, six-feet-one, with bright eyes and very light hair and whiskers, a hot temper, a thoroughly good heart, and with a pair of shoulders which would think nothing of a sack of

99

wheat. It was known to all Plumplington that he had not a shilling in the world, and that he earned forty shillings a week from Messrs. Mealing's establishment at Barchester. Men said of him that he was likely to do well in the world, but nobody thought that he would have the impudence to make up to Polly Peppercorn.

But all the girls saw it and many of the old women, and some even of the men. And at last Polly told him that if he had anything to say to her he must say it to her father. "And you mean to have him, then?" said Bessy Rolt in surprise. Her lover was by at the moment, though not exactly within hearing of Bessy's question. But Polly when she was alone with Bessy spoke up her mind freely. "Of course I mean to have him, if he pleases. What else? You don't suppose I would go on with a young man like that and mean nothing. I hate such ways."

"But what will your father say?"

"Why shouldn't he like it? I heard papa say that he had but 7s. 6d. a week when he first came to Du Boungs. He got poor mamma to marry him, and he never was a good-looking man."

"But he had made some money."

"Jack has made no money as yet, but he is a good-looking fellow. So they're quits. I believe that father would do anything for me, and when he knows that I mean it he won't let me break my heart."

But a week after that a change had come over the scene. Jack had gone to Mr. Hickory Peppercorn, and Mr. Peppercorn had given him a rough word or two. Jack had not borne the rough word well, and old Hickory, as he was called, had said in his wrath, "Impudent cub! you've got nothing. Do you know what my girl will have?"

"I've never asked."

"You knew she was to have something."

"I know nothing about it. I'm ready to take the rough and smooth together. I'll marry the young lady and wait till you give her something." Hickory couldn't turn him out on the spur of the moment because there was business to be done, but warned him not to go into his private house. "If you speak

100

another word to Polly, old as I am, I'll measure you across the back with my stick." But Polly, who knew her father's temper, took care to keep out of her father's sight on that occasion.

Polly after that began the battle in a fashion that had been invented by herself. No one heard the words that were spoken between her and her father, — her father who had so idolized her; but it appeared to the people of Plumplington that Polly was holding her own. No disrespect was shown to her father, not a word was heard from her mouth that was not affectionate or at least decorous. But she took upon herself at once a certain lowering of her own social standing. She never drank tea with Emily Greenmantle, or accosted her in the street with her old friendly manner. She was terribly humble to Dr. Freeborn, who however would not acknowledge her humility on any account. "What's come over you?" said the Doctor. "Let me have none of your stage plays or I shall take you and shake you."

"You can shake me if you like it, Dr. Freeborn," said Polly, "but I know who I am and what my position is."

"You are a determined young puss," said the Doctor, "but I am not going to help you in opposing your own father." Polly said not a word further, but looked very demure as the Doctor took his departure.

But Polly performed her greatest stroke in reference to a change in her dress. All her new silks, that had been the pride of her father's heart, were made to give way to old stuff gowns. People wondered where the old gowns, which had not been seen for years, had been stowed away. It was the same on Sundays as on Mondays and Tuesdays. But the due gradation was kept between Sundays and week-days. She was quite well enough dressed for a brewer's foreman's daughter on one day as on the other, but neither on one or on the other was she at all the Polly Peppercorn that Plumplington had known for the last couple of years. And there was not a word said about it. But all Plumplington knew that Polly was fitting herself, as regarded her outside garniture, to be the wife of Jack Hollycombe with 40s. a week. And all Plumplington said that she would carry her purpose, and that Hickory Peppercorn would break down under stress of the artillery brought to bear against him. He could not put out her clothes for her, or force her into wearing them as her mother might have done, had her mother been living. He could only tear his hair and greet, and swear to himself that under no such artillery as this would he give away. His girl should never marry Jack Hollycombe. He thought he knew his girl well enough to be sure that she would not marry without his consent. She might make him very unhappy by wearing dowdy clothes, but she would not quite break his heart. In the meantime Polly took care that her father should have no opportunity of measuring Jack's back.

With the affairs of Miss Greenmantle much more ceremony was observed, though I doubt whether there was more earnestness felt in the matter. Mr. Peppercorn was very much in earnest, as was Polly, — and Jack Hollycombe. But Peppercorn talked about it publicly, and Polly showed her purpose, and Jack exhibited the triumphant lover to all eyes. Mr. Greenmantle was silent as death in respect to the great trouble that had come upon him. He had spoken to no one on the subject except to the peccant lover, and just a word or two to old Dr. Freeborn. There was no trouble in the town that did not reach Dr. Freeborn's ears; and Mr. Greenmantle, in spite of his little jealousy, was no exception. To the Doctor he had said a word or two as to Emily's bad behaviour. But in the stiffness of his back, and the length of his face, and the continual frown which was gathered on his brows, he was eloquent to all the town. Peppercorn had no powers of looking as he looked. The gloom of the bank was awful. It was felt to be so by the two junior clerks, who hardly knew whether to hate or to pity most Mr. Philip Hughes. And if Mr. Greenmantle's demeanour was hard to bear down below, within the bank, what must it have been up-stairs in the family sitting-room? It was now, at this time, about the middle of November; and with Emily everything had been black and clouded for the last two months past. Polly's misfortune had only begun about the first of November. The two young ladies had had their own ideas about their own young men from nearly the same date. Philip Hughes and Jack Hollycombe had pushed themselves into prominence about the same time. But Emily's trouble had declared itself six weeks before Polly had sent her young man to her father. The first scene which took place with Emily and Mr. Greenmantle, after young Hughes had declared himself, was very impressive. "What is this, Emily?"

"What is what, papa?" A poor girl when she is thus cross-questioned hardly knows what to say.

"One of the young men in the bank has been to me." There was in this a great slur intended. It was acknowledged by all Plumplington that Mr. Hughes was the cashier, and was hardly more fairly designated as one of the young men than would have been Mr. Greenmantle himself, — unless in regard to age.

"Philip, I suppose," said Emily. Now Mr. Greenmantle had certainly led the way into this difficulty himself. He had been allured by some modesty in the young man's demeanour, — or more probably by something pleasant in his manner which had struck Emily also, — to call him Philip. He had, as it were, shown a parental regard for him, and those who had best known Mr. Greenmantle had been sure that he would not forget his manifest good intentions towards the young man. As coming from Mr. Greenmantle the use of the Christian name had been made. But certainly he had not intended that it should be taken up in this manner. There had been an ingratitude in it, which Mr. Greenmantle had felt very keenly.

"I would rather that you should call the young man Mr. Hughes in anything that you may have to say about him."

"I thought you called him Philip, papa."

"I shall never do so again, — never. What is this that he has said to me? Can it be true?"

"I suppose it is true, papa."

"You mean that you want to marry him?"

"Yes, papa."

"Goodness gracious me!" After this Emily remained silent for a while. "Can you have realized the fact that the young man has — nothing; literally nothing!" What is a young lady to say when she is thus appealed to? She knew that though the young man had nothing, she would have a considerable portion of her own. She was her father's only child. She had not "cared for" young Gresham, whereas she had "cared for" young Hughes. What would be all the world to her if she must marry a man she did not care for? That, she was resolved, she would not do. But what would all the world be to her if she were not allowed to marry the man she did love? And what good would it be to her to be the only daughter of a rich man if she were to be baulked in this manner? She had thought it all over, assuming to herself perhaps greater privileges than she was entitled to expect.

But Emily Greenmantle was somewhat differently circumstanced from Polly Peppercorn. Emily was afraid of her father's sternness, whereas Polly was not in the least afraid of her governor, as she was wont to call him. Old Hickory was, in a good-humoured way, afraid of Polly. Polly could order the things, in and about the house, very much after her own fashion. To tell the truth Polly had but slight fear but that she would have her own way, and when she laid by her best silks she did not do it as a person does bid farewell to those treasures which are not to be seen again. They could be made to do very well for the future Mrs. Hollycombe. At any rate, like a Marlborough or a Wellington, she went into the battle thinking of victory and not of defeat. But Wellington was a long time before he had beaten the French, and Polly thought that there might be some trouble also for her. With Emily there was no prospect of ultimate victory.

Mr. Greenmantle was a very stern man, who could look at his daughter as though he never meant to give way. And, without saying a word, he could make all Plumplington understand that such was to be the case. "Poor Emmy," said the old Doctor to his old wife; "I'm afraid there's a bad time coming for her." "He's a nasty cross old man," said the old woman. "It always does take three generations to make a 'gentleman.'" For Mrs. Freeborn's ancestors had come from the time of James I.

"You and I had better understand each other," said Mr. Greenmantle, standing up with his back to the fireplace, and looking as though he were all poker from the top of his head to the heels of his boots. "You cannot marry Mr. Philip Hughes." Emily said nothing but turned her eyes down upon the ground. "I don't suppose he thinks of doing so without money."

"He has never thought about money at all."

"Then what are you to live upon? Can you tell me that? He has £220 from the bank. Can you live upon that? Can you bring up a family?" Emily blushed as she still looked upon the ground. "I tell you fairly that he shall never have the spending of my money. If you mean to desert me in my old age, — go."

"Papa, you shouldn't say that."

"You shouldn't think it." Then Mr. Greenmantle looked as though he had uttered a clenching argument, "You shouldn't think it. Now go away, Emily, and turn in your mind what I have said to you."

"Down I Shall Go"

Then there came about a conversation between the two young ladies which was in itself very interesting. They had not met each other for about a fortnight when Emily Greenmantle came to Mr. Peppercorn's house. She had been thoroughly unhappy, and among her causes for sorrow had been the severance which seemed to have taken place between her and her friend. She had discussed all her troubles with Dr. Freeborn, and Dr. Freeborn had advised her to see Polly. "Here's Christmas-time coming on and you are all going to quarrel among yourselves. I won't have any such nonsense. Go and see her."

"It's not me, Dr. Freeborn," said Emily. "I don't want to quarrel with anybody; and there is nobody I like better than Polly." Thereupon Emily went to Mr. Peppercorn's house when Peppercorn would be certainly at the brewery, and there she found Polly at home.

Polly was dressed very plainly. It was manifest to all eyes that the Polly Peppercorn of to-day was not the same Polly Peppercorn that had been seen about Plumplington for the last twelve months. It was equally manifest that Polly intended that everybody should see the difference. She had not meekly put on her poorer dress so that people should see that she was no more than her father's child; but it was done with some ostentation. "If father says that Jack and I are not to have his money I must begin to reduce myself by times." That was what Polly intended to say to all Plumplington. She was sure that her father would have to give way under such shots as she could fire at him.

"Polly, I have not seen you, oh, for such a long time."

105

Polly did not look like quarrelling at all. Nothing could be more pleasant than the tone of her voice. But yet there was something in her mode of address which at once excited Emily Greenmantle's attention. In bidding her visitor welcome she called her Miss Greenmantle. Now on that matter there had been some little trouble heretofore, in which the banker's daughter had succeeded in getting the better of the banker. He had suggested that Miss Peppercorn was safer than Polly; but Emily had replied that Polly was a nice dear girl, very much in Dr. Freeborn's good favours, and in point of fact that Dr. Freeborn wouldn't allow it. Mr. Greenmantle had frowned, but had felt himself unable to stand against Dr. Freeborn in such a matter. "What's the meaning of the Miss Greenmantle?" said Emily sorrowfully.

"It's what I'm come to," said Polly, without any show of sorrow, "and it's what I mean to stick to as being my proper place. You have heard all about Jack Hollycombe. I suppose I ought to call him John as I'm speaking to you."

"I don't see what difference it will make."

"Not much in the long run; but yet it will make a difference. It isn't that I should not like to be just the same to you as I have been, but father means to put me down in the world, and I don't mean to quarrel with him about that. Down I shall go."

"And therefore I'm to be called Miss Greenmantle."

"Exactly. Perhaps it ought to have been always so as I'm so poorly minded as to go back to such a one as Jack Hollycombe. Of course it is going back. Of course Jack is as good as father was at his age. But father has put himself up since that and has put me up. I'm such poor stuff that I wouldn't stay up. A girl has to begin where her husband begins; and as I mean to be Jack's wife I have to fit myself for the place."

"I suppose it's the same with me, Polly."

"Not quite. You're a lady bred and born, and Mr. Hughes is a gentleman. Father tells me that a man who goes about the country selling malt isn't a gentleman. I suppose father is right. But Jack is a good enough gentleman to my thinking. If he had a share of father's money he would break out in quite a new place."

"Mr. Peppercorn won't give it to him?"

"Well! That's what I don't know. I do think the governor

loves me. He is the best fellow anywhere for downright kindness. I mean to try him. And if he won't help me I shall go down as I say. You may be sure of this, — that I shall not give up Jack."

"You wouldn't marry him against your father's wishes?"

Here Polly wasn't quite ready with her answer. "I don't know that father has a right to destroy all my happiness," she said at last. "I shall wait a long time first at any rate. Then if I find that Jack can remain constant, — I don't know what I shall do."

"What does he say?"

"Jack? He's all sugar and promises. They always are for a long time. It takes a deal of learning to know whether a young man can be true. There is not above one in twenty that do come out true when they are tried."

"I suppose not," said Emily sorrowfully.

"I shall tell Mr. Jack that he's got to go through the ordeal. Of course he wants me to say that I'll marry him right off the reel and that he'll earn money enough for both of us. I told him only this morning ——"

"Did you see him?"

"I wrote him, — out quite plainly. And I told him that there were other people had hearts in their bodies besides him and me. I'm not going to break father's heart, — not if I can help it. It would go very hard with him if I were to walk out of this house and marry Jack Hollycombe, quite plain like."

"I would never do it," said Emily with energy.

"You are a little different from me, Miss Greenmantle. I suppose my mother didn't think much about such things, and as long as she got herself married decent, didn't trouble herself much what her people said."

"Didn't she?"

"I fancy not. Those sort of cares and bothers always come with money. Look at the two girls in this house. I take it they only act just like their mothers, and if they're good girls, which they are, they get their mothers' consent. But the marriage goes on as a matter of course. It's where money is wanted that parents become stern and their children become dutiful. I mean to be dutiful for a time. But I'd rather have Jack than father's money."

"Dr. Freeborn says that you and I are not to quarrel. I am sure I don't see why we should."

"What Dr. Freeborn says is very well." It was thus that Polly carried on the conversation after thinking over the matter for a moment or two. "Dr. Freeborn is a great man in Plumplington, and has his own way in everything. I'm not saying a word against Dr. Freeborn, and goodness knows I don't want to quarrel with you, Miss Greenmantle."

"I hope not."

"But I do mean to go down if father makes me, and if Jack proves himself a true man."

"I suppose he'll do that," said Miss Greenmantle. "Of course you think he will."

"Well, upon the whole I do," said Polly. "And though I think father will have to give up, he won't do it just at present, and I shall have to remain just as I am for a time."

"And wear——" Miss Greenmantle had intended to inquire whether it was Polly's purpose to go about in her second-rate clothes, but had hesitated, not quite liking to ask the question.

"Just that," said Polly. "I mean to wear such clothes as shall be suitable for Jack's wife. And I mean to give up all my airs. I've been thinking a deal about it, and they're wrong. Your papa and my father are not the same."

"They are not the same, of course," said Emily.

"One is a gentleman, and the other isn't. That's the long and the short of it. I oughtn't to have gone to your house drinking tea and the rest of it; and I oughtn't to have called you Emily. That's the long and the short of that," said she, repeating herself.

"Dr. Freeborn thinks ——"

"Dr. Freeborn mustn't quite have it all his own way. Of course Dr. Freeborn is everything in Plumplington; and when I'm Jack's wife I'll do what he tells me again."

"I suppose you'll do what Jack tells you then."

"Well, yes; not exactly. If Jack were to tell me not to go to church, — which he won't, — I shouldn't do what he told me. If he said he'd like to have a leg of mutton boiled, I should boil it. Only legs of mutton wouldn't be very common with us, unless father comes around."

"I don't see why all that should make a difference between you and me."

"It will have to do so," said Polly with perfect self-assurance. "Father has told me that he doesn't mean to find money to buy legs of mutton for Jack Hollycombe. Those were his very words. I'm determined I'll never ask him. And he said he wasn't going to find clothes for Jack Hollycombe's brats. I'll never go to him to find a pair of shoes for Jack Hollycombe or one of his brats. I've told Jack as much, and Jack says that I'm right. But there's no knowing what's inside a young man till you've tried him. Jack may fall off, and if so there's an end of him. I shall come round in time, and wear my fine clothes again when I settle down as an old maid. But father will never make me wear them, and I shall never call you anything but Miss Greenmantle unless he consents to my marrying Jack."

Such was the eloquence of Polly Peppercorn as spoken on that occasion. And she certainly did fill Miss Greenmantle's mind with a strong idea of her persistency. When Polly's last speech was finished the banker's daughter got up, and kissed her friend, and took her leave. "You shouldn't do that," said Polly with a smile. But on this one occasion she returned the caress; and then Miss Greenmantle went her way thinking over all that had been said to her.

"I'll do it too, let him persuade me ever so." This was Polly's soliloquy to herself when she was left alone, and the "him" spoken of on this occasion was her father. She had made up her own mind as to the line of action she would follow, and she was quite resolved never again to ask her father's permission for her marriage. Her father and Jack might fight that out among themselves, as best they could. There had already been one scene on the subject between herself and her father in which the brewer's foreman had acted the part of stern parent with considerable violence. He had not beaten his girl, nor used bad words to her, nor, to tell the truth, had he threatened her with any deprivation of those luxuries to which she had become accustomed; but he had sworn by all the oaths which he knew by heart that if she chose to marry Jack Hollycombe she should go "bare as a tinker's brat." "I don't want anything better," Polly had said. "He'll want something else though," Peppercorn had replied, and had bounced out of the room and banged the door.

Miss Greenmantle, in whose nature there was perhaps something of the lugubrious tendencies which her father exhibited, walked away home from Mr. Peppercorn's house with a sad heart. She was very sorry for Polly Peppercorn's grief, and she was very sorry also for her own. But she had not that amount of high spirits which sustained Polly in her troubles. To tell the truth Polly had some hope that she might get the better of her father, and thereby do a good turn both to him and to herself. But Emily Greenmantle had but little hope. Her father had not sworn at her, nor had he banged the door, but he had pressed his lips together till there was no lip really visible. And he had raised his forehead on high till it looked as though one continuous poker descended from the crown of his head passing down through his entire body. "Emily, it is out of the question. You had better leave me." From that day to this not a word had been spoken on the "subject." Young Gresham had been once asked to dine at the bank, but that had been the only effort made by Mr. Greenmantle in the matter.

Emily had felt as she walked home that she had not at her command weapons so powerful as those which Polly intended to use against her father. No change in her dress would be suitable to her, and were she to make any it would be altogether inefficacious. Nor would her father be tempted by his passion to throw in her teeth the lack of either boots or legs of mutton which might be the consequence of her marriage with a poor man. There was something almost vulgar in these allusions which made Emily feel that there had been some reason for her papa's exclusiveness, — but she let that go by. Polly was a dear girl, though she had found herself able to speak of the brats' feet without even a blush. "I suppose there will be brats, and why shouldn't she, — when she's talking only to me. It must be so I suppose." So Emily had argued to herself, making the excuse altogether on behalf of her friend. But she was sure that if her father ¹ ad heard Polly he would have been offended.

But ·vhat was Emily to do on her own behalf? Harry Gresham had come to dinner, but his coming had been altogether without effect. She was quite sure that she could never care for Harry Gresham, and she did not quite believe that Harry Gresham cared very much for her. There was a rumour about in the country that Harry Gresham wanted money, and she knew well that

Harry Gresham's father and her own papa had been closeted together. She did not care to be married after such a fashion as that. In truth Philip Hughes was the only young man for whom she did care.

She had always felt her father to be the most impregnable of men, — but now on this subject of her marriage he was more impregnable than ever. He had never yet entirely digested that poker which he had swallowed when he had gone so far as to tell his daughter that it was "entirely out of the question." From that hour her home had been terrible to her as a home, and had not been in the least enlivened by the presence of Harry Gresham. And now how was she to carry on the battle? Polly had her plans all drawn out, and was preparing herself for the combat seriously. But for Emily, there was no means left for fighting.

And she felt that though a battle with her father might be very proper for Polly, it would be highly unbecoming for herself. There was a difference in rank between herself and Polly of which Polly clearly understood the strength. Polly would put on her poor clothes, and go into the kitchen, and break her father's heart by preparing for a descent into regions which would be fitting for her were she to marry her young man without a fortune. But to Miss Greenmantle this would be impossible. Any marriage, made now or later, without her father's leave, seemed to her out of the question. She would only ruin her "young man" were she to attempt it, and the attempt would be altogether inefficacious. She could only be unhappy, melancholy, — and perhaps morose; but she could not be so unhappy and melancholy, — or morose, as was her father. At such weapons he could certainly beat her. Since that unhappy word had been spoken, the poker within him had not been for a moment lessened in vigour. And she feared even to appeal to Dr. Freeborn. Dr. Freeborn could do much, — almost everything in Plumplington, — but there was a point at which her father would turn even against Dr. Freeborn. She did not think that the Doctor would ever dare to take up the cudgels against her father on behalf of Philip Hughes. She felt that it would be more becoming for her to abstain and to suffer in silence than to apply to any human being for assistance. But she could be miserable; — outwardly miserable as well as inwardly; — and very miserable she was determined that she would be! Her father no doubt would be miserable too; but she was sad at heart as she bethought herself that her father would rather like it. Though he could not easily digest a poker when he had swallowed it, it never seemed to disagree with him. A state of misery in which he would speak to no one seemed to be almost to his taste. In this way poor Emily Greenmantle did not see her way to the enjoyment of a happy Christmas.

Mr. Greenmantle Is Much Perplexed

That evening Mr. Greenmantle and his daughter sat down to dinner together in a very unhappy humour. They always dined at half-past seven; not that Mr. Greenmantle liked to have his dinner at that hour better than any other, but because it was considered to be fashionable. Old Mr. Gresham, Harry's father, always dined at half-past seven, and Mr. Greenmantle rather followed the habits of a county gentleman's life. He used to dine at this hour when there was a dinner-party, but of late he had adopted it for the family meal. To tell the truth there had been a few words between him and Dr. Freeborn while Emily had been talking over matters with Polly Peppercorn. Dr. Freeborn had not ventured to say a word as to Emily's love affairs; but had so discussed those of Jack Hollycombe and Polly as to leave a strong impression on the mind of Mr. Greenmantle. He had quite understood that the Doctor had been talking at himself, and that when Jack's name had been mentioned, or Polly's, the Doctor had intended that the wisdom spoken should be intended to apply to Emily and to Philip Hughes. "It's only because he can give her a lot of money," the Doctor had said. "The young man is a good man, and steady. What is Peppercorn that he should want anything better for his child? Young Hollycombe has taken her fancy, and why shouldn't she have him?"

"I suppose Mr. Peppercorn may have his own views," Mr.

Greenmantle had answered.

"Bother his views," the Doctor had said. "He has no one else to think of but the girl and his views should be confined to making her happy. Of course he'll have to give way at last, and will only make himself ridiculous. I shouldn't say a word about it only that the young man is all that he ought to be."

Now in this there was not a word which did not apply to Mr. Greenmantle himself. And the worst of it was the fact that Mr. Greenmantle felt that the Doctor intended it.

But as he had taken his constitutional walk before dinner, a walk which he took every day of his life after bank hours, he had sworn to himself that he would not be guided, or in the least affected, by Dr. Freeborn's opinion in the matter. There had been an underlying bitterness in the Doctor's words which had much aggravated the banker's ill-humour. The Doctor would not so have spoken of the marriage of one of his own daughters, — before they had all been married. Birth would have been considered by him almost before anything. The Peppercorns and the Greenmantles were looked down upon almost from an equal height. Now Mr. Greenmantle considered himself to be infinitely superior to Mr. Peppercorn, and to be almost, if not altogether, equal to Dr. Freeborn. He was much the richer man of the two, and his money was quite sufficient to outweigh a century or two of blood.

Peppercorn might do as he pleased. What became of Peppercorn's money was an affair of no matter. The Doctor's argument was no doubt good as far as Peppercorn was concerned. Peppercorn was not a gentleman. It was that which Mr. Greenmantle felt so acutely. The one great line of demarcation in the world was that which separated gentlemen from non-gentlemen. Mr. Greenmantle assured himself that he was a gentleman, acknowledged to be so by all the county. The old Duke of Omnium had customarily asked him to dine at his annual dinner at Gatherum Castle. He had been in the habit of staying occasionally at Greshamsbury, Mr. Gresham's county seat, and Mr. Gresham had been quite willing to forward the match between Emily and his younger son. There could be no doubt that he was on the right side of the line of demarcation. He was therefore quite determined that his daughter should not marry the Cashier in his own bank.

As he sat down to dinner he looked sternly at his daughter, and thought with wonder at the viciousness of her taste. She looked at him almost as sternly as she thought with awe of his cruelty. In her eyes Philip Hughes was quite as good a gentleman as her father. He was the son of a clergyman who was now dead, but had been intimate with Dr. Freeborn. And in the natural course of events might succeed her father as manager of the Bank. To be manager of the Bank at Plumplington was not very much in the eyes of the world; but it was the position which her father filled. Emily vowed to herself as she looked across the table into her father's face, that she would be Mrs. Philip Hughes, — or remain unmarried all her life. "Emily, shall I help you to a mutton cutlet?" said her father with solemnity.

"No thank you, papa," she replied with equal gravity.

"On what then do you intend to dine?" There had been a sole of which she had also declined to partake. "There is nothing else, unless you will dine off rice pudding."

"I am not hungry, papa." She could not decline to wear her customary clothes as did her friend Polly, but she could at any rate go without her dinner. Even a father so stern as was Mr. Greenmantle could not make her eat. Then there came a vision across her eyes of a long sickness, produced chiefly by inanition, in which she might wear her father's heart out. And then she felt that she might too probably lack the courage. She did not care much for her dinner; but she feared that she could not persevere to the breaking of her father's heart. She and her father were alone together in the world, and he in other respects had always been good to her. And now a tear trickled from her eye down her nose as she gazed upon the empty plate. He ate his two cutlets one after another in solemn silence and so the dinner was ended.

He, too, had felt uneasy qualms during the meal. "What shall I do if she takes to starving herself and going to bed, all along of that young rascal in the outer bank?" It was thus that he had thought of it, and he too for a moment had begun to tell himself that were she to be perverse she must win the battle. He knew himself to be strong in purpose, but he doubted whether he would be strong enough to stand by and see his daughter starve herself. A week's starvation or a fortnight's he might bear, and it was possible that she might give way before that time had come.

Then he retired to a little room inside the bank, a room that was half private and half official, to which he would betake himself to spend his evening whenever some especially gloomy fit would fall upon him. Here, within his own bosom, he turned over all the circumstances of the case. No doubt he had with him all the laws of God and man. He was not bound to give his money to any such interloper as was Philip Hughes. On that point he was quite clear. But what step had he better take to prevent the evil? Should he resign his position at the bank, and take his daughter away to live in the south of France? It would be a terrible step to which to be driven by his own Cashier. He was as efficacious to do the work of the bank as ever he had been, and he would leave this enemy to occupy his place. The enemy would then be in a condition to marry a wife without a fortune; and who could tell whether he might not show his power in such a crisis by marrying Emily! How terrible in such a case would be his defeat! At any rate he might go for three months, on sick leave. He had been for nearly forty years in the bank, and had never yet been absent for a day on sick leave. Thinking of all this he remained alone till it was time for him to go to bed.

On the next morning he was dumb and stiff as ever, and after breakfast sat dumb and stiff, in his official room behind the bank counter, thinking over his great trouble. He had not spoken a word to Emily since yesterday's dinner beyond asking her whether she would take a bit of fried bacon. "No thank you, papa," she had said; and then Mr. Greenmantle had made up his mind that he must take her away somewhere at once, lest she should be starved to death. Then he went into the bank and sat there signing his name, and meditating the terrible catastrophe which was to fall upon him. Hughes, the Cashier, had become Mr. Hughes, and if any young man could be frightened out of his love by the stern look and sterner voice of a parent, Mr. Hughes would have been so frightened.

Then there came a knock at the door, and Mr. Peppercorn having been summoned to come in, entered the room. He had expressed a desire to see Mr. Greenmantle personally, and having proved his eagerness by a double request, had been allowed to have his way. It was quite a common affair for him to visit the bank on matters referring to the brewery; but now it was evident to any one with half an eye that such at present was not Mr. Peppercorn's business. He had on the clothes in which he habitually went to church instead of the light-coloured pepper and salt tweed jacket in which he was accustomed to go about among the malt and barrels. "What can I do for you, Mr. Peppercorn?" said the banker. But the aspect was the aspect of a man who had a poker still fixed within his head and gullet.

"'Tis nothing about the brewery, sir, or I shouldn't have troubled you. Mr. Hughes is very good at all that kind of thing." A further frown came over Mr. Greenmantle's face, but he said nothing. "You know my daughter Polly, Mr. Greenmantle?"

"I am aware that there is a Miss Peppercorn," said the other. Peppercorn felt that an offence was intended. Mr. Greenmantle was of course aware. "What can I do on behalf of Miss Peppercorn?"

"She's as good a girl as ever lived."

"I do not in the least doubt it. If it be necessary that you should speak to me respecting Miss Peppercorn, will it not be well that you should take a chair?"

Then Mr. Peppercorn sat down, feeling that he had been snubbed. "I may say that my only object in life is to do every mortal thing to make my girl happy." Here Mr. Greenmantle simply bowed. "We sit close to you in church, where, however, she comes much more reg'lar than me, and you must have observed her scores of time."

"I am not in the habit of looking about among young ladies at church time, but I have occasionally been aware that Miss Peppercorn has been there."

"Of course you have. You couldn't help it. Well, now, you know the sort of appearance she has made."

"I can assure you, Mr. Peppercorn, that I have not observed Miss Peppercorn's dress in particular. I do not look much at the raiment worn by young ladies even in the outer world, — much less in church. I have a daughter of my own ———"

"It's her as I'm coming to." Then Mr. Greenmantle frowned more severely than ever. But the brewer did not at the moment say a word about the banker's daughter, but reverted to his own. "You'll see next Sunday that my girl won't look at all like herself."

"I really cannot promise ——"

"You cannot help yourself, Mr. Greenmantle. I'll go bail that everyone in church will see it. Polly is not to be passed over in a crowd; — at least she didn't used to be. Now it all comes of her wanting to get herself married to a young man who is altogether beneath her. Not as I mean to say anything against John Holly-combe as regards his walk of life. He is an industrious young man, as can earn forty shillings a week, and he comes over here from Barchester selling malt and such like. He may rise himself to £3 some of these days if he looks sharp about it. But I can give my girl —; well, what is quite unfit that he should think of looking for with a wife. And it's monstrous of Polly wanting to throw herself away in such a fashion. I don't believe in a young man being so covetous."

"But what can I do, Mr. Peppercorn?"

"I'm coming to that. If you'll see her next Sunday you'll think of what my feelings must be. She's a-doing of it all just because she wants to show me that she thinks herself fit for nothing better than to be John Hollycombe's wife. When I tell her that I won't have it, — this sudden changing of her toggery, she says it's only fitting. It ain't fitting at all. I've got the money to buy things for her, and I'm willing to pay for it. Is she to go poor just to break her father's heart?"

"But what can I do, Mr. Peppercorn?"

"I'm coming to that. The world does say, Mr. Greenmantle, that your young lady means to serve you in the same fashion."

Hereupon Mr. Greenmantle waxed very wroth. It was terrible to his ideas that his daughter's affairs should be talked of at all by the people at Plumplington at large. It was worse again that his daughter and the brewer's girl should be lumped together in the scandal of the town. But it was worse, much worse, that this man Peppercorn should have dared to come to him, and tell him all about it. Did the man really expect that he, Mr. Greenmantle, should talk unreservedly as to the love affairs of his Emily? "The world, Mr. Peppercorn, is very impertinent in its usual scanda-lous conversations as to its betters. You must forgive me if I do not intend on this occasion to follow the example of the world. Good morning, Mr. Peppercorn."

"It's Dr. Freeborn as has coupled the two girls together."

"I can not believe it."

"You ask him. It's he who has said that you and I are in a boat together."

"I'm not in a boat with any man."

"Well; — in a difficulty. It's the same thing. The Doctor seems to think that young ladies are to have their way in everything. I don't see it. When a man has made a tidy bit of money, as have you and I, he has a right to have a word to say as to who shall have the spending of it. A girl hasn't the right to say that she'll give it all to this man or to that. Of course, it's natural that my money should go to Polly. I'm not saying anything against it. But I don't mean that John Hollycombe shall have it. Now if you and I can put our heads together, I think we may be able to see our way out of the wood."

"Mr. Peppercorn, I cannot consent to discuss with you the affairs of Miss Greenmantle."

"But they're both alike. You must admit that."

"I will admit nothing, Mr. Peppercorn."

"I do think, you know, that we oughtn't to be done by our own daughters."

"Really, Mr. Peppercorn ———"

"Dr. Freeborn was saying that you and I would have to give way at last."

"Dr. Freeborn knows nothing about it. If Dr. Freeborn coupled the two young ladies together he was I must say very impertinent; but I don't think he ever did so. Good morning, Mr. Peppercorn. I am fully engaged at present and cannot spare time for a longer interview." Then he rose up from his chair, and leant upon the table with his hands by way of giving a certain signal that he was to be left alone. Mr. Peppercorn, after pausing a moment, searching for an opportunity for another word, was overcome at last by the rigid erectness of Mr. Greenmantle and withdrew.

Jack Hollycombe

Mr. Peppercorn's visit to the bank had been no doubt inspired by Dr. Freeborn. The Doctor had not actually sent him to the bank, but had filled his mind with the idea that such a visit might be made with good effect. "There are you two fathers going to make two fools of yourselves," the Doctor had said. "You have each of you got a daughter as good as gold, and are determined to break their hearts because you won't give your money to a young man who happens to want it."

"Now, Doctor, do you mean to tell me that you would have married your young ladies to the first young man that came and asked for them?"

"I never had much money to give my girls, and the men who came happened to have means of their own."

"But if you'd had it, and if they hadn't, do you mean to tell me you'd never have asked a question?"

"A man should never boast that in any circumstances of his life he would have done just what he ought to do, — much less when he has never been tried. But if the lover be what he ought to be in morals and all that kind of thing, the girl's father ought not to refuse to help them. You may be sure of this, — that Polly means to have her own way. Providence has blessed you with a girl that knows her own mind." On receipt of this compliment Mr. Peppercorn scratched his head. "I wish I could say as much for my friend Greenmantle. You two are in a boat together, and ought to make up your mind as to what you should do." Peppercorn resolved that he would remember the phrase about the boat, and began to think that it might be good that he should see Mr. Greenmantle. "What on earth is it you two want? It is not as though you were dukes, and looking for proper alliances for two ducal spinsters."

Now there had no doubt been a certain amount of intended venom in this. Dr. Freeborn knew well the weak points in Mr. Greenmantle's character, and was determined to hit him where he was weakest. He did not see the difference between the banker and the brewer nearly so clearly as did Mr. Greenmantle. He

119

would probably have said that the line of demarcation came just below himself. At any rate, he thought that he would be doing best for Emily's interest if he made her father feel that all the world was on her side. Therefore it was that he so contrived that Mr. Peppercorn should pay his visit to the bank.

On his return to the brewery the first person that Peppercorn saw standing in the doorway of his own little sanctum was Jack Hollycombe. "What is it you're wanting?" he asked gruffly.

"I was just desirous of saying a few words to yourself, Mr. Peppercorn."

"Well, here I am!" There were two or three brewers and porters about the place, and Jack did not feel that he could plead his cause well in their presence. "What is it you've got to say, — because I'm busy? There ain't no malt wanted for the next week; but you know that, and as we stand at present you can send it in without any more words, as it's needed."

"It ain't about malt or anything of that kind."

"Then I don't know what you've got to say. I'm very busy just at present, as I told you."

"You can spare me five minutes inside."

"No I can't." But then Peppercorn resolved that neither would it suit him to carry on the conversation respecting his daughter in the presence of the workmen, and he thought that he perceived that Jack Hollycombe would be prepared to do so if he were driven. "Come in if you will," he said; "we might as well have it out." Then he led the way into the room, and shut the door as soon as Jack had followed him. "Now what is it you have got to say? I suppose it's about that young woman down at my house."

"It is, Mr. Peppercorn."

"Then let me tell you that the least said will be soonest mended. She's not for you, — with my consent. And to tell you the truth I think that you have a mortal deal of brass coming to ask for her. You've no edication suited to her education, — and what's wus, no money." Jack had shown symptoms of anger when his deficient education had been thrown in his teeth, but had cheered up somewhat when the lack of money had been insisted upon. "Them two things are so against you that you haven't a leg to stand on. My word! what do you expect that I should say when such a one as you comes a-courting to a girl like that?"

"I did, perhaps, think more of what she might say."

"I daresay; — because you knew her to be a fool like yourself. I suppose you think yourself to be a very handsome young man."

"I think she's a very handsome young woman. As to myself I never asked the question."

"That's all very well. A man can always say as much as that for himself. The fact is you're not going to have her."

"That's just what I want to speak to you about, Mr. Peppercorn."

"You're not going to have her. Now I've spoken my intentions, and you may as well take one word as a thousand. I'm not a man as was ever known to change my mind when I'd made it up in such a matter as this."

"She's got a mind too, Mr. Peppercorn."

"She have, no doubt. She have a mind and so have you. But you haven't either of you got the money. The money is here," and Mr. Peppercorn slapped his breeches pocket. "I've had to do with earning it, and I mean to have to do with giving it away. To me there is no idea of honesty at all in a chap like you coming and asking a girl to marry you just because you know that she's to have a fortune."

"That's not my reason."

"It's uncommon like it. Now you see there's somebody else that's got to be asked. You think I'm a good-natured fellow. So I am, but I'm not soft like that."

"I never thought anything of the kind, Mr. Peppercorn."

"Polly told you so, I don't doubt. She's right in thinking so, because I'd give Polly anything in reason. Or out of reason for the matter of that, because she is the apple of my eye." This was indiscreet on the part of Mr. Peppercorn, as it taught the young man to think that he himself must be in reason or out of reason, and that in either case Polly ought to be allowed to have him. "But there's one thing I stop at; and that is a young man who hasn't got either edication, or money, — nor yet manners."

"There's nothing against my manner, I hope, Mr. Peppercorn."

"Yes; there is. You come a-interfering with me in the most

delicate affair in the world. You come into my family, and want to take away my girl. That I take it is the worst of manners."

"How is any young lady to get married unless some young fellow comes after her?"

"There'll be plenty to come after Polly. You leave Polly alone, and you'll find that she'll get a young man suited to her. It's like your impudence to suppose that there's no other young man in the world so good as you. Why; — dash my wig; who are you? What are you? You're merely acting for them corn-factors over at Barchester."

"And you're acting for them brewers here at Plumplington. What's the difference?"

"But I've got the money in my pocket, and you've got none. That's the difference. Put that in your pipe and smoke it. Now if you'll please to remember that I'm very busy, you'll walk yourself off. You've had it out with me, which I didn't intend; and I've explained my mind very fully. She's not for you; — at any rate my money's not."

"Look here, Mr. Peppercorn."

"Well?"

"I don't care a farthing for your money."

"Don't you now?"

"Not in the way of comparing it with Polly herself. Of course money is a very comfortable thing. If Polly's to be my wife——"

"Which she ain't."

"I should like her to have everything that a lady can desire."

"How kind you are."

"But in regard to money for myself I don't value it that." Here Jack Hollycombe snapped his fingers. "My meaning is to get the girl I love."

"Then you won't."

"And if she's satisfied to come to me without a shilling, I'm satisfied to take her in the same fashion. I don't know how much you've got, Mr. Peppercorn, but you can go and found a Hiram's Hospital with every penny of it." At this moment a discussion was going on respecting a certain charitable institution in Barchester, — and had been going on for the last forty years, — as to which Mr. Hollycombe was here expressing the popular opinion of the day. "That's the kind of thing a man should do who don't choose to leave his money to his own child." Jack was now angry, having had his deficient education twice thrown in his teeth by one whom he conceived to be so much less educated than himself. "What I've got to say to you, Mr. Peppercorn, is that Polly means to have me, and if she's got to wait — why, I'm so minded that I'll wait for her as long as ever she'll wait for me." So saying Jack Hollycombe left the room.

Mr. Peppercorn thrust his hat back upon his head, and stood with his back to the fire, with the tails of his coat appearing over his hands in his breeches pockets, glaring out of his eyes with anger which he did not care to suppress. This man had presented to him a picture of his future life which was most unalluring. There was nothing he desired less than to give his money to such an abominable institution as Hiram's Hospital. Polly, his own dear daughter Polly, was intended to be the recipient of all his savings. As he went about among the beer barrels, he had been a happy man as he thought of Polly bright with the sheen which his money had provided for her. But it was of Polly married to some gentleman that he thought at these moments; — of Polly surrounded by a large family of little gentlemen and little ladies. They would all call him grandpapa; and in the evenings of his days he would sit by the fire in that gentleman's parlour, a welcome guest, because of the means which he had provided; and the little gentlemen and the little ladies would surround him with their prattle and their noises and caresses. He was not a man whom his intimates would have supposed to be gifted with a strong imagination, but there was the picture firmly set before his mind's eye. "Edication," however, in the intended son-in-law was essential. And the son-in-law must be a gentleman. Now Jack Hollycombe was not a gentleman, and was not educated up to that pitch which was necessary for Polly's husband.

But Mr. Peppercorn, as he thought of it all, was well aware that Polly had a decided will of her own. And he knew of himself that his own will was less strong than his daughter's. In spite of all the severe things which he had just said to Jack Hollycombe, there was present to him a dreadful weight upon his heart, as he thought that Polly would certainly get the better of him. At this moment he hated Jack Hollycombe with most un-Christian rancour. No misfortune that could happen to Jack, either sudden

123

death, or forgery with flight to the antipodes, or loss of his good looks, — which Mr. Peppercorn most unjustly thought would be equally efficacious with Polly, — would at the present moment of his wrath be received otherwise than as a special mark of good-fortune. And yet he was well aware that if Polly were to come and tell him that she had by some secret means turned herself into Mrs. Jack Hollycombe, he knew very well that for Polly's sake he would have to take Jack with all his faults, and turn him into the dearest son-in-law that the world could have provided for him. This was a very trying position, and justified him in standing there for a quarter of an hour with his back to the fire, and his coat-tails over his arms, as they were thrust into his trousers pockets.

In the meantime Jack had succeeded in obtaining a few minutes' talk with Polly, — or rather the success had been on Polly's side, for she had managed the business. On coming out from the brewery Jack had met her in the street, and had been taken home by her. "You might as well come in, Jack," she had said, "and have a few words with me. You have been talking to father about it, I suppose."

"Well; I have. He says I am not sufficiently educated. I suppose he wants to get some young man from the colleges."

"Don't you be stupid, Jack. You want to have your own way, I suppose."

"I don't want him to tell me I'm uneducated. Other men that I've heard of ain't any better off than I am."

"You mean himself, — which isn't respectful."

"I'm educated up to doing what I've got to do. If you don't want more, I don't see what he's got to do with it."

"As the times go of course a man should learn more and more. You are not to compare him to yourself; and it isn't respectful. If you want to say sharp things against him, Jack, you had better give it all up; — for I won't bear it."

"I don't want to say anything sharp."

"Why can't you put up with him? He's not going to have his own way. And he is older than you. And it is he that has got the money. If you care about it——"

"You know I care."

"Very well. Suppose I do know, and suppose I don't. I hear

you say you do, and that's all I've got to act upon. Do you bide your time if you've got the patience, and all will come right. I shan't at all think so much of you if you can't bear a few sharp words from him."

"He may say whatever he pleases."

"You ain't educated, — not like Dr. Freeborn, and men of that class."

"What do I want with it?" said he.

"I don't know that you do want it. At any rate I don't want it; and that's what you've got to think about at present. You just go on, and let things be as they are. You don't want to be married in a week's time."

"Why not?" he asked.

"At any rate I don't; and I don't mean to. This time five years will do very well."

"Five years! You'll be an old woman."

"The fitter for you, who'll still be three years older. If you've patience to wait leave it to me."

"I haven't over much patience."

"Then go your own way and suit yourself elsewhere."

"Polly, you're enough to break a man's heart. You know that I can't go and suit myself elsewhere. You are all the world to me, Polly."

"Not half so much as a quarter of malt if you could get your own price for it. A young woman is all very well just as a play-thing; but business is business; — isn't it, Jack?"

"Five years! Fancy telling a fellow that he must wait five years."

"That'll do for the present, Jack. I'm not going to keep you here idle all the day. Father will be angry when I tell him that you've been here at all."

"It was you that brought me."

"Yes, I did. But you're not to take advantage of that. Now I say, Jack, hands off. I tell you I won't. I'm not going to be kissed once a week for five years. Well. Mark my words, this is the last time I ever ask you in here. No; I won't have it. Go away." Then she succeeded in turning him out of the room and closing the house door behind his back. "I think he's the best young man I see about anywhere. Father twits him about his education. It's

125

my belief there's nothing he can't do that he's wanted for. That's the kind of education a man ought to have. Father says it's because he's handsome I like him. It does go a long way, and he is handsome. Father has got ideas of fashion into his head which will send him crazy before he has done with them." Such was the soliloquy in which Miss Peppercorn indulged as soon as she had been left by her lover.

"Educated! Of course I'm not educated. I can't talk Latin and Greek as some of those fellows pretend to, — though for the matter of that I never heard it. But two and two make four, and ten and ten make twenty. And if a fellow says that it don't he is trying on some dishonest game. If a fellow understands that, and sticks to it, he has education enough for my business, — or for Peppercorn's either." Then he walked back to the inn yard where he had left his horse and trap.

As he drove back to Barchester he made up his mind that Polly Peppercorn would be worth waiting for. There was the memory of that kiss upon his lips which had not been made less sweet by the severity of the words which had accompanied it. The words indeed had been severe; but there had been an intention and a purpose about the kiss which had altogether redeemed the words. "She is just one in a thousand, that's about the truth. And as for waiting for her; — I'll wait like grim death, only I hope it won't be necessary!" It was thus he spoke of the lady of his love as he drove himself into the town under Barchester Towers.

Dr. Freeborn and Philip Hughes

Things went on at Plumplington without any change for a fortnight, — that is without any change for the better. But in truth the ill-humour both of Mr. Greenmantle and of Mr. Peppercorn had increased to such a pitch as to add an additional blackness to the general haziness and drizzle and gloom of the

November weather. It was now the end of November, and Dr. Freeborn was becoming a little uneasy because the Christmas attributes for which he was desirous were still altogether out of sight. He was a man specially anxious for the mundane happiness of his parishioners and who would take any amount of personal trouble to insure it; but he was in fault perhaps in this, that he considered that everybody ought to be happy just because he told them to be so. He belonged to the Church of England certainly, but he had no dislike to Papists or Presbyterians, or dissenters in general, as long as they would arrange themselves under his banner as "Freebornites." And he had such force of character that in Plumplington, — beyond which he was not ambitious that his influence should extend, — he did in general prevail. But at the present moment he was aware that Mr. Greenmantle was in open mutiny. That Peppercorn would yield he had strong hope. Peppercorn he knew to be a weak, good fellow, whose affection for his daughter would keep him right at last. But until he could extract that poker from Mr. Greenmantle's throat, he knew that nothing could be done with him.

At the end of the fortnight Mr. Greenmantle called at the Rectory about half an hour before dinner time, when he knew that the Doctor would be found in his study before going up to dress for dinner. "I hope I am not intruding, Dr. Freeborn," he said. But the rust of the poker was audible in every syllable as it fell from his mouth.

"Not in the least. I've a quarter of an hour before I go and wash my hands."

"It will be ample. In a quarter of an hour I shall be able sufficiently to explain my plans." Then there was a pause, as though Mr. Greenmantle had expected that the explanation was to begin with the Doctor. "I am thinking," the banker continued after a while, "of taking my family abroad to some foreign residence." Now it was well known to Dr. Freeborn that Mr. Greenmantle's family consisted exclusively of Emily.

"Going to take Emily away?" he said.

"Such is my purpose, — and myself also."

"What are they to do at the bank?"

"That will be the worst of it, Dr. Freeborn. The bank will be the great difficulty."

"But you don't mean that you are going for good?"

"Only for a prolonged foreign residence; — that is to say for six months. For forty years I have given but very little trouble to the Directors. For forty years I have been at my post and have never suggested any prolonged absence. If the Directors cannot bear with me after forty years I shall think them unreasonable men." Now in truth Mr. Greenmantle knew that the Directors would make no opposition to anything that he might propose; but he always thought it well to be armed with some premonitory grievance. "In fact my pecuniary matters are so arranged that should the Directors refuse I shall go all the same."

"You mean that you don't care a straw for the Directors."

"I do not mean to postpone my comfort to their views, — or my daughter's."

"But why does your daughter's comfort depend on your going away? I should have thought that she would have preferred Plumplington at present."

That was true, no doubt. And Mr. Greenmantle felt; — well; that he was not exactly telling the truth in putting the burden of his departure upon Emily's comfort. If Emily, at the present crisis of affairs, were carried away from Plumplington for six months, her comfort would certainly not be increased. She had already been told that she was to go, and she had clearly understood why. "I mean as to her future welfare," said Mr. Greenmantle very solemnly.

Dr. Freeborn did not care to hear about the future welfare of young people. What had to be said as to their eternal welfare he thought himself quite able to say. After all there was something of benevolent paganism in his disposition. He liked better to deal with their present happiness, — so that there was nothing immoral in it. As to the world to come he thought that the fathers and mothers of his younger flock might safely leave that consideration to him. "Emily is a remarkably good girl. That's my idea of her."

Mr. Greenmantle was offended even at this. Dr. Freeborn had no right, just at present, to tell him that his daughter was a good girl. Her goodness had been greatly lessened by the fact that in regard to her marriage she was anxious to run counter to her father. "She is a good girl. At least I hope so."

"Do you doubt it?"

"Well, no; — or rather yes. Perhaps I ought to say no as to her life in general."

"I should think so. I don't know what a father may want, — but I should think so. I never knew her to miss church yet, — either morning or evening."

"As far as that goes she does not neglect her duties."

"What is the matter with her that she is to be taken off to some foreign climate for prolonged residence?" The Doctor among his other idiosyncrasies entertained an idea that England was the proper place for all Englishmen and Englishwomen who were not driven out of it by stress of pecuniary circumstances. "Has she got a bad throat or a weak chest?"

"It is not on the score of her own health that I propose to move her," said Mr. Greenmantle.

"You did say her comfort. Of course that may mean that she likes the French way of living. I did hear that we were to lose your services for a time, because you could not trust your own health."

"It is failing me a little, Dr. Freeborn. I am already very near sixty."

"Ten years my junior," said the Doctor.

"We cannot all hope to have such perfect health as you possess."

"I have never frittered it away," said the Doctor, "by prolonged residence in foreign parts." This quotation of his own words was most harassing to Mr. Greenmantle, and made him more than once inclined to bounce in anger out of the Doctor's study. "I suppose the truth is that Miss Emily is disposed to run counter to your wishes in regard to her marriage, and that she is to be taken away not from consumption or a weak throat, but from a dangerous lover." Here Mr. Greenmantle's face became black as thunder. "You see, Greenmantle, there is no good in our talking about this matter unless we understand each other."

"I do not intend to give my girl to the young man upon whom she thinks that her affections rest."

"I suppose she knows."

"No, Dr. Freeborn. It is often the case that a young lady does not know; she only fancies, and where that is the case absence is the best remedy. You have said that Emily is a good girl."

"A very good girl."

"I am delighted to hear you express yourself. But obedience to parents is a trait in character which is generally much thought of. I have put by a little money, Dr. Freeborn."

"All Plumplington knows that."

"And I shall choose that it shall go somewhat in accordance with my wishes. The young man of whom she is thinking——"

"Philip Hughes, an excellent fellow. I've known him all my life. He doesn't come to church quite so regularly as he ought, but that will be mended when he's married."

"Hasn't got a shilling in the world," continued Mr. Green-mantle, finishing his sentence. "Nor is he — just, — just — just what I should choose for the husband of my daughter. I think that when I have said so he should take my word for it."

"That's not the way of the world, you know."

"It's the way of my world, Dr. Freeborn. It isn't often that I speak out, but when I do it's about something that I've got a right to speak of. I've heard this affair of my daughter talked about all over the town. There was one Mr. Peppercorn came to me——"

"One Mr. Peppercorn? Why, Hickory Peppercorn is as well known in Plumplington as the church-steeple."

"I beg your pardon, Dr. Freeborn; but I don't find any reason in that for his interfering about my daughter. I must say that I took it as a great piece of impertinence. Goodness gracious me! If a man's own daughter isn't to be considered peculiar to himself I don't know what is. If he'd asked you about your daughters, — before they were married?" Dr. Freeborn did not answer this, but declared to himself that neither Mr. Peppercorn nor Mr. Green-mantle could have taken such a liberty. Mr. Greenmantle evidently was not aware of it, but in truth Dr. Freeborn and his family belonged altogether to another set. So at least Dr. Freeborn told himself. "I've come to you now, Dr. Freeborn, because I have not liked to leave Plumplington for a prolonged residence in foreign parts without acquainting you."

"I should have thought that unkind."

"You are very good. And as my daughter will of course go with me, and as this idea of a marriage on her part must be entirely given up; —" the emphasis was here placed with much weight on the word entirely; — "I should take it as a great kindness if you would let my feelings on the subject be generally known. I will own that I should not have cared to have my daughter talked about, only that the mischief has been done."

"In a little place like this," said the Doctor, "a young lady's marriage will always be talked about."

"But the young lady in this case isn't going to be married."

"What does she say about it herself?"

"I haven't asked her, Dr. Freeborn. I don't mean to ask her. I shan't ask her."

"If I understand her feelings, Greenmantle, she is very much set upon it."

"I cannot help it."

"You mean to say then that you intend to condemn her to unhappiness merely because this young man hasn't got as much money at the beginning of his life as you have at the end of yours?"

"He hasn't got a shilling," said Mr. Greenmantle.

"Then why can't you give him a shilling? What do you mean to do with your money?" Here Mr. Greenmantle again looked offended. "You come and ask me, and I am bound to give you my opinion for what it's worth. What do you mean to do with your money? You're not the man to found a Hiram's Hospital with it. As sure as you are sitting there your girl will have it when you're dead. Don't you know that she will have it?"

"I hope so."

"And because she's to have it, she's to be made wretched about it all her life. She's to remain an old maid, or else to be married to some well-born pauper, in order that you may talk about your son-in-law. Don't get into a passion, Greenmantle, but only think whether I'm not telling you the truth. Hughes isn't a spendthrift."

"I have made no accusation against him."

"Nor a gambler, nor a drunkard, nor is he the sort of man to treat a wife badly. He's there at the bank so that you may keep him under your own eye. What more on earth can a man want in a son-in-law?"

Blood, thought Mr. Greenmantle to himself; an old family name; county associations, and a certain something which he

131

felt quite sure that Philip Hughes did not possess. And he knew well enough that Dr. Freeborn had married his own daughters to husbands who possessed these gifts; but he could not throw the fact back into the Rector's teeth. He was in some way conscious that the Rector had been entitled to expect so much for his girls, and that he, the banker, was not so entitled. The same idea passed through the Rector's mind. But the Rector knew how far the banker's courage would carry him. "Good night, Dr. Freeborn," said Mr. Greenmantle suddenly.

"Good night, Greenmantle. Shan't I see you again before you go?" To this the banker made no direct answer, but at once took his leave.

"That man is the greatest ass in all Plumplington," the Doctor said to his wife within five minutes of the time of which the hall door was closed behind the banker's back. "He's got an idea into his head about having some young county swell for his son-in-law."

"Harry Gresham. Harry is too idle to earn money by a profession, and therefore wants Greenmantle's money to live upon. There's Peppercorn wants something of the same kind for Polly. People are such fools." But Mrs. Freeborn's two daughters had been married much after the same fashion. They had taken husbands nearly as old as their father, because Dr. Freeborn and his wife had thought much of "blood."

On the next morning Philip Hughes was summoned by the banker into the more official of the two back parlours. Since he had presumed to signify his love for Emily, he had never been asked to enjoy the familiarity of the other chamber. "Mr. Hughes, you may probably have heard it asserted that I am about to leave Plumplington for a prolonged residence in foreign parts." Mr. Hughes had heard it and so declared. "Yes, Mr. Hughes, I am about to proceed to the South of France. My daughter's health requires attention, — and indeed on my own behalf I am in need of some change as well. I have not as yet officially made known my views to the Directors."

"There will be, I should think, no impediment with them."

"I cannot say. But at any rate I shall go. After forty years of service in the Bank I cannot think of allowing the peculiar views of men who are all younger than myself to interfere with my comfort. I shall go."

"I suppose so, Mr. Greenmantle."

"I shall go. I say it without the slightest disrespect for the Board. But I shall go."

"Will it be permanent, Mr. Greenmantle?"

"That is a question which I am not prepared to answer at a moment's notice. I do not propose to move my furniture for six months. It would not, I believe, be within the legal power of the Directors to take possession of the Bank house for that period."

"I am quite sure they would not wish it."

"Perhaps my assurance on that subject may be of more avail. At any rate they will not remove me. I should not have troubled you on this subject were it not that your position in the Bank must be affected more or less."

"I suppose that I could do the work for six months," said Philip Hughes.

But this was a view of the case which did not at all suit Mr. Greenmantle's mind. His own duties at Plumplington had been, to his thinking, the most important ever confided to a Bank Manager. There was a peculiarity about Plumplington of which no one knew the intricate details but himself. The man did not exist who could do the work as he had done it. But still he had determined to go, and the work must be intrusted to some man of lesser competence. "I should think it probable," he said, "that some confidential clerk will be sent over from Barchester. Your youth, Mr. Hughes, is against you. It is not for me to say what line the Directors may determine to take."

"I know the people better than any one can do in Barchester."

"Just so. But you will excuse me if I say you may for that reason be the less efficient. I have thought it expedient, however, to tell you of my views. If you have any steps that you wish to take you can now take them."

Then Mr. Greenmantle paused, and had apparently brought the meeting to an end. But there was still something which he wished to say. He did think that by a word spoken in due season, — by a strong determined word, he might succeed in putting an end to this young man's vain and ambitious hopes. He did not wish to talk to the young man about his daughter; but, if the strong word might avail here was the opportunity. "Mr.

Hughes," he began.

"Yes, sir."

"There is a subject on which perhaps it would be well that I should be silent." Philip, who knew the manager thoroughly, was now aware of what was coming, and thought it wise that he should say nothing at the moment. "I do not know that any good can be done by speaking of it." Philip still held his tongue. "It is a matter no doubt of extreme delicacy, — of the most extreme delicacy I may say. If I go abroad as I intend, I shall as a matter of course take with me — Miss Greenmantle."

"I suppose so."

"I shall take with me — Miss Greenmantle. It is not to be supposed that when I go abroad for a prolonged sojourn in foreign parts, that I should leave — Miss Greenmantle behind me."

"No doubt she will accompany you."

"Miss Greenmantle will accompany me. And it is not improbable that my prolonged residence may in her case be — still further prolonged. It may be possible that she should link her lot in life to some gentleman whom she may meet in those realms."

"I hope not," said Philip.

"I do not think that you are justified, Mr. Hughes, in hoping anything in reference to my daughter's fate in life."

"All the same, I do."

"It is very, — very, —! I do not wish to use strong language, and therefore I will not say impertinent."

"What am I to do when you tell me that she is to marry a foreigner?"

"I never said so. I never thought so. A foreigner! Good heavens! I spoke of a gentleman whom she might chance to meet in those realms. Of course I meant an English gentleman."

"The truth is, Mr. Greenmantle, I don't want your daughter to marry anyone unless she can marry me."

"A most selfish proposition."

"It's a sort of matter in which a man is apt to be selfish, and it's my belief that if she were asked she'd say the same thing. Of course you can take her abroad and you can keep her there as long as you please."

"I can; — and I mean to do it."

"I am utterly powerless to prevent you, and so is she. In this contention between us I have only one point in my favour."

"You have no point in your favour, sir."

"The young lady's good wishes. If she be not on my side, — why then I am nowhere. In that case you needn't trouble yourself to take her out of Plumplington. But if——"

"You may withdraw, Mr. Hughes," said the banker. "The interview is over." Then Philip Hughes withdrew, but as he went he shut the door after him in a very confident manner.

The Young Ladies Are To Be Taken Abroad

How should Philip Hughes see Emily before she had been carried away to "foreign parts" by her stern father? As he regarded the matter it was absolutely imperative that he should do so. If she should be made to go, in her father's present state of mind, without having reiterated her vows, she might be persuaded by that foreign-living English gentleman whom she would find abroad, to give him her hand. Emily had no doubt confessed her love to Philip, but she had not done so in that bold unshrinking manner which had been natural to Polly Peppercorn. And her lover felt it to be incumbent upon him to receive some renewal of her assurance before she was taken away for a prolonged residence abroad. But there was a difficulty as to this. If he were to knock at the door of the private house and ask for Miss Greenmantle, the servant, though she was in truth Philip's friend in the matter, would not dare to show him up. The whole household was afraid of Mr. Greenmantle, and would receive any hint that his will was to be set aside with absolute dismay. So Philip at last determined to take the bull by the horns and force his way into the drawing-room. Mr. Greenmantle could not be made more hostile than he was; and then it was quite on the cards, that he might be kept in ignorance of the intrusion. When therefore the banker was sitting in his own more private room, Philip passed through from the bank into the house, and made

135

his way up-stairs with no one to announce him.

With no one to announce him he passed straight through into the drawing-room, and found Emily sitting very melancholy over a half-knitted stocking. It had been commenced with an idea that it might perhaps be given to Philip, but as her father's stern severity had been announced, she had given up that fond idea, and had increased the size, so as to fit them for the paternal feet. "Good gracious, Philip," she exclaimed, "how on earth did you get here?"

"I came up-stairs from the bank."

"Oh, yes; of course. But did you not tell Mary that you were coming?"

"I should never have been let up had I done so. Mary has orders not to let me put my foot within the house."

"You ought not to have come; indeed you ought not."

"And I was to let you go abroad without seeing you! Was that what I ought to have done? It might be that I should never see you again. Only think of what my condition must be."

"Is not mine twice worse?"

"I do not know. If it be twice worse than mine then I am the happiest man in all the world."

"Oh, Philip, what do you mean?"

"If you will assure me of your love——"

"I have assured you."

"Give me another assurance, Emily," he said sitting down beside her on the sofa. But she started up quickly to her feet. "When you gave me the assurance before, then — then——"

"One assurance such as that ought to be quite enough."

"But you are going abroad."

"That can make no difference."

"Your father says, that you will meet there some Englishman who will——"

"My father knows nothing about it. I shall meet no Englishman, and no foreigner; at least none that I shall care about. You oughtn't to get such an idea into your head."

"That's all very well, but how am I to keep such ideas out? Of course there will be men over there; and if you come across some idle young fellow who has not his bread to earn as I do, won't it be natural that you should listen to him?"

136

"No; it won't be natural."

"It seems to me to be so. What have I got that you should continue to care for me?"

"You have my word, Philip. Is that nothing?" She had now seated herself on a chair away from the sofa, and he, feeling at the time some special anxiety to get her into his arms, threw himself down on his knees before her, and seized her by both her hands. At that moment the door of the drawing-room was opened, and Mr. Greenmantle appeared within the room. Philip Hughes could not get upon his feet quick enough to return the furious anger of the look which was thrown on him. There was a difficulty even in disembarrassing himself of poor Emily's hands; so that she, to her father, seemed to be almost equally a culprit with the young man. She uttered a slight scream, and then he very gradually rose to his legs.

"Emily," said the angry father, "retire at once to your chamber."

"But, papa, I must explain."

"Retire at once to your chamber, miss. As for this young man, I do not know whether the laws of his country will not punish him for this intrusion."

Emily was terribly frightened by this allusion to her country's laws. "He has done nothing, papa; indeed he has done nothing."

"His very presence here, and on his knees! Is that nothing? Mr. Hughes, I desire that you will retire. Your presence in the bank is required. I lay upon you my strict order never again to presume to come through that door. Where is the servant who announced you?"

"No servant announced me."

"And did you dare to force your way into my private house, and into my daughter's presence unannounced? It is indeed time that I should take her abroad to undergo a prolonged residence in some foreign parts. But the laws of the country which you have outraged will punish you. In the meantime why do you not withdraw? Am I to be obeyed?"

"I have just one word which I wish to say to Miss Greenmantle."

"Not a word. Withdraw! I tell you, sir, withdraw to the bank. There your presence is required. Here it will never be needed."

"Good-bye, Emily," he said, putting out his hand in his vain attempt to take hers.

"Withdraw, I tell you." And Mr. Greenmantle, with all the stiffness of the poker apparent about him, backed poor young Philip Hughes through the doorway on to the staircase, and then banged the door behind him. Having done this, he threw himself on to the sofa, and hid his face with his hands. He wished it to be understood that the honour of his family had been altogether disgraced by the lightness of his daughter's conduct.

But his daughter did not see the matter quite in the same light. Though she lacked something of that firmness of manner which Polly Peppercorn was prepared to exhibit, she did not intend to be altogether trodden on. "Papa," she said, "why do you do that?"

"Good heavens!"

"Why do you cover up your face?"

"That a daughter of mine should have behaved so disgracefully!"

"I haven't behaved disgracefully, papa."

"Admitting a young man surreptitiously to my drawing-room!"

"I didn't admit him; he walked in."

"And on his knees! I found him on his knees."

"I didn't put him there. Of course he came, — because, — because——"

"Because what?" he demanded.

"Because he is my lover. I didn't tell him to come; but of course he wanted to see me before we went away."

"He shall see you no more."

"Why shouldn't he see me? He's a very good young man, and I am very fond of him. That's just the truth."

"You shall be taken away for a prolonged residence in foreign parts before another week has passed over your head."

"Dr. Freeborn quite approves of Mr. Hughes," pleaded Emily. But the plea at the present moment was of no avail. Mr. Greenmantle in his present frame of mind was almost as angry with Dr. Freeborn as with Emily or Philip Hughes. Dr. Freeborn was joined in this frightful conspiracy against him.

"I do not know," said he grandiloquently, "that Dr. Freeborn has any right to interfere with the private affairs of my family.

Dr. Freeborn is simply the Rector of Plumplington, — nothing more."

"He wants to see the people around him all happy," said Emily.

"He won't see me happy," said Mr. Greenmantle with awful pride.

"He always wishes to have family quarrels settled before Christmas."

"He shan't settle anything for me." Mr. Greenmantle, as he so expressed himself, determined to maintain his own independence. "Why is he to interfere with my family quarrels because he's the Rector of Plumplington? I never heard of such a thing. When I shall have taken up my residence in foreign parts he will have no right to interfere with me."

"But, papa, he will be my clergyman all the same."

"He won't be mine, I can tell him that. And as for settling things by Christmas, it is all nonsense. Christmas, except for going to church and taking the Sacrament, is no more than any other day."

"Oh, papa!"

"Well, my dear, I don't quite mean that. What I do mean is that Dr. Freeborn has no more right to interfere with my family at this time of year than at any other. And when you're abroad, which you will be before Christmas, you'll find that Dr. Freeborn will have nothing to say to you there."

"You had better begin to pack up at once," he said on the following day.

"Pack up?"

"Yes, pack up. I shall take you first to London, where you will stay for a day or two. You will go by the afternoon train to-morrow."

"To-morrow!"

"I will write and order beds to-day."

"But where are we to go?"

"That will be made known to you in due time," said Mr. Greenmantle.

"But I've got no clothes," said Emily.

"France is a land in which ladies delight to buy their dresses."

"But I shall want all manner of things, — boots and underclothing, — and — and linen, papa."

"They have all those things in France."

"But they won't fit me. I always have my things made to fit me. And I haven't got any boxes."

"Boxes! what boxes? work-boxes?"

"To put my things in. I can't pack up unless I've got something to pack them in. As to going to-morrow, papa, it's quite impossible. Of course there are people I must say good-bye to. The Freeborns——"

"Not the slightest necessity," said Mr. Greenmantle. "Dr. Freeborn will quite understand the reason. As to boxes, you won't want the boxes till you've bought the things to put in them."

"But papa, I can't go without taking a quantity of things with me. I can't get everything new; and then I must have my dresses made to fit me." She was very lachrymose, very piteous, and full of entreaties; but still she knew what she was about. As the result of the interview, Mr. Greenmantle did almost acknowledge that they could not depart for a prolonged residence abroad on the morrow.

Early on the following morning Polly Peppercorn came to call. For the last month she had stuck to her resolution, — that she and Miss Greenmantle belonged to different sets in society, and could not be brought together, as Polly had determined to wear her second-rate dresses in preparation for a second-rate marriage, — and this visit was supposed to be something altogether out of the way. It was clearly a visit with a cause, as it was made at eleven o'clock in the morning. "Oh, Miss Greenmantle," she said, "I hear that you're going away to France, — you and your papa, quite at once."

"Who has told you?"

"Well, I can't quite say; but it has come round through Dr. Freeborn." Dr. Freeborn had in truth told Mr. Peppercorn, with the express view of exercising what influence he possessed so as to prevent the rapid emigration of Mr. Greenmantle. And Mr. Peppercorn had told his daughter, threatening her that something of the same kind would have to happen in his own family if she proved obstinate about her lover. "It's the best thing going," said Mr. Peppercorn, "when a girl is upsetting and determined to have her own way." To this Polly made no reply, but came away early on the following morning, so as to converse with her late friend, Miss Greenmantle.

"Papa says so; but you know it's quite impossible."

"What is Mr. Hughes to do?" asked Polly in a whisper.

"I don't know what anybody is to do. It's dreadful, the idea of going away from home in this sudden manner."

'Indeed it is."

"I can't do it. Only think, Polly, when I talk to him about clothes, he tells me I'm to buy dresses in some foreign town. He knows nothing about a woman's clothes; — nor yet a man's for the matter of that. Fancy starting to-morrow for six months. It's the sort of thing that Ida Pfeiffer used to do."

"I didn't know her," said Polly.

"She was a great traveller, and went about everywhere almost without anything. I don't know how she managed it, but I'm sure that I can't."

"Dr. Freeborn says that he thinks it's all nonsense." As Polly said this she shook her head and looked uncommonly wise. Emily, however, made no immediate answer. Could it be true that Dr. Freeborn had thus spoken of her father? Emily did think that it was all nonsense, but she had not yet brought herself to express her thoughts openly. "To tell the truth, Miss Greenmantle," continued Polly, "Dr. Freeborn thinks that Mr. Hughes ought to be allowed to have his own way." In answer to this Emily could bring herself to say nothing; but she declared to herself that since the beginning of things Dr. Freeborn had always been as near an angel as any old gentleman could be. "And he says that it's quite out of the question that you should be carried off in this way."

"I suppose I must do what papa tells me."

"Well; yes. I don't know quite about that. I'm all for doing everything that papa likes, but when he talks of taking me to France, I know I'm not going. Lord love you, he couldn't talk to anybody there." Emily began to remember that her father's proficiency in the French language was not very great. "Neither could I for the matter of that," continued Polly. "Of course, I learned it at school, but when one can only read words very slowly one can't talk them at all. I've tried it, and I know it. A precious figure father and I would make finding our way about France."

"Does Mr. Peppercorn think of going?" asked Emily.

"He says so; — if I won't drop Jack Hollycombe. Now I don't mean to drop Jack Hollycombe; not for father nor for anyone. It's only Jack himself can make me do that."

"He won't, I suppose."

"I don't think he will. Now it's absurd, you know, the idea of our papas both carrying us off to France because we've got lovers in Plumplington. How all the world would laugh at them! You tell your papa what my papa is saying, and Dr. Freeborn thinks that that will prevent him. At any rate, if I were you, I wouldn't go and buy anything in a hurry. Of course, you've got to think of what would do for married life."

"Oh, dear, no!" exclaimed Emily.

"At any rate I should keep my mind fixed upon it. Dr. Freeborn says that there's no knowing how things may turn out." Having finished the purport of her embassy, Polly took her leave without even having offered one kiss to her friend.

Dr. Freeborn had certainly been very sly in instigating Mr. Peppercorn to proclaim his intention of following the example of his neighbour the banker. "Papa," said Emily when her father came in to luncheon, "Mr. Peppercorn is going to take his daughter to foreign parts."

"What for?"

"I believe he means to reside there for a time."

"What nonsense! He reside in France! He wouldn't know what to do with himself for an hour. I never heard anything like it. Because I am going to France is all Plumplington to follow me? What is Mr. Peppercorn's reason for going to France?" Emily hesitated; but Mr. Greenmantle pressed the question, "What object can such a man have?"

"I suppose it's about his daughter," said Emily. Then the truth flashed upon Mr. Greenmantle's mind, and he became aware that he must at any rate for the present abandon the idea. Then, too, there came across him some vague notion that Dr. Freeborn had instigated Mr. Peppercorn and an idea of the object with which he had done so.

"Papa," said Emily that afternoon, "am I to get the trunks I spoke about?"

"What trunks?"

"To put my things in, papa. I must have trunks if I am to go abroad for any length of time. And you will want a large portmanteau. You would get it much better in London than you would at Plumplington." But here Mr. Greenmantle told his daughter that she need not at present trouble her mind about either his travelling gear or her own.

A few days afterwards Dr. Freeborn sauntered into the bank, and spoke a few words to the cashier across the counter. "So Mr. Greenmantle, I'm told, is not going abroad," said the Rector.

"I've heard nothing more about it," said Philip Hughes.

"I think he has abandoned the idea. There was Hickory Peppercorn thinking of going, too, but he has abandoned it. What do they want to go travelling about France for?"

"What indeed, Dr. Freeborn; — unless the two young ladies have something to say to it."

"I don't think they wish it, if you mean that."

"I think their fathers thought of taking them out of harm's way."

"No doubt. But when the harm's way consists of a lover it's very hard to tear a young lady away from it." This was said so that Philip only could hear it. The two lads who attended the bank were away at their desks in distant parts of the office. "Do you keep your eyes open, Philip," said the Rector, "and things will run smoother yet than you expected."

"He is frightfully angry with me, Dr. Freeborn. I made my way up into the drawing-room the other day, and he found me there."

"What business had you to do that?"

"Well, I was wrong, I suppose. But if Emily was to be taken away suddenly I had to see her before she went. Think, Doctor, what a prolonged residence in a foreign country means. I mightn't see her again for years."

"And so he found you up in the drawing-room. It was very improper; that's all I can say. Nevertheless, if you'll behave yourself, I shouldn't be surprised if things were to run smoother before Christmas." Then the Doctor took his leave.

"Now, father," said Polly, "you're not going to carry me off to foreign parts."

"Yes, I am. As you're so willful it's the only thing for you."

"What's to become of the brewery?"

"The brewery may take care of itself. As you won't want the money for your husband there'll be plenty for me. I'll give it up. I ain't going to slave and slave all my life and nothing come of it. If you won't oblige me in this the brewery may go and take care of itself."

"If you're like that, father, I must take care of myself. Mr. Greenmantle isn't going to take his daughter over."

"Yes; he is."

"Not a bit of it. He's as much as told Emily that she's not to get her things ready." Then there was a pause, during which Mr. Peppercorn showed that he was much disturbed. "Now, father, why don't you give way, and show yourself what you always were, — the kindest father that ever a girl had."

"There's no kindness in you, Polly. Kindness ought to be reciprocal."

"Isn't it natural that a girl should like her young man?"

"He's not your young man."

"He's going to be. What have you got to say against him? You ask Dr. Freeborn."

"Dr. Freeborn, indeed! He isn't your father!"

"He's not my father, but he's my friend. And he's yours, if you only knew it. You think of it, just for another day, and then say that you'll be good to your girl." Then she kissed him, and as she left him she felt that she was about to prevail.

The Young Ladies Are To Remain at Home

Miss Emily Greenmantle had always possessed a certain character for delicacy. We do not mean delicacy of sentiment. That of course belonged to her as a young lady, — but delicacy of health. She was not strong and robust, as her friend Polly Peppercorn. When we say that she possessed that character, we intend to imply that she perhaps made a little use of it. There had never been much the matter with her, but she had always been a little delicate. It seemed to suit her, and prevented the necessity of overexertion. Whereas Polly, who had never been delicate, felt herself always called upon to "run round," as the Americans say. "Running round" on the part of a young lady implies a readiness and a willingness to do everything that has to be done in domestic life. If a father wants his slippers or a mother her thimble, or a cook a further supply of sauces, the active young lady has to "run round." Polly did run round; but Emily was delicate and did not. Therefore when she did not get up one morning, and complained of a headache, the doctor was sent for. "She's not very strong, you know," the doctor said to her father. "Miss Emily always was delicate."

"I hope it isn't much," said Mr. Greenmantle.

"There is something I fear disturbing the even tenor of her thoughts," said the doctor, who had probably heard of the hopes entertained by Mr. Philip Hughes and favoured them. "She should be kept quite quiet. I wouldn't prescribe much medicine, but I'll tell Mixet to send her in a little draught. As for diet she can have pretty nearly what she pleases. She never had a great appetite." And so the doctor went his way. The reader is not to suppose that Emily Greenmantle intended to deceive her father, and play the old soldier. Such an idea would have been repugnant to her nature. But when her father told her that she was to be taken abroad for a prolonged residence, and when it of course followed that her lover was to be left behind, there came upon her a natural feeling that the best thing for her would be to lie in bed, and so to avoid all the troubles of life for the present moment.

"I am very sorry to hear that Emily is so ill," said Dr. Freeborn, calling on the banker further on in the day.

"I don't think it's much, Dr. Freeborn."

"I hope not; but I just saw Miller, who shook his head. Miller never shakes his head quite for nothing."

In the evening Mr. Greenmantle got a little note from Mrs. Freeborn. "I am *so unhappy* to hear about *dear* Emily. The poor child always was *delicate*. *Pray* take care of her. She must see Dr. Miller twice every day. Changes do take place so *frequently*. If you think she would be better here, we would be *delighted* to have her. There is so much in having the attention of a *lady*."

"Of course I am nervous," said Mr. Philip Hughes next morning to the banker. "I hope you will excuse me, if I venture to ask for one word as to Miss Greenmantle's health."

"I am very sorry to hear that Miss Greenmantle has been taken so poorly," said Mr. Peppercorn, who met Mr. Greenmantle in the street. "It is not very much, I have reason to hope," said the father, with a look of anger. Why should Mr. Peppercorn be solicitous as to his daughter?

"I am told that Dr. Miller is rather alarmed." Then Polly called at the front door to make special inquiry after Miss Greenmantle's health.

Mr. Greenmantle wrote to Mrs. Freeborn thanking her for the offer, and expressing a hope that it might not be necessary to move Emily from her own bed. And he thanked all his other neighbours for the pertinacity of their inquiries, — feeling however all the while that there was something of a conspiracy being hatched against him. He did not quite think his daughter guilty, but in his answer made to the inquiry of Philip Hughes, he spoke as though he believed that the young man had been the instigator of it. When on the third day his daughter could not get up, and Mr. Miller had ordered a more potent draught, Mr. Greenmantle almost owned to himself that he had been beaten. He took a walk by himself and meditated on it. It was a cruel case. The money was his money, and the girl was his girl, and the young man was his clerk. He ought according to the rules of justice in the world to have had plenary power over them all. But it had come to pass that his power was nothing. What is a father to do when a young lady goes to bed and remains there? And how is a soft-hearted father to make any use of his own money when all his neighbours turn against him?

"Miss Greenmantle is to have her own way, father," Polly said to Mr. Peppercorn on one of these days. It was now the second week in December, and the whole ground was hard with frost. "Dr. Freeborn will be right after all. He never is much wrong. He declared that Emily would be given to Philip Hughes as a Christmas-box."

"I don't believe it a bit," said Mr. Peppercorn.

"It is so all the same. I knew that when she became ill her

father wouldn't be able to stand his ground. There is no knowing what these delicate young ladies can do in that way. I wish I were delicate."

"You don't wish anything of the kind. It would be very wicked to wish yourself to be sickly. What should I do if you were running up a doctor's bill?"

"Pay it, — as Mr. Greenmantle does. You've never had to pay half-a-crown for a doctor for me, I don't know when."

"And now you want to be poorly."

"I don't think you ought to have it both ways, you know. How am I to frighten you into letting me have my own lover? Do you think that I am not as unhappy about him as Emily Greenmantle? There he is now going down to the brewery. You go after him and tell him that he shall have what he wants."

Mr. Peppercorn turned round and looked at her. "Not if I know," he said.

"Then I shall go to bed," said Polly, "and send for Dr. Miller to-morrow. I don't see why I'm not to have the same advantage as other girls. But, father, I wouldn't make you unhappy, and I wouldn't cost you a shilling I could help, and I wouldn't not wait upon you for anything. I wouldn't pretend to be ill, — not for Jack Hollycombe."

"I should find you out if you did."

"I wouldn't fight my battle except on the square for any earthly consideration. But, father——"

"What do you want of me?"

"I am broken-hearted about him. Though I look red in the face, and fat, and all that, I suffer quite as much as Emily Greenmantle. When I tell him to wait perhaps for years, I know I'm unreasonable. When a young man wants a wife, he wants one. He has made up his mind to settle down, and he doesn't expect a girl to bid him remain as he is for another four or five years."

"You've got no business to tell him anything of the kind."

"When he asks me I have a business, — if it's true. Father!"

"Well!"

"It is true. I don't know whether it ought to be so, but it is true. I'm very fond of you."

"You don't show it."

"Yes, I am. And I think I do show it, for I do whatever you tell

147

me. But I like him the best."

"What has he done for you?"

"Nothing; — not half so much as I have done for him. But I do like him the best. It's human nature. I don't take on to tell him so; — only once. Once I told him that I loved him better than all the rest, — and that if he chose to take my word for it, once spoken, he might have it. He did choose, and I'm not going to repeat it, till I tell him when I can be his own."

"He'll have to take you just as you stand."

"May be; but it will be worthwhile for him to wait just a little, till he shall see what you mean to do. What do you mean to do with it, father? We don't want it at once."

"He's not edicated as a gentleman should be."

"Are you?"

"No; but I didn't try to get a young woman with money. I made the money, and I've a right to choose the sort of son-in-law my daughter shall marry."

"No; never!" she said.

"Then he must take you just as you are; and I'll make ducks and drakes of the money after my own fashion. If you were married to-morrow what do you mean to live upon?"

"Forty shillings a week. I've got it all down in black and white."

"And when children come; — one after another, year by year."

"Do as others do. I'll go bail my children won't starve; — or his. I'd work for them down to my bare bones. But would you look on the while, making ducks and drakes of your money, or spending at the pothouse, just to break the heart of your own child? You speak of yourself as though you were strong as iron. There isn't a bit of iron about you; — but there's something a deal better. You are one of those men, father, who are troubled with a heart."

"You're one of those women," said he, "who trouble the world by their tongues." Then he bounced out of the house and banged the door.

He had seen Jack Hollycombe through the window going down to the brewery, and he now slowly followed the young man's steps. He went very slowly as he got to the entrance to the brewery yard, and there he paused for a while thinking over the condition of things. "Hang the fellow," he said to himself; "what on earth has he done that he should have it all his own way? I never had it all my way. I had to work for it; — and precious hard too. My wife had to cook the dinner with only just a slip of a girl to help her make the bed. If he'd been a gentleman there'd have been something in it. A gentleman expects to have things ready to his hand. But he's to walk into all my money just because he's good-looking. And then Polly tells me, that I can't help myself because I'm good-natured. I'll let her know whether I'm good-natured! If he wants a wife he must support a wife; — and he shall." But though Mr. Peppercorn stood in the doorway murmuring after this fashion he knew very well that he was about to lose the battle. He had come down the street on purpose to signify to Jack Hollycombe that he might go up and settle the day with Polly; and he himself in the midst of all his objurgations was picturing to himself the delight with which he would see Polly restored to her former mode of dressing. "Well, Mr. Hollycombe, are you here?"

"Yes, Mr. Peppercorn, I am here."

"So I perceive, — as large as life. I don't know what on earth you're doing over here so often. You're wasting your employers' time, I believe."

"I came over to see Messrs. Grist and Grindall's young man."

"I don't believe you came to see any young man at all."

"It wasn't any young woman, as I haven't been to your house, Mr. Peppercorn."

"What's the good of going to my house? There isn't any young woman there can do you any good." Then Mr. Peppercorn looked round and saw that there were others within hearing to whom the conversation might be attractive. "Do you come in here. I've got something to say to you." Then he led the way into his own little parlour, and shut the door. "Now, Mr. Hollycombe, I've got something to communicate."

"Out with it, Mr. Peppercorn."

"There's that girl of mine up there is the biggest fool that ever was since the world began."

"It's astonishing," said Jack, "what different opinions different people have about the same thing."

"I daresay. That's all very well for you; but I say she's a fool. What on earth can she see in you to make her want to give you all my money?"

"She can't do that unless you're so pleased."

"And she won't neither. If you like to take her, there she is."

"Mr. Peppercorn, you make me the happiest man in the world."

"I don't make you the richest; — and you're going to make yourself the poorest. To marry a wife upon forty shillings a week! I did it myself, however, — upon thirty-five, and I hadn't any stupid old father-in-law to help me out. I'm not going to see her break her heart; and so you may go and tell her. But you needn't tell her as I'm going to make her any regular allowance. Only tell her to put on some decent kind of gown, before I come home to tea. Since all this came up the slut has worn the same dress she bought three winters ago. She thinks I didn't know it."

And so Mr. Peppercorn had given way; and Polly was to be allowed to flaunt it again this Christmas in silks and satins. "Now you'll give me a kiss," said Jack when he had told his tale.

"I've only got it on your bare word," she answered, turning away from him.

"Why; he sent me here himself; and says you're to put on a proper frock to give him his tea in."

"No."

"But he did."

"Then, Jack, you shall have a kiss. I am sure the message about the frock must have come from himself. Jack, are you not the happiest young man in all Plumplington?"

"How about the happiest young woman," said Jack.

"Well; I don't mind owning up. I am. But it's for your sake. I could have waited, and not have been a bit impatient. But it's so different with a man. Did he say, Jack, what he meant to do for you?"

"He swore that he would not give us a penny."

"But that's rubbish. I am not going to let you marry till I know what's fixed. Nor yet will I put on my silk frock."

"You must. He'll be sure to go back if you don't do that. I shouldn't risk it all now, if I were you."

"And so make a beggar of you. My husband shall not be

dependent on any man, — not even on father. I shall keep my clothes on as I've got 'em till something is settled."

"I wouldn't anger him if I were you," said Jack cautiously.

"One has got to anger him sometimes, and all for his own good. There's the frock hanging up-stairs, and I'm as fond of a bit of finery as any girl. Well; — I'll put it on to-night because he has made something of a promise; but I'll not continue it till I know what he means to do for you. When I'm married my husband will have to pay for my clothes, and not father."

"I guess you'll pay for them yourself."

"No, I shan't. It's not the way of the world in this part of England. One of you must do it, and I won't have it done by father, — not regular. As I begin so I must go on. Let him tell me what he means to do and then we shall know how we're to live. I'm not a bit afraid of you and your forty shillings."

"My girl!" Here was some little attempt at embracing, which, however, Polly checked.

"There's no good in all that when we're talking business. I look upon it now that we're to be married as soon as I please. Father has given way as to that, and I don't want to put you off."

"Why no! You ought not to do that when you think what I have had to endure."

"If you had known the picture which father drew just now of what we should have to suffer on your forty shillings a week!"

"What did he say, Polly?"

"Never mind what he said. Dry bread would be the best of it. I don't care about the dry bread; — but if there is to be anything better it must be all fixed. You must have the money for your own."

"I don't suppose he'll do that."

"Then you must take me without the money. I'm not going to have him giving you a five-pound note at the time and your having to ask for it. Nor yet am I going to ask for it. I don't mind now. And to give him his due, I never asked him for a sovereign but what he gave me two. He's very generous."

"Is he now?"

"But he likes to have the opportunity. I won't live in the want of any man's generosity, — only my husband's. If he chooses to do anything extra that'll be as he likes it. But what we have to live upon, — to pay for meat and coals and such like, — that must be your own. I'll put on the dress to-night because I won't vex him. But before he goes to bed he must be made to understand all that. And you must understand it too, Jack. As we mean to go on so must we begin!" The interview had ended, however, in an invitation given to Jack to stay in Plumplington and eat his supper. He knew the road so well that he could drive himself home in the dark.

"I suppose I'd better let them have two hundred a year to begin with," said Peppercorn to himself, sitting alone in his little parlour. "But I'll keep it in my own hands. I'm not going to trust that fellow further than I can see him."

But on this point he had to change his mind before he went to bed. He was gracious enough to Jack as they were eating their supper, and insisted on having a hot glass of brandy and water afterwards, — all in honour of Polly's altered dress. But as soon as Jack was gone Polly explained her views of the case, and spoke such undoubted wisdom as she sat on her father's knee, that he was forced to yield. "I'll speak to Mr. Scribble about having it all properly settled." Now Mr. Scribble was the Plumplington attorney.

"Two hundred a year, father, which is to be Jack's own, — forever. I won't marry him for less, — not to live as you propose."

"When I say a thing I mean it," said Peppercorn. Then Polly retired, having given him a final kiss.

About a fortnight after this Mr. Greenmantle came to the Rectory and desired to see Dr. Freeborn. Since Emily had been taken ill there had been many signs of friendship between the Greemantle and the Freeborn houses. But now there he was in the Rectory hall, and within five minutes had followed the Rectory footman into Dr. Freeborn's study. "Well, Greenmantle, I'm delighted to see you. How's Emily?"

Mr. Greenmantle might have been delighted to see the Doctor but he didn't look it. "I trust that she is somewhat better. She has risen from her bed to-day."

"I'm glad to hear that," said the Doctor.

"Yes; she got up yesterday, and to-day she seems to be restored to her usual health."

"That's good news. You should be careful with her and not let her trust too much to her strength. Miller said that she was very weak, you know."

"Yes; Miller has said so all through," said the father; "but I'm not quite sure that Miller has understood the case."

"He hasn't known all the ins and outs you mean, — about Philip Hughes." Here the Doctor smiled, but Mr. Greenmantle moved about uneasily as though the poker were at work. "I suppose Philip Hughes had something to do with her malady."

"The truth is——," began Mr. Greenmantle.

"What's the truth?" asked the Doctor. But Mr. Greenmantle looked as though he could not tell his tale without many efforts. "You heard what old Peppercorn has done with his daughter? — Settled £250 a year on her forever, and has come to me asking me whether I can't marry them on Christmas Day. Why if they were to be married by banns there would not be time."

"I don't see why they shouldn't be married by banns," said Mr. Greenmantle, who amidst all these difficulties disliked nothing so much as that he should be put into the category with Mr. Peppercorn, or Emily with Polly Peppercorn.

"I say nothing about that. I wish everybody was married by banns. Why shouldn't they? But that's not to be. Polly came to me the next day, and said that her father didn't know what he was talking about."

"I suppose she expects a special licence like the rest of them," said Mr. Greenmantle.

"What the girls think mostly of is their clothes. Polly wouldn't mind the banns the least in the world; but she says she can't have her things ready. When a young lady talks about her things a man has to give up. Polly says that February is a very good month to be married in."

Mr. Greenmantle was again annoyed, and showed it by the knitting of his brow, and the increased stiffness of his head and shoulders. The truth may as well be told. Emily's illness had prevailed with him and he too had yielded. When she had absolutely refused to look at her chicken-broth for three consecutive days her father's heart had been stirred. For Mr. Greenmantle's character will not have been adequately described unless it be explained that the stiffness lay rather in the neck and shoulders

153

than in the organism by which his feelings were conducted. He was in truth very like Mr. Peppercorn, though he would have been infuriated had he been told so. When he found himself alone after his defeat, — which took place at once when the chicken-broth had gone down untasted for the third time, — he was ungainly and ill-natured to look at. But he went to work at once to make excuses for Philip Hughes, and ended by assuring himself that he was a manly honest sort of fellow, who was sure to do well in his profession; and ended by assuring himself that it would be very comfortable to have his married daughter and her husband living with him. He at once saw Philip, and explained to him that he had certainly done very wrong in coming up to his drawing-room without leave. "There is an etiquette in those things which no doubt you will learn as you grow older." Philip thought that the etiquette wouldn't much matter as soon as he had married his wife. And he was wise enough to do no more than beg Mr. Greenmantle's pardon for the fault which he had committed. "But as I am informed by my daughter," continued Mr. Greenmantle, "that her affections are irrevocably settled upon you," — here Philip could only bow, — "I am prepared to withdraw my opposition, which has only been entertained as long as I thought it necessary for my daughter's happiness. There need be no words now," he continued, seeing that Philip was about to speak, "but when I shall have made up my mind as to what it may be fitting that I shall do in regard to money, then I will see you again. In the meantime you're welcome to come into my drawing-room when it may suit you to pay your respects to Miss Greenmantle." It was speedily settled that the marriage should take place in February, and Mr. Greenmantle was now informed that Polly Peppercorn and Mr. Hollycombe were to be married in the same month!

He had resolved, however, after much consideration, that he would himself inform Dr. Freeborn that he had given way, and had now come for this purpose. There would be less of triumph to the enemy, and less of disgrace to himself, if he were to declare the truth. And there no longer existed any possibility of a permanent quarrel with the Doctor. The prolonged residence abroad had altogether gone to the winds. "I think I will just step over and tell the Doctor of this alteration in our plans." This he had said to Emily, and Emily had thanked him and kissed him, and once again had called him "her own dear papa." He had suffered greatly during the period of his embittered feelings, and now had his reward. For it is not to be supposed that when a man has swallowed a poker the evil results will fall only upon his companions. The process is painful also to himself. He cannot breathe in comfort so long as the poker is there.

"And so Emily too is to have her lover. I am delighted to hear it. Believe me she hasn't chosen badly. Philip Hughes is an excellent young fellow. And so we shall have the double marriage coming after all." Here the poker was very visible. "My wife will go and see her at once, and congratulate her; and so will I as soon as I have heard that she's got herself properly dressed for drawing-room visitors. Of course I may congratulate Philip."

"Yes, you may do that," said Mr. Greenmantle very stiffly.

"All the town will know all about it before it goes to bed to-night. It is better so. There should never be a mystery about such matters. Good-bye, Greenmantle, I congratulate you with all my heart."

Christmas-Day

"Now I'll tell you what we'll do," said the Doctor to his wife a few days after the two marriages had been arranged in the manner thus described. It yet wanted ten days to Christmas, and it was known to all Plumplington that the Doctor intended to be more than ordinarily blithe during the present Christmas holidays. "We'll have these young people to dinner on Christmas-day, and their fathers shall come with them."

"Will that do, Doctor?" said his wife.

"Why should it not do?"

"I don't think that Mr. Greenmantle will care about meeting Mr. Peppercorn."

"If Mr. Peppercorn dines at my table," said the Doctor with a certain amount of arrogance, "any gentleman in England may meet him. What! not meet a fellow townsman on Christmas-day and on such an occasion as this!"

"I don't think he'll like it," said Mrs. Freeborn.

"Then he may lump it. You'll see he'll come. He'll not like to refuse to bring Emily here especially, as she is to meet her betrothed. And the Peppercorns and Jack Hollycombe will be sure to come. Those sort of vagaries as to meeting this man and not that, in sitting next to one woman and objecting to another, don't prevail on Christmas-day, thank God. They've met already at the Lord's Supper, or ought to have met; and they surely can meet afterwards at the parson's table. And we'll have Harry Gresham to show that there is no ill-will. I hear that Harry is already making up to the Dean's daughter at Barchester."

"He won't care whom he meets," said Mrs. Freeborn. "He has got a position of his own and can afford to meet anybody. It isn't quite so with Mr. Greenmantle. But of course you can have it as you please. I shall be delighted to have Polly and her husband at dinner with us."

So it was settled and the invitations were sent out. That to the Peppercorns was despatched first, so that Mr. Greenmantle might be informed whom he would have to meet. It was conveyed in a note from Mrs. Freeborn to Polly, and came in the shape of an order rather than a request. "Dr. Freeborn hopes that your papa and Mr. Hollycombe will bring you to dine with us on Christmas-day at six o'clock. We'll try and get Emily Greenmantle and her lover to meet you. You must come because the Doctor has set his heart upon it."

"That's very civil," said Mr. Peppercorn. "Shan't I get any dinner till six o'clock?"

"You can have lunch, father, of course. You must go."

"A bit of bread and cheese when I come out of church — just when I'm most famished. Of course I'll go. I never dined with the Doctor before."

"Nor did I; but I've drunk tea there. You'll find he'll make himself very pleasant. But what are we to do about Jack?"

"He'll come, of course."

"But what are we to do about his clothes?" said Polly. "I don't think he's got a dress coat; and I'm sure he hasn't a white tie. Let him come just as he pleases, they won't mind on Christmas-day as long as he's clean. He'd better come over and go to church with us; and then I'll see as to making him up tidy." Word was sent to say that Polly and her father and her lover would come, and the necessary order was at once despatched to Barchester.

"I really do not know what to say about it," said Mr. Greenmantle when the invitation was read to him. "You will meet Polly Peppercorn and her husband as is to be," Mrs. Freeborn had written in her note; "for we look on you and Polly as the two heroines of Plumplington for this occasion." Mr. Greenmantle had been struck with dismay as he read the words. Could he bring himself to sit down to dinner with Hickory Peppercorn and Jack Hollycombe; and ought he to do so? Or could he refuse the Doctor's invitation on such an occasion? He suggested at first that a letter should be prepared declaring that he did not like to take his Christmas dinner away from his own house. But to this Emily would by no means consent. She had plucked up her spirits greatly since the days of the chicken-broth, and was determined at the present moment to rule both her future husband and her father. "You must go, papa. I wouldn't not go for all the world."

"I don't see it, my dear; indeed I don't."

"The Doctor has been so kind. What's your objection, papa?"

"There are differences, my dear."

"But Dr. Freeborn likes to have them."

"A clergyman is very peculiar. The rector of a parish can always meet his own flock. But rank is rank you know, and it behoves me to be careful with whom I shall associate. I shall have Mr. Peppercorn slapping my back and poking me in the ribs some of these days. And moreover they have joined your name with that of the young lady in a manner that I do not quite approve. Though you each of you may be a heroine in your own way, you are not the two heroines of Plumplington. I do not choose that you shall appear together in that light."

"That is only his joke," said Emily.

"It is a joke to which I do not wish to be a party. The two heroines of Plumplington! It sounds like a vulgar farce."

Then there was a pause, during which Mr. Greenmantle was thinking how to frame the letter of excuse by which he would

157

avoid the difficulty. But at last Emily said a word which settled him. "Oh, papa, they'll say that you were too proud, and then they'll laugh at you." Mr. Greenmantle looked very angry at this, and was preparing himself to use some severe language to his daughter. But he remembered how recently she had become engaged to be married, and he abstained. "As you wish it, we will go," he said. "At the present crisis of your life I would not desire to disappoint you in anything." So it happened that the Doctor's proposed guests all accepted; for Harry Gresham too expressed himself as quite delighted to meet Emily Greenmantle on the auspicious occasion.

"I shall be delighted also to meet Jack Hollycombe," Harry had said. "I have known him ever so long and have just given him an order for twenty quarters of oats."

They were all to be seen at the Parish Church of Plumplington on that Christmas morning; — except Harry Gresham, who, if he did so at all, went to church at Greshamsbury, — and the Plumplington world all looked at them with admiring eyes. As it happened the Peppercorns sat just behind the Greenmantles, and on this occasion Jack Hollycombe and Polly were exactly in the rear of Philip Hughes and Emily. Mr. Greenmantle as he took his seat observed that it was so, and his devotions were, we fear, disturbed by the fact. He walked up proudly to the altar among the earliest and most aristocratic recipients, and as he did so could not keep himself from turning round to see whether Hickory Peppercorn was treading on his kibes. But on the present occasion Hickory Peppercorn was very modest and remained with his future son-in-law nearly to the last.

At six o'clock they all met in the Rectory drawing-room. "Our two heroines," said the Doctor as they walked in, one just after the other, each leaning on her lover's arm. Mr. Greenmantle looked as though he did not like it. In truth he was displeased, but he could not help himself. Of the two young ladies Polly was by far the most self-possessed. As long as she had got the husband of her choice she did not care whether she were or were not called a heroine. And her father had behaved very well on that morning as to money. "If you come out like that, father," she said, "I shall have to wear a silk dress every day." "So you ought," he said with true Christmas generosity. But the income then promised had been a solid assurance, and Polly was the best contented young woman in all Plumplington.

They all sat down to dinner, the Doctor with a bride on each side of him, the place of honour to his right having been of course accorded to Emily Greenmantle; and next to each young lady was her lover. Miss Greenmantle, as was her nature was very quiet, but Philip Hughes made an effort and carried on, as best he could, a conversation with the Doctor. Jack Hollycombe till after pudding-time said not a word, and Polly tried to console herself through his silence by remembering that the happiness of the world did not depend upon loquacity. She herself said a little word now and again, always with a slight effort to bring Jack into notice. But the Doctor with his keen power of observation understood them all, and told himself that Jack was to be a happy man. At the other end of the table Mr. Greenmantle and Mr. Peppercorn sat opposite to each other, and they too, till after pudding-time, were very quiet. Mr. Peppercorn felt himself to be placed a little above his proper position, and could not at once throw off the burden. And Mr. Greenmantle would not make the attempt. He felt that an injury had been done him in that he had been made to sit opposite to Hickory Peppercorn. And in truth the dinner party as a dinner party would have been a failure, had it not been for Harry Gresham, who, seated in the middle between Philip and Mr. Peppercorn, felt it incumbent upon him in his present position to keep up the rattle of the conversation. He said a good deal about the "two heroines," and the two heroes, till Polly felt herself bound to quiet him by saying that it was a pity that there was not another heroine also for him.

"I'm an unfortunate fellow," said Harry, "and am always left out in the cold. But perhaps I may be a hero too some of these days."

Then when the cloth had been removed, — for the Doctor always had the cloth taken off his table, — the jollity of the evening really began. The Doctor delighted to be on his legs on such an occasion and to make a little speech. He said that he had on his right and on his left two young ladies both of whom he had known and had loved throughout their entire lives, and now they were to be delivered over by their fathers, whom he delight-ed to welcome this Christmas-day at his modest board, each to

159

the man who for the future was to be her lord and her husband. He did not know any occasion on which he, as a pastor of the church, could take greater delight, seeing that in both cases he had ample reason to be satisfied with the choice which the young ladies had made. The bridegrooms were in both instances of such a nature and had made for themselves such characters in the estimation of their friends and neighbours as to give all assurance of the happiness prepared for their wives. There was much more of it, but this was the gist of the Doctor's eloquence. And then he ended by saying that he would ask the two fathers to say a word in acknowledgment of the toast.

This he had done out of affection to Polly, whom he did not wish to distress by calling upon Jack Hollycombe to take a share in the speech-making of the evening. He felt that Jack would require a little practice before he could achieve comfort during such an operation; but the immediate effect was to plunge Mr. Greenmantle into a cold bath. What was he to say on such an opportunity? But he did blunder through, and gave occasion to none of that sorrow which Polly would have felt had Jack Hollycombe got upon his legs, and then been reduced to silence. Mr. Peppercorn in his turn made a better speech than could have been expected from him. He said that he was very proud of his position that day, which was due to his girl's manner and education. He was not entitled to be there by anything that he had done himself. Here the Doctor said, "Yes, yes, yes, certainly." But Peppercorn shook his head. He wasn't specially proud of himself, he said, but he was awfully proud of his girl. And he thought that Jack Hollycombe was about the most fortunate young man of whom he had ever heard. Here Jack declared that he was quite aware of it.

After that the jollity of the evening commenced; and they were very jolly till the Doctor began to feel that it might be difficult to restrain the spirits which he had raised. But they were broken up before a very late hour by the necessity that Harry Gresham should return to Greshamsbury. Here we must bid farewell to the "two heroines of Plumplington," and to their young men, wishing them many joys in their new capacities. One little scene however must be described, which took place as the brides were putting on their hats in the Doctor's study. "Now

I can call you Emily again," said Polly, "and now I can kiss you; though I know I ought to do neither the one nor the other."

"Yes, both, both, always do both," said Emily. Then Polly walked home with her father, who, however well satisfied he might have been in his heart, had not many words to say on that evening.

"The Two Heroines of Plumplington" appeared for the first time in 1882 in the Good Cheer (Christmas) issue of Good Words.

The Widow's Mite

BUT, I'M NOT A WIDOW, and I haven't got two mites."

"My dear, you are a widow, and you have got two mites."

"I'll tell both of you something that will astonish you. I've made a calculation, and I find that if everybody in England would give up their Christmas dinner; that is, in Scotland and Ireland, too —"

"They never have any in Ireland, Bob."

"Hold your tongue till I've done, Charley. They do have Christmas dinners in Ireland. It's pretty nearly the only day that they do, and I don't count much upon them either. But if everybody gave up his special Christmas dinner, and dined as he does on other days, the saving would amount to two millions and a half."

Charley whistled.

"Two millions and a half is a large sum of money," said Mrs. Granger, the elder lady of the party.

"Those calculations never do any good," said the younger lady, who had declared herself not to be a widow.

"Those calculations do a great deal of good," continued Bob, carrying on his argument with continued warmth. "They show us what a great national effort would do."

"A little national effort I should call that," said Mrs. Granger. "But I should doubt the two millions and a half."

163

"Half a crown a head on thirty million people would do it. You are to include all the beer, wine, and whisky. But suppose you take off one-fifth for the babies and young girls, who don't drink."

"Thank you, Bob," said the younger lady, — Nora Field by name.

"And two more fifths for the poor, who haven't got the half-crown a head," said the elder lady.

"And you'd ruin the grocer and butcher," said Charley.

"And never get your half-crown after all," said Nora.

It need hardly be said that the subject under discussion was the best mode of abstracting from the pockets of the non-suffering British public a sufficiency of money to sustain the suffering portion during the period of the cotton famine. Mr. Granger was the rector of Plumstock, a parish in Cheshire, sufficiently near to the manufacturing districts to give to every incident of life at that time a colouring taken from the distress of the neighbourhood; but which had not itself ever depended on cotton, — for Plumstock boasted that it was purely agricultural. Mr. Granger was the chairman of a branch relief committee, which had its centre in Liverpool, and the subject of the destitution, with the different modes by which it might be, should be, or should not be relieved, was constantly under discussion in the rectory. Mr. Granger himself was a practical man, somewhat hard in his manners, but by no means hard in his heart, who had in these times taken upon himself the business of almsbegging on a large scale. He declined to look at the matter in a political, statistical, or economical point of view, and answered all questions as to rates, rates in aid, loans, and the Consolidated Fund, with a touch of sarcasm, which showed the bent of his own mind.

"I've no doubt you'll have settled all that in the wisest possible way by the time that the war is over, and the river full of cotton again."

"Father," Bob replied, pointing across the Cheshire flats to the Mersey, "that river will never again be full of American cotton."

"It will be all the same for the present purpose, if it comes from India," said the rector, declining all present argument on

the great American question. To collect alms was his immediate work, and he would do nothing else. Five-pound notes,
sovereigns, half-crowns, shillings, and pence! In search of
these he was urgent, we may almost say day and night, begging with a pertinacity which was disagreeable, but irresistible.
The man who gave him five sovereigns, instantly became the
mark for another petition. "When you have got your dinner,
you have not done with the butcher forever," he would say in
answer to reproaches. "Of course, we must go on as long as
this thing lasts." Then his friends and neighbours buttoned up
their pockets; but Mr. Granger would extract coin from them
even when buttoned.

The two young men who had taken part in the above argument were his sons. The elder, Charles, was at Oxford, but
now in these Christmas days — for Christmas was close at
hand — had come home. Bob, the second son, was in a merchant's house in Liverpool, intending to become, in the ful-
ness of time, a British merchant prince. It had been hinted to
him, however, more than once, that if he would talk a little
less, and work a little harder, the path to his princedom
would be quicker found than if his present habits were main-
tained. Nora Field was Mrs. Granger's niece. She was Miss
Field, and certainly not a widow in the literal sense of the
word; but she was about to become a bride a few weeks after
Christmas. "It is spoil from the Amalekites," Mr. Granger had
said, when she had paid in some contribution from her slender
private stores to his treasury; — "spoil from the Amalekites,
and therefore the more precious." He had called Nora Field's
two sovereigns spoil from the Amalekites, because she was
about to marry an American.

Frederic Frew, or Frederic F. Frew, as he delighted to hear
himself called, for he had been christened Franklin as well as
Frederic, — and to an American it is always a point of honour that, at any rate, the initial of his second Christian name
should be remembered by all men, — was a Pennsylvanian
from Philadelphia; a strong Democrat, according to the politics of his own country, hating the Republicans, as the Tories
used to hate the Whigs among us, before political feeling had
become extinct; speaking against Lincoln the President, and

Seward his minister, and the Fremonts, and Sumners, and Philipses, and Beechers of the Republican party, fine hard racy words of powerful condemnation, such as used to be spoken against Earl Grey and his followers, but nevertheless as steady for the war as Lincoln, or Seward, or any Republican of them all; — as steady for the war, and as keen in his bitterness against England. His father had been a partner in a house of business, of which the chief station had been in Liverpool. That house had now closed its transactions, and young Frew was living and intended to live an easy idle life on the moderate fortune which had been left him; but the circumstances of his family affairs had made it necessary for him to pass many months in Liverpool, and during that sojourn he had become engaged to Nora Field. He had travelled much, going everywhere with his eyes open, as Americans do. He knew many things, had read many books, and was decided in his opinion on most subjects. He was good-looking too, and well-mannered; was kindly-hearted, and capable of much generosity. But he was hard, keen in his intelligence, but not broad in his genius, thin and meagre in his aspirations, — not looking to or even desirous of anything great, but indulging a profound contempt for all that is very small. He was a well-instructed, but by no means learned man, who greatly despised those who were ignorant. I fear that he hated England in his heart; but he did not hate Nora Field, and was about to make her his wife in three or four weeks from the present time.

When Nora declared to her aunt that she was not a widow, and that she possessed no two mites, and when her aunt flatly contradicted her, stating that she was a widow, and did possess two mites, they had not intended to be understood by each other literally. It was an old dispute between them. "What the widow gave," said Nora, "she gave off her own poor back, and therefore was very cold. She gave it out of her own poor mouth, and was very hungry afterwards in consequence. I have given my two pounds, but I shall not be cold or hungry. I wish I was a widow with two mites; only, the question is whether I should not keep them for my own back after all, and thus gain nothing by the move."

"As to that," replied her aunt, "I cannot speak. But the widowhood and two mites are there for us all, if we choose to make use of them."

"In these days," said Bob, "the widows with two mites should not be troubled at all. We can do it all without them if we go to work properly."

"If you had read your Bible properly, sir," said Mrs. Granger, "you would understand that the widows would not thank you for the exemption."

"I don't want the widows to thank me. I only want to live, and allow others to live, according to the existing circumstances of the world." It was manifest from Bob's tone that he regarded his mother as little better than an old fogy.

In January, Nora was to become Mrs. Frederic F. Frew, and be at once taken away to new worlds, new politics, and new loves and hatreds. Like a true, honest-hearted girl as she was, she had already become half an American in spirit. She was an old Union American, and as such was strong against the South; and in return for her fervour in that matter, her future husband consented to abstain from any present loud abuse of things English, and generously allowed her to defend her own country when it was abused. This was much as coming from an American. Let us hope that the same privilege may be accorded to her in her future home in Philadelphia. But in the meantime, during these last weeks of her girlhood, these cold, cruel weeks of desperate want, she strove vigorously to do what little might be in her power for the poor of the country she was leaving. All this want had been occasioned by the wretched rebels of the South. This was her theory. And she was right in much of this. Whether the Americans of the South are wretched or are rebels we will not say here; but of this there can be no doubt, that they have created all this misery which we are enduring. "But I have no way of making myself a widow," she said again. "Uncle Robert would not let me give away the cloak he gave me the other day."

"He would have to give you another," said Mrs. Granger.

"Exactly. It is not so easy, after all, to be a widow with two mites!"

Nora Field had no fortune of her own, nor was her uncle in a position to give her any. He was not a poor man; but, like many

167

men who are not poor, he had hardly a pound of his own in the shape of ready money. To Nora and to her cousins, and to certain other first cousins of the same family, had been left, some eighteen months since, by a grand-aunt, a hundred pounds apiece, and with this hundred pounds Nora was providing for herself her wedding *trousseau*. A hundred pounds do not go far in such provision, as some young married women who may read this will perhaps acknowledge; but Mr. Frederic F. Frew had been told all about it, and he was contented. Miss Field was fond of nice clothes, and had been tempted more than once to wish that her greataunt had left them all two hundred pounds apiece instead of one.

"If I were to cast in my wedding veil?" said Nora.

"That will be your husband's property," said her aunt.

"Ah, but before I'm married."

"Then why have it at all?"

"It is ordered, you know."

"Couldn't you bedizen yourself with one made of false lace?" said her uncle. "Frew would never find it out, and that would be a most satisfactory spoiling of the Amalekite."

"He isn't an Amalekite, uncle Robert. Or if he is, I'm another."

"Just so; and therefore false lace will be quite good enough for you. Molly" — Mrs. Granger's name was Molly — "I've promised to let them have the use of the great boiler in the back-kitchen once a week, and you are to furnish them with fuel."

"Oh, dear!" said Mrs. Granger, upon whose active charity this loan of her own kitchen boiler made a strain that was almost too severe. But she recovered herself in half a minute. "Very well, my dear. But you won't expect any dinner on that day."

"No; I shall expect no dinner; only some food in the rough. You may boil that in the copper too, if you like it."

"You know, my dear, you don't like anything boiled."

"As for that, Molly, I don't suppose any of them like it. They'd all prefer roast-mutton."

"The copper will be your two mites," whispered the niece.

"Only I have not thrown them in of my accord," said Mrs. Granger.

Mr. Frew, who was living in Liverpool, always came over to

Plumstock on Friday evening, and spent Saturday and Sunday
with the rector and his family. For him those Saturdays were
happy days, for Frederic F. Frew was a good lover. He liked to be
with Nora, to walk with her, and to talk with her. He liked to
show her that he loved her, and to make himself gracious and
pleasant. I am not so sure that his coming was equally agreeable
to Mr. Granger. Mr. Frew *would* talk about American politics,
praising the feeling and spirit of his countrymen in the North;
whereas Mr. Granger, when driven into the subject, was constrained to make a battle for the South. All his prejudices, and
what he would have called his judgment, went with the South;
and he was not ashamed of his opinion; but he disliked arguing
with Frederic F. Frew. I fear it must be confessed that Frederic F.
Frew was too strong for him in such arguments. Why it should be
so I cannot say; but an American argues more closely on politics
than does an Englishman. His convictions are not the truer on
that account; very often the less true, as are the conclusions of a
logician, because he trusts to syllogisms which are often false,
instead of to the experience of his life and daily workings of his
mind. But though not more true in his political convictions than
an Englishman, he is more unanswerable, and therefore Mr.
Granger did not care to discuss the subject of the American war
with Frederic F. Frew.

"It riles me," Frew said, as he sat after dinner in the Plumstock
drawing-room on the Friday evening before Christmas day, "to
hear your folks talking of our elections. They think the war will
come to an end, and the rebels of the South will have their own
way, because the Democrats have carried their ticket."

"It will have that tendency," said the parson.

"Not an inch; any more than your carrying the Reform Bill or
repealing the Corn Laws had a tendency to put down the throne.
It's the same sort of argument. Your two parties were at daggers'
drawn about the Reform Bill; but that did not cause you to split
on all other matters."

"But the throne wasn't in question," said the parson.

"Nor is the war in question; not in that way. The most popular
Democrat in the States at this moment is M'Clellan —"

"And they say no one is so anxious to see the war ended."

"Whoever says so slanders him. If you don't trust his deeds,

169

look at his words."

"I believe in neither," said the parson.

"Then put him aside as a nobody. But you can't do that, for he is the man whom the largest party in the Northern States trusts most implicitly. The fact is, sir" — and Frederic F. Frew gave the proper twang to the last letter of the last word — "you, none of you here, understand our politics. You can't realize the blessings of a —"

"Molly, give me some tea," said the rector, in a loud voice. When matters went as far as this he did not care by what means he stopped the voice of his future relative.

"All I say is this," continued Frew, "you will find out your mistake if you trust to the Democratic elections to put an end to the war, and bring cotton back to Liverpool."

"And what is to put an end to the war?" asked Nora.

"Victory and union," said Frederic F. Frew.

"Exhaustion," said Charley from Oxford.

"Compromise," said Bobby from Liverpool.

"The Lord Almighty, when he shall have done his work," said the parson. "And, in the meantime, Molly, do you keep plenty of fire under the kitchen boiler."

That was clearly the business of the present hour for all in Mr. Granger's part of the country; — we may say, indeed, for all on Mr. Granger's side of the water. It mattered little, then, in Lancashire, whether New York might have a Democratic or a Republican governor. The old cotton had been burned; the present crop could not be garnered; the future crop — the crop which never would be future, could not get itself sown. Mr. Granger might be a slow politician, but he was a practical man, understanding the things immediately around him; and they all were aware — Frederic F. Frew with the rest of them — that he was right when he bade his wife keep the fire well hot beneath the kitchen boiler.

"Isn't it almost wicked to be married in such a time as this?" It was much later in the evening when Nora, still troubled in her mind about her widow's mite, whispered these words into her lover's ears. If she were to give up her lover for twelve months, would not that be a throwing in of something to the treasury from off her own back and out of her own mouth? But then this matter of her marriage had been so fully settled that she feared to think of disturbing it. He would never consent to such a postponement. And then the offering, to be of avail for her, must be taken from her own back, not from his; and Nora had an idea that in the making of such an offering as that suggested, Mr. Frederic F. Frew would conceive that he had contributed by far the greater part. Her uncle called him an Amalekite, and she doubted whether it would be just to spoil an Amalekite after such a fashion as that. Nevertheless, into his ears she whispered her little proposition.

"Wicked to get married!" said Frederic. "Not according to my idea of the Christian religion."

"Oh! but you know what I mean;" and she gave his arm a slight caressing pinch. At this time her uncle had gone to his own room; her cousins had gone to their studies, — by which I believe they intended to signify the proper smoking of a pipe of tobacco in the rectory kitchen; and Mrs. Granger, seated in her easy-chair, had gone to her slumbers, dreaming of the amount of fuel with which that kitchen boiler must be supplied.

"I shall bring a breach of promise against you," said Frederic, "if you don't appear in church with bridal array on Monday, the 12th of January, and pay the pounds into the war-treasury. That would be a spoiling of the Amalekite." Then he got hold of the fingers which had pinched him.

"Of course I shan't put it off, unless you agree."

"Of course you won't."

"But, dear Fred, don't you think we ought?"

"No; certainly not. If I thought you were in earnest I would scold you."

"I am in earnest — quite. You need not look in that way, for you know very well how truly I love you. You know I want to be your wife above all things."

"Do you?" And then he began to insinuate his arm round her waist; but she got up and moved away, not as in anger at his caress, but as showing that the present moment was unfit for it.

"I do," she said, "above all things. I love you so well that I could hardly bear to see you go away again without taking me with you. I could hardly bear it, — but I could bear it."

"Could you? Then I couldn't. I'm a weaker vessel than you,

and your strength must give way to my weakness."

"I know I've no right to tax you, — if you really care about it." Frederic F. Frew made no answer to this in words, but pursued her in her retreat from the sofa on which they had sat.

"Don't, Fred. I am so much in earnest. I wish I knew what I ought to do to throw in my two mites."

"Not throw me over certainly, and break all the promises you have made for the last twelve months. You can't be in earnest. It's out of the question, you know."

"Oh! I am in earnest."

"I never heard of such a thing in my life. What good would it do? It wouldn't bring the cotton in. It wouldn't feed the poor. It wouldn't keep your aunt's boiler hot."

"No; that it wouldn't," said Mrs. Granger, starting up; "and coals are such a terrible price." Then she went to sleep again, and ordered in large supplies in her dreams.

"But I should have done as much as the widow did. Indeed I should, Fred. Oh, dear! — to have to give you up! But I only meant for a year."

"As you are so very fond of me" —

"Of course, I'm fond of you. Should I let you do like that if I was not?" At the moment of her speaking he had again got his arm round her waist.

"Then I'm too charitable to allow you to postpone your happiness for a day. We'll look at it in that way."

"You won't understand me, or rather you do understand me, and pretend that you don't, which is very wrong."

"I always was very wicked."

"Then why don't you make yourself better? Do not you too wish to be a widow? You ought to wish it."

"I should like to have an opportunity of trying married life first."

"I won't stay any longer with you, sir, because you are scoffing. Aunt, I'm going to bed." Then she returned again across the room, and whispered to her lover: "I'll tell you what, sir; I'll marry you on Monday the 12th of January, if you'll take me just as I am now: with a bonnet on, and a shawl over my dress: exactly as I walked out with you before dinner. When I made the promise, I never said anything about fine clothes."

"You may come in an old red cloak, if you like it."

"Very well; now mind I've got your consent. Good-night, sir. After all it will only be half a mite." She had turned towards the door, and had her hand upon the lock; but she came back into the room, close up to him. "It will not be a quarter of a mite," she said. "How can it be anything if I get you?" Then she kissed him, and hurried away out of the room, before he could again speak to her.

"What, what, what!" said Mrs. Granger, waking up. "So Nora has gone, has she?"

"Gone; yes, just this minute," said Frew, who had turned his face to the fire, so that the tear in his eyes might not be seen. As he took himself off to his bed, he swore to himself that Nora Field was a trump, and that he had done well in securing for himself such a wife; but it never occurred to him that she was in any way in earnest about her wedding dress. She was a trump because she was so expressive in her love to himself, and because her eyes shone so brightly when she spoke eagerly on any matter; but as to her appearing at the altar in a red cloak, or, as was more probable, in her own customary thick woollen shawl, he never thought about it. Of course she would be married as other girls are married.

Nor had Nora thought of it till that moment in which she made the proposition to her lover. As she had said before, her veil was ordered, and so was her white silk dress. Her bonnet also had been ordered, with its bridal wreath, and the other things assorting therewith. A vast hole was to be made in her grand-aunt's legacy for the payment of all this finery; but, as Mrs. Granger had said to her, in so spending it, she would best please her future husband. He had enough of his own, and would not care that she should provide herself with articles which he could afterwards give her, at the expense of that little smartness at his wedding which an American likes, at any rate, as well as an Englishman. Nora, with an honesty which some ladies may not admire, had asked her lover the question in the plainest language. "You will have to buy my things so much the sooner," she had said. "I'd buy them all to-morrow, only you'll not let me." "I should rather think not, Master Fred." Then she had gone off with her aunt, and ordered her wedding-clothes. But now as she

prepared for bed after the conversation which has just been recorded, she began to think in earnest whether it would not be
well to dispense with white silk and orange wreaths while so
many were dispensing with — were forced to dispense with bread
and fuel. Could she bedizen herself with finery from Liverpool,
while her uncle was, as she well knew, refusing himself a set of
new shirts which he wanted sorely, in order that he might send
to the fund at Liverpool the money which they would cost him?
He was throwing in his two mites daily, as was her aunt, who
toiled unceasingly at woollen shawls and woollen stockings, so
that she went on knitting even in her sleep. But she, Nora, since
the earnestness of these bad days began, had done little or nothing. Her needle, indeed, had been very busy, but it had been
busy in preparation for Mr. Frederic F. Frew's nuptials. Even Bob
and Charley worked for the Relief Committee; but she had done
nothing: nothing but given her two pounds. She had offered
four, but her uncle, with a self-restraint never before or afterwards practised by him, had chucked her back two, saying that
he would not be too hard even upon an Amalekite. As she
thought of the word, she asked herself whether it was not more
incumbent on her, than on anyone else, to do something in the
way of self-sacrifice. She was now a Briton, but would shortly be
an American. Should it be said of her that the distress of her own
countrywomen, the countrywomen whom she was leaving, did
not wring her heart? It was not without a pang that she prepared
to give up that nationality, which all its owners rank as the first
in the world, and all who do not own it, rank, if not as the first,
then as the second. Now it seemed to her as though she were
deserting her own family in its distress, deserting her own ship in
the time of its storm, and she was going over to those from whom
this distress and this storm had come! Was it not needful that she
should do something; that she should satisfy herself that she had
been willing to suffer in the cause?

She would throw in her two mites if she only knew where to
find them. "I could only do it in truth," she said to herself, as she
rose from her prayers, "by throwing in him. I have got one very
great treasure, but I have not got anything else that I care about.
After all, it isn't so easy to be a widow with two mites." Then she
sat down and thought about it. As to postponing her marriage,

that she knew to be in truth quite out of the question. Even if she could bring herself to do it, everybody about her would say that she was mad, and Mr. Frederic F. Frew might not impossibly destroy himself with one of those pretty revolvers which he sometimes brought out from Liverpool for her to play with. But was it not practicable for her to give up her wedding-clothes? There would be considerable difficulty even in this. As to their having been ordered, that might be overcome by the sacrifice of some portion of the price. But then her aunt and even her uncle would oppose her; her cousins would cover her with ridicule — in the latter matter she might, however, achieve something of her widowhood; — and, after all, the loss would fall more upon F. F. Frew than upon herself. She really did not care for herself in what clothes she was married, so that she was made his wife. But as regarded him, might it not be disagreeable to him to stand before the altar with a dowdy creature in an old gown? And then there was one other consideration. Would it not seem that she was throwing in her two mites publicly before the eyes of all men, as a Pharisee might do it? Would there not be an ostentation in her widowhood? But as she continued to reflect, she cast this last thought behind her. It might be so said of her, but if such saying were untrue, if the offering were made in a widow's spirit, and not in the spirit of a Pharisee, would it not be cowardly to regard what men might say? Such false accusation would make some part of the two mites. "I'll go into Liverpool about it on Monday," she said to herself as she finally tucked the clothes around her.

Early in the following morning she was up and out of her room, with the view of seeing her aunt before she came down to breakfast; but the first person she met was her uncle. He accosted her in one of the passages. "What, Nora, this is early for you! Are you going to have a morning lovers' walk with Frederic Franklin?"

"Frederic Franklin, as you choose to call him, uncle, never comes out of his room much before breakfast time. And it's raining hard."

"Such a lover as he is ought not to mind rain."

"But I should mind it, very much. But, uncle, I want to speak to you, very seriously. I have been making up my mind about something."

"There's nothing wrong, is there, my dear?"

"No; there's nothing very wrong. It is not exactly about anything being wrong. I hardly know how to tell you what it is." And then she paused, and he could see by the light of the candle in his hand that she blushed.

"Hadn't you better speak to your aunt?" said Mr. Granger.

"That's what I meant to do when I got up," said Nora; "but as I have met you, if you don't mind —"

He assured her that he did not mind, and putting his hand upon her shoulder caressingly, promised her any assistance in his power. "I'm not afraid that you will ask anything I ought not to do for you."

Then she revealed to him her scheme, turning her face away from him as she spoke. "It will be so horrid," she said, "to have a great box of finery coming home when you are all giving up everything for the poor people. And if you don't think it would be wrong —"

"It can't be wrong," said her uncle. "It may be a question of whether it would be wise."

"I mean wrong to him. If it was to be any other clergyman, I should be ashamed of it. But as you are to marry us —"

"I don't think you need mind about the clergyman."

"And of course I should tell the Foster girls."

"The Foster girls?"

"Yes; they are to be my bridesmaids, and I am nearly sure they have not bought anything new yet. Of course they would think it all very dowdy, but I don't care a bit about it. I should just tell them that we had all made up our minds that we couldn't afford wedding-clothes. That would be true; wouldn't it?"

"But the question is about that wild American."

"He isn't a wild American."

"Well, then; about the tamed American. What will he say?"

"He said I might come in an old cloak."

"You have told him, then?"

"But I'm afraid he thought I was only joking. But, uncle, if you'll help me, I think I can bring him round."

"I daresay you can — to anything, just at present."

"I didn't at all mean that. Indeed, I'm sure I couldn't bring

176

him round to putting off the marriage."

"No, no, no; not to that; to anything else."

"I know you are laughing at me, but I don't much mind being laughed at. I should save very nearly fifteen pounds, if not quite. Think of that."

"And you'd give it all to the soup-kitchen?"

"I'd give it all to you for the distress."

Then her uncle spoke to her somewhat gravely. "You're a good girl, Nora; a dear good girl. I think I understand your thoughts on this matter, and I love you for them. But I doubt whether there be any necessity for you to make this sacrifice. A marriage should be a gala festival according to the means of the people married, and the bridegroom has a right to expect that his bride shall come to him fairly arrayed, and bright with wedding trappings. I think we can do, my pet, without robbing you of your little braveries."

"Oh, as for that, of course you can do without me."

There was a little soreness in her tone; not because she was feeling herself to be misunderstood, but because she knew that she could not explain herself further. She could not tell her uncle that the poor among the Jews might have been relieved without the contribution of those two mites, but that the widow would have lost all had she not so contributed. She had hardly arranged her thoughts as to the double blessing of charity, and certainly could not express them with reference to her own case; but she felt the need of giving in this time of trouble something that she herself valued. She was right when she had said that it was hard to be a widow. How many among us, when we give, give from off our own backs, and from out of our own mouths? Who can say that he has sacrificed a want of his own; that he has abandoned a comfort; that he has worn a thread-bare coat, when coats with their gloss on have been his customary wear; that he has fared roughly on cold scraps, whereas a well-spread board has been his usual daily practice? He who has done so, has thrown in his two mites, and for him will charity produce her double blessing.

Nora thought that it was not well in her uncle to tell her that he could do without her wedding-clothes. Of course he could do without them. But she soon threw those words behind her, and went back upon the words which had preceded them: "The bridegroom has a right to expect that the bride shall come to him fairly arrayed." After all, that must depend upon circumstances. Suppose the bride had no means of arraying herself fairly without getting into debt; what would the bridegroom expect in that case? "If he'll consent, you will?" she said, as she prepared to leave her uncle.

"You'll drive him to offer to pay for the things himself."

"I daresay he will, and then he'll drive me to refuse. You may be quite sure of this, uncle, that whatever clothes I do wear, he will never see the bill of them"; and then that conference was ended.

"I've made that calculation again," said Bob at breakfast, "and I feel convinced that if an Act of Parliament could be passed restricting the consumption of food in Christmas week, the entire week, mind, to that of ordinary weeks, we should get two millions of money, and that those two millions would tide us over till the Indian cotton comes in. Of course I mean by food, butchers' meat, groceries, spirits, and wines. Only think, that by one measure, which would not entail any real disappointment on anyone, the whole thing would be done."

"But the Act of Parliament wouldn't give us the money," said his father.

"Of course I don't really mean an Act of Parliament; that would be absurd. But the people might give up their Christmas dinners."

"A great many will, no doubt. Many of those most in earnest are pretty nearly giving up their daily dinners. Those who are indifferent will go on feasting the same as ever. You can't make a sacrifice obligatory."

"It would be no sacrifice if you did," said Nora, still thinking of her wedding-clothes.

"I doubt whether sacrifices ever do any real good," said Frederic F. Frew.

"Oh, Fred!" said Nora.

"We have rather high authority as to the benefit of self-denial," said the parson.

"A man who can't sacrifice himself must be selfish," said Bobby; "and we are all agreed to hate selfish people."

"And what about the widow's mite?" said Mrs. Granger.

"That's all very well, and you may knock me down with the Bible if you like, as you might do also if I talked about pre-Adamite formations. I believe every word of the Bible, but I do not believe that I understand it all thoroughly."

"You might understand it better if you studied it more," said the parson.

"Very likely. I won't be so uncourteous as to say the same thing of my elders. But now, about these sacrifices. You wouldn't wish to keep people in distress that you might benefit yourself by releasing them?"

"But the people in distress are there," said Nora.

"They oughtn't to be there; and as your self-sacrifices, after all, are very insufficient to prevent distress, there certainly seems to be a question open whether some other mode should not be tried. Give me the country in which the humanitarian principle is so exercised that no one shall be degraded by the receipt of charity. It seems to me that you like poor people here in England that you may gratify yourselves by giving them, not as much to eat as they want, but just enough to keep their skins from falling off their bones. Charity may have its double blessing, but it may also have its double curse."

"Not charity, Mr. Frew," said Mrs. Granger.

"Look at your Lady Bountifuls."

"Of course it depends on the heart," continued the lady; "but charity, if it be charity" —

"I'll tell you what," said Frederic F. Frew, interrupting her. "In Philadelphia, which in some matters is the best organized city I know" —

"I'm going down to the village," said the parson, jumping up; "who is to come with me?" and he escaped out of the room before Frew had had an opportunity of saying a word further about Philadelphia.

"That's the way with your uncle always," said he, turning to Nora, almost in anger. "It certainly is the most conclusive argument I know — that of running away."

"Mr. Granger meant it to be conclusive," said the elder lady.

"But the pity is that it never convinces."

"Mr. Granger probably had no desire of convincing."

179

"Ah! Well, it does not signify," said Frew. "When a man has a pulpit of his own, why should he trouble himself to argue in any place where counter arguments must be met and sustained?"

Nora was almost angry with her lover, whom she regarded as stronger and more clever than any of her uncle's family, but tyrannical and sometimes overbearing in the use of his strength. One by one her aunt and cousins left the room, and she was left alone with him. He had taken up a newspaper as a refuge in his wrath, for in truth he did not like the manner in which his allusions to his own country were generally treated at the parsonage. There are Englishmen who think that every man differing with them is bound to bet with them on any point in dispute. "Then you decline to back your opinion," such men say when the bet is refused. The feeling of an American is the same as to those who are unwilling to argue with him. He considers that every intelligent being is bound to argue whenever matter of argument is offered to him; nor can he understand that any subject may be too sacred for argument. Frederic F. Frew, on the present occasion, was as a dog from whose very mouth a bone had been taken. He had given one or two loud, open growls, and now sat with his newspaper, showing his teeth as far as the spirit of the thing went. And it was in this humour that Nora found herself called upon to attack him on the question of her own proposed charity. She knew well that he could bark, even at her, if things went wrong with him. "But then he never bites," she said to herself. He had told her that she might come to her wedding in an old cloak if she pleased, but she had understood that there was nothing serious in this permission. Now, at this very moment, it was incumbent on her to open his eyes to the reality of her intention.

"Fred," she said, "are you reading that newspaper because you are angry with me?"

"I am reading the newspaper because I want to know what there is in it."

"You know all that now, just as well as if you had written it. Put it down, sir!" And she put her hand on to the top of the sheet. "If we are to be married in three weeks' time, I expect that you will be a little attentive to me now. You'll read as many papers as you like after that, no doubt."

"Upon my word, Nora. I think your uncle is the most unfair man I ever met in my life."

"Perhaps he thinks the same of you, and that will make it equal."

"He can't think the same of me. I defy him to think that I'm unfair. There's nothing so unfair as hitting a blow, and then running away when the time comes for receiving the counter-blow. It's what your Lord Chatham did, and he never ought to have been listened to in Parliament again."

"That's a long time ago," said Nora, who probably felt that her lover should not talk to her about Lord Chatham just three weeks before their marriage.

"I don't know that the time makes any difference."

"Ah; — but I have got something else that I want to speak about. And, Fred, you mustn't turn up your nose at what we are all doing here, — as to giving away things, I mean."

"I don't turn up my nose at it. Haven't I been begging of every American in Liverpool till I'm ashamed of myself?"

"I know you have been very good, and now you must be more good still, — good to me specially, I mean — That isn't being good. That's only being foolish." What little ceremony had led to this last assertion I need not perhaps explain. "Fred, I'm an Englishwoman to-day, but in a month's time I shall be an American."

"I hope so, Nora, — heart and soul."

"Yes, that is what I mean. Whatever is my husband's country must be mine. And you know how well I love your country; do you not? I never run away when you talk to me about Philadelphia, — do I? And you know how I admire all your institutions — my institutions, as they will be."

"Now, I know you're going to ask some very great favour."

"Yes, I am; and I don't mean to be refused, Master Fred. I'm to be an American almost tomorrow, but as yet I am an Englishwoman, and I am bound to do what little I can before I leave my country. Don't you think so?"

"I don't quite understand."

"Well, it's about my wedding-clothes. It does seem stupid talking about them, I know. But I want you to let me do without them altogether. Now you've got the plain truth. I want to give

181

uncle Robert the money for his soup-kitchen, and to be married just as I am now. I do not care one straw what any other creature in the world may say about it, so long as I do not displease you."

"I think it's nonsense, Nora."

"Oh, Fred, don't say so. I have set my heart upon it. I'll do anything for you afterwards. Indeed, for the matter of that, I'd do anything on earth for you, whether you agree or whether you do not. You know that."

"But, Nora, you wouldn't wish to make yourself appear foolish? How much money will you save?"

"Very nearly twenty pounds altogether."

"Let me give you twenty pounds, so that you may leave it with your uncle by way of your two mites, as you call it."

"No, no; certainly not. I might just as well send you the milliner's bill; might I not?"

"I don't see why you shouldn't do that."

"Ah, but I do. You wouldn't wish me to be guilty of the pretence of giving a thing away, and then doing it out of your pocket. I have no doubt that what you are saying about the evil of promiscuous charity is quite true." And then, as she flattered him with this wicked flattery, she looked up with her bright eyes into his face. "But now, as the things are, we must be charitable; or the people will die. I feel almost like a rat leaving a falling house, in going away at this time; and if you would postpone it —"

"Nora!"

"Then I must be like a rat; but I won't be a rat in a white silk gown. Come now, say that you agree. I never asked you for anything before."

"Everybody will think that you're mad, and that I'm mad, and that we are all mad together."

"Because I go to church in a merino dress? Well; if that makes madness, let us be mad. Oh, Fred, do not refuse me the first thing I've asked you! What difference will it make? Nobody will know it over in Philadelphia!"

"Then you are ashamed of it?"

"No; not ashamed. Why should I be ashamed? But one does not wish to have that sort of thing talked about by everybody."

"And you are so strong-minded, Nora, that you do not care

about finery yourself?"

"Fred, that's ill-natured. You know very well what my feelings are. You are sharp enough to understand them without any further explanation. I do like finery; quite well enough, as you'll find out to your cost some day. And if ever you scold me for extravagance, I shall tell you about this."

"It's downright Quixotism."

"Quixotism leads to nothing, but this will lead to twenty pounds' worth of soup; — and to something else too."

When he pressed her to explain what that something else was, she declined to speak further on the subject. She could not tell him that the satisfaction she desired was that of giving up something, — of having made a sacrifice, — of having thrown into the treasury her two mites, — two mites off her own back, as she had said to her aunt, and out of her own mouth. He had taxed her with indifference to a woman's usual delight in gay plumage, and had taxed her most unjustly. "He ought to know," she said to herself, "that I should not take all this trouble about it, unless I did care for it." But, in truth, he did understand her motives thoroughly, and half approved them. He approved the spirit of self-abandonment, but disapproved the false political economy by which, according to his light, that spirit was accompanied. "After all," said he, "the widow would have done better to have invested her small capital in some useful trade."

"Oh, Fred, — but never mind now. I have your consent, and now I've only got to talk over my aunt." So saying, she left her lover to turn over in his mind the first principles of that large question of charity.

"The giving of pence and halfpence, of scraps of bread and sups of soup is, after all, but the charity of a barbarous, half-civilized race. A dog would let another dog starve before he gave him a bone, and would see his starved fellow-dog die without a pang. We have just got beyond that, only beyond that, as long as we dole out sups of soup. But Charity, when it shall have made itself perfect, will have destroyed this little trade of giving, which makes the giver vain and the receiver humble. The Charity of the large-hearted is that which opens to every man the profit of his own industry; to every man and to every woman." Then having gratified himself with the enunciation of this fine theory, he allowed his mind to run away to a smaller subject, and began to think of his own wedding garments. If Nora insisted on carrying out this project of hers, in what guise must he appear on the occasion? He also had ordered new clothes. "It's just the sort of thing that they'll make a story of in Chestnut Street." Chestnut Street, as we all know, is the West End of Philadelphia.

When the morning came of the twelfth of January, — the morning that was to make Nora Field a married woman, she had carried her point; but she was not allowed to feel that she had carried it triumphantly. Her uncle had not forbidden her scheme, but had never encouraged it. Her lover had hardly spoken to her on the subject since the day on which she had explained to him her intention. "After all, it's a mere bagatelle," he had said; "I am not going to marry your clothes." One of her cousins, Bob, had approved; but he had coupled his approval with an intimation that something should be done to prevent any other woman from wearing bridal wreaths for the next three months. Charley had condemned her altogether, pointing out that it was bad policy to feed the cotton spinners at the expense of the milliners. But the strongest opposition had come from her aunt and the Miss Fosters. Mrs. Granger, though her heart was in the battle which her husband was fighting, could not endure to think that all the time-honoured ceremonies of her life should be abandoned. In spite of all that was going on around her, she had insisted on having mince-pies on the table on Christmasday. True, there were not many of them, and they were small and flavourless. But the mince-pies were there, with whisky to burn with them instead of brandy, if any of the party chose to go through the ceremony. And to her the idea of a wedding without wedding-clothes was very grievous. It was she who had told Nora that she was a widow with two mites, or might make herself one, if she chose to encounter self-sacrifice. But in so saying she had by no means anticipated such a widowhood as this. "I really think, Nora, you might have one of those thinner silks, and you might do without a wreath; but you should have a veil, — indeed you should." But Nora was obstinate. Having overcome her future lord, and quieted her uncle, she was not at all prepared to yield to the mild remonstrances of her aunt. The two Miss Fosters were very much shocked, and for three days there was a disagreeable coolness between them and the Plumstock family. A friend's bridal is always an occasion for a new dress, and the Miss Fosters naturally felt that they were being robbed of their rights.

"Sensible girl," said old Foster, when he heard of it. "When you're married, if ever you are, I hope you'll do the same."

"Indeed we won't, papa," said the two Miss Fosters. But the coolness gradually subsided, and the two Miss Fosters consented to attend in their ordinary Sunday bonnets.

It had been decided that they should be married early, at eight o'clock; that they should then go to the parsonage for breakfast, and that the married couple should start for London immediately afterwards. They were to remain there for a week, and then return to Liverpool for one other remaining week before their final departure for America. "I should only have had them on for about an hour if I'd got them, and then it would have been almost dark," she said to her aunt.

"Perhaps it won't signify very much," her aunt replied. Then when the morning came, it seemed that the sacrifice had dwindled down to a very little thing. The two Miss Fosters had come to the parsonage overnight, and as they sat up with the bride over a bed-room fire, had been good-natured enough to declare that they thought it would be very good fun.

"You won't have to get up in the cold to dress me," said Nora, "because I can do it all myself; that will be one comfort."

"Oh, we shouldn't have minded that; and as it is, of course, we'll turn you out nice. You'll wear one of your other new dresses; won't you?"

"Oh, I don't know, just what I'm to travel in. It isn't very old. Do you know after all I'm not sure that it isn't a great deal better."

"I suppose it will be the same thing in the end," said the younger Miss Foster.

"Of course it will," said the elder.

"And there won't be all that bother of changing my dress," said Nora.

Frederic F. Frew came out to Plumstock by an early train, from Liverpool, bringing with him a countryman of his own as his friend on the occasion. It had been explained to the friend that he was to come in his usual habiliments.

"Oh, nonsense," said the friend, "I guess I'll see you turned off in a new waistcoat." But Frederic F. Frew had made it understood that an old waistcoat was imperative.

"It's something about the cotton, you know. They're all beside themselves here, as though there was never going to be a bit more in the country to eat. That's England all over. Never mind; do you come just as if you were going into your counting-house. Brown cotton gloves, with a hole in the thumbs, will be the thing, I should say."

There were candles on the table when they were all assembled in the parsonage drawing-room previous to the marriage. The two gentlemen were there first. Then came Mrs. Granger, who rather frightened Mr. Frew by kissing him, and telling him that she should always regard him as a son-in-law.

"Nora has always been like one of ourselves, you know," she said, apologizingly.

"And let me tell you, Master Frew," said the parson, "that you're a very lucky fellow to get her."

"I say, isn't it cold?" said Bob, coming in — "where are the girls?"

"Here are the girls," said Miss Foster, heading the procession of three which now entered the room, Nora, of course, being the last. Then Nora was kissed by everybody, including the strange American gentleman, who seemed to have made some mistake as to his privilege in the matter. But it all passed off very well, and I doubt if Nora knew who kissed her. It was very cold, and they were all wrapped close in their brown shawls and greatcoats, and the women looked very snug and comfortable in their ordinary winter bonnets.

"Come," said the parson, "we mustn't wait for Charley; he'll follow us to church." So the uncle took his niece on his arm, and the two Americans took the two bridesmaids, and Bob took his mother, and went along the beaten path over the snow to the church, and, as they got to the door, Charley rushed after them quite out of breath.

"I haven't even got a pair of gloves at all," he whispered to his mother.

"It doesn't matter; nobody's to know," said Mrs. Granger.

Nora by this time had forgotten the subject of her dress altogether, and it may be doubted if even the Misses Foster were as keenly alive to it as they thought they would have been. For myself, I think they all looked more comfortable on that cold winter morning without the finery which would have been customary than they could have done with it. It had seemed to them all beforehand that a marriage without veils and wreaths, without white gloves and new gay dresses, would be but a *triste* affair; but the idea passed away altogether when the occasion came. Mr. Granger and his wife and the two lads clustered round Nora as they made themselves ready for the ceremony, uttering words of warm love, and it seemed as though even the clerk and the servants took nothing amiss. Frederic F. Frew had met with a rebuff in the hall of the parsonage, in being forbidden to take his own bride under his own arm; but when the time for action came, he bore no malice, but went through his work manfully. On the whole, it was a pleasant wedding, homely, affectionate, full of much loving greeting; not without many sobs on the part of the bride and of Mrs. Granger, and some slight suspicion of an eagerly-removed tear in the parson's eye; but this, at any rate, was certain, that the wedding-clothes were not missed. When they all sat down to their breakfast in the parsonage dining-room, that little matter had come to be clean forgotten. No one knew, not even the Misses Foster, that there was anything at all extraordinary in their garb. Indeed, as to all gay apparel, we may say that we only miss it by comparison. It is very sad to be the wearer of the only frock-coat in company, to carry the one solitary black silk handkerchief at a dinner party. But I do not know but that a dozen men so arrayed do not seem to be as well dressed as though they had obeyed the latest rules of fashion as to their garments. One thing, however, had been made secure. That sum of twenty pounds, saved from the milliners, had been duly paid over into Mr. Granger's hands.

"It has been all very nice," said Mrs. Granger, still sobbing, when Nora went upstairs to tie on her bonnet before she started. "Only you are going!"

"Yes, I'm going now, aunt. Dear aunt! But, aunt, I have failed in one thing — absolutely failed."

"Failed in what, my darling?"

187

"There has been no widow's mite. It is not easy to be a widow with two mites."

"What you have given will be blessed to you, and blessed to those who will receive it."

"I hope it may; but I almost feel that I have been wrong in thinking of it so much. It has cost me nothing. I tell you, aunt, that it is not easy to be a widow with two mites."

When Mrs. Granger was alone with her husband after this, the two Miss Fosters having returned to Liverpool under the discreet protection of the two younger Grangers, for they had positively refused to travel with no other companion than the strange American — she told him all that Nora had said. "And who can tell us," he replied, "that it was not the same with the widow herself? She threw in all that she had, but who can say that she suffered aught in consequence? It is my belief that all that is given in a right spirit comes back instantly, in this world, with interest."

"I wish my coals would come back," said Mrs. Granger.

"Perhaps you have not given them in a right spirit, my dear."

"The Widow's Mite" appeared for the first time in 1863 in the January issue of Good Words.

The Two Generals

A Christmas Story of the War in Kentucky

C HRISTMAS OF 1860 is now three years past, and the civil war which was then being commenced in America is still raging without any apparent sign of an end. The prophets of that time who prophesied the worst never foretold anything so black as this. On that Christmas day Major Anderson, who then held the command of the forts in Charleston harbour on the part of the United States Government, removed his men and stores from Fort Moultrie to Fort Sumter, thinking that he might hold the one though not both against any attack from the people of Charleston, whose State, that of South Carolina, had seceded five days previously. That was in truth the beginning of the war, though at that time Mr. Lincoln was not yet President. He became so on the 4th March, 1861, and on the 15th of April following Fort Sumter was evacuated by Major Anderson, on the part of the United States Government, under fire from the people of Charleston. So little bloody, however, was that affair that no one was killed in the assault; — though one poor fellow perished in the saluting fire with which the retreating officer was complimented as he retired with the so-called honours of war. During the three years that have since passed, the combatants have better learned the use of their weapons of war.

No one can now laugh at them for bloodless battles. Never have the sides of any stream been so bathed in blood as have the shores of those Virginian rivers whose names have lately become familiar to us. None of those old death-dooming generals of Europe whom we have learned to hate for the cold-blooded energy of their trade, — Tilly, Gustavus Adolphus, Frederic, or Napoleon; — none of these ever left so many carcases to the kites as have the Johnsons, Jacksons, and Hookers of the American armies, who come and go so fast, that they are almost forgotten before the armies they have led have melted into clay.

Of all the states of the old union, Virginia has probably suffered the most, but Kentucky has least deserved the suffering which has fallen to her lot. In Kentucky the war has raged hither and thither, every town having been subject to inroads from either army. But she would have been loyal to the Union if she could; — nay, on the whole she has been loyal. She would have thrown off the plague chain of slavery if the prurient virtue of New England would have allowed her to do so by her own means. But virtuous New England was too proud of her own virtue to be content that the work of abolition should thus pass from her hands. Kentucky, when the war was beginning, desired nothing but to go on in her own course. She wished for no sudden change. She grew no cotton. She produced corn and meat, and was a land flowing with milk and honey. Her slaves were not as the slaves of the Southern States. They were few in number; tolerated for a time because their manumission was understood to be of all questions the most difficult; — rarely or never sold from the estates to which they belonged. When the war broke out Kentucky said that she would be neutral. Neutral, — and she lying on the front lines of the contest! Such neutrality was impossible to her, — impossible to any of her children!

Near to the little State capital of Frankfort there lived at that Christmas time of 1860 an old man, Major Reckenthorpe by name, whose life had been marked by many circumstances which had made him well known throughout Kentucky. He had sat for nearly thirty years in the Congress of the United States at Washington, representing his own State sometimes as senator, and sometimes in the lower house. Though called a major he was by profession a lawyer, and as such had lived successfully. Time had been when friends had thought it possible that he might fill the President's chair; but his name had been too much and too long in men's mouths for that. Who had heard of Lincoln, Pierce, or Polk, two years before they were named as candidates for the Presidency? But Major Reckenthorpe had been known and talked of in Washington longer perhaps than any other living politician.

Upon the whole he had been a good man, serving his country as best he knew how, and adhering honestly to his own political convictions. He had been and now was a slaveowner, but had voted in the Congress of his own State for the abolition of slavery in Kentucky. He had been a passionate man, and had lived not without the stain of blood on his hands, for duels had been familiar to him. But he had lived in a time and in a country in which it had been hardly possible for a leading public man not to be familiar with a pistol. He had been known as one whom no man could attack with impunity; but he had also been known as one who would not willingly attack anyone. Now at the time of which I am writing, he was old, — almost on the shelf, — past his duellings and his strong short invectives on the floors of Congress; but he was a man whom no age could tame, and still he was ever talking, thinking, and planning for the political well-being of his State.

In person he was tall, still upright, stiff and almost ungainly in his gait, with eager grey eyes which the waters of age could not dim, with short, thick, grizzled hair which age had hardly thinned, but which ever looked rough and uncombed, with large hands, which he stretched out with extended fingers when he spoke vehemently; — and of the Major it may be said that he always spoke with vehemence. But now he was slow in his steps, and infirm on his legs. He suffered from rheumatism, sciatica, and other maladies of the old, which no energy of his own could repress. In these days he was a stern, unhappy, all but broken-hearted old man; for he saw that the work of his life had been wasted.

And he had another grief which at this Christmas of 1860

191

had already become terrible to him, and which afterwards bowed him with sorrow to the ground. He had two sons, both of whom were then at home with him, having come together under the family roof tree that they might discuss with their father the political position of their country, and especially the position of Kentucky. South Carolina had already seceded, and other Slave States were talking of secession. What should Kentucky do? So the Major's sons, young men of eight-and-twenty and five-and-twenty, met together at their father's house; — they met and quarrelled deeply, as their father had well known would be the case.

The eldest of these sons was at that time the owner of the slaves and land which his father had formerly possessed and farmed. He was a Southern gentleman, living on the produce of slave labour, and as such had learned to vindicate, if not love, that social system which has produced as its result the war which is still raging at this Christmas of 1863. To him this matter of secession or non-secession was of vital import. He was prepared to declare that the wealth of the South was derived from its agriculture, and that its agriculture could only be supported by its slaves. He went further than this, and declared also that no further league was possible between a Southern gentleman and a Puritan from New England. His father, he said, was an old man, and might be excused by reason of his age from any active part in the contest that was coming. But for himself there could be but one duty; — that of supporting the new Confederacy, to which he would belong, with all his strength and with whatever wealth was his own.

The second son had been educated at Westpoint, the great military school of the old United States, and was now an officer in the National Army. Not on that account need it be supposed that he would, as a matter of course, join himself to the Northern side in the war, — to the side which, as being in possession of the capital and the old Government establishments, might claim to possess a right to his military services. A large proportion of the officers in the pay of the United States leagued themselves with Secession, — and it is difficult to see why such an act would be more disgraceful in them than in others. But with Frank Reckenthorpe such was not the case. He declared that he would be loyal to the Government which he served; and in saying so, seemed to imply that the want of such loyalty in any other person, soldier or non-soldier, would be disgraceful, as in his opinion it would have been disgraceful in himself.

"I can understand your feeling," said his brother, who was known as Tom Reckenthorpe, "on the assumption that you think more of being a soldier than of being a man; but not otherwise."

"Even if I were no soldier, I would not be a rebel," said Frank.

"How a man can be a rebel for sticking to his own country, I cannot understand," said Tom.

"Your own country!" said Frank. "Is it to be Kentucky or South Carolina? And is it to be a republic or a monarchy; — or shall we hear of Emperor Davis? You already belong to the greatest nation on earth, and you are preparing yourself to belong to the least; — that is, if you should be successful. Luckily for yourself, you have no chance of success."

"At any rate I will do my best to fight for it."

"Nonsense, Tom," said the old man, who was sitting by.

"It is no nonsense, sir. A man can fight without having been at Westpoint. Whether he can do so after having his spirit drilled and drummed out of him there, I don't know."

"Tom!" said the old man.

"Don't mind him, father," said the younger. "His appetite for fighting will soon be over. Even yet I doubt whether we shall ever see a regiment in arms sent from the Southern States against the Union."

"Do you?" said Tom. "If you stick to your colours, as you say you will, your doubts will soon be set at rest. And I'll tell you what, if your regiment is brought into the field, I trust that I may find myself opposite to it. You have chosen to forget that we are brothers, and you shall find that I can forget it also."

"Tom!" said the father, "you should not say such words as that; at any rate, in my presence."

"It is true, sir," said he. "A man who speaks as he speaks does not belong to Kentucky, and can be no brother of mine. If I were to meet him face to face, I would as soon shoot him as another;

— sooner, because he is a renegade."

"You are very wicked, — very wicked," said the old man, rising from his chair, — "very wicked." And then, leaning on his stick, he left the room.

"Indeed, what he says is true," said a sweet, soft voice from a sofa in the far corner of the room. "Tom, you are very wicked to speak to your brother thus. Would you take on yourself the part of Cain?"

"He is more silly than wicked, Ada," said the soldier. "He will have no chance of shooting me, or of seeing me shot. He may succeed in getting himself locked up as a rebel; but I doubt whether he'll ever go beyond that."

"If I ever find myself opposite to you with a pistol in my grasp," said the elder brother, "may my right hand —"

But his voice was stopped, and the imprecation remained un-uttered. The girl who had spoken rushed from her seat and put her hand before his mouth. "Tom," she said, "I will never speak to you again if you utter such an oath, — never." And her eyes flashed fire at his and made him dumb.

Ada Forster called Mrs. Reckenthorpe her aunt, but the con-nection between them was not so near as that of aunt and niece. Ada nevertheless lived with the Reckenthorpes, and had done so for the last two years. She was an orphan, and on the death of her father had followed her father's sister-in-law from Maine down to Kentucky; — for Mrs. Reckenthorpe had come from that farthest and most straitlaced State of the Union, in which people bind themselves by law to drink neither beer, wine, nor spirits, and all go to bed at nine o'clock. But Ada Forster was an heiress, and therefore it was thought well by the elder Recken-thorpes that she should marry one of their sons. Ada Forster was also a beauty, with slim, tall form, very pleasant to the eye; with bright, speaking eyes and glossy hair; with ivory teeth of the whitest, — only to be seen now and then when a smile could be won from her; and therefore such a match was thought desirable also by the younger Reckenthorpes. But unfortunately it had been thought desirable by each of them, whereas the father and mother had intended Ada for the soldier.

I have not space in this short story to tell how progress had been made in the troubles of this love affair. So it was now, that

Ada had consented to become the wife of the elder brother, — of Tom Reckenthorpe, with his home among the slaves, — although she, with all her New England feelings strong about her, hated slavery and all its adjuncts. But when has Love stayed to be guided by any such consideration as that? Tom Reckenthorpe was a handsome, high-spirited, intelligent man. So was his brother Frank. But Tom Reckenthorpe could be soft to a woman, and in that, I think, had he found the means of his success. Frank Reckenthorpe was never soft.

Frank had gone angrily from home when, some three months since, Ada had told him her determination. His brother had been then absent, and they had not met till this their Christmas meeting. Now it had been understood between them, by the intervention of their mother, that they would say nothing to each other as to Ada Forster. The elder had, of course, no cause for saying aught, and Frank was too proud to wish to speak on such a matter before his successful rival. But Frank had not given up the battle. When Ada had made her speech to him, he had told her that he would not take it as conclusive. "The whole tenor of Tom's life," he had said to her, "must be distasteful to you. It is impossible that you should live as the wife of a slaveowner."

"In a few years there will be no slaves in Kentucky," she had answered.

"Wait till then," he had answered; "and I also will wait." And so he had left her, resolving that he would bide his time. He thought that the right still remained to him of seeking Ada's hand, although she had told him that she loved his brother. "I know that such a marriage would make each of them miserable," he said to himself over and over again. And now that these terrible times had come upon them, and that he was going one way with the Union, while his brother was going the other way with Secession, he felt more strongly than ever that he might still be successful. The political predilections of American women are as strong as those of American men. And Frank Reckenthorpe knew that all Ada's feelings were as strongly in favour of the Union as his own. Had not she been born and bred in Maine? Was she not ever keen for total abolition, till even the old Major, with all his gallantry for womanhood and all his love

195

for the young girl who had come to his house in his old age, would be driven occasionally by stress of feeling to rebuke her? Frank Reckenthorpe was patient, hopeful, and firm. The time must come when Ada would learn that she could not be a fit wife for his brother. The time had, he thought, perhaps come already; and so he spoke to her a word or two on the evening of that day on which she had laid her hand upon his brother's mouth.

"Ada," he had said, "there are bad times coming to us."

"Good times, I hope," she had answered. "No one could expect that the thing could be done without some struggle. When the struggle has passed we shall say that good times have come." The thing of which she spoke was that little thing of which she was ever thinking, the enfranchisement of four millions of slaves.

"I fear that there will be bad times first. Of course I am thinking of you now."

"Bad or good they will not be worse to me than to others."

"They would be very bad to you if this State were to secede, and if you were to join your lot to my brother's. In the first place, all your fortune would be lost to him and to you."

"I do not see that; but of course I will caution him that it may be so. If it alters his views, I shall hold him free to act as he chooses."

"But Ada, should it not alter yours?"

"What, — because of my money? — or because Tom could not afford to marry a girl without a fortune?"

"I did not mean that. He might decide that for himself. But your marriage with him under such circumstances as those which he now contemplates, would be as though you married a Spaniard or a Greek adventurer. You would be without country, without home, without fortune, and without standing-ground in the world. Look you, Ada, before you answer. I frankly own that I tell you this because I want you to be my wife, and not his."

"Never, Frank; I shall never be your wife, — whether I marry him or no."

"All I ask of you now is to pause. This is no time for marrying or for giving in marriage."

"There I agree with you; but as my word is pledged to him, I shall let him be my adviser in that."

Late on that same night Ada saw her betrothed and bade him adieu. She bade him adieu with many tears, for he came to tell her that he intended to leave Frankfort very early on the following morning. "My staying here now is out of the question," said he. "I am resolved to secede, whatever the State may do. My father is resolved against secession. It is necessary, therefore, that we should part. I have already left my father and mother, and now I have come to say good-bye to you."

"And your brother, Tom?"

"I shall not see my brother again."

"And is that well after such words as you have spoken to each other? Perhaps it may be that you will never see him again. Do you remember what you threatened?"

"I do remember what I threatened."

"And did you mean it?"

"No; of course I did not mean it. You, Ada, have heard me speak many angry words, but I do not think that you have known me do many angry things."

"Never one, Tom: — never. See him then before you go, and tell him so."

"No, — he is hard as iron, and would take any such telling from me amiss. He must go his way, and I mine."

"But though you differ as men, Tom, you need not hate each other as brothers."

"It will be better that we should not meet again. The truth is, Ada, that he always despises anyone who does not think as he thinks. If I offered him my hand he would take it, but while doing so he would let me know that he thought me a fool. Then I should be angry, and threaten him again, and things would be worse. You must not quarrel with me, Ada, if I say that he has all the faults of a Yankee."

"And the virtues too, sir, while you have all the faults of a Southern—. But, Tom, as you are going from us, I will not scold you. I have, too, a word of business to say to you."

"And what's the word of business, dear?" said Tom, getting nearer to her as a lover should do, and taking her hand in his.

"It is this. You and those who think like you are dividing yourselves from your country. As to whether that be right or wrong, I will say nothing now, — nor will I say anything as to your chance of success. But I am told that those who go with the South will not be able to hold property in the North."

"Did Frank tell you that?"

"Never mind who told me, Tom."

"And is that to make a difference between you and me?"

"That is just the question that I am asking you. Only you ask me with a reproach in your tone, and I ask you with none in mine. Till we have mutually agreed to break our engagement you shall be my adviser. If you think it better that it should be broken, — better for your own interests, be man enough to say so."

But Tom Reckenthorpe either did not think so, or else he was not man enough to speak his thoughts. Instead of doing so he took the girl in his arms and kissed her, and swore that whether with fortune or no fortune she should be his, and his only. But still he had to go, — to go now, within an hour or two of the very moment at which they were speaking. They must part, and before parting must make some mutual promise as to their future meeting. Marriage now, as things stood at this Christmas time, could not be thought of even by Tom Reckenthorpe. At last he promised that if he were then alive he would be with her again, at the old family house in Frankfort, on the next coming Christmas day. So he went, and as he let himself out of the old house Ada, with her eyes full of tears, took herself up to her bedroom.

During the year that followed — the year 1861 — the American war progressed only as a school for fighting. The most memorable action was that of Bull's Run, in which both sides ran away, not from individual cowardice in either set of men, but from that feeling of panic which is engendered by ignorance and inexperience. Men saw waggons rushing hither and thither, and thought that all was lost. After that the year was passed in drilling and in camp-making, — in the making of soldiers, of gunpowder, and of cannons. But of all the articles of war made in that year, the article that seemed easiest of fabrication was a general officer. Generals were made with the greatest rapidity, owing their promotion much more frequently to local interest than to military success. Such a State sent such and such regiments, and therefore must be rewarded by having such and such generals nominated from among its citizens. The wonder perhaps is that with armies so formed battles should have been fought so well.

Before the end of 1861 both Major Reckenthorpe's sons had become general officers. That Frank, the soldier, should have been so promoted was, at such a period as this, nothing strange. Though a young man he had been soldier, or learning the trade of a soldier, for more than ten years, and such service as that might well be counted for much in the sudden construction of an army intended to number seven hundred thousand troops, and which at one time did contain all those soldiers. Frank too was a clever fellow, who knew his business, and there were many generals made in those days who understood less of their work than he did. As much could not be said for Tom's quick military advancement. But this could be said for them in the South, — that unless they did make their generals in this way, they would hardly have any generals at all, and General Reckenthorpe, as he so quickly became, — General Tom as they used to call him in Kentucky, — recommended himself specially to the Confederate leaders by the warmth and eagerness with which he had come among them. The name of the old man so well known throughout the Union, who had ever loved the South without hating the North, would have been a tower of strength to them. Having him they would have thought that they might have carried the State of Kentucky into open secession. He was now worn out and old, and could not be expected to take upon his shoulders the crushing burden of a new contest. But his eldest son had come among them, eagerly, with his whole heart; and so they made him a general.

The poor old man was in part proud of this and in part grieved. "I have a son a general in each army," he said to a stranger who came to his house in those days; "but what strength is there in a fagot when it is separated? of what use is a house that is divided against itself? The boys would kill each other if they met."

"It is very sad," said the stranger.

"Sad!" said the old man. "It is as though the Devil were let loose upon the earth; — and so he is; so he is."

The family came to understand that General Tom was with the Confederate army which was confronting the Federal army of the Potomac and defending Richmond; whereas it was well known that Frank was in Kentucky with the army on the Green River, which was hoping to make its way into Tennessee, and which did so early in the following year. It must be understood that Kentucky, though a slave state, had never seceded, and that therefore it was divided off from the Southern States, such as Tennessee and that part of Virginia which had seceded, by a cordon of pickets; so that there was no coming up from the Confederate army to Frankfort in Kentucky. There could, at any rate, be no easy or safe coming up for such a one as General Tom, seeing that being a soldier he would be regarded as a spy, and certainly treated as a prisoner if found within the Northern lines. Nevertheless, General as he was, he kept his engagement with Ada, and made his way into the gardens of his father's house on the night of Christmas-eve. And Ada was the first who knew that he was there. Her ear first caught the sound of his footsteps, and her hand raised for him the latch of the garden door.

"Oh, Tom, it is not you?"

"But it is though, Ada, my darling!" Then there was a little pause in his speech. "Did I not tell you that I should see you to-day?"

"Hush. Do you know who is here? You brother came across to us from the Green River yesterday."

"The mischief he did. Then I shall never find my way back again. If you knew what I have gone through for this!"

Ada immediately stepped out through the door and on to the snow, standing close up against him as she whispered to him, "I don't think Frank would betray you," she said. "I don't think he would."

"I doubt him, — doubt him hugely. But I suppose I must trust him. I got through the pickets close to Cumberland Gap, and I left my horse at Stoneley's, half way between this and Lexington. I cannot go back to-night now that I have come so far!"

"Wait, Tom; wait a minute, and I will go in and tell your mother. But you must be hungry. Shall I bring you food?"

"Hungry enough, but I will not eat my father's victuals out here in the snow."

"Wait a moment, dearest, till I speak to my aunt." Then Ada slipped back into the house and soon managed to get Mrs. Reckenthorpe away from the room in which the Major and his second son were sitting. "Tom is here," she said, "in the garden. He has encountered all this danger to pay us a visit because it is Christmas. Oh, aunt, what are we to do? He says that Frank would certainly give him up!"

Mrs. Reckenthorpe was nearly twenty years younger than her husband, but even with this advantage on her side Ada's tidings were almost too much for her. She, however, at last managed to consult the Major, and he resolved upon appealing to the generosity of his younger son. By this time the Confederate General was warming himself in the kitchen, having declared that his brother might do as he pleased; — he would not skulk away from his father's house in the night.

"Frank," said the father, as his younger son sat silently thinking of what had been told him, "it cannot be your duty to be false to your father in his own house."

"It is not always easy, sir, for a man to see what is his duty. I wish that either he or I had not come here."

"But he is here; and you, his brother, would not take advantage of his coming to his father's house?" said the old man.

"Do you remember, sir, how he told me last year that if ever he met me on the field he would shoot me like a dog?"

"But, Frank, you know that he is the last man in the world to carry out such a threat. Now he has come here with great danger."

"And I have come with none; but I do not see that that makes any difference."

"He has put up with it all that he may see the girl he loves."

"Psha!" said Frank, rising up from his chair. "When a man has work to do, he is a fool to give way to play. The girl he loves! Does he not know that it is impossible that she should ever marry him? Father, I ought to insist that he should leave this house as a prisoner. I know that that would be my duty."

"You would have, sir, to bear my curse."

"I should not the less have done my duty. But, father, independently of your threat, I will neglect that duty. I cannot bring myself to break your heart and my mother's. But I will not see him. Good-bye, sir. I will go up to the hotel, and will leave the place before daybreak to-morrow."

After some few further words Frank Reckenthorpe left the house without encountering his brother. He also had not seen Ada Forster since that former Christmas when they had all been together, and he had now left his camp and come across from the army much more with the view of inducing her to acknowledge the hopelessness of her engagement with his brother, than from any domestic idea of passing his Christmas at home. He was a man who would not have interfered with his brother's prospects, as regarded either love or money, if he had thought that in doing so he would in truth have injured his brother. He was a hard man, but one not wilfully unjust. He had satisfied himself that a marriage between Ada and his brother must, if it were practicable, be ruinous to both of them. If this were so, would not it be better for all parties that there should be another arrangement made? North and South were as far divided now as the two poles. All Ada's hopes and feelings were with the North. Could he allow her to be taken as a bride among perishing slaves and ruined whites?

But when the moment for his sudden departure came he knew that it would be better that he should go without seeing her. His brother Tom had made his way to her through cold, and wet, and hunger, and through infinite perils of a kind sterner even than these. Her heart now would be full of softness towards him. So Frank Reckenthorpe left the house without seeing any one but his mother. Ada, as the front door closed behind him, was still standing close by her lover over the kitchen fire, while the slaves of the family, with whom Master Tom had always been the favourite, were administering to his little comforts.

Of course General Tom was a hero in the house for the few days that he remained there, and of course the step he had taken was the very one to strengthen for him the affection of the girl whom he had come to see. North and South were even more bitterly divided now than they had been when the former parting had taken place. There were fewer hopes of reconciliation; more positive certainty of war to the knife; and they who adhered strongly to either side, and those who did not adhere strongly to either side were very few, — held their opinions now with more acrimony than they had then done. The peculiar bitterness of civil war, which adds personal hatred to national enmity, had come upon the minds of the people. And here, in Kentucky, on the borders of the contest, members of the same household were, in many cases, at war with each other. Ada Forster and her aunt were passionately Northern, while the feelings of the old man had gradually turned themselves to that division in the nation to which he naturally belonged. For months past the matter on which they were all thinking, — the subject which filled their minds morning, noon, and night, — was banished from their lips because it could not be discussed without the bitterness of hostility. But, nevertheless, there was no word of bitterness between Tom Reckenthorpe and Ada Forster. While these few short days lasted it was all love. Where is the woman whom one touch of romance will not soften, though she be ever so impervious to argument? Tom could sit up-stairs with his mother and his betrothed, and tell them stories of the gallantry of the South, — of the sacrifices women were making, and of the deeds men were doing, — and they would listen and smile and caress his hand, and all for a while would be pleasant; while the old Major did not dare to speak before them of his Southern hopes. But down in the parlour, during the two or three long nights which General Tom passed in Frankfort, open secession was discussed between the two men. The old man now had given away altogether. The Yankees, he said, were too bitter for him. "I wish I had died first; that is all," he said. "I wish I had died first. Life is wretched now to a man who can do nothing." His son tried to comfort him, saying that secession would certainly be accomplished in twelve months, and that every Slave State would certainly be included in the Southern Confederacy. But the Major shook his head. Though he hated the political bitterness of the men whom he called Puritans and Yankees, he knew their strength and acknowledged their power. "Nothing good can come in my time," he said; "not in my time, — not in my time."

In the middle of the fourth night General Tom took his departure. An old slave arrived with his horse a little before midnight, and he started on his journey. "Whatever turns up, Ada," he said, "you will be true to me."

"I will; though you are a rebel, all the same for that."

"So was Washington."

"Washington made a nation; — you are destroying one."

"We are making another, dear; that's all. But I won't talk secesh to you out here in the cold. Go in, and be good to my father; and remember this, Ada, I'll be here again next Christmas-eve, if I'm alive."

So he went, and made his journey back to his camp in safety. He slept at a friend's house during the following day, and on the next night again made his way through the Northern lines back into Virginia. Even at that time there was considerable danger in doing this, although the frontier to be guarded was so extensive. This arose chiefly from the paucity of roads, and the impossibility of getting across the country where no roads existed. But General Tom got safely back to Richmond, and no doubt found that the tedium of his military life had been greatly relieved by his excursion.

Then, after that, came a year of fighting, — and there has since come another year of fighting; of such fighting that we, hearing the accounts from day to day, have hitherto failed to recognise its extent and import. Every now and then we have even spoken of the inaction of this side or of that, as though the drawn battles which have lasted for days, in which men have perished by tens of thousands, could be renewed as might the old German battles, in which an Austrian general would be ever retreating with infinite skill and military efficacy. For constancy, for blood, for hard determination to win at any cost of life or material, history has known no such battles as these. That the South has fought the best as regards skill no man can doubt. As regards pluck and resolution there has not been a pin's choice between them. They have both fought as Englishmen fight when they are equally in earnest. As regards result, it has been almost altogether in favour of the North, because they have so vast a superiority in numbers and material.

General Tom Reckenthorpe remained during the year in Virginia, and was attached to that corps of General Lee's army which was commanded by Stonewall Jackson. It was not probable, therefore, that he would be left without active employment. During the whole year he was fighting, assisting in the wonderful raids that were made by that man whose loss was worse to the Confederates than the loss of Vicksburg or of New Orleans. And General Tom gained for himself mark, name, and glory, — but it was the glory of a soldier rather than of a general. No one looked upon him as the future commander of an army; but men said that if there was a rapid stroke to be stricken, under orders from some more thoughtful head, General Tom was the hand to strike it. Thus he went on making wonderful rides by night, appearing like a warrior ghost leading warrior ghosts in some quiet valley of the Federals, seizing supplies and cutting off cattle, till his name came to be great in the State of Kentucky, and Ada Forster, Yankee though she was, was proud of her rebel lover.

And Frank Reckenthorpe, the other general, made progress also, though it was progress of a different kind. Men did not talk of him so much as they did of Tom; but the War Office at Washington knew that he was useful, — and used him. He remained for a long time attached to the western army, having been removed from Kentucky to St. Louis, in Missouri, and was there when his brother last heard of him. "I am fighting day and night," he once said to one who was with him from his own State, "and, as far as I can learn, Frank is writing day and night. Upon my word, I think that I have the best of it."

It was but a couple of days after this, the time then being about the latter end of September, that he found himself on horseback at the head of three regiments of cavalry near the foot of one of those valleys which lead up into the Blue Mountain ridge of Virginia. He was about six miles in advance of Jackson's army, and had pushed forward with the view of intercepting certain Federal supplies which he and others had hoped might be within his reach. He had expected that there would be fighting, but he had hardly expected so much fighting as came that day in his way. He got no supplies. Indeed, he got nothing but blows, and though on that day the Confederates would not admit that they had been worsted, neither could they claim to have done more than hold their own. But General Tom's fighting was in that day brought to an end.

It must be understood that there was no great battle fought on this occasion. General Reckenthorpe, with about 1500 troopers, had found himself suddenly compelled to attack about double that number of Federal infantry. He did so once, and then a second time, but on each occasion without breaking the lines to which he was opposed; and towards the close of the day he found himself unhorsed, but still unwounded, with no weapon in his hand but his pistol, immediately surrounded by about a dozen of his own men, but so far in advance of the body of his troops as to make it almost impossible that he should find his way back to them. As the smoke cleared away and he could look about him, he saw that he was close to an uneven, irregular line of Federal soldiers. But there was still a chance, and he had turned for a rush, with his pistol ready for use in his hand, when he found himself confronted by a Federal officer. The pistol was already raised, and his finger was on the trigger, when he saw that the man before him was his brother.

"Your time has come," said Frank, standing his ground very calmly. He was quite unarmed, and had been separated from his men and ridden over; but hitherto he had not been hurt.

"Frank!" said Tom, dropping his pistol arm, "is that you?"

"And you are not going to do it, then?" said Frank.

"Do what?" said Tom, whose calmness was altogether gone. But he had forgotten that threat as soon as it had been uttered, and did not even know to what his brother was alluding.

But Tom Reckenthorpe, in his confusion at meeting his brother, had lost whatever chance there remained to him of escaping. He stood for a moment or two, looking at Frank, and wondering at the coincidence which had brought them together, before he turned to run. Then it was too late. In the hurry and scurry of the affair all but two of his own men had left him, and he saw that a rush of Federal soldiers was coming up around him. Nevertheless he resolved to start for a run. "Give me a chance, Frank," he said, and prepared to run. But as he went, — or rather before he had left the ground on which he was standing before his brother, a shot struck him, and he was disabled. In a minute he was as though he were stunned; then he smiled faintly, and slowly sunk upon the ground. "It's all up, Frank," he said, "and you are in at the death."

Frank Reckenthorpe was soon kneeling beside his brother amidst a crowd of his own men. "Spurrell," he said to a young officer who was close to him, "it is my own brother." — "What, General Tom?" said Spurrell. "Not dangerously, I hope?"

By this time the wounded man had been able, as it were, to

feel himself and to ascertain the amount of the damage done him. "It's my right leg," he said; "just on the knee. If you'll believe me, Frank, I thought it was my heart at first. I don't think much of the wound, but I suppose you won't let me go?"

Of course they wouldn't let him go, and indeed if they had been minded so to do, he could not have gone. The wound was not fatal, as he had at first thought; but neither was it a matter of little consequence as he afterwards asserted. His fighting was over, unless he could fight with a leg amputated between the knee and the hip.

Before nightfall General Tom found himself in his brother's quarters, a prisoner on parole, with his leg all but condemned by the surgeon. The third day after that saw the leg amputated. For three weeks the two brothers remained together, and after that the elder was taken to Washington, — or rather to Alexandria, on the other side of the Potomac, as a prisoner, there to wait his chance of exchange. At first the intercourse between the two brothers was cold, guarded, and uncomfortable; but after a while it became more kindly than it had been for many a day. Whether it were cold or kindly, its nature, we may be sure, was such as the younger brother made it. Tom was ready enough to forget all personal animosity as soon as his brother would himself be willing to do so; though he was willing enough also to quarrel, — to quarrel bitterly as ever, — if Frank should give him occasion. As to that threat of the pistol, it had passed away from Tom Reckenthorpe, as all his angry words passed from him. It was clean forgotten. It was not simply that he had not wished to kill his brother, but that such a deed was impossible to him. The threat had been like a curse that means nothing, — which is used by passion as its readiest weapon when passion is impotent. But with Frank Reckenthorpe words meant what they were intended to mean. The threat had rankled in his bosom from the time of its utterance, to that moment when a strange coincidence had given the threatener the power of executing it. The remembrance of it was then strong upon him, and he had expected that his brother would have been as bad as his word. But his brother had spared him; and now, slowly, by degrees, he began to remember that also.

"What are your plans, Tom?" he said, as he sat one day by his brother's bed before the removal of the prisoner to Alexandria.

"Plans," said Tom. "How should a poor fellow like me have plans? To eat bread and water in prison at Alexandria, I suppose."

"They'll let you up to Washington on your parole, I should think. Of course I can say a word for you."

"Well, then, do say it. I'd have done as much for you, though I don't like your Yankee politics."

"Never mind my politics now, Tom."

"I never did mind them. But at any rate, you see I can't run away."

It should have been mentioned a little way back in this story that the poor old Major had been gathered to his fathers during the past year. As he had said to himself, it would be better for him that he should die. He had lived to see the glory of his country, and had gloried in it. If further glory or even further gain were to come out of this terrible war, — as great gains to men and nations do come from contests which are very terrible while they last, — he at least would not live to see it. So when he was left by his sons, he turned his face to the wall and died. There had of course been much said on this subject between the two brothers when they were together, and Frank had declared how special orders had been given to protect the house of the widow if the waves of the war in Kentucky should surge up around Frankfort. Land very near to Frankfort had become debatable between the two armies, and the question of flying from their house had more than once been mooted between the aunt and her niece; but, so far, that evil day had been staved off, and as yet Frankfort, the little capital of the State, was Northern territory.

"I suppose you will get home?" said Frank, after musing awhile, "and look after my mother and Ada?"

"If I can I shall, of course. What else can I do with one leg?"

"Nothing in this war, Tom, of course." Then there was another pause between them. "And what will Ada do?" said Frank.

"What will Ada do? Stay at home with my mother."

"Ah, — yes. But she will not remain always as Ada Forster."

"Do you mean to ask whether I shall marry her; — because of

my one leg? If she will have me, I certainly shall."

"And will she? Ought you to ask her?"

"If I found her seamed all over with small-pox, with her limbs broken, blind, disfigured by any misfortune which could have visited her, I would take her as my wife all the same. If she were pennyless it would make no difference. She shall judge for herself; but I shall expect her to act by me, as I would have acted by her." Then there was another pause. "Look here, Frank," continued General Tom; "if you mean that I am to give her up as a reward to you for being sent home, I will have nothing to do with the bargain."

"I had intended no such bargain," said Frank, gloomily.

"Very well; then you can do as you please. If Ada will take me, I shall marry her as soon as she will let me. If my being sent home depends upon that, you will know how to act now."

Nevertheless he was sent home. There was not another word spoken between the two brothers about Ada Forster. Whether Frank thought that he might still have a chance through want of firmness on the part of the girl; or whether he considered that in keeping his brother away from home he could at least do himself no good; or whether, again, he resolved that he would act by his brother as a brother should act, without reference to Ada Forster, I will not attempt to say. For a day or two after the above conversation he was somewhat sullen, and did not talk freely with his brother. After that he brightened up once more, and before long the two parted on friendly terms. General Frank remained with his command, and General Tom was sent to the hospital at Alexandria, — or to such hospitalities as he might be able to enjoy at Washington in his mutilated state, — till that affair of his exchange had been arranged.

In spite of his brother's influence at headquarters this could not be done in a day; nor could permission be obtained for him to go home to Kentucky till such exchange had been effected. In this way he was kept in terrible suspense for something over two months, and mid-winter was upon him before the joyful news arrived that he was free to go where he liked. The officials in Washington would have sent him back to Richmond had he so pleased, seeing that a Federal general officer, supposed to be of equal weight with himself, had been sent back from some Southern prison in his place; but he declined any such favour, declaring his intention of going home to Kentucky. He was simply warned that no pass South could after this be granted to him, and then he went his way.

Disturbed as was the state of the country, nevertheless railways ran from Washington to Baltimore, from Baltimore to Pittsburgh, from Pittsburgh to Cincinnati, and from Cincinnati to Frankfort. So that General Tom's journey home, though with but one leg, was made much faster, and with less difficulty, than that last journey by which he reached the old family house. And again he presented himself on Christmas-eve. Ada declared that he remained purposely at Washington, so that he might make good his last promise to the letter; but I am inclined to think that he allowed no such romantic idea as that to detain him among the amenities of Washington.

He arrived again after dark, but on this occasion did not come knocking at the back door. He had fought his fight, had done his share of the battle, and now had reason to be afraid of no one. But again it was Ada who opened the door for him. "Oh, Tom; oh, my own one." There never was a word of question between them as to whether that unseemly crutch and still unhealed wound was to make any difference between them. General Tom found before three hours were over that he lacked the courage to suggest that he might not be acceptable to her as a lover with one leg. There are times in which girls throw off all their coyness, and are as bold in their loves as men. Such a time was this with Ada Forster. In the course of another month the elder General simply sent word to the younger that they intended to be married in May, if the war did not prevent them; and the younger General simply sent back word that his duties at headquarters would prevent his being present at the ceremony.

And they were married in May, though the din of war was going on around them on every side. And from that time to this the din of war is still going on, and they are in the thick of it. The carnage of their battles, the hatreds of their civil contests, are terrible to us when we think of them; but may it not be that the beneficient power of Heaven, which they acknowledge as we do, is thus cleansing their land from that stain of slavery, to abolish which no human power seemed to be sufficient?

"The Two Generals" appeared for the first time in 1863 in the December issue of Good Words.

Catherine Carmichael; or,
Three Years Running

C

Christmas Day. No. 1

ATHERINE CARMICHAEL, whose name is prefixed to this story, was very early in her life made acquainted with trouble. That name became hers when she was married, but the reader must first know her as Catherine Baird. Her father was a Scotchman of good birth, and had once been possessed of fair means. But the world had gone against him, and he had taken his family out to New Zealand when Catherine was yet but ten years old. Of Mr. Baird and his misfortunes little need be said, except that for nearly a dozen years he followed the precarious and demoralizing trade of a gold-digger at Hokitika. Sometimes there was money in plenty, sometimes there was none. Food there was, always plenty, though food of the roughest. Drink there was, generally, much more than plenty. Everything around the young Bairds was rough. Frequently changing their residence from one shanty to another, the last shanty inhabited by them would always be the roughest. As for the common decencies of life, they seemed to become ever scarcer and more scarce with them, although the females among them had a taste for decency, and although they lived in a region which then seemed to be running over with gold. The mother was ever decent in language, in manners, and in morals, and strove gallantly for her children. That they could read and write, and had some taste for such pursuits, was due to her; for the father, as years passed over him, and as he became more and more hardened to the rough usages of a digger's life, fell gradually into the habits of a mere miner. A year before his death no one would have thought he had been the son of Fergus Baird, Esq., of Killach, and that when he had married the daughter of a neighbouring laird, things had smiled pleasantly on him and his young wife.

Then his wife died, and he followed her within one year. Of the horrors of that twelve months it is useless now to tell. A man's passion for drink, if he be not wholly bad, may be moderated by a wife, and then pass all bounds when she is no longer there to restrain him. So it was with him; and for a while there was danger that it should be so with his boys also. Catherine was the eldest daughter, and was then twenty-two. There was a brother older, then four younger, and after them three other girls. That year to Catherine was very hard, — too hard, almost, for endurance. But there came among them at the diggings, where they were still dwelling, a young man whose name was John Carmichael, whose presence there gave something of grace to her days. He, too, had come for gold and had joined himself to the Bairds in consequence of some distant family friendship.

Within twelve months the father of the family had followed the mother, and the eight children were left without protection and without anything in the world worthy of the name of property. The sons could fight for themselves, and were left to do so. The three younger children were carried back to Scotland, a sister of their mother's having undertaken to maintain them; but Catherine was left. When the time came in which the three younger sisters were sent, it was found that a home presented itself for Catherine; and as the burden of providing for even the younger orphans was very great, it was thought proper that Catherine should avail herself of the home which was offered her.

John Carmichael, when he came among the diggers at Hokitika, — on the western coast of the southern of the two New Zealand islands, — had done so chiefly because he had

quarrelled with his cousin, Peter Carmichael, a squatter settled across the mountains in the Canterbury Province, with
whom he had been living for the last three or four years. This
Peter Carmichael, who was now nearly fifty, had for many
years been closely connected with Baird, and at one period
had been in partnership with him at the diggings. John had
heard of Baird and Hokitika, and when the quarrel had become, as he thought, unbearable, he had left the Canterbury
sheep-farm, and had tried his fortune in a gold-gully.

Then Baird died, and what friends there were laid their
heads together to see how best the family should be main-
tained. The boys and John Carmichael with them, would stick
to the gold. Word came out from the aunt in Scotland that
she would do what was needed. Let the burden not be made
too heavy for her. If it were found necessary to send children
home, let them, if possible, be young. Peter Carmichael himself came across the mountains to Hokitika and arranged
things for the journey; — and before he left, he had arranged
things also for Catherine. Catherine should go with him
across the mountains, and live with him at Mount Warriwa,
— as his home was called, — and be his wife.

Catherine found everything to be settled for her almost before she was able to say a word as to her own desire in the
matter. It was so evident that she could not be allowed to increase the weight of the burden which was to be imposed
upon the aunt at home! It was so evident that her brothers
were not able to find a home for her! It was so evident that
she could not live alone in that wild country! And it seemed
also to be quite evident that John Carmichael had no proposition of his own to make to her! Peter Carmichael was odious
to her, but the time was such that she could not allow herself
to think of her own dislikings.

There had never been a word of overt outspoken love between John Carmichael and Catherine Baird. The two were
nearly of an age, and, as such, the girl had seemed to be the
elder. They had come to be friends more loving than any
other that either had. Catherine, in those gloomy days, in
which she had seen her father perishing and her brothers too
often straying in the wrong path, had had much need of a

friend. And he had been good to her, keeping himself to sober, hard-working ways, because he might so best assist her in her difficulties. And she had trusted him, begging him to watch over the boys, and to help her with the girls. Her conduct had been beyond all praise; and he also, — for her sake following her example, — had been good. Of course she had loved him, but of course she had not said so, as he had not chosen to speak first.

Then had come the second death and the disruption. The elder Carmichael had come over, and had taken things into his own hands. He was known to be a very hard man, but nevertheless he spent some small sums of money for them, eking out what could be collected from the sale of their few goods. He settled this, and he settled that, as men do settle things when they have money to spend. By degrees, — not very slowly, but still gradually, — it was notified to Catherine that she might go across the mountains, and become mistress of Warriwa. It was very little that he said to her in the way of love-making.

"You might as well come home with me, Kate, and I'll send word on, and we'll get ourselves spliced as we go through Christchurch."

When he put it thus clearly to her, she certainly already knew what was intended. Her elder brother had spoken of it. It did not surprise her, nor did she start back and say at once that it should not be so.

From the moment in which Peter Carmichael had appeared upon the scene all Kate's intimacy with John seemed to come to an end. The two men, whose relationship was distant, did not renew their quarrel. The elder, indeed, was gracious, and said something to his younger kinsman as to the expediency of his returning to Warriwa. But John seemed to be oppressed by the other's presence, and certainly offered no advice as to Kate's future life. Nor did Kate say a word to him. When first an allusion to the suggested marriage was made in her presence she did not dare, indeed, to look at him, but she could perceive that neither did he look at her. She did not look, but yet she could see. There was not a start, not a change of colour, not a motion even of her foot. He expressed no consent, but she told herself that, by his silence, he gave it. There was no need for a question, even had it been possible that she could ask one.

And so it was settled. Peter Carmichael was a just man, in his way, but coarse, and altogether without sentiment. He spoke of the arrangement that had been made as he might have done of the purchase of a lot of sheep, not, however, omitting to point out that in this bargain he was giving everything and getting almost nothing. As a wife, Catherine might, perhaps, be of some service about the house; but he did not think that he should have cared to take a wife really for the sake of the wife. But it would do. They could get themselves married as they went through Christchurch, and then settle down comfortably. The brothers had nothing to say against it, and to John it seemed to be a matter of indifference. So it was settled. What did it signify to Catherine, as no one else cared for her?

Peter Carmichael was a hard-working man, who had the name of considerable wealth. But he was said to be hard of hand and hard of heart, — a stern, stubborn man, who was fond only of his money. There had been much said about him between John and Catherine before he had come to Hokitika, — when there had been no probability of his coming. "He is just," John had said, "but so ungenial that it seems to me impossible that a human being should stay with him." And yet this young man, of whose love she had dreamt, had not had a word to say when it was being arranged that she should be taken off to live all her future life with this companionship and no other! She would not condescend to ask even a question about her future home. What did it matter? She must be somewhere, because she could not be got rid of and buried at once beneath the sod. Nobody wanted her. She was only a burden. She might as well be taken to Warriwa and die there as elsewhere, — and so she went.

They travelled for two days and two nights across the mountains to Christchurch, and there they were married, as it happened, on Christmas Day, — on Christmas Day, because they passed that day and no other in the town as they went on. There was a further journey, two other days and two other nights, down nearly to the southern boundary of the Canterbury Province; and thither they went on with no great change between them, hav-

217

ing become merely man and wife during that day they had remained at Christchurch. As they passed one great river after another on their passage down Kate felt how well it would be that the waters should pass over her head. But the waters refused to relieve her of the burden of her life. So she went on and reached her new home at Warriwa.

Catherine Carmichael, as she must now be called, was a well-grown, handsome young woman, who, through all the hardships of her young life, still showed traces of the gentle blood from which she had sprung. And ideas had come to her from her mother of things better than those around her. To do something for others, and then something, if possible, for herself, — these had been the objects nearest to her. Of the amusements, of the lightness and pleasures of life, she had never known anything. To sit vacant for an hour dreaming over a book had never come to her; nor had it been for her to make the time run softly with some apology for women's work in her hands. The hard garments, fit for a miner's work, passed through her hands. The care of the children, the preparation of their food, the doing the best she could for the rough household, — these things had kept her busy from her early rising till she would go late to her bed. But she had loved her work because it had been done for her father and her mother, for her brothers and her sisters. And she had respected herself, never despising the work she did; no man had ever dared to say an uncivil word to Kate Baird among all those rough miners with whom her father associated. Something had come to her from her mother which, while her mother lived, — even while her father lived, — had made her feel herself to be mistress of herself. But all that independence had passed away from her, — all that consciousness of doing the best she could, — as soon as Peter Carmichael had crossed her path.

It was not till the hard, dry, middle-aged man had taken possession of her that she acknowledged to herself that she had really loved John Carmichael. When Peter had come among them, he had seemed to dominate her as well as the others. He and he only had money. He and he only could cause aught to be done. And then it had seemed that for all the others there was a way of escape open, but none for her. No one wanted her, unless it was this dry old man. The young man certainly did not want her. Then in her sorrow she allowed herself to be crushed, in spite of the strength for which she had given herself credit. She was astounded, almost stupefied, so that she had no words with which to assert herself. When she was told that the hard, dry man would find a home for her, she had no reason to give why it should not be so. When she did not at first refuse to be taken away across the mountains, she had failed to realize what it all meant. When she reached Warriwa, and the waters in the pathless, unbridged rivers had not closed over her head, — then she realized it.

She was the man's wife, and she hated him. She had never known before what it was to hate a human being. She had always been helpful, and it is our nature to love those we help. Even the rough men who would lure her father away to drink had been her friends. "Oh, Dick," she would say, to the roughest of the rough, putting her hand prayerfully on the man's sleeve, "do not ask him to-night;" and the rough man would go from the shanty for the time. She would have mended his jacket for him willingly, or washed his shirt. Though the world had been very hard to her, she had hated no one. Now, she hated a man with all the strength of her heart, and he was her husband.

It was good for the man, though whether good for herself or not she could never tell, that he did not know that he was hated. "Now, old woman; here you'll have a real home," he said, as he allowed her to jump out of the buggy in which he had driven her all the way from Christchurch; "you'll find things tidier than you ever had 'em away at Hokitika." She jumped down on the yard into which he had driven, with a bandbox in her hand, and passed into the house by a back door. As she did so a very dirty old woman, — fouler looking, certainly, than any she had ever seen away among the gold-diggings, — followed her from the kitchen, which was built apart, a little to the rear of the house. "So you be the new wife, be ye?" said the old woman.

"Yes; I am Mr. Carmichael's wife. Are you the servant?"

"I don't know nothing about servants. I does for 'un, — what he can't do for 'unself. You'll be doing for 'un all now, I guess." Then her husband followed her in and desired her to come and help to unload the buggy. Anything to be done was a relief to her. If she could load and unload the buggy night and day it

219

would be better than anything else she could see in prospect before her. Then there came a Maori in a blanket, to assist in carrying the things. The man was soft and very silent, — softly and silently civil, so that he seemed to be a protection to her against the foul old woman, and that lord of hers, who was so much fouler to her imagination.

Then her home life began. A woman can generally take an interest in the little surroundings of her being, feeling that the tables and the chairs, the beds and the linen are her own. Being her own, they are dear to her and will give a constancy of employment which a man cannot understand. She tried her hand at this, though the things were not her own, — were only his. But he told her so often that they were his that she could not take them to her heart. There was not much there for a woman to love; but little as there was, she could have loved it for the man's sake, had the man been lovable. The house consisted of three rooms, in the centre of which they lived, sleeping in one of the others. The third was unfurnished and unoccupied, except by sheepskins, which, as they were taken by the shepherds from the carcases of sheep that had died about the run, were kept there till they could be sent to the market. A table or two, with a few chairs; a bedstead with an old feather bed upon it; a washing-basin with a broken jug, with four or five large boxes in lieu of presses, made up nearly all the furniture. An iron pot or two and a frying-pan, with some ill-matched broken crockery, completed the list of domestic goods. How was she to love such as these with such an owner for them?

He had boasted that things were tidier there than she had known them at the diggings. The outside of the house was so, for the three rooms fronting on to the wide prairie-land of the sheep-run had a verandah before them, and the place was not ruinous. But there had been more of comfort in the shanty which her father and brothers had built for their home down in the gold-gully. As to food, to which she was indifferent, there was no question but that it had been better and more plentiful at the diggings. For the food she would not have cared at all, — but she did care for the way in which it was doled out to her hands, so that at every dole she came to hate him more. The meat was plentiful enough. The men who took their rations from the station came there and cut it from the sheep as they were slaughtered, almost as they would. Peter would count the sheep's heads every week, and would then know that, within a certain wide margin, he had not been robbed. Could she have made herself happy with mutton she might have lived a blessed life. But of other provisions every ounce was weighed to her, as it was to the station hands. So much tea for the week, so much sugar, so much flour, and so much salt. That was all, — unless when he was tempted to buy a sack of potatoes by some itinerant vendor, when he would count them out almost one by one. There was a storeroom attached to the kitchen, double-locked, the strongest of all the buildings about the place. Of this, for some month or two, he never allowed her to see the inside. She became aware that there were other delicacies there besides the tea and sugar, — jam and pickles, and boxes of sardines. The station-hands about the place, as the shepherds were called, would come and take the pots and bottles away with them, and Peter would score them down in his book and charge them in his account of wages against the men, with a broad profit to himself. But there could be no profit in sending such luxuries into the house. And then, as the ways of these people became gradually known to her, she learned that the rations which had been originally allowed for Peter himself and the old woman and the Maori had never been increased at her coming. Rations for three were made to do as rations for four. "It's along of you that he's a-starving of us," said the old woman. Why on earth should he have married her and brought her there, seeing that there was so little need for her!

But he had known what he was about. Little though she found for her to do, there was something which added to his comfort. She could cook, — an art which the old woman did not possess. She could mend his clothes, and it was something for him to have some one to speak to him. Perhaps in this way he liked her, though it was as a man may like a dog whom he licks into obedience. Though he would tell her that she was sulky, and treat her with rough violence if she answered him, yet he never repented him of his bargain. If there was work which she could do, he took care not to spare her, — as when the man came for the sheepskins, and she had to hand them out across the verandah, counting them as she did so. But there was, in truth, little

221

for her to do.

There was so little to do that the hours and days crept by with feet so slow that they never seemed to pass away. And was it to be thus with her for always, — for her, with her young life, and her strong hands, and her thoughts always full? Could there be no other life than this? And if not, could there be no death? And then she came to hate him worse and worse, — to hate him and despise him, telling herself that of all human beings he was the meanest. Those miners who would work for weeks among the clay, — working almost day and night, — with no thought but of gold, and who then, when gold had been found, would make beasts of themselves till the gold was gone, were so much better than him! Better! why, they were human; while this wretch, this husband of hers, was meaner than a crawling worm! When she had been married to him about eight months, it was with difficulty that she could prevail upon herself not to tell him that she hated him.

The only creature about the place that she could like was the Maori. He was silent, docile, and uncomplaining. His chief occupation was that of drawing water and hewing wood. If there was aught else to do, he would be called upon to do it, and in his slow manner he would set about the task. About twice a month he would go to the nearest post-office, which was twenty miles off, and take a letter, or, perhaps, fetch one. The old woman and the squatter would abuse him for everything or nothing; and the Maori, to speak the truth, seemed to care little for what they said. But Catherine was kind to him, and he liked her kindness. Then there fell upon the squatter a sense of jealousy, — or feeling, probably, that his wife's words were softer to the Maori than to himself, — and the Maori was dismissed. "What's that for?" asked Catherine sulkily.

"He is a lazy skunk."

"Who is to get the wood?"

"What's that to you? When you were down at Hokitika you could get wood for yourself." Not another word was said, and for a week she did cut the wood. After that, there came a lad who had been shepherding, and was now well-nigh idiotic; but with such assistance as Catherine could give him, he did manage to hew the wood and draw the water.

Then one day a great announcement was made to her. "Next week John Carmichael will be here."

"John!"

"Yes; why not John? He will have that room. If he wants a bed, he must bring it with him." When this was said November had come round again, and it wanted about six weeks to Christmas.

Christmas Day. No. 2

John Carmichael was to come! And she understood that he was to come there as a resident; — for Peter had spoken of the use of that bedroom as though it were to be permanent. With no direct telling, but by degrees, something of the circumstances of the run at Warriwa had become known to her. There were on it 15,000 sheep, and these, with the lease of the run, were supposed to be worth £15,000. The sheep and all were the property of her husband. Some years ago he had taken John, when he was a boy, to act with him as his foreman or assistant, and the arrangement had been continued till the quarrel had sprung up. Peter had more than once declared his purpose of leaving all that he possessed to the young man, and John had never doubted his word. But, in return for all this future wealth, it was expected, not only that the lad should be his slave, but that the lad, grown into a man should remain so as long as Peter might live. As Peter was likely to live for the next twenty years, and as the slavery was hard to bear, John had quarrelled with his kinsman, and had gone away to the diggings. Now, it seemed, the quarrel had been arranged, and John was to come back to Warriwa. That someone was needed to ride round among the four or five shepherds, — someone beyond Peter himself, — someone to overlook the shearing, someone to attend to the young lambs, someone to see that the water-holes did not run dry, had become manifest even to Kate herself. It had leaked out from Peter's dry mouth that someone must come, and now she was told that John Carmichael would return to his old home.

Though she hated her husband, Kate knew what was due to him. Hating him as she had learned to do, hating him as she acknowledged to herself that she did, still she had endeavoured to do her duty by him. She could not smile upon him, she could not even speak to him with a kind voice; but she could make his bed, and iron his shirts, and cook his dinner, and see that the things confided to her charge were not destroyed by the old woman or the idiot boy. Perhaps he got from her all that he wanted to get. He did not complain that her voice was not loving. He was harsh, odious in his ways with her, sometimes almost violent; but it may be doubted whether he would have been less so had she attempted to turn him by any show of false affection. She had learned to feel that if she served him she did for him all that he required, and that duty demanded no more. But now! would not duty demand more from her now?

Since she had been brought home to Warriwa, she had given herself up freely to her thoughts, telling herself boldly that she hated her husband, and that she loved that other man. She told herself, also, that there was no breach of duty in this. She would never again see that other man. He had crossed her path and had gone. There was nothing for her left in the world, except her husband Peter and Warriwa. As for her hating the one man, not to do that would be impossible. As for loving the other man, there was nothing in it but a dream. Her thoughts were her own, and therefore she went on loving him. She had no other food for her thoughts, except the hope that death might come to her, and some vague idea that that last black fast-running river, over which she had been ferried in the dark, might perhaps be within her reach, should death be too long in coming of its own accord. With such thoughts running across her brain, there was, she thought, no harm in loving John Carmichael, — till now, when she was told that John was to be brought here to live under the same roof with her.

Now there must be harm in it! Now there would be crime in loving him! And yet she knew that she could not cease to love him because he should be there, meeting her eye every day. How comely he was, with that soft brown hair of his, and the broad, open brow, and the smile that would curl round his lips! How near they had once been to swearing that they would be each, all things to the other! "Kate!" he had said, "Kate!" as she had stood close to him, fastening a button to his shirt. Her finger had trembled against his neck, and she knew that he had felt the quiver. The children had come upon them at the moment, and no other word had been said. Then Peter had come there, — Peter who was to be her husband, — and after that John Carmichael had spoken no word at all to her. Though he had been so near to loving her while her finger had touched him in its trembling, all that had passed away when Peter came. But it had not passed away from her heart, nor would she be able to stifle it when he should be there, sitting daily at the same board with her. Though the man himself was so odious, there was something sacred to her in the name of husband, — something very sacred to her in the name of wife. "Why should he be coming?" she said to her husband the day after the announcement had been made to her, when twenty-four hours for thinking had been allowed to her.

"Because it suits," he said, looking up at her from the columns of a dirty account-book, in which he was slowly entering figures.

What could she say to him that might be of avail? How much could she say to him? Should she tell him everything, and then let him do as he pleased? It was in her mind to do so, but she could not bring herself to speak the words. He would have thought——! Oh! what might he not have thought! There was no dealing in fair words with one so suspicious, so unmanly, so inhuman.

"It won't suit," she said, sullenly.

"Why not? what have you got to do with it?"

"It won't suit; he and I will be sure to, — sure to, — sure to have words."

"Then you must have 'em. Ain't he my cousin? Do you expect me to be riding round among them lying, lazy varmint every day of my life, while you sit at home twiddling your thumbs?" Here she knew that allusion was made both to the sheep and to the shepherds. "If anything happens to me, who do you think is to have it all after me?" One day at Hokitika he had told her coarsely that it was a good thing for a young woman to marry an

225

old man, because she would be sure to get everything when he was dead. "I suppose that's why you don't like John," he added, with a sneer.

"I do like him," she said, with a clear, loud voice; "I do like him." Then he leered round at her, shaking his head at her, as though declaring that he was not to be taken in by her devices, and after that he went on with his figures.

Before the end of November John arrived. Something, at any rate, she could do for his comfort. Wherever she got them, there, when he came, were the bed and bedstead for his use. At first she asked simply after her brothers. They had been tempted to go off to other diggings in New South Wales, and he had not thought well to follow them. "Sheep is better nor gold, Jack," said Peter, shaking his head and leering.

She tried to be very silent with him; — but she succeeded so far that her very silence made him communicative. In her former intercourse she had always talked the most, — a lass of that age having always more to say for herself than a lad. But now he seemed to struggle to find chance opportunities. As a rule he was always out early in the morning on horseback, and never home till Peter was there also. But opportunities would, of course, be forthcoming. Nor would it be wise that she should let him feel that she avoided them. It was not only necessary that Peter should not suspect, but that John, too, should be kept in the dark. Indeed, it might be well that Peter should suspect a little. But if he were to suspect, — that other he, — and then he were to speak out, how should she answer him?

"Kate," he said to her one day, "do you ever think of Hokitika?"

"Think, indeed! — of the place where father and mother lie."

"But of the time when you and I used to fight it out for them? I used not to think in those days, Kate, that you would ever be over here, — mistress of Warriwa."

"No, indeed, nobody would have thought it."

"But Kate——"

It was clearly necessary that she should put an end to these reminiscences, difficult as it might be to do so. "John," she said, "I think you'd better make a change."

"What change?"

She struggled not to blush as she answered him, and she succeeded. "I was a girl in those days, but now I'm a married woman. You had better not call me Kate any more."

"Why? what's the harm?"

"Harm! no, there's no harm; but it isn't the proper thing when a young woman's married, unless he be her brother, or her cousin at furthest; you don't call me by my name before him."

"Didn't I?"

"No, you call me nothing at all. What you do before him, you must do behind his back."

"And we were such friends!" But as she could not stand this, she left the room, and did not come back from the kitchen till Peter had returned.

So a month went on, and still there was the word Kate sounding in her ears whenever the old man's back was turned. And it sounded now as it sounded on that one day when her finger was trembling at his throat. Why not give way to the sound! Why not ill-treat the man who had so foully ill-treated her? What did she owe to him but her misery? What had he done for her but make a slave of her? And why should she, living there in the wild prairie, beyond the ken of other women, allow herself to be trammelled by the laws which the world had laid down for her sex? To other women the world made some return for true obedience. The love of one man, the strong protecting arm of one true friend, the consciousness of having one to buckler her against the world, one on whom she might hang with trust! This was what other women have in return for truth; — but was any of this given to her when he would turn round and leer at her, reminding her by his leer that he had caught her and made a slave of her? And then there was this young man, sweeter to her now than ever, and dearer!

As she thought of all this she came suddenly, — in a moment, — to a resolution, striking her hand violently on the table as she did so. She must tell her husband everything. She must do that, or else she must become a false wife. As she thought of that possibility of being false, an ecstasy of sweetness for a moment pervaded her senses. To throw herself on his bosom and tell him that she loved him would be compensation almost sufficient to the misery of the last twelve months. Then the word wife crept

227

into her ears, and she remembered words that she had read as to woman's virtue. She thought of her father and her mother! And how would it be with her when, after a while, she would awake from her dream? She had sat silent for an hour alone, now melting into softness, and then rousing herself to all the strength of womanhood. At last a frown came across her brow, very dark; and then, dashing her clenched hand down upon the table, she expressed her purpose in spoken words: "I will tell it him all!"

Then she told him all, after her fashion. It was the custom of the two men to go forth together almost at dawn, and it was her business to prepare their meal for them before they went. On the first morning after her resolution had been formed, she bade her husband to stay awhile. She had thought to say it in the seclusion of their own room; but she had felt that it would be better that John should not be in the house when it was spoken. Peter stayed at her bidding, looking eagerly into her face, as she stood at the back door watching till the young man had started on his horse. Then she turned round to her husband. "He must go away from this," she said, pointing over her shoulder to the retreating figure of the horseman.

"Why is he to go? What has he been and done?" This last question he asked, lowering his voice to a whisper, as though thinking that she had detected his cousin in some delinquency.

There was a savage purpose in her heart to make the revelation as bitter to him as it might be. He must know her own purity, but he must know also her thorough contempt for himself. There was no further punishment that he could inflict upon her, save that of thinking her to be false. Though he were to starve her, beat her, murder her, she would care for that not at all. He had carried her away helpless to his foul home, and all that was left her was to preserve herself strong against disgrace.

"He is a man, a young man, and I am a woman. You had better let him go." Then he stood for a while with his mouth open, holding her by the arm, not looking at her, but with his eyes fixed on the spot whence his cousin was disappearing. After a moment or two, his lips came together and produced a long low whistle. He still clutched her, and still looked out upon the far-retreating figure; but he was for a while as though he had been stricken dumb. "You had better let him go," she repeated.

Then he whispered some word into her ear. She threw up the arm that he was holding so violently that he was forced to start back from her, and to feel how much stronger she was than he, should she choose to put out her strength. "I tell you all," she said, "that you have to know. Little as you deserve, you have fallen into honest hands. Let him go."

"And he hasn't said a word?"

"I have told you all that you are to hear."

"I would kill him."

"If you are beast enough to accuse him, he will kill you; — or I will do it, if you ever tell him what I have said to you. Bid him go; and let that be all." Then she turned away from him, and passing through the house, crossed the verandah, and went out upon the open space on the other side. He lingered about the place for half an hour, but did not follow her. Then he mounted his old horse, and rode away across the prairie after his sheep.

"Have you told him?" she said, that night when they were alone.

"Told him what?"

"That he must go." He shook his head, not angrily, but in despair. Since that morning he had learned to be afraid of her. "If you do not," she said very slowly, looking him full in the face — "if you do not — I will. He shall be told to-night, before he goes to his bed."

"Am I to say that he — that he——?" As he endeavoured to ask the question, he was white with despair.

"You are to say nothing to him but that he must quit Warriwa at once. If you will say that, he will understand you."

What took place between the two men on the next day she did not know. It may be doubted whether she would ever know it. Peter said not a word further to her on the matter. But on the morning of the second day there was the buggy ready, and Peter with it, prepared to drive his cousin away. It was apparent to her that her husband had not dared to say an evil word of her, nor did she believe that he suspected her. She felt that, poor a creature as he was, she had driven him to respect her. But the thing was settled as she would have it, and the young man was to go.

During those last two days there was not a word spoken between her and John unless when she handed him his food. When he was away across the land she took care that not a stitch should be wanting to his garments. She washed his things and laid them smooth for him in his box, — oh, with such loving hands! As she kneeled down to her work, she looked round to the door of the room to see that it was closed, and to the window, lest the eyes of that old woman should be prying in; and then she stooped low, and burying her face beneath the lid, kissed the linen which her hands had smoothed. This she could do, and not feel herself disgraced; — but when the morning came she could let him go and not speak a word. She came out before he was up and prepared the breakfast, and then went back to her own room, so that they two might eat it together and then start. But he could not bring himself to go without one word of farewell. "Say good-bye, at any rate," he sobbed, standing at her door, which opened out upon the verandah. Peter the while was looking on with a lighted pipe in his mouth.

"Good-bye, John." The words were heard, but the sobs were almost hidden.

"Give me your hand," said he. Then there came forth a hand, — nothing but a hand. He took it in his, and for a moment thought that he would touch it with his lips. But he felt, — feeling like a man, — that it behoved him to spare her all he could. He pressed it in his grasp for a moment, and then the hand disappeared.

"If we are to go, we might as well be off," said Peter. So they mounted the buggy and went away.

The nearest town to Warriwa was a place called Timaru, through which a coach, running from Dunedin to Christchurch, passed three times a week. This was forty miles off, and here was transacted what business was necessary for the carrying on of the sheep-station. Stores were bought at Timaru, such as sugar, tea, and flour, and here Peter Carmichael generally sold his wool. Here was the bank at which he kept his money, and in which his credit always stood high. There were not many journeys made from Warriwa to Timaru; but when one became necessary it was always a service of pleasure to Peter. He could, as it were, finger his money by looking at the bank which contained it, and he could learn what might probably be the price which the merchants would give him for his next clip. On this occasion he seemed to be quite glad of an excuse for driving into Timaru, though it can hardly be imagined that he and his companion were pleasant to each other in the buggy. From Warriwa the road, or track rather, was flat the whole way to Timaru. There was nothing to be seen on either way but a long everlasting plain of grey, stunted, stony grass. At Warriwa the outlines of the distant mountains were just visible in the west, but the traveller, as he went eastward towards the town and the road, soon lost sight of the hills, and could see nothing but the grey plain. There were, however, three rivers to be passed, the Warriwa, and two others, which, coming down from the northwest, ran into the Warriwa. Of these the Warriwa itself was the widest, and the deepest, and the fastest. It was in crossing this, within ten miles of her home, — crossing it after dark, — that Catherine had thought how well it would be that the waters should pass over her head, so that she might never see that home. Often, since that, she had thought how well it would have been for her had she been saved from the horrors of her home by the waters of the river.

We may suppose that very little was said by the two men as they made their way into Timaru. Peter was one who cared little for conversation, and could be quite content to sit for hours together in his buggy, calculating the weight of his wool, and the money which would come from it. At Timaru they dined together, still, we may say, without many words. Then the coach came, and John Carmichael was carried away, — whither his cousin did not even inquire. There was some small money transaction between them, and John was carried away to follow out his own fortune.

Had it been possible Peter would have returned at once, so as to save expense, but the horses made it necessary that he should remain that night in town. And, having done so, he stayed the greater part of the following day, looking after his money and his wool, and gathering his news. At about two he started, and made his way back over the two smaller rivers in safety. At the Warriwa there was but one ferryman, and in carrying a vehicle with horses over it was necessary that the man in charge of them should work also. On the former day, though the rivers had been very high, there had been daylight, and John Carmichael had been there. Now it was pitch dark, though it was in the middle of summer, and the waters were running very strong. The ferryman refused at first to put the buggy on the raft, bidding old Carmichael wait till the next morning. It was Christmas Eve, he said, and he did not care to be drowned on Christmas Eve.

Nor was such to be his destiny. But it was the destiny of Peter Carmichael. The waters went over him and one of his horses. At three o'clock in the morning his body was brought home to Warriwa, lying across the back of the other. The ferryman had been unable to save the man's life, but had got the body, and had brought it home to the young widow just twelve months after the day on which she had become a wife.

Christmas Day. No. 3

There she was, on the morning of that Christmas Day, with the ferryman and that old woman, with the half-idiot boy, and the body of her dead husband! She was so stunned that she sat motionless for hours, with the corpse close to her, lying stretched out on the verandah, with a sheet over it. It is a part of the cruelty of the life which is lived in desolate places, far away, that when death comes, the small incidents of death are not mitigated to the sufferer by the hands of strangers.

If the poorest wife here at home becomes a widow, some attendant hands will close the glazed eye and cover up the limbs, and close the coffin which is there at hand; and then it will be taken away and hidden forever. There is an appropriate spot, though it be but under the poorhouse wall. Here there was no appropriate spot, no ready hand, no coffin, no coroner with his authority, no parish officer ready with his directions. She sat there numb, motionless, voiceless, thinking where John Carmichael might be. Could it be that he would come back to her, and take from her that ghastly duty of getting rid of the object that was lying within a yard or two of her arm?

She tried to weep, telling herself that, as a wife now widowed, she was bound to weep for her husband. But there was not a tear, nor a sob, nor a moan. She argued it with herself, saying that she would grieve for him now that he was dead. But she could not grieve, — not for that; only for her own wretchedness and desolation. If the waters had gone over her instead of him, then how merciful would heaven have been to her! The misery of her condition came home to her with its full weight, — her desolation, her powerlessness, her friendlessness, the absence of all interest in life, of all reason for living; but she could not induce herself to say, even to herself, that she was struck with anguish on account of him. That voice, that touch, the cunning leer of that eye, would never trouble her again. She had been freed from something. She became angry with herself because it was in this way that she regarded it; but it was thus that she continued to regard it. She had threatened once to kill him, — to kill him should he speak a word as to which she bade him to be silent. Now he was dead, — whether he had spoken that word or not. Then she wondered whether he had spoken it, and she wondered, also, what John Carmichael would say or do when he should hear that his kinsman was no more. So she sat motionless for hours within her room, but with the door open on to the verandah, and the feet of the corpse within a few yards of her chair.

The old ferryman took the horse, and went out under the boy's guidance in quest of the shepherds. Distances are large on these sheepruns, and a shepherd with his flock is not always easily found. It was nearly evening before he returned with two of these men, and then they dug the grave, — not very far away, as the body must be carried in their arms; and then they buried him, putting up a rough palisade around the spot to guard it, if it might be so guarded for a while, from the rats. She walked with them as they carried it, and stood there as they did their work; and the old woman went with them, helping a little. But the widow spoke not a word, and when returning, seated herself again in the same chair. Not once did there come to her the relief of a tear, or even a sob.

The ferryman went back to his river, and the shepherds to

their sheep, and the old woman and the boy remained with her, preparing what food was eaten. The key of the store-room was now in her possession, having been taken out of his pocket before they laid him in his grave, and they could do what they pleased with what it contained. So she remained for a fortnight, altogether inactive, having as yet resolved upon nothing. Thoughts no doubt there were running through her mind. What was now to become of her? To whom did the place belong, and the sheep, and the money, which, as she knew, was lying in the bank? It had all been promised to John, before her marriage. Then the old man had hinted to her, in his coarse way, that it would be hers. Then he had hinted again that John was to be brought back, and to live here. How would it be? Without the speaking of words, even to herself, it was settled in her heart that John Carmichael should be, ought to be, must be, the owner of Warriwa. Then how different would Warriwa become? But she strove gallantly against feeling that, for herself, there would be any personal interest in such a settlement. She would have kept her thoughts away from that if it had been possible; — if it had been possible.

At the end of a fortnight there came out to her from Timaru a young man, who declared himself to be the clerk of a solicitor established there, and this young man brought with him a letter from the manager of the bank. The purport of the letter was this: Mr. Carmichael, as he had passed through Timaru on his way home from Christchurch after his marriage, had then executed a will, which he had deposited at the bank. In this he had named the manager as his sole executor, and had left everything of which he was possessed to his wife. The writer of the letter then went on to explain that there might have been a subsequent will made. He was aware that John Carmichael had been again at Warriwa, and it was possible that Peter Carmichael might have reverted to his old intention of making his kinsman his heir. There had been a former will to that effect, which had been destroyed in the presence of the banker. There was no such document at Timaru. If anywhere, it must be at Warriwa. Would Mrs. Carmichael allow the young man to search? If no such document could be found, the money and the property would be hers. It would be well that she should return with the young man to the town, and take up her abode there in lodgings for a few weeks till things should have settled themselves.

And thus she found herself mistress of Warriwa, owner of the sheep, and possessor of all the money. Of course, she obeyed the counsel given her, and went into the town. No other will was found; no other claimant came forward. Week after week went by, and month after month, very slowly, and at the end of six months she found that everything was undoubtedly hers. An agent had been hired to live at Warriwa, and her signature was recognized at the bank as commanding all that money. The sum seemed so large that it was a wonder to her that the old man should have lived in such misery at home. Then two of her brothers came to her, across from New South Wales. They had come to her because she was alone. No, they said; they did not want her help, though a little money would go a long way with them. They had come because she was alone.

Then she laid a task upon them, and told them her plans. Yes; she had been very much alone; — altogether without counsel in this particular matter; but she had formed her plans. If they would assist her, no doubt they would be compensated for their time. Where was John Carmichael? They had not heard of John Carmichael since they had left him when they went away from Hokitika.

Thereupon she explained to them that none of all that property was hers; — that none of it all should ever be hers; that, to her view of the matter, the station, with the run, and the sheep, and the money, all belonged to John Carmichael. When they told her that she had been the man's wife, and, therefore, much nearer than John Carmichael, she only shook her head. She could not explain to them her thoughts and feelings. She could not say to them that she would not admit herself to have been the wife of a man whom she had ever hated, — for whom, not for a single moment, had she ever entertained anything of wifely feeling. "I am here," she said, "only as his care-taker; — only as such will I ever spend a farthing of the money." Then she showed them a letter, of which she had sent copies addressed to him at the post-offices of various towns in New Zealand, having spent many of her hours in making the copies, and the letter was as follows; —

235

"If you will return to Warriwa, you will find that everything has been kept for you as well as I have known how to keep it. The sheep are nearly up to the number. The money is at the bank at Timaru, except a very little which I have taken to pay the wages and just to support myself, — till I can go away and leave it all. You should hurry to Warriwa, because I cannot go away till you come.   CATHERINE."

It was not, perhaps, a very wise letter. An advertisement in the New Zealand papers would have done better, and have cost less trouble. But that was her way of setting about her work, — till her brothers had come to her, and then she sent them forth upon her errand. It was in vain that they argued with her. They were to go and find him, and send him, — not to her, — but to Warriwa. On his arrival he should find that everything was ready for him. There would be some small thing for the lawyer to arrange, but that could be arranged at once. When the elder brother asked at the bank about his sister, the manager told him that all Timaru had failed to understand the purposes of the heiress. That old Peter Carmichael had been a miser, everybody had known, and that a large sum was lying in the bank, and that the sheep were out on the run at Warriwa. They knew, too, that the widow had inherited it all. But they could not understand why she should be careful with the money as old Peter had been; why she should live there in lodgings, seeing no one; why she should be taken out to Warriwa once a month; and why on these occasions she should remain there a day or two, going through every figure, as it was said that she did do. If she liked the life of a squatter, why did she not live there and make the place comfortable? If, as was more probable, the place could hardly be delightful to her, why not sell it, and go away among her friends? There would be friends enough now to make her welcome. For, though she had written the letters, and sent them out, one or two at a time, she had told no one of her purpose till her brothers came to her. Then the banker understood it all, and the brothers probably understood something also.

They got upon his traces at last, and found him in Queensland, up to his throat in mud, looking for gold in a gully. "Luck? Yes; he had got a little, and spent the most of it. There was gold, no doubt, but he was not much in love with the spot." 'Tis

236

always thus the wandering gold-digger speaks of his last adventure. When they told him that Peter Carmichael was dead, he jumped out of the gully, leaving the cradle behind him in which he had been washing the dirt, searching for specks of gold. "And Warriwa?" he said. Then they explained the nature of the will. "And the money, too?" Yes; the money also had been left to the widow. "It would have been hers any way," he said, "whether he left a will or not. Well, well! So Kate is a rich woman." Then he jumped into the gully again, and went to work at his cradle. By degrees they explained it all to him, — as much, at least, as they could explain. He must go to Warriwa. She would do nothing till he had been there.

"She says it is to be all yours," said the younger brother.

"Don't you say no more than you know," said the elder. "Let him go and find it out for himself."

"But Kate said so."

"Kate is a woman, and may change her mind as well as another. Let him go and find it out for himself." So he sold his claim at the gully for what little it would fetch, and started off once again for New Zealand and Warriwa.

He had himself landed at Dunedin in order that he might not be seen and questioned in passing through Timaru, and from Dunedin he made his way across the country direct to Warriwa. I need not trouble my readers with New Zealand geography, but at a little place called Oamaru he hired a buggy and a pair of horses, and had himself driven across the country to the place. He knew that Catherine was living in the town, and not at the station; but even though the distance were forty miles, he thought that it would be better to send for her than to discuss such things as would have to be discussed before the bankers and the attorney, and all the eager eyes and ears of Timaru. What it was that he would have to discuss he hardly yet knew; but he did know, or thought that he knew, that he had been banished from Warriwa because old Peter Carmichael had not chosen to have "a young fellow like that hopping about round his wife." It was thus that Peter had explained his desire in that matter of John's departure. Now he had been sent for, because of the property. The property was the property of the widow. He did not in the least doubt that. Christmas had again come around, and it was just a year,

— a year and a day, — since she had put her hand out to him through the closed door and had bade him good-bye.

There she was, when he entered the house, sitting at that little side-table, with the very books before her at which Peter had spent so many of his hours. "Kate," he said, as he entered, "I have come, you see, — because you sent for me."

She jumped up, rushing at him, as though to throw her arms round him, forgetting, — forgetting that there had been no love spoken between them. Then she stopped herself, and stood a moment looking at him. "John," she said, "John Carmichael, I am so glad you have come at last. I am tired minding it, — very tired, and I know that I do not do it as it should be."

"Do what, Kate?"

"Mind it all, — for you. No one else could do it, because I had to sign the papers. Now you have come, and may do as you please with it. Now you have come, — and I may go."

"He left it to you; all of it, — the money, and the sheep, and the station."

Then there came a frown across her brow, — not of anger, but of perplexity. How should she explain it? How should she let him know that it must be as she would have it, — that he must have it all; and have it not from her, but as heir to his kinsman? How could she do all this and teach him at the same time that there need be nothing of gratitude in it all, — nothing certainly of love?

"John," she said, "I will not take it from him as his widow. I never loved him. I never had a kindly feeling towards him. It would kill me to take it. I will not have it. It must be yours."

"And you?"

"I will go away."

"Whither will you go? Where will you live?" Then she stood there dumb before him, frowning at him. What was it to him where she might go? She thought of the day when she had sewn the button on his shirt, when he might have spoken to her. And she remembered, too, how she had prepared his things for him, when he had been sent away, at her bidding, from Warriwa. What was it to him what might become of her?

"I am tired of this," she said. "You must come to Timaru, so that the lawyer may do what is necessary. There must be papers prepared. Then I will go away."

"Kate!" She only stamped her foot. "Kate, — why was it that he made me go?"

"He could not bear to have people about the place, eating and drinking."

"Was it that?"

"Or perhaps he hated you. It is easy, I think, to hate in a place so foul as this."

"And not easy to love?"

"I have had no chance of loving. But what is the use of all that? Will you do as I bid you?"

"What! — take it all from your hands?"

"No; not from mine, — from his. I will not take it, coming to me from him. It is not mine, and I cannot give it; but it is yours. You need not argue, for it must be so." Then she turned away, as though going; — but she knew not whither to go, and stopped at the end of the verandah, looking towards the spot at which the grave was marked by the low railings.

There she stood for some minutes before she stirred. Then he followed her, and, laying his hand upon her shoulder, spoke the one word which was necessary. "Kate, will you take it, if not from him, then from me?" She did not answer him at once, and then his arm was passed round her waist. "If not from him, then from me?"

"Yes; from you," she said. "Anything from you." And so it was.

"Catherine Carmichael" appeared for the first time in 1878 in the Christmas number of The Masonic Magazine.

Not If I Know It

NOT IF I KNOW IT." It was an ill-natured answer to give, made in the tone that was used, by a brother-in-law to a brother-in-law, in the hearing of the sister of the one and wife of the other, — made, too, on Christmas Eve, when the married couple had come as visitors to the house of him who made it! There was no joke in the words, and the man who had uttered them had gone for the night. There was to be no other farewell spoken indicative of the brightness of the coming day. "Not if I know it!" and the door was slammed behind him. The words were very harsh in the ears even of a loving sister.

"He was always a cur," said the husband.

"No; not so. George has his ill-humours and his little periods of bad temper; but he was not always a cur. Don't say so of him, Wilfred."

"He always was so to me. He wanted you to marry that fellow Cross because he had a lot of money."

"But I didn't," said the wife, who now had been three years married to Wilfred Horton.

"I cannot understand that you and he should have been children of the same parents. Just the use of his name, and there would be no risk."

"I suppose he thinks that there might have been risk," said the wife. "He cannot know you as I do."

"Had he asked me I would have given him mine without

241

thinking of it. Though he knows that I am a busy man, I have never asked him to lend me a shilling. I never will."

"Wilfred!"

"All right, old girl — I am going to bed; and you will see that I shall treat him to-morrow just as though he had refused me nothing. But I shall think that he is a cur." And Wilfred Horton prepared to leave the room.

"Wilfred!"

"Well, Mary, out with it."

"Curs are curs——"

"Because other curs make them so; that is what you are going to say."

"No, dear, no; I will never call you a cur, because I know well that you are not one. There is nothing like a cur about you." Then she took him in her arms and kissed him. "But if there be any signs of ill-humour in a man, the way to increase it is to think much of it. Men are curs because other men think them so; women are angels sometimes, just because some loving husband like you tells them that they are. How can a woman not have something good about her when everything she does is taken to be good? I could be as cross as George is if only I were called cross. I don't suppose you want the use of his name so very badly."

"But I have condescended to ask for it. And then to be answered with that jeering pride! I wouldn't have his name to a paper now, though you and I were starving for the want of it. As it is, it doesn't much signify. I suppose you won't be long before you come." So saying, he took his departure.

She followed him, and went through the house till she came to her brother's apartments. He was a bachelor, and was living all alone when he was in the country at Hallam Hall. It was a large, rambling house, in which there had been of custom many visitors at Christmas time. But Mrs. Wade, the widow, had died during the past year, and there was nobody there now but the owner of the house, and his sister, and his sister's husband. She followed him to his rooms, and found him sitting alone, with a pipe in his mouth, and as she entered she saw that preparations had been made for the comfort of more than one person. "If there be anything that I hate," said George Wade, "it is to be asked for the use of my name. I would sooner lend money to a fellow at once, — or give it to him."

"There is no question about money, George."

"Oh, isn't there? I never knew a man's name wanted when there was no question about money."

"I suppose there is a question — in some remote degree." Here George Wade shook his head. "In some remote degree," she went on repeating her words. "Surely you know him well enough not to be afraid of him."

"I know no man well enough not to be afraid of him where my name is concerned."

"You need not have refused him so crossly, just on Christmas Eve."

"I don't know much about Christmas where money is wanted."

"'Not if I know it!' you said."

"I simply meant that I did not wish to do it. Wilfred expects that everybody should answer him with such constrained courtesy! What I said was as good a way of answering him as any other; and if he didn't like it — he must lump it."

"Is that the message that you send him?" she asked.

"I don't send it as a message at all. If he wants a message you may tell him that I'm extremely sorry, but that it's against my principles. You are not going to quarrel with me as well as he?"

"Indeed, no," she said, as she prepared to leave him for the night. "I should be very unhappy to quarrel with either of you." Then she went.

"He is the most punctilious fellow living at this moment, I believe," said George Wade, as he walked alone up and down the room. There were certain regrets which did make the moment bitter to him. His brother-in-law had on the whole treated him well, — had been liberal to him in all those matters in which one brother comes in contact with another. He had never asked him for a shilling, or even for the use of his name. His sister was passionately devoted to her husband. In fact, he knew Wilfred Horton to be a fine fellow. He told himself that he had not meant to be especially uncourteous, but that he had been at the moment startled by the expression of Horton's wishes. But looking back over his own conduct, he could remember that in the course of their intimacy he himself had been occasionally rough to his brother-in-law, and he could remember that his brother-in-law had not liked it. "After all what does it mean, 'Not if I know it?' It is just a form of saying that I had rather not." Nevertheless, Wilfred Horton could not persuade himself to go to bed in a good humour with George Wade.

"I think I shall get back to London to-morrow," said Mr. Horton, speaking to his wife from beneath the bedclothes, as soon as she had entered the room.

"To-morrow?"

"It is not that I cannot bear his insolence, but that I should have to show by my face that I had made a request, and had been refused. You need not come."

"On Christmas Day?"

"Well, yes. You cannot understand the sort of flutter I am in. 'Not if I know it!' The insolence of the phrase in answering such a request! The suspicion that it showed! If he had told me that he had any feeling about it, I would have deposited the money in his hands. There is a train in the morning. You can stay here and go to church with him, while I run up to town."

"That you two should part like that on Christmas Day; you two dear ones! Wilfred, it will break my heart." Then he turned round and endeavoured to make himself comfortable among the bedclothes. "Wilfred, say that you will not go out of this to-morrow."

"Oh, very well! You have only to speak and I obey. If you could only manage to make your brother more civil for the one day it would be an improvement."

"I think he will be civil. I have been speaking to him, and he seems to be sorry that he should have annoyed you."

"Well, yes; he did annoy me. 'Not if I know it!' in answer to such a request! As if I had asked him for five thousand pounds! I wouldn't have asked him or any man alive for five thousand pence. Coming down to his house at Christmastime, and to be suspected of such a thing!" Then he prepared himself steadily to sleep, and she, before she stretched herself by his side, prayed that God's mercy might obliterate the wrath between these men, whom she loved so well, before the morrow's sun should have come and gone.

The bells sounded merry from Hallam Church tower on the following morning, and told to each of the inhabitants of the old hall a tale that was varied according to the minds of the three inhabitants whom we know. With her it was all hope, but hope accompanied by that despondency which is apt to afflict the weak in the presence of those that are stronger. With her husband it was anger, — but mitigated anger. He seemed, as he came into his wife's room while dressing, to be aware that there was something which should be abandoned, but which still it did his heart some good to nourish. With George Wade there was more of Christian feeling, but of Christian feeling which it was disagreeable to entertain. "How on earth is a man to get on with his relatives, if he cannot speak a word above his breath?" But still he would have been very willing that those words should have been left unsaid.

Any observer might have seen that the three persons as they sat down to breakfast were each under some little constraint. The lady was more than ordinarily courteous, or even affectionate, in her manner. This was natural on Christmas Day, but her too apparent anxiety was hardly natural. Her husband accosted his brother-in-law with almost loud good humour. "Well, George, a merry Christmas, and many of them. My word; — how hard it froze last night! You won't get any hunting for the next fortnight. I hope old Burnaby won't spin us a long yarn."

George Wade simply kissed his sister, and shook hands with his brother-in-law. But he shook hands with more apparent zeal than he would have done but for the quarrel, and when he pressed Wilfred Horton to eat some devilled turkey, he did it with more ardour than was usual with him. "Mrs. Jones is generally very successful with devilled turkey." Then, as he passed round the table behind his sister's back, she put out her hand to touch him, and as though to thank him for his goodness. But any one could see that it was not quite natural.

The two men as they left the house for church, were thinking of the request that had been made yesterday, and which had been refused. "Not if I know it!" said George Wade to himself. "There is nothing so unnatural in that, that a fellow should think so much of it. I didn't mean to do it. Of course, if he had said that he wanted it particularly I should have done it."

245

"Not if I know it!" said Wilfred Horton. "There was an insolence about it. I only came to him just because he was my brother-in-law. Jones, or Smith, or Walker would have done it without a word." Then the three walked into church, and took their places in the front seat, just under Dr. Burnaby's reading-desk.

We will not attempt to describe the minds of the three as the Psalms were sung, and as the prayers were said. A twinge did cross the minds of the two men as the coming of the Prince of Peace was foretold to them; and a stronger hope did sink into the heart of her whose happiness depended so much on the manner in which they two stood with one another. And when Dr. Burnaby found time, in the fifteen minutes which he gave to his sermon, to tell his hearers why the Prophet had specially spoken of Christ as the Prince of Peace, and to describe what the blessings were, hitherto unknown, which had come upon the world since a desire for peace had filled the minds of men, a feeling did come on the hearts of both of them, — to one that the words had better not have been spoken, and to the other that they had better have been forgiven. Then came the Sacrament, more powerful with its thoughts than its words, and the two men as they left the church were ready to forgive each other — if they only knew how.

There was something a little sheep-faced about the two men as they walked up together across the grounds to the old hall, — something sheep-faced which Mrs. Horton fully understood, and which made her feel for the moment triumphant over them. It is always so with a woman when she knows that she has for the moment got the better of a man. How much more so when she has conquered two? She hovered about among them as though they were dear human beings subject to the power of some beneficent angel. The three sat down to lunch, and Dr. Burnaby could not but have been gratified had he heard the things that were said of him. "I tell you, you know," said George, "that Burnaby is a right good fellow, and awfully clever. There isn't a man or woman in the parish that he doesn't know how to get to the inside of."

"And he knows what to do when he gets there," said Mrs. Horton, who remembered with affection the gracious old parson as he had blessed her at her wedding.

"No; I couldn't let him do it for me." It was thus Horton spoke to his wife as they were walking together about the gardens. "Dear Wilfred, you ought to forgive him."

"I have forgiven him. There!" And he made a sign as of blowing his anger away to the winds. "I do forgive him. I will think no more about it. It is as though the words had never been spoken, — though they were very unkind. 'Not if I know it!' All the same, they don't leave a sting behind."

"But they do."

"Nothing of the kind. I shall drink prosperity to the old house and a loving wife to the master just as cheerily by and by as though the words had never been spoken."

"But there will not be peace, — not the peace of which Dr. Burnaby told us. It must be as though it had really — really never been uttered. George has not spoken to me about it, not to-day, but if he asks, you will let him do it?"

"He will never ask — unless at your instigation."

"I will not speak to him," she answered, — "not without telling you. I would never go behind your back. But whether he does it or not, I feel that it is in his heart to do it." Then the brother came up and joined them in their walk, and told them of all the little plans he had in hand in reference to the garden. "You must wait till *she* comes, for that, George," said his sister.

"Oh, yes; there must always be a she when another she is talking. But what will you say if I tell you there is to be a she?"

"Oh, George!"

"Your nose is going to be put out of joint, as far as Hallam Hall is concerned." Then he told them all his love story, and so the afternoon was allowed to wear itself away till the dinner hour had nearly come.

"Just come in here, Wilfred," he said to his brother-in-law when his sister had gone up to dress. "I have something I want to say to you before dinner."

"All right," said Wilfred. And as he got up to follow the master of the house, he told himself that after all his wife would prove herself too many for him.

"I don't know the least in the world what it was you were asking me to do yesterday."

"It was a matter of no consequence," said Wilfred, not able to avoid assuming an air of renewed injury.

"But I do know that I was cross," said George Wade.

"After that," said Wilfred, "everything is smooth between us. No man can expect anything more straightforward. I was a little hurt, but I know that I was a fool. Every man has a right to have his own ideas as to the use of his name."

"But that will not suffice," said George.

"Oh! yes it will."

"Not for me," repeated George. "I have brought myself to ask your pardon for refusing, and you should bring yourself to accept my offer to do it."

"It was nothing. It was only because you were my brother-in-law, and therefore the nearest to me. The Turco-Egyptian New Waterworks Company simply requires somebody to assert that I am worth ten thousands pounds."

"Let me do it, Wilfred," said George Wade. "Nobody can know your circumstances better than I do. I have begged your pardon, and I think that you ought now in return to accept this at my hand."

"All right," said Wilfred Horton. "I will accept it at your hand." And then he went away to dress. What took place up in the dressingroom need not here be told. But when Mrs. Horton came down to dinner the smile upon her face was a truer index of her heart than it had been in the morning.

"I have been very sorry for what took place last night," said George afterwards in the drawing-room, feeling himself obliged, as it were, to make full confession and restitution before the assembled multitude, — which consisted, however, of his brother-in-law and his sister. "I have asked pardon, and have begged Wilfred to show his grace by accepting from me what I had before declined. I hope that he will not refuse me."

"Not if I know it," said Wilfred Horton.

"Not If I Know It" appeared for the first time in 1882 in the Christmas number of Life.